A Master of the Century Past

IN A FINAL COMMENT ON THE CAILLOU FORGERIES, THE noted art connoisseur and critic HMB has written that "forgery is the calling of an artist who lacks a true lifework."

It was a comment typical of HMB—terse and enigmatic. Some of the more "knowledgeable" (that was a favorite word of HMB's), those who had been reading him for some thirty years, might have found the tone a little self-righteous. Some of the more long-standing "knowledge-ables" might have recalled the complex relationship in which the noted critic stood to the forger, the well-known portrait painter Jack Birnbaum. But HMB was not disposed to rehearse this matter.

The forger, of course, recognized that he was the addressee of this coded message. And I, Jack Birnbaum, am that addressee.

We go way back, HMB and I. I knew him when the butterfly that is HMB was only the caterpillar that was Henry Berger, no middle initial. Indeed, I must acknowledge the debt I owe to Henry Berger. It was to his initial encouragement that I owe my decision to pursue a life in art rather than in dentistry, a career into which my father had hoped I would follow himself. It is characteristic of HMB not to credit me by name with the authorship of the Caillous. The *métier* I practice, portrait painting, I grant, does not these days qualify as a "lifework." It has degenerated into the merest labor of commemoration. I say this despite the fact that it is portrait painting that has earned me a place in the National Academy of Design (not to mention an income in middle six figures).

But others had found promise in the early work I exhibited under my own name. It was in judgment on these works, on the other hand, that HMB had long ago rescinded his own blessing, cast me out into dark-ness, and henceforth forbade himself the mention of my name.

Can I really be blamed—HMB was now covertly pleading with the knowledgeables—if the accursed man has chosen a life of crime? HMB would never have put it that way of course, for it was one of the hall-marks of HMB's critical style—he regarded it as a commitment to "objectivity"—that he always referred to himself in the third person.

The question was posed in the written opinion that accompanied the act of passing sentence on the worth of the Caillou forgeries. It lurked in the reminder to the knowledgeables that it had been HMB who first exposed the forger, painting under his own signature, as an inauthentic modernist, a painter of kitsch. They were two of HMB's favorite expressions, "inauthentic" and "kitsch."

I should like to mention another commentary on the Caillou forgeries here at the outset. In his contribution to the festschrift for Dr. Roland Hightower, *The Psychopathology of Art* (London: Imago Press, 1985), Dr. Wolfgang Von Lust zu Todt, M.D., discusses my work along with those of several other important forgers, principally Hans van Meegeren. Dr. Hightower, who specializes in the treatment of depression, is of course well known for his work on depression neurosis and its connection with the artistic personality. I myself have consulted Dr. Hightower on occasion.

Dr. Todt is also well known—for his interest in the psychoanalysis of works of art. I was flattered by his high opinion of my forgeries, even though he is, I am afraid, a mere dabbler in matters of connoisseurship. It was he who coined the phrase "a master of the century past" for my Caillou persona.

I was particularly interested in his analysis of my motives. "This art forger is no mere con man," Todt says emphatically. There is no criminal sociopathology (*Schwindeltrieb*) manifest here, he says, but something much deeper.

We must search, he says, for a displacement (*Versetzung*), triggered by trauma (*Trauma*). Artists, as is well known, are subject to depression (*Niederdrückung*). It is also widely recognized that obsessional neurosis (*Besessene Nervenstärkung*) is also a factor in the artistic psyche. In cases like Birnbaum's, the artist's own creative drive (*Schaffenstrieb*) becomes *identified* with another artistic personality and seeks gratification in a kind of fixated mimesis. (I could not have put it better myself!)

2

His study of the forgeries, he contends, supports this thesis. The creation of the pseudo-Caillous started long before the forger had any intention of foisting them on the art public. He cites my myriad studies of all the Caillou paintings known—starting with the genuine Caillou (now in the Carter Museum). I did this for years before any move was made to market them. (I apologize for these earlier amateurish efforts. I confess to having a horror of destroying any of my work, as many artists do.) There follows a description of my labors to master the techniques of the early impressionists. In his account, central to my efforts was the rejection of soft chiaroscuro (which I continued to use in my portrait painting), the mastery of "descriptive" brush stroke, the use of the palette knife, the wet-on-wet technique. (Frankly, I find all these patents of scholarship on his part a bit tedious.)

He continues: According to technical experts, it is more difficult to detect fraudulent work in the era of impressionism than in painters of the more distant past, for canvas and paint pigments were standardized and mass produced by the time of impressionism. He cites the fact that what definitely established the work as forgery were those first early esquisses on materials that would easily have revealed their recent origins. "If Birnbaum's motives had been the mere pecuniary, would he have gone to the trouble of preserving the laborious evidence of his fraud?" he asks. "No, decidedly not!" he answers.

"If Birnbaum is to be believed, one must view the oeuvre of this master —and I dare to call Birnbaum a master—as inspired by a different kind of drive [*Trieb*]."

He cites the existence of my *Catalogue Raisonné of the Works of Jean-Jacques Caillou* (complete with color plates) as evidence of obsessional fixation. The entries catalog an imagined exhibition of the work of Caillou, a grand retrospective, a lifework. It was, of course, he says, pure adolescent fantasy. But the choice of Caillou is significant. A man who died too young, a might-have-been-great painter. It shows that Birnbaum was a lonely, misunderstood man, easily victimized and taken advantage of. "This identification—and 'identification' is not too strong a word for his feelings for Caillou—was forged by his failure to achieve recognition in his own right." (Sometimes the good doctor gets carried away.)

3

Todt's article ends with a "psychocritique" of one of the entries in the catalog: "The Bathers" (No. 4, see Plate 5).

> This work may have been influenced by Bazille's "The Bathers" (1866), but it is more dramatic. One may also conjecture that it exerted an influence on Renoir's masterpiece "The Boating Party," now in the Philips Museum. The attitude and pose of the second swimmer bears a remarkable resemblance to a figure in the later work.

According to Todt, the painting was actually inspired by a film made by the painter's son, the great film director Jean Renoir: the little black-and-white masterpiece *Partie de Campagne*. The Caillou contains two male figures in striped swimming suits and straw hats. The center of attention is the swimmer who is playing a wood flute in a Pan-like attitude. The other swimmer is standing and regarding him with amusement. Two ladies, in fashionable dress, recline on the grass, also looking in the direction of the flute player.

He reports, with justifiable pride, on his own researches into the source of this little masterwork. The film was shown twice during the year of its composition, 1966—at the Thalia on Broadway at Ninety-seventh Street (January 5–7 and August 3–5) and at the St. Mark's Place Cinema once (the week of March 7). (I must confess that a visit to the St. Mark's Place Cinema was the source of my inspiration.)

What Dr. Todt finds in my painting is a strong adolescent wish (probably only momentarily conscious and then quickly suppressed) to have the whole subterfuge revealed. In an aside, he finds it absolutely staggering that the "cognoscenti" failed to see "that the forger was pulling the leg of the collective art world." He continues, "No one spotted the obvious when it was acquired in a private sale by the Louvre in 1974. Why otherwise would Birnbaum foist such an obvious howler on the public?" (I am not really impressed by all this palaver about my quickly suppressed motives.)

You will not find among my hundreds of works a self-portrait. I've painted my wife, my children, my lovers, my enemies. I have approached all of these with due feeling. Often the love of subject shines

4

forth from the finished work. Without sentimentality, mind you. But I have never painted myself! I wonder why.

Great artists have not infrequently taken themselves as subject, sometimes slyly inserting themselves into mythology or group portraiture (Perugino), sometimes within some allegory (Titian). We enjoy Rubens' lust for life. We are moved by the story of Rembrandt, documented in his magnificent series of self-portraits. We can hardly bear the suffering of Van Gogh, amid his overwhelming artistry.

I am now painting my self-portrait. Since I am verging on old age, it is too late for me to try to recapture my former figure. I was never handsome, but more than one woman has found me comely.

I have never really liked working from photographs. Great photographs are poetry or short fiction. Snapshots are not fiction, it is true, but it is always in the nature of a snapshot that one requires a gloss to know what one is looking at.

How could I try to recapture on canvas one of the former manifestations of myself? I have a theory that all of us, as we grow nearer old age, tend to maintain in our minds an unchanging picture of our own appearance. Mine is fixed in my early forties. It was a time when I had a slim figure and a neat little mustache. There is always this shock when I look into a mirror. I see a face I recognize, but it is without mustache and it is has aged so much.

I have looked at old photographs of myself, closed my eyes, and imagined the following scene. The background looks rather like the Plaza Hotel. I am watching a revolving door. There I emerge, in a corduroy jacket, unmustachioed, brown hair brushed back in a modest pompadour. Nothing excessive. I can't be more than twenty-five. I wave in a friendly fashion. I reenter. When I emerge again, I am wearing a business suit, obviously of a very good cut. My hairline has receded noticeably, but the color is still more brown than gray, and I sport that little mustache that I grew. Roxie Carter loved it. I nod and then wink broadly. I reenter.

The figure that next emerges is closer to my present age. I have shaved off that grotesque body ornament on my upper lip. My wife, Lee, always hated it. But somehow my hairline is more or less where it was last time, and I haven't put on the weight I know I had acquired in

5

the meanwhile. The appearance has simply not aged in a natural way. I must give up this thought-experiment.

So, I choose to paint myself, looking as I do now in the mirror, in my studio, sitting at my easel, working on one of the canvases by which I wish to be remembered. It is the large "Afternoon Garden." It contains portraits of my wife, Lee; my brother-in-law, Monty; and his wife, Roxie. At the left my child and her Carter cousin (all now fully grown) are playing ring-around-the-rosy. It is work that bears subtle references to paintings by Bazille, Renoir, Manet, and Caillou. Of course, Caillou.

On the walls behind me are pictures that "quote" other of my works, among them the gorgeous "Odalisque," now unfortunately destroyed.

I am wearing an open-necked shirt, gray flannel slacks, loafers, no smock. A bit old-fashioned perhaps, but I am unusually clean for a working painter. My bearing suggests an enjoyment of earthly pleasures, success, elegance. *Surtout, l'élégance!*

I am wearing a beret to cover my baldness. I have a prominent nose, which suggests perhaps a bit of arrogance, a sensual mouth, lips from which might burst, occasionally, a great peal of laughter, and eyes blue and luminous. I am trying to give the impression that there is little going on around my person that they miss. Frankly, that's a bit of the painter's license to flatter. The cheeks have perhaps grown a little flabby. I have tried to be honest about some things. It is a refined face, but not really a noble face. It suggests a touchiness, a quickness to take offense. I am not sure how true all that is, whether Dr. Todt would find that in my character, but it is what I see in my mirror. And in any case, it makes for a more interesting piece of work.

I am not dissatisfied, technically speaking. But I must admit it is, at best, an idealization of my character.

Please excuse this digression.

Of course, it is also true—if bizarre—that it was I, the accursed Jack Birnbaum, who was primarily responsible for rescuing from obscurity the important proto-impressionist Jean-Jacques Caillou—whose work I then proceeded to forge. Many years ago, I found the Caillou masterpiece "Portrait of M. Auguste Renoir" (now in the Carter Museum of Representational Art) in the flea market in Paris.

6

I FIRST SAW CAILLOU'S "PORTRAIT OF M. AUGUSTE Renoir" in the company of Marthe de Saint Veran. Her husband, Commandant le Comte de Saint Veran—she never referred to him in any other way—was away fighting Ho Chi Minh. We were then at the height of our mutual passion.

I was twenty-five and I was her lover. I suppose that would have made her my mistress. But that word gives a totally wrong impression. For she was, by then in her late forties, financially independent of Monsieur Le Comte. And in matters of love I was her pupil. But please don't get the idea that I was being kept. I was independent in my own way, so to speak—studying painting on the GI Bill.

Marthe was slim, with an endearing, bird-like, animated little face. She had small but ravishing breasts and narrow hips. She was no great beauty, but I found her very hospitable. The left nipple was missing its tip. She had a scar from a badly done appendectomy. I was also ravished by these imperfections.

She had a good position as a set designer. She called herself *une femme sérieuse*. That still had a meaning in France of the 1950s. I doubt that it is an idiom in current use today, but it was part of what enchanted American men about French women, and they lamented the lack of it in American women. It meant that when Monsieur le Comte was at home, Marthe devoted herself to their life together. When he was away, she felt free to shower these devotions generously on other men. "Art" was a word she used profusely—as in *l'art de la cuisine, l'art du jardin,* and so forth. She was the mistress of so many of these arts. They formed a kind of curriculum with the overall course title of *l'art de vivre.*

She owned a charming house in the Sixteenth. In her dining room I learned much about *l'art gastronomique.* Repairing to her bedroom, I would then receive instruction in the art of love. I owe so much to

Marthe. She is the reason why to this day I am often taken to be a native speaker of French. Speaking good French is also an art, and the boudoir is a splendid place to learn.

It was one of those halcyon days in spring. Marthe was shopping for furnishings for a Feydeau play for the actress Edwige Feuillère. She needed *bibelots* for the set. I had gone along, because I could not at the time bear to be away from Marthe.

Something caught my eye in a stall nearby.

It was a stall full of old paintings and other *objets d'art*. Bronze angels, naked waifs, Second Empire near-erotica. It was the kind of place one might go looking for frames rather than the paintings in them.

What had caught my eye was an unframed canvas, about three and a half feet high and two and a half wide. It was a portrait of an artist working on a canvas on his easel—a bearded, rather severe looking young man, absorbed in the act of creation, palette and brushes in his left hand, in his right hand a thin brush which touched the painting. The subject of the canvas on the right was a nude female, viewed from the rear, one arm supported on a pedestal, the other raised to her beturbaned head. The painting reflected the orientalism popular in French painting of the 1850s and 1860s. It was, I surmised, a reference to a popular work of the period. I did not recognize it.

Behind the painter, on the wall, were several other paintings. It was the kind of transitional painting not quite independent of the traditions of the Academy or the influence of French romanticism. But it had an impressionist look to it—the kind of painting Degas, Manet, Renoir were doing before they went out of doors. My first thought was to dismiss it as a copy of some painting in the Jeu de Paume unknown to me. The overall painting surface was very dirty, but I saw immediately that it was a striking image.

I held it up to the light. It was darkened by decades of grime. I felt Marthe's hand on my shoulder.

"Not bad," she said. "It is a copy, but I do not recognize the original. Possibly Renoir? No, Bazille."

I hadn't thought of Bazille.

"There is a signature. But I cannot read it. It is so dirty," she said.

"Nice though. You want it?" she said in English. Her English had improved steadily under my tutelage.

I asked the stall owner about it. He said he had no idea who had done it. How much did he want for it? He quoted a figure. The equivalent of three hundred dollars. Out of my range, I replied.

But Marthe, for whom shopping was also one of the arts, jumped in. That was too much for a copy, even a good copy of who knows what obscure painter. And the condition, it was deplorable. You couldn't even read the signature of the painter.

The stall-keeper shrugged.

She said she would buy it. The figure she gave was the equivalent of fifty dollars. He laughed. She went up twenty-five. He shrugged. They settled on the equivalent of one hundred dollars. That was still beyond my range. But Marthe bought it. The dealer wrapped it, and Marthe and I lugged it to the *metro*.

"What does that idiot know about painting! It is not a copy. I'll wager it is an original. We find out whose initials are on it," she said.

When we got back to Marthe's home in Passy, we unwrapped the painting and reexamined it.

I hadn't paid any attention before to the other paintings hung on the wall behind the artist. Now I saw they were a street scene in the snow, a lady contemplating a vase of flowers, and a boating scene. They all looked vaguely familiar.

"What have we here?" I asked.

"Aucune idée, chéri!"

"It's an impressionist, but I don't know which one. They were a gregarious bunch. They painted and partied together. They quoted their own and each others' work in their paintings. I think we have found something, Marthe."

She began rewrapping the picture.

"What are you doing?" I asked.

"Taking it to an expert. Labiche. Charles Labiche, he is a cousin of my husband."

"Oh!"

"He is a conservator. You say that? Anyway, he does work for the

9

Louvre, the National Gallery, all the museums of Europe. He knows this period."

She went to the telephone and arranged to take the painting to Labiche.

For some reason, she had told Labiche on the phone that the painting belonged to "a friend." She mentioned my name. She said "Jacques" had brought the painting to her, and she had suggested he show it to Labiche. When could they bring it by? Why not now, he said.

Labiche worked at home. He lived in a once elegant townhouse in the Place des Vosges. Labiche was young for the reputation accorded him by Marthe. He greeted us at the door, wearing a laboratory coat. He kissed Marthe on both cheeks and shook hands with me.

He ushered us into his studio which was on the first floor. He put the painting down on a table, unwrapped it, and turned a bright light upon it.

He studied it in silence for several minutes. He turned it over and examined the underside of the canvas and the wood stretcher.

"Well, Charles. Do you recognize it? Is it a copy?" Marthe asked.

"To the first question, the answer is no. To the second, it is also no, at least probably no. I cannot say for sure, I think it is old—the eighteen sixties. It is curious."

"Why curious?" she asked.

"You do not recognize the painter?"

"No, should I?"

He did not answer her, but disappeared momentarily. When he returned, he was bearing a large volume in his hand. I could read the name on the front cover: Degas. Labiche opened it and found what he was looking for. He pointed triumphantly to a figure in a black-and-white reproduction. The title read "The Critique at the Studio of M. Manet (1869)." It was one of those odd pieces, partly serious, mostly in fun, of a group of artists assembled in a studio, doing the kind of pantomime that suggests their line of work. It was full of dark, frock-coated figures in top hats. It had that kind of strong contrast of light that shows the influence of photography upon proto-impressionism.

There was a cartouche to the side of the photograph, one of those profile outlines with numbers keyed to a list of names, just like an old

10

school yearbook. It was a pretty impressive gathering. Degas had included himself. Besides Manet, the names of Fantin-Latour, Sisley, Monet, Bazille, and Renoir were familiar.

"Your picture is of Auguste Renoir," Labiche announced. "Just look!" We did. He was dead right.

"But why should Renoir be working on such a painting? None of his nudes has that look or pose *à la Ingres. C'est bizarre, ça.*"

He made a gesture to indicate he hadn't the faintest idea. "Maybe it is a joke!"

"Who is it by?" I asked. "Could it be a Renoir self-portrait?"

"No, I do not think so. You are perhaps thinking that it is like Renoir's portrait of his friend Frédéric Bazille? It bears a resemblance, but no, I do not think so."

"Could it be a Bazille?" Marthe asked. "If Renoir paints Bazille at his *chevalet*, maybe Bazille returns the favor."

"That is possible, but I do not think so. I think it is a portrait of M. Auguste Renoir by a less well-known contemporary. The painting was clearly done by someone who knew their work very well. Look at the paintings on the wall. This one looks like one of Monet's snow scenes of the road to Louveciennes, which was done in the 1860s. This one—ach, I cannot see. We shall have to clean the canvas. Then we can read the signature. It looks like it is only initials, but that should give us an idea who it was."

"You think it is worth cleaning?" I asked.

"Oh definitely. It is a mystery. It piques the curiosity, *n'est-ce pas?* Can you leave it with me for a month or two?" he asked, assuming that I was the owner.

I looked at Marthe. She nodded to me.

As he put it in a cupboard, Labiche was still ruminating on the inappropriateness of the female nude. "That shall have to be cleared up."

Labiche was industrious. Still under the impression that it belonged to me, he sent it back to me care of Marthe. When I first saw it in its cleaned state, I was overwhelmed. It was a striking image. The first thing to be noted were the initials, now clear: J.-J.C.

No major impressionist bore those initials. Clearly, it was not one of the major impressionists. Not a major financial coup. The details of the pictures on the wall were also considerably clearer.

There was a note attached: to M. Jack Birnbaum, from M. Le Comte Charles Labiche:

> Your painting is, as I surmised, a portrait of Auguste Renoir. It was done by his fellow student and friend, Jean-Jacques Caillou (1841–1870).
>
> Caillou had been a student, along with Renoir, Bazille, Sisley, and Monet, of Gleyre at the *École des Beaux Arts* in the early 1860s.
>
> Indeed, he was clearly Gleyre's favorite. He was one of the "petit bourgeois" impressionists—an artisan background like Renoir's.
>
> The portrait of Renoir cannot have been done before 1869.
>
> The primary evidence for my identification are the initials J-J-C in the lower right hand corner. But there is other internal evidence as well.
>
> First, there are the pictures "quoted" on the wall behind the artist. The locus at Louveciennes on the road to Versailles was the scene of multiple studies by various impressionists who were visiting Pissarro, who was living there in 1869. There is a study by Pissarro himself and by Monet. This image corresponds to none of their known works. But I have found a reference in a Monet letter to Renoir, after Caillou's death in 1870, which makes Caillou a party to the group at Louveciennes during the winter of '69. The locus of the boating scene is La Grenouillère on the Seine, to which Monet, Renoir, and Bazille repaired in the summer of 1869, along with Manet. Again there is evidence from letters that Caillou was also a party to the expedition. The perspective is not the same as any of the known studies, leading me to conjecture that the painting like the one just discussed is from the hand of Caillou. The third picture suggests, in conception, a picture Manet painted of his *protégée*, Mme. Alvarez (the older sister of Berthe Morisot) but I identify the picture here being quoted as a portrait of Berthe Morisot herself done by Caillou and submitted to the Salon in 1867 but rejected. There is a record of Caillou's submitting a painting called "Woman With Flowers" and the dimensions mentioned are consonant with the size here depicted. Correspondence again suggests the subject was Berthe Morisot.
>
> Finally, there is the nude female subject on the *chevalet*. As you know, this baffled me when I initially saw your canvas. I did not think it referred to a painting by Renoir, who is perhaps the most extensively catalogued figure in French Impressionism. But the mystery is explained if the canvas is not by Renoir but by Caillou. For one of Caillou's pictures, rejected by the Salon, found its way into the *Refusés* show of

that year. It was referred to in the 1867 catalogue as *"Femme au Bain."*

The fact that it has the look and pose of an Ingres odalisque also confirms the authorship of Caillou. There was some discussion in the press as to whether a subject suggested by another painter should be exhibited as an original work. That was the reason given for its refusal by the Salon jury of 1867. But clearly, Caillou had taken little more than the pose and the voluptuous lines of the body from Ingres. The light is not Ingres's cool light but Manet's harsh "flashpowder" lighting. *Vide* the *"Olympe,"* exhibited in the *Salon des Refusés* the year before. All this can be seen from this canvas.

But why is Renoir working on it? My hypothesis is that it is a kind of joke. The members of the *Atelier* Gleyre were known to retouch each other's work. Moreover in Renoir's famous portrait of their mutual friend Bazille, probably painted about the same time as this one, the pictures on the wall are by other members of the circle.

Caillou volunteered in 1870 and was killed in November of that year. He was only twenty-nine. He had not begun painting till late so that there was not a great output of mature work. Unfortunately, none of these is known to have survived the fire which destroyed his mother's house in St. Pierre, Meuse, where he had stored his work at the time of his enlistment.

Up until the time of your discovery, it was believed that all of Caillou's works had been consumed in that fire. Although not a major discovery, it is now known, thanks to you, that one of his works has survived. With your permission, I should like to publish a note in the *Cahiers d'Histoire d' Arts* and I have made, for that purpose, a black and white photograph of this painting. Would that be contrary to your wishes, dear sir?

Please be assured, dear sir, of my sentiment. . . .

Charles Labiche.

Marthe and I read the letter together, then took another look at the painting. A mere footnote it might be, but it ravished me. I was charmed by its high seriousness. It was the tribute by one artist of the greatest promise (Caillou) to another of almost as great promise (Renoir).

"He was a man with a vocation," I said. "With a capital V!"

"A vocation?" she laughed. "What do you mean?"

"A man who *must* paint. Like Van Gogh. What a waste that he was killed in the 1870 war. He might have been a greater painter than Renoir."

13

"You really think so?" she asked doubtfully. She adored Renoir. He was at the height of his reputation. I had my doubts about him.

"I was hoping it was a Bazille. I could sell it to one of you rich Americans," she said wistfully.

This was the first time in my life I had ever had the opportunity to explore the riot of pleasures of lovemaking. I was obsessed! I simply could not keep my hands off Marthe. And Marthe simply loved to be touched. It was a period in which I was not seriously pursuing my high calling. And such matters as finding a minor impressionist were charming distractions.

One afternoon, not long after the Caillou had come back cleaned, I arrived at Marthe's house, carrying in my mind the map of the day's experimentations. But first, dinner. I rang the bell. I heard the footfalls and the release of the latch. But the door did not open to receive me. And the footsteps retreated.

I pushed gently on the door. It opened. As I entered the hallway, I caught sight of Marthe. She was retreating. She waved to me over her shoulder. My heart skipped a beat, as it always did when I caught sight of her naked.

She had a towel drapped about her head. I assumed she had just taken a bath. I rearranged my schedule. Dinner could wait.

It turned out to be a summons more than a wave. She disappeared into her studio, which was on the first floor. Puzzled, I followed her.

The studio was an inferno of light. She had borrowed a battery of stage lights and they were focused upon a central area along the back wall. There she had placed a large mirror. Nearby was hung the Caillou painting. I understood immediately. She was copying the "Odalisque" —the painting on the easel in the painting.

She was working on a canvas on her easel, about three feet by two feet in dimensions. She was now holding in her right hand a brush, in her left a palette. She faced me briefly, smiling mysteriously. Then she went back to her canvas. My eye took in the image on the canvas and then turned to a personal piece of connoisseurship—of her figure.

She had already painted in the odalisque's head, in profile looking

14

over the shoulder. She had made a very good copy of it. She had completed the outlines of the body from the Caillou original. She was now using her own figure to complete the painting. The figure in the painting was far more ample. It was not the modeling of that she was now seeking. I understood what concerned her. She was trying to recapture how the harsh "flashpowder lighting" would illuminate the contours. My eyes traveled to Marthe's body. Those beloved parts were covered with little beads of sweat that caught and reflected the light. She was immersed in her painting, which I had for the moment the tact to respect.

A moment later Marthe put down the palette and stepped back and inspected her arched back in the mirror. I tiptoed over to examine her work. She had captured the lighting rather well, I thought. I admired her facility. The odalisque was, after all, only quoted in the Caillou work, hardly more than an oil sketch. And the spectator views the Ingres-like painting in the Caillou work at such an oblique angle.

When she returned to the canvas, I could not resist any longer. I saluted her artistry by planting a kiss on her right buttock. It tasted pleasingly saline.

She smiled but not with the usual encouragement. *"Méchant!* Can't you see that I am working?"

I retreated.

I sat down in a chair and waited. But she did not lay down the palette and the brush. After a while, I got up and searched for pencil and paper. I found some gray paper and red chalk. I took up a drawing board upon which I tacked the paper. Then I began sketching Marthe, still prancing around, arching her back, studying herself over her shoulder in the mirror. Working rapidly, I did my own version. The body lacked the fullness of the Caillou image, but, then, my inspiration did not come from the canvas.

I became absorbed in my work. I was not aware that she herself had finished until I felt her hand on my shoulder. I looked up to see that she was standing in front of my chair. She took the board from my hand and studied my work.

"Bravo, mon gosse!" she said, *"Très belle! Très érotique!"*

I responded to the compliment by leaning down and running my lips

15

over the hairline of her pubis, ending up at her appendix scar. I felt a hand lightly tracing playful patterns over my head.

That was in fact the last time Marthe and I made love. A week later she sent me a *pneumatique*. She had something to tell me. She suggested lunch at a certain restaurant off *Boulevard Montparnasse*. Her news concerned the imminent return of Commandant le Comte de Saint Veran. We held hands. I shed tears, but I accepted my sentence. I ordered a bottle of champagne and asked her to grant my one request. As a souvenir, I added. And what is that, *chéri*, she asked. I wanted her recently completed work inspired by the Caillou.

A day later I received by special messenger a large package. It could only have been a wrapped canvas. I tore the wrapping off. It was not what I expected. It was the Caillou painting itself.

She had written me a note. In English, mostly.

"You already have a very good 'odalisque,' so I keep mine! *Tu sais, c'est un souvenir d'un grand amour, chéri!*"

Not a memento of *her* great love, nor a memento of *our* great love, but of *a* great love. How the French love precision!

I READ MANNY SHINE'S OBITUARY IN THE *TIMES* YESTER-day. There was a picture of him in late middle age. Very respectable he looked. And the lead proclaimed him to be "an acknowledged master among the early abstract expressionists, a seminal influence on a gener-ation of younger painters." It neglected to mention that Manny had died very rich, which happens now, more often than you think. It's no mystery. It's a matter of good marketing and increased life-expectancy.

That business of "seminal influence" gave me a particular chuckle. Even in the days when he and I shared a cold-water flat in the West Village, Manny was aware of his "seminal influence." That was still

16

before his abstract expressionist period. But he felt assured of an influence on future generations, even when he was a mere tyro, doing what he called "social commentary."

It wasn't a happy relationship—Manny and me. We fought a lot. Otherwise, we usually didn't talk.

It was a tiny apartment. He would have a date with a "debutante"—that was the way he would put it. And I was supposed to vacate the apartment for a couple of hours. I spent a lot of time at the Waldorf Cafeteria on Sixth Avenue and Eighth Street. Along with the Trotskyites, the Schachtmanites, and the Lovestoneites. In those days the Waldorf was open twenty-four hours a day.

In the early days of our relationship, I had had the chance to watch Manny work. We would be having a beer at the Pine Tavern and some "debutante" would catch his eye. If he managed to trap her in conversation, he'd relate the story of his life, that he was a real comer, one of the future greats, Peggy was going to give him a one-man show. Then he'd invite the debutante up to the apartment to see his work. It was the old come-up-and-see-my-etchings routine. If she consented, he'd show her a couple of canvases and then invite her "to fuck one of the future greats." That was the way he'd put it. She'd have something to tell her grandchildren. As I said, even in those days Manny was aware of his profound seminal influence.

He was a big man. Red hair. There was always a rich red bristle on his chin. He almost never bathed. I remember once telling Manny he needed a bath. His reply was: "You should try *not* bathing, Birnbaum. It's a known fact that skirts are aroused by the male odor. You'd get more ass. From the look of you, you need it."

All this was before Manny discovered "post-easel painting." Someone called one of his big canvases a malediction. Something like that. The closest one could come to a curse in the language of abstraction. I think it was Clement Greenberg. No, actually that sounds more like HMB. But even in his realist days there was a certain fury in Manny's canvases.

After one of our many fights, he painted something he called "Portrait of Jack Birnbaum." The subject was actually a potted palm. Off to the left you could just see a cat creeping away. Manny had used as a model the palm tree that our landlord kept in the downstairs hall. It smelled of cat piss because the landlord's cat would relieve himself there when it was too cold to go out.

Manny was proud enough of this little work to show it to Hack Ferkin when Hack came to do a guest critique at the studio where Manny and I were both studying. I took along one of my studies of an aquarium of tropical fish. Hack didn't like Manny's work much, but he was much impressed with mine.

I always thought Manny was a bad painter. But I am in a minority. I saw a reference to that "portrait" a couple of years ago. It was in the catalog of a small museum in Houston. It still bears the title "Portrait of Jack Birnbaum."

When I had started doing fish, Manny's comments were not encouraging. Even when we were talking, he would usually speak only to execrate my work. It was a habit to which I'd adjusted. One of the earlier fish studies drew the comment: "I feel like I need glasses to look at that. It makes me nauseous. Excuse me, while I go puke."

A little wave of pleasure passed through my frame. That was exactly the effect I wanted. I have always loved the luminescent colors of tropical fish. I knew that they are very short-sighted. I was after the world view of a fish. The canvas was darkly primed, very flat in perspective, with sharp luminescent shapes close to the picture plane, receding very quickly into a vague background.

Hack first saw it at the studio in New York, as I've mentioned.

I had put it on the easel right after he had dismissed Manny's palm tree. He circled my painting, viewing it from all angles. Then he viewed it from various distances. We all silently watched as he approached the edge of the shallow dais on which the easel stood. Then he tripped and fell. He flashed me a wan smile. As he picked himself up, he asked me whether my painting had that effect on everybody. That was the beginning of my association with Hack, my very brief period of triumph as a creative artist.

Haskell Ferkin was then about sixty-five. He was a thin, bald, pasty-faced man, who always wore a corduroy suit and a bow tie. He looked as if he were at death's door. He had terrible rheumatism from underheated Paris apartments and New York cold-water flats, a rasping cough from all those *Gauloises,* a perpetual *crise de foie* from cheap marc. People who had known Hack for forty years said he had always looked as if he were at death's door.

Hack was a sculptor. He has pieces in major museums, but his place in the history of modernism is as a theorist of Dada and, more important, as an impresario.

One sees Haskell Ferkin in lots of photographs of the early Dada activities. There is a wonderful one of him in a Dada cabaret as one of the show girls along with Duchamp's "Rose Selavy." In another, he is part of a *tableau vivant* wearing nothing but a fig leaf.

There he is at the entrance to *À bas l'Image,* the infamous show he mounted in 1926. The "viewer," if that is what he can be called, is introduced into a totally darkened room and must feel his way along a wall of various textures and temperatures: painted canvas, steel wool, cloth, hair, marble, false teeth, wooden phalluses, and vulvas. About a year later, he mounted his famous "Smell a painting" show. Beneath a series of paintings he placed vaporizers that exuded an appropriate scent: beneath a Picasso Rose Period picture a delicate but somewhat cloying scent of flowers; beneath a Cézanne still-life of fruit, the strong smell of fermenting apples. In front of an Utrillo street scene that featured a *pissoir,* there was also a characteristic odor.

A show he staged in 1939, right before the outbreak of war, he called "To Be a Bat." It was very dark. In so far as one could see anything, all one could see was vague black and white outlines of unidentifiable objects. The room was a resonating cavern of distorted, amplified noises.

And there he is in the *Life* photograph of 1942, among his fellow Surrealists, all refugees, each dressed in a business suit, each sitting next to some former friend with whom he had had a quarrel, to whom he had not spoken up to that very moment.

I followed Hack Ferkin back to Paris.

Someday Hack's art theory might be revived. I suppose some future art historian might see it as a precursor to conceptual or multimedia art. Painting is a dead end, he felt. Touch—that's our real connection with reality. Vision is a derived mode of perception. You can't get behind the surface in painting. Or in sculpture, for that matter.

That highly controversial notion gave the direction to his thought. "We need to find out how things feel, how they smell and taste, but mostly how they feel, before we are mislead by seeing," he was wont to say.

Once, while sitting on the terrace of the Dome Café—he lived nearby—I saw him illustrate this little lecture. He had ordered a beer and was waiting for it to come. Then, all of a sudden, he picked up the red rose from the bud vase on our table and began to explore the texture of the bud very gently with his finger. He put it to his nose and drew a great breath. Then he put it to his lips and began licking it.

Then he pulled a petal and began chewing it. I looked on, open-mouthed in astonishment. I had never seen a man eat a rose before.

There was nothing repulsive about the experience. It was with the greatest refinement that he ate that rose. It was as if he were consuming some long-denied delicacy. The first artichoke of the season, perhaps. He had attracted the attention of several surrounding tables, but seemed absolutely unaware of that. It made me think that the episode was a kind of pantomime. The story he was telling concerned the search for the truth behind the visual surfaces of the rose. His face registered delight at the scent. It betrayed curiosity about the taste, then disappointment. How could something that smelled so wonderful have such an earthy, bitter taste?

The idea for *Sous-Mer* came several years later.

It came to Hack one day when he was shopping for food. I happened to be along.

For Hack, food shopping was always a feast in itself, not just the preparation for a feast. He collected sensations like other men collect coins, postage stamps, or sexual experiences. He would find his way to one of Paris' outdoor markets. There he would lovingly caress the vegetables and savor the scents of fruit, cheeses, sausage. All the vendors knew him. They would joke about his food fetishes.

On this particular prowl, we went very early to the fish stalls at *Les Halles*. Ferkin especially loved fish. He loved the shape and color of them, he loved rubbing his hands over their unscaled bodies. He even loved the smell that lingered on his fingers after the touching. I myself found it repellent.

All of a sudden, I saw Hack's face light up. I was too far away to hear the conversation between him and the fishmonger. What I saw was Hack wildly gesticulating to the fish vendor, a process that ended when he purchased an enormous fish.

The fishmonger made motions as if to scale the fish only to be wildly warned off by Hack. The fishmonger looked astonished but complied. I heard the vendor mutter something about selling fish *pour nourrir, pas pour les trophées.*

When we left the market, Hack also had with him a mass of fish skeletons, fish heads, fins, and other things. He was not doing his usual potato-sack shuffle.

"Where are we going?" I asked.

"Home, laddy. We have work to do."

Usually when we got home from a shopping expedition, the first thing Hack did was make himself a stiff drink. Not today. He marched right into the kitchen, armed himself with a boning knife, sharpened it with vigorous strokes, and proceeded to eviscerate the fish. I sat down at the kitchen table, amazed at his display of energy.

"What are you doing, Hack?"

"Honest work, m'lad. Taxidermy."

"May one inquire as to why you want the *raw feel* of stuffing animals? Is taxidermy now, like cooking, one of the higher arts? If so, have you also revalued undertaking?"

"Don't be flippant. I am not planning a career change at my advanced age!"

It took most of the day for Hack to stuff the fish. When I left that evening, he was still at it. He hardly seemed to notice I was going, but I was ordered to return next morning prepared to paint.

When I arrived the next day, Hack was still in the clothes he was wearing the day before. He had finished stuffing the fish and had mounted it, in a manner of speaking, by cutting a hole in an immense piece of wooden paneling and placing it there, off center. He had outlines of other fish shapes on the board, front and back.

"We are going to create a see-and-touchscape. S-e-e," he announced. "Oh?"

"Have you ever wanted to touch a painting?"

"I wouldn't think of it," I said, joking of course, knowing Ferkin's feeling about painting. "Of course not!"

"This is a work you'll want to touch. And it will be okay to do so. Run your hands over the fish."

I did. I felt a prick on the tip of a finger. I put it to my mouth and tasted the blood.

Hack put his hand on my shoulder, ignoring the fact that the fish scales had lacerated my finger.

"It's the ultimate primal scream," he intoned with great solemnity. "Water is a frightening place for us. You and I are going to create the Underwater Nightmare."

It was the beginning of *Sous-Mer*.

It took us a year to prepare for the show. Hack persuaded the dealer Levinsohn to let us take over his space in the *Rue Jacob*.

The viewer entered from the street into a black antechamber. His only sensation was the sound of some eerie chorus. Actually, it was a record of the mating song of humpback whales, which played continuously. Then one noticed the tiny floor lights at one's feet and followed them, along with a trail of coral rocks, into the next room. People who came in sandals complained of cuts to their feet. Then the spectator went down into an underground salon through a fine mist of salt water, sprayed face high. Some spectators complained that they couldn't get the odor of salt out of their clothes after visiting the show.

The lighting was uncanny. The room was dark except for the lights that illuminated the see-and-touchscapes. Those lights went on and off randomly, so that one got a brief view of the seascapes, then another, then a third. Since they aimed at the magnification of size, the effect of the sudden encounter was overwhelming. Some people were so terrified, they literally stumbled into the paintings, putting their hands out to protect themselves. They got the shock of wet fish-scales or of the

22

noxious secretion of some unknown sea creature. There was an eel that emitted a small electric charge and a ray whose antenna were set in violent motion when the surface was touched anywhere. At the rear, was mounted, full-face, the head of a killer shark. From the very start, the exhibition was jammed.

The art critic for *Le Monde* pronounced it the ultimate monstrosity. *Canard Enchainé* featured Hack and me swimming in an aquarium amid sharks and octopi. The critic for the Paris *Herald Tribune* singled me out. He said the show was a throwback to the great days of Dada and surrealism—"morbid, sick, self-destructive, but alive!" In a letter from Paris published in the *New Yorker*, Genet hailed me as a new star on the horizon.

M Y WIFE LEE, WHO DESCRIBES HERSELF AS A "JUNGIAN determinist," believes that we all conform to certain personality types that are exemplified in myths. The sources for these mythic types are usually Indian, or Greek, or Norse, so there's a certain ethnic bias to the whole enterprise. In my case it's even more complicated, for the source of my mythic being (my Dasein, as she would say) is the biblical patriarch Jacob. She worked most of this out on the basis of my name (Jack), her name (Lee), her brother's name (everybody calls him Monty, but his given name is Lawrence, and for Lee that's a close enough fit to Laban), and her sister-in-law, whose name is Roxie (a good enough surrogate for Rachel). I have pointed out—repeatedly— that there are certain facts that just don't fit. Monty is not my father-in- law but her brother. She retorts: But you slaved as the shepherd of his lambs—okay metaphorical lambs. And you lusted after what was his— his wife.

It does no good to point out discrepancies to Lee. Mythic Daseins, she feels, can never be exact. When the fact that I was an art forger came to light, she already had a ready explanation. Just consult the part of the story about the speckled kind, she told everybody.

I can only take so much mythologizing. But there is something that does seem to me to fit. It is that mysterious business where Jacob wrestles all night with the stranger, who turns out to be an angel sent from the Lord. In the course of the wrestling, the angel injures Jacob's hip. And before allowing him to depart, Jacob exacts from the angel a blessing.

My personal angel is the famous critic HMB, whom I had known as the boy Henry Berger. The boy Henry Berger gave me his blessing. Later the critic HMB rescinded it. So, mythically speaking, the angel gave me the blessing first and then broke my hip. But Jungian determinism is not strict; it tolerates such minor discrepancies.

Let me go back, for just a moment, to my youth. When I attended D.W. Clinton H.S. in the Bronx, Henry Berger was my best friend. He was a prodigy, all our teachers thought so. I was in awe of him. I counted myself among the elect when he called me friend.

I had been sketching and painting as long as I could remember. I had confided this to Berger early on. I had avowed that painting was what I most wanted to do in life. Not dentistry, art. Berger knew about my father's hostility to the idea. My mother had a brother, my uncle Ben, a commercial artist, who also lived in the Bronx. Ben was a failure in life. He couldn't make a living by his own labors. His wife had to work. It was a bad situation, according to my father. They could never leave the Bronx. His wife "wore the pants." The unspoken moral, whenever the subject of my future came up, was: You don't want that kind of life.

Through much of our early relations I resisted showing my new friend any of my work. I already knew how uncompromising his standards were. And I lacked the requisite confidence to face his judgment. I still remember very vividly the day when I summoned my courage. We were in my room, after school, horsing around. Suddenly Berger stopped and said:

"Come on, Birnbaum. Let me see your oeuvre."

I had heard it now so often. So, reluctantly, I agreed. I locked the door, to exclude the attention of "the philistines"—as Berger sometimes referred to my mother and father. And I held my first exhibition.

At first, I handed my sketches to Berger, who was sitting on the bed.

24

But he objected and made me put up my easel and position it for the best light. One by one, I brought out my "oeuvre," as he walked around each of them in a wide arc until he found the proper viewing angle. On some he came up very close in order to examine the brush stroke. Occasionally, stroking his chin, he would say, "Just so!" But he was reserving comment, signaling with a snap of his fingers when he wanted to see the next.

I was in agony, but finally Berger had been shown all the works I thought fit to exhibit. Save one, a small canvas of a pretty girl I had once gone out with on a double date along with Berger. She had taken a profound dislike to Berger. I did not want to remind my friend of that catastrophe.

Berger came over and put his hand on my shoulder. He rarely descended to such a show of affection. A tremor of fear passed through me. He is softening me for the worst, I thought. His hand still on my shoulder, he maintained a pregnant silence.

"I have been trying to find the right word for it. What immediately comes to mind is the German word *Beruf*. Max Weber uses it in a seminal work in the sociology of religion. I deplore, incidentally, the provincial reaction to all things German because of the abominable Adolph Hitler. But for the moment, I can't think of the right word in English."

"I don't think I can help." It was an expression I had not heard before. Then his features lit up. He had found the right word. In English.

"I have found it," he said. "You have a *calling!*"

I thought my oeuvre had found favor, but I wasn't sure.

"I mean a 'calling' in the sense in which someone has something they just *have* to do. It's a mission to which they are *summoned* by some force outside themselves. Like Joan of Arc and her voices. 'Calling!' I like that. It's better than *Beruf*, which can also mean "profession." We usually don't ask someone what their calling is when we want to know how they make a living. Do we?"

"Do you think they are good, Berger, I mean *mon oeuvre?*"

"*Mes oeuvres*, old fellow. Are they good? I really can't say. What I do see is intensity, vulnerability. They are *une oeuvre sérieuse. Sans doute.*"

Berger fell silent. Then he removed his hand from my shoulder.

25

"You would be wasted in dentistry. Just as Gauguin was in stock-brokering."

He took a handkerchief out of his pocket and touched it to his eye. He seemed to be brushing away a tear. "I am much moved."

He looked at me and smiled bravely. "Forgive me. I envy you. You see, I don't feel yet that I have found a true calling. Talent, maybe. Even probably. But a calling? No, not yet."

I doubt that I was recalling this episode when I returned to New York in the late 1950s. I had long since lost contact with Henry Berger. And I felt I was the darling of the gods. Sufficient rumor of *Sous-Mer* had reached these shores to attract Consuela Connery, the well-known champion of modernism, to view our show. She then contacted me about including some of my canvases in her upcoming show of "younger trend-setters." She was, of course, an old chum of Hack's.

Consuela was a slight, gray-haired, dumpy woman in her fifties. She was wearing a wool suit and low-heeled shoes when she came to select a couple of canvases. She had that cultivated sing-song that people were wont to use to caricature Mrs. Roosevelt's speech. Like Mrs. Roosevelt, her whole being suggested that she had emerged from privilege to do something serious with her life. Her brochure proclaimed she "had devoted herself without reserve to the Various Causes of Modernism."

She selected four of my canvases: Aquarium VIII through XI.

"It's not *quite* what I am showing these days," she said, somewhat wistfully. "But there must always be continuity as well as change."

I was not sure I liked that.

"You'll be in good company. Manny Shine, Ruth ... "

"Excuse me, Mrs. Connery, did you say, Manny Shine?" I asked. "S-H-I-N-E," I spelled the name for her.

"Yes, of course. You've heard of him?"

"He's a big man? With red hair?"

"Yes, of course. HMB discovered him and brought him to me. He thinks he'll be as *important* as Jack Pollack. Between you and me, I think HMB is still burned up over the fact that it was Clement Greenberg who got the credit for recognizing Pollack's genius. But he's right. Shine will be a real force."

26

I smiled weakly and said I knew the name. It was the first time I'd heard a reference to HMB. It was really a very small world, how small I had no idea.

As it happened, Hack also had business in New York and planned to stay until the Connery opening, when I would burst upon the New York art scene like a new meteor. So we found a place for the two of us. He was interviewed for a piece in *New York* magazine, which referred to him as one of "the grand old men of modern art" but mistakenly said he had been in the great Armory show. He gave some lectures at the New School. Usually afterwards some acolyte would deliver him back to me dead drunk, and I would put him to bed.

We were both encountering the initials H-M-B with greater and greater frequency. In various articles in the popular press that bore that byline or in pieces that quoted or referred to an entity that bore that chop. I, of course, was still waiting in the wings to be taken notice of in the New York press. But Hack had become, in a minor way, a subject of interest to the critic.

In self-defense, Hack had begun reading the criticism of HMB in various New York magazines. He read me passages.

One piece was called "The Gospel According to HMB." In it the critic acknowledged the great power of art criticism and dedicated himself to being "fair, open, and free from the sin of subjectivity." The rule guiding his connoisseurship, he proclaimed, would be to dedicate himself to "authentic modernism," distinguishing it from "modernist *kitsch*." He gave examples of both. The latter list included both Hack Ferkin and his close friend Boris Korbanov. Ferkin, HMB said, some critics had too kindly allowed "to become, as it were, a footnote to modernism."

Hack, who usually showed an indifference to any review of his work, did a slow burn. He regarded his friend Korbanov as one of the genuine between-the-war giants. He started referring to HMB as the "noted critic Harrummb" or "the well-known connoisseur Harrummb." He made it sound like there was an annoying deposit of phlegm in his throat.

We usually didn't go out very much, but Hack one day decided he wanted to attend a party to which he had been invited. It was a whim. I was not invited, but I knew that Hack couldn't go without me. He was far gone by then. Besides, the invitation billed the occasion as an "installation" and that meant a big crowd. The party-giver was a well-known plastics manufacturer. Consuela had said he was one of her best customers. The installation was to take place on a Sunday afternoon.

Hack probably wouldn't have thought of going before he came across a preview of the installation in the *New York Times*. The plastics manufacturer and his wife, the Neugelds, had redesigned a town house on the east side around their collection of paintings. The photographs featured the Neugelds' master bedroom on the top floor. One whole wall was dominated by a Manny Shine. Otherwise, the room looked almost as if the Neugelds hadn't moved in yet. The *Times* writer had been most impressed by the salon, where walls had been torn out to give an unobstructed view of a Sally Bentnick—"the well-known color-field illusionist." "The brilliant, shimmering acrylics of the full wall painting have been carried over into the furnishings with striking effect. I loved it," the home furnishing writer said. Unfortunately, the photograph of the salon was not in color.

After reading the piece, Hack decided we had to go. "We must show the flag," he announced.

We were greeted by Mr. and Mrs. Neugeld at the door. Mrs. Neugeld, a motherly looking woman, was dressed in a multicolored cocktail dress. Over her shoulder, I caught sight of the Sally Bentnick. Her dress was a miniature version of the mural—all brilliant, shimmering acrylic. Mr. Neugeld was dressed in a complementary emerald green outfit, also a quotation from the painting.

The room was too full of people for the full effect of the decor to be felt. The furniture had the proper clean modernist look. The tables and chairs were plastic clones of the painted stripes, the floor a glowing white, exactly matching the canvas priming. The *Times* piece had said the effect was at the same time both spartan and overwhelming.

Hack was wearing a dark corduroy suit. His bow tie drooped with fatigue. A bandanna—I suppose it could be considered a kind of flag—dangled from the breast pocket. I was wearing a suit I had recovered from my parents' attic. I couldn't remember the last time I had worn it. The suit and I had become strangers to each other.

28

At the door, when I caught a glimpse of the already assembled guests, I wanted to retreat. "I feel like we are Mormon missionaries going door-to-door," I whispered to Hack.

"Let me get you a drink and a nosh, Mr. Ferkin. And what's you're name again, son?"

"Jack Birnbaum!"

"Are you also an artist?"

"I am."

"Do you do acrylics? Isn't that Bentnick a modern miracle?"

"It's—how shall I put it—spartan and at the same time overwhelming!"

"Well put, Jack. Let me show you the Shine I have upstairs. It will knock your socks off. Manny was supposed to come, but hasn't shown yet. Do you know Manny?"

"I've had the pleasure."

Mercifully, Mr. Neugeld was called away by his wife to greet a new arrival.

There seemed to be no one in the room either of us knew, so we lingered over the buffet. Hack, who had declined the "nosh," started sniffing at the offerings, thereby attracting the attention of a lady standing nearby. He smiled at her.

"The *chèvre* is from a farm near Gordes. South of France. You can tell by the clover. It's unique to the area. The smoked mackerel is from Zabar's. You get better from Wolfowitz and Daughter. That's just off Houston Street," he said smiling at her amiably. He was showing off.

She looked at him quizzically.

"Are you a caterer?"

"Perish the thought, dear lady. You might call me a fetishist. I wouldn't be offended. But let me assure you that I do not sniff for a living."

He smiled again at her. She quickly excused herself.

We began again to survey the gathering. A tall man caught Hack's eye and the two exchanged nods.

"Who was that?" I asked.

"Robert Motherwell!" Hack answered. He then pointed out several other celebrities in the crowd. Then his eye fell on a group who was hanging on the words of a thin, bespectacled, sharp-featured young man. I followed Hack's eye. The man was dressed in a severe black suit with a matching black knit tie.

"I don't know who that is," Hack said, pointing in the direction of the man who seemed to be delivering a monologue. "He looks like an undertaker."

Perhaps it was Hack's remark that triggered the chain of memory that led me back to Henry Berger and then forward to the severe-looking young man.

"I'll be damned!" I exclaimed. My jaw hung slack in astonishment.

"You know that quaint bit of Americana?" Hack inquired. "He looks like one of the dress-ups you see at historical recreations. The Pilgrims are landing at Plymouth Rock."

"His name is Henry Berger. We were close friends in high school. I must go over and say hello."

I dashed over. Hack trailed along.

Berger was in mid-sentence, intent on finishing. But I could see that he had taken note of our arrival. The sentence extended to paragraph length. I was bursting with impatience to inform him who I was.

Later, between phrases, he managed to give us an acknowledging nod, all without dropping a word.

" ... some *knowledgeable* people—not necessarily of the crude chauvinist variety—might say that there is an American school." He raised both hands, wiggling the second and third fingers, as if he were a conductor cuing his orchestra. He continued, "Although HMB is often taken to be the voice of such a movement, HMB has said that he declines to be responsive to this question. It is an *inauthentic* question."

The speaker paused momentarily.

Hack coughed. Then his face registered an odd, gleeful kind of amazement. He had discovered the true identity of the speaker. In my impatience to be recognized, it had not yet registered on me that I was in the presence not only of Henry Berger but of HMB.

"You may not recognzie me, Berger. I'm Birnbaum."

I extended my hand to him. He declined to take it.

"*Jack* Birnbaum?" I said. My voice rose. Its questioning tone sounded decidedly uncomfortable to my ear. Still my hand remained untaken.

"Have we met?" he asked coolly.

30

"We went to high school together. DeWitt Clinton. DeWitt C in the Bronx. Has it been so long?"

"Quite so! I hope you are well. . . ." I knew I had committed a gaffe, but I was not clear as to its exact nature. He certainly should have known who I was. Had there been some slight on my part that he had never forgiven? Or was he trying to hide his traces? I'd been stiffed, but for what crime?

"Well, as I was saying, if you take selected groups of painters—Motherwell, Rothko, Shine, there are family resemblances. Take others like Barnett Newman and Sally Bentnick, the same is true. But if you try to pair one from the first group with one from the second, there is much less similarity. Do you all know the *Philosophical Investigations* of the Austrian philosopher Ludwig Wittgenstein? I take the notion of a 'family resemblance' from him. It's a difficult work, but rewarding. It deserves a wider audience than the pack of logic-choppers who inhabit our philosophy departments."

Still mystified, I was only half listening. I was still reviewing our relations in high school. Indeed, our classmates had baptized us "the B and Bs." That had come about because he had started insisting on addressing me by my last name and on being called "Berger" in return. I couldn't be wrong. We had been friends.

Baffled, I tried to catch the eye of the once-Berger. The darting brown eyes of the once-Berger were having none of it. Only once in the following moments did I feel the force of those see-all spectacles as they made a quick sweep over my features. And for a bare nanosecond did my identity seem to be acknowledged. Not with pleasure, exactly. Nor with displeasure, exactly. Just noted, just quickly appraised. It was as if I was a work of possible interest, on which he might be asked to render judgment. The eyes had turned away, as it were, with a Gallic shrug: *Aucune importance.* Then the eyes turned on Hack and gave him the once over. He appeared to be a more significant object of attention. But further study would be required.

"HMB, what do you think of the new tack that Manny Shine is taking?"

Hack exchanged a look with me, confirming that we were in the company of a legend. The idea still boggled my mind, but I was adjusting. There seemed to be something almost predestined about the boy Henry Berger being father to the man who was HMB.

Hack could hardly restrain himself. He was laughing as discreetly as he could. But he was obviously a distraction. And HMB would have to take cognizance of it. He turned and looked in Hack's direction with a vaguely threatening mien.

"I said something amusing, Mr. . . . ?"

"Ferkin. Hack Ferkin, Mr. Harrummb." The circle around HMB looked surprised. Was the gentleman clearing his throat?

"Ah yes, the well-known *artiste de cabaret*," HMB responded testily. "A new tack?" He made the little movement with the two fingers of both hands that properly punctuated the phrase. "We shall just have to wait and see—when Consuela opens her new show."

He turned to Hack with mock amiability. "Do you know Manny Shine's work, Mr. Ferkin? HMB played some part in calling the attention of the knowledgeable to his work. But you've been away, haven't you?"

"Everybody calls me Hack, Harrummb," Hack said with his usual air of urbanity. This time there could be no doubt. The gutteral drum-roll was intended. We were about to be treated to fireworks. "I've seen it. But then what do I know about painting? I am only a sculptor and a mere footnote to modernism—at best."

"Ah, just so. Originally, even HMB failed to see the significance of Shine's work. He saw only incoherence, albeit a shining kind of incoherence. It disoriented him. He thought it lacked focus. But then HMB was going through a bad period personally. *Une crise de coeur.*"

HMB smiled benignly and tapped his chest gently.

"And he is the first to admit that such subjective states of mind can interfere with true understanding."

Again his smile swept his circle of listeners.

"So he took another look. And he was rewarded. It was nothing short of a revelation. What HMB took to be a kind of coded obscenity was really a profound expression of disgust. The kind of fury you see in a great painter like Bosch. There is vulgarity, even obscenity, in Shine's work. But it is the daring-to-be-vulgar you find only in the greatest masters. Like Caravaggio. I would say that among the painters who are called abstract expressionists"—again HMB made the little gesture with the fingers of both hands, thereby imparting with great economy his suspicion of labels—"Shine is the only one doing significant social commentary. And I hope he doesn't lose that fury in his new work."

He looked around the circle, letting his eyes rest longest on Ferkin. But Hack declined to respond.

"Sally Bentnick was another one of your discoveries, wasn't she, HMB?"

The question came from the young woman who had retreated so quickly from Hack. Now she was standing very near HMB.

He smiled. "That's right. And again HMB did not see the point—not immediately. At first he thought her painting lacked something he couldn't quite put his finger on. His eye seemed constantly to wander to the surrounding space—above, to the left, to the right. She seemed to want HMB to look away from the work. Again, he realized that it was his own limitations. We critics, you know, must be modest in our judgments. *Re*-vision is not a mortal sin, not even a venal sin. On *re*-view,"—he drew the hyphen with a short but graceful gesture—"he realized that was precisely the intent of the artist. The thought occurred to him that Bentnick was indulging in a kind of inverse *trompe-l'oeil*— something akin to the perspectival jokes the sixteenth century was so fond of. Sally was doing the same thing with color. It was, in the language of abstraction, the unframed, the inverted *trompe-l'oeil*. What a bravura conception!"

He beamed at having given such winged words to his perception. And then he saw that Hack was looking puzzled.

"Have I said something puzzling, Mr. Ferkin? A philosopher, I forget whom, once said that he knew Wittgenstein was deep because Wittgenstein looked puzzled whenever he, the philosopher, lectured."

"It's really nothing, Harrummb."

This time, Hack's air of good fellowship seemed a trifle forced. Again the throat clearing drew attention away from HMB to his stooped figure. "But do you always begin in puzzlement and . . . "

"Of course. It's a mark of authenticity in art. Just as familiarity is a mark of kitsch."

HMB smiled. The last words were conveyed without the need for amplification. HMB had scored. Everybody present knew his opinion of Ferkin's work. They all smiled. Except for Hack. And me.

"You don't like Bentnick's work, Ferkin?" HMB pressed. "You are not swept on wings of color into the surrounding space by that gorgeous object?" HMB's hand was outstretched toward the painting. Then it swept full circle round the room. "But then you are a sculptor. Space and color are perhaps not sculptural values, in your view."

Hack Ferkin's face now darkened. It was the first time that I had ever seen my friend really angry.

"That's not painting, you jackass. That's *home furnishing*," Ferkin countered savagely.

I stole a look at my former friend, the famous critic. The great brow of HMB was twisted into a Gordian knot of perplexity. It was the kind of expression perhaps seen at appropriate moments on the face of the celebrated Wittgenstein. HMB had been rendered speechless. It was the first time I could remember seeing Henry Berger rendered speechless.

T HE EXCHANGE OF OPINIONS JUST REPORTED ARE NOW part of the oral history of that period. At least one recent writer on contemporary art history claims to be one of the knowledgeables present at the encounter. The incident has passed into history, of course, because HMB was, and continues to be, such a dominant figure. Hack is, as he himself acknowledged, a mere footnote and I, who was perhaps the *casus belli*, simply do not figure at all in the accounts.

Word spread rapidly throughout New York art circles. In the days immediately following, Consuela Connery brought it up with me. Her show was to open in about two weeks. She was apprehensive. It was not good public relations, she suggested.

Her concern simply did not register on me. For I was shrouded in grief. Two days after that Sunday conversation, early in the morning, I knocked at Hack's bedroom door. I got no answer. I knocked again. Still no answer. I went into the room.

Hack was still in bed. His eyes and mouth were open. It was clear he was dead.

He could only have died a little while before, for rigor mortis had not yet taken over his limbs. I closed his eyes and mouth. That gave his face a composed, half-amused look. I spied a bud vase on a nearby table containing a fresh rose. I seized it and put it in his hand. I moved the hand so that the rose touched his nostrils. He could no longer delight in its fragrance, of course, but I thought that's how he would have wanted to be remembered

The *Times* published a brief obituary. On the Obituary Page. No picture. He was, after all, only a footnote to modernism.

His remains were cremated. There were few people at the memorial ceremony, mostly relatives, who had come to take the ashes back to Nebraska. His time had passed, he was never a major figure. But I am sure some people didn't come who would otherwise have been there. I think they stayed away out of fear that it might get back to HMB that they were among the mourners.

Perhaps these thoughts are colored by what happened to me subsequently. For I cannot hide the strong conviction that HMB, no longer able to vent his wrath on Hack, simply turned on me, and waged a particularly mean-spirited vendetta against me.

When Consuela Connery's show of "younger trend-setters" opened, with four of my canvases, it was widely reviewed, in the *Times, Art News,* the *Bulletin of the College Art Association,* even in the *New Yorker.* Manny Shine's "new tack" received the lion's share of attention. But in all of these publications, my name received some mention. And a sentence or two of cautious but usually not unfavorable comment

But one New York critic did devote a whole paragraph in his long review of the show to my work. Writing in *New York Magazine,* HMB said:

Finally, it should be noted that the show at the Connery contains four canvases by the until recently expatriate painter, Jack Birnbaum. Many had been looking forward to his first show here, since news of his Paris collaboration with the late Haskell Ferkin had been much ballyhooed. This critic missed the Paris show called *Sous-Mer*. Frankly, he has never been an admirer of Ferkin. Minus the carnival atmosphere that always seemed to surround Ferkin's work—and to hide Ferkin's flaws—Birnbaum's canvases appear at best inoffensive and at worst modernist *kitsch*. HMB finds it painful to pass this judgment, since he had in the distant past found promise in Birnbaum's work. Indeed he tended to distrust his first impression that the work was bland and derivative. Perhaps it was the critic's fault. He had recently had an attack of an old ailment, a minor *crise de foie*. So he returned again to the Connery gallery, alas and alack, only to find his initial reaction confirmed. HMB now regrets his early mistake. He apologizes to the painter for misleading him into abandoning a career in dentistry.

In the months that followed, I came to recognize the power my former friend now wielded. Consuela returned my paintings unsold. The few appointments I could get in Fifty-seventh Street or in Madison Avenue galleries usually ended with rejection and some comments to the effect that my work was innocuous. God, how I hate that word! I would have preferred to hear someone say it made them want to vomit. Few used exactly the vocabulary of HMB, but it was clear that the dealers who viewed my work were all speaking his language.

By the beginning of the next year, I had given up on those centers of power. I was showing my works in the outskirts, at sidewalk art shows in the Village and Brooklyn Heights.

I was trying to cope with the loss of Hack. I had never realized how much he meant to me. He would have scoffed at the idea that he had been a substitute father to me. But in the year that followed his death, I constantly fought against a sense of numbness. I was without hope. I wandered the streets, not knowing where I was. I couldn't paint. I spent a lot of time in old movie houses and in museums.

I must now tell you about the event that marked a new beginning in my art. Bear in mind the double blow I had suffered—the death of Hack and the Fall from Grace. I was also running out of money. But I don't think that was a major factor in my state of depression. I could always mooch a little from my brother Morton, now a rising star at Columbia Physicians and Surgeons, if I was willing to put up with a lecture from

Morton's wife, Phyllis. The subject was always the same, about getting a grip on myself and being a *Mensch*, like her husband. I would go to Sunday dinner at my parents'—they had now moved to Central Park West—and my mother would slip me a twenty while my father pointed to himself as an example of what dentistry and America, in that order, could do for a Jewish boy with ambition.

But in one of the rare moments when I considered where my next meal was coming from, I took out the Caillou painting. I was wondering how much it would fetch, where I could sell it. I was overcome by its beauty. I can only describe that moment as an epiphany. I know that sounds extravagant. But before then, it had been only a prized souvenir. Now in a bolt of lightening it had acquired transcendence. I had looked at hundreds of impressionist paintings. Now I was having that wonderful experience of looking at something familiar and *seeing* it for the first time, seeing that it deserved to be enshrined, knowing that it had become a part of me and that I could never part with it.

Suddenly, I realized I was sobbing. I hadn't cried in years. It was so long ago I couldn't remember when. I hadn't cried during the war when I had been wounded by shrapnel. I hadn't even cried when I discovered Hack's body.

My first thought was that this was a delayed release of grief for Hack, for I was aware of a feeling of loss, of mourning, that seemed to accompany my tears.

"Why are you crying, you twit?" I asked myself.

And then, from somewhere within me a voice that didn't seem to be mine said, "Because of a soldier, killed by a Prussian bullet. Because life is short. And because art is simply not long enough."

It was not long after that I started making Caillou studies. It was little more than doodling when it all began, first some sketches in oil of the snow scene on the wall of the portrait, then of the lady with the vase of flowers. They were very unsatisfactory. They made me feel how little I knew about the techniques of impressionism.

After a few hours devoted to these subjects, I myself began to wonder exactly what I was doing. I rationalized it as experiments in a new style. But that sounds far too deliberative. Art is one of the fundamental forms of play. I remember Hack telling me that, more than once, usually invoking some example of a child finding out what he can make a rattle do. Fantasy is also important. Since fantasies are part of the private self, they are private, even secret, forms of play. These were secret forms of play. One day I was surprised to find that I was no longer painting in the *Sous-Mer* style.

So, without really noticing it, my fantasy was taking over the part of my conscious life devoted to painting. I suddenly wanted to paint again, but when I began I simply could no longer do anything abstract.

I now spent a lot of time in museums. Previously I had been pretty catholic in my taste. Now I found that the only rooms I was drawn into housed the impressionists. One day I realized that I had lost interest in everything painted after 1870.

I would be standing before an early Monet or a Renoir or a Pissarro and suddenly I would become aware that some fellow viewer was looking at me. With curiosity, sometimes with annoyance.

Once a little old lady tapped me on the shoulder with her umbrella.

"Young man, you are making a pest of yourself. Would you kindly stop it!"

"I am sorry," I said, coloring. "What was I doing?"

"You were talking to yourself! If you didn't realize it, you had probably better seek help."

I reddened and stammered a further apology.

I had not realized that there were eavesdroppers on these private seminars, where there was usually only one question to be answered: How would Caillou have done that?

One day I began a subject not suggested in the Caillou portrait of Renoir. It was a bathing scene. I had recently been to Washington and looked at "The Boating Party" in the Phillips. A day or two later, I had gone to the St. Mark's Cinema to see the artist's son Jean's little movie, *Partie de Campagne.* I was struck by similarities that must have been intended. But for days I wondered how Papa Renoir's friend Caillou would have handled the lights, the colors, the gentleman's mustache, the lady's flirtatious smile.

I worked on it feverishly. When it was finished, I was absolutely overjoyed with what I had wrought. It was a breakthrough.

That night, as I fantasized my way into sleep, my reverie took the

38

form of a great exhibit, literally rooms and rooms of Caillous. Soon thereafter, I began the catalog of this grand retrospective. It took twenty years to finish.

I HAVE HAD LEAN YEARS, I CAN TELL YOU. I, TOO, HAVE suffered for my art. There was a long period when you might have seen me, cowering in a folding chair, wearing a ratty old sweater, a knitted cap pulled down over my eyes to hide my shame. I see myself in those years of misery at the shopping malls with easy access off the Jersey Turnpike, amid the makers of crewel, the carvers of scrimshaw, the welders of jewelry, less reticent, more businesslike than myself. They would arrive in caravans of recreational vehicles. I, the old-fashioned walking peddler, would arrive from the nearest working Pennsy station, my wares upon my back. I had become a bohemian caricature haunting the shopping malls—seeking some buyers for my paintings of tropical fish.

My first commission came in 1957. It came from an unexpected source—my father, Dr. Jack Birnbaum. He was that year the treasurer of the New York Dental Association.

I got a call from him in late spring. It was a summons to his office on Eighty-sixth Street. I had not seen my parents for months, but I thought I knew what he wanted to see me about. Every year at this time, he would renew his offer of assistance. If I applied to a school of dental technology in the city, I could count on his support. "You are no spring chicken, Jack. It's time to think about taking your place in society," I could hear him saying to me.

That year I did not know whether I would finally succumb.

When I arrived at his office, he had just finished with his last patient.

I could hear his voice. "Remember, Father, floss! Floss! Think of it as confession. You are absolving yourself from sin!" I heard his hearty

39

laugh. He was feeling expansive. The next moment a youngish priest came out of his office. He flashed me a smile of renewed innocence.

"Come on in, *Jungling!*" my father called to me. I didn't like the sound of that *Jungling*.

He was still wearing his short lab jacket and he was washing his hands. He went over to the closet, took off the lab jacket. Then he donned his elegant suitcoat. He was no longer in the ready-to-wear class.

"Come, walk me home!" he said, "I have a proposition." Then he stopped and looked at me aghast. "Don't you have something decent to wear? I am ashamed to be seen with you."

I bent my head to inspect my corduroys. They were indeed shabby. But they were clean. I held my head up and returned his stare defiantly.

He picked a route that stayed mostly on Broadway. Perhaps he felt he'd look less out of place with me there. He kept to general topics until we passed Zabar's, where he ducked in to buy some smoked fish. When he returned, he was ready for business. I thought I knew what was to follow.

"I think I have a commission for you," he announced. I was surprised. It was not about dental technology. I could feel his eyes on me, waiting for me to show enthusiasm. But I wasn't sure where I was being led. My mind was still on dental technology.

"A painting," he said. "A portrait," he continued.

"Oh," I said, trying to show enthusiasm.

"The president's term is up this year—Dr. Sean Balfour. Our presidents have always had their portraits painted before leaving office."

I looked puzzled.

"The president of the New York Dental Association! Who do you think I'm talking about, the president of General Motors? Anyway, I've mentioned your name and it was received—well not exactly enthusiastically, but let's say—open-mindedly. They want you to go for an interview."

"I've never painted a portrait."

"I know. That's part of the problem, but I showed them your clippings from that Paris show—you know, what's its name. They were particularly impressed with what the *New Yorker* said about you."

40

"I suppose I could do it. How much would it pay?"

"That's up to you. What the traffic will bear. But remember you are supposed to be a famous artist, not a bum!"

"I've no idea what the traffic will bear."

My father thought for a moment. I could see him doing a mental calculation. Then he gave me his opinion.

"A full upper plate would cost between twelve and fifteen hundred. Both upper and lower would be in the range of three thousand. I don't think they'd go that high. Fifteen hundred. I'd say. Because you're a famous artist. Otherwise, I don't think they'd go beyond twelve. Have you got a suit?"

I shook my head. He stopped and handed me the bag of goodies. He looked me over and turned me around. "I think it'll work. We'll have one of my older suits made over."

He took his smoked fish back and slapped me playfully on the back.

If you are desperate enough to become a portrait painter, you should expect to be at the mercy of a committee. My patrons are usually institutions, not individuals. It is a committee that usually gives me my commission and sits in judgment on my finished work. The portrait must of course reproduce a flattering image of the subject—the judgment of associates counts more in this respect than does that of the subject. But such portraits are, after all, only office furniture. They are intended to render an aura of dignity, of high seriousness, of experience, soundness, and continuity.

They are trappings of power. Do not expect that anyone will examine them as art. I have never had illusions as to why my services were sought. Typically, a painting occupies a greater space than a photograph. It therefore confers greater status on its subject. It shows greater respect.

In any case, the Dental Association committee was impressed enough by my manner or my father's suit or my credentials—I am not sure which—to commission me to paint Dr. Sean Balfour's portrait. And, coached by my father, I got them to agree to a fee equivalent to the cost of a full upper plate. At first, they expected me to work from photographs—the portraits of presidents past had all been done from photographs. It was an inspired bit of salesmanship that I insisted on live sittings. For when the committee inspected the finished work, they pronounced it "more lifelike" than its companions, a quality they ascribed to my insistence on sittings. And since then, I have been commissioned to paint the portraits of all the subsequent presidents.

That same year my brother Morton was on a similar committee at Presbyterian. My work was, of course, not reviewed anywhere, but I never had to advertise. It was word-of-mouth advertising.

I occasionally see some of my work from those days. I have never seen any of which I have cause to feel ashamed. It's funny how instantly I can recognize the work as my own even when, as usually, I have not the foggiest recollection of the face.

But sometimes I come across someone I painted whose features I do remember. A while back I was in Columbia P and S and I passed a whole gallery of paintings I had done during that early period. I was walking the length of the gallery bemused by the fact that I had no memory of any of them. Then suddenly I came upon one I remembered. I recognized the tattersall vest and the bowtie first. He was a sharp-featured, bespectacled old gnome. I knew instantly his name, without having to consult the nameplate: Dr. Newton Trueheart. I felt flushed. Suddenly I was blushing. After all these years!

I remember Dr. Trueheart because during the sittings I had wanted so much to shut him up. He had just been elected President of the College of Obstetrics and Gynecology—something like that—when he came to my studio. Yes, I had acquired a studio by then.

I usually tried to get my subjects to talk while they were sitting. So long as it did not disturb the pose, it relaxed them and often gave me some hint of that elusive smile or gesture that make a portrait look less like an overgrown passport photo.

Dr. Trueheart made it immediately clear that he had no time for small talk. He brought a small tape recorder out of his briefcase and started to dictate even before I had arranged him in a pose. Nothing thereafter could stop him. He was revising his book, he told me. "It is standard in the field," he said. "On disorders of the uterus," he added, after which he addressed himself exclusively to the machine. He spoke

42

as if he were addressing the assembled students and staff of Physicians and Surgeons on disorders of the uterus. Dr. Trueheart's voice was high, penetrating, and nasal.

The revisions, so far as I could tell, consisted mostly of discussions of his cases since the last edition. I could tell he came from distant New England, but I could never penetrate the layers of disordered uteruses that surrounded him to discover from where. One thing I was reasonably certain of—he was a lifelong bachelor. According to my brother Morton, misogyny is epidemic among gynecologists.

I almost didn't finish that commission. I remember him discoursing with clinical detachment. He had a true "calling" for medicine, you might say. I, on the other hand, suffered from episodes of nausea and retching. Dr. Trueheart seemed completely oblivious to the discomfort he was causing me.

Anyway, halfway through the sittings, I went out and bought a TV. It was my first set, black and white—an act of pure self-defense against Dr. Trueheart. I hooked it up in my studio and turned up the volume. I found I could paint and between dabs look at the screen.

I had to do that only once, thank God. We were getting close to finished. It was a night sitting. And the only thing I could find to watch was the election returns. It was the primaries in the gubernatorial elections. I would have preferred baseball, but I reconciled myself to learning, at the least, who the candidates were.

As it happens, I tuned in at the moment when the losing candidate for lieutenant governor on the Republican ticket was expected to make his concession speech. He had been resoundingly rejected by his party, poor man whoever he was, and I was feeling sorry for him. The audience in the rented hotel ballroom was busy chanting something. It sounded like "Ontym! Ontym! Ontym." I later deciphered that as: "Monty, Monty, Monty."

One heard those cheers before the camera finally settled on a door through which a well-dressed man was leading a woman. He was much younger than I expected for a seeker of such high office. He appeared to be about my own age. So did his wife. The network commentator recounted his history and that of his campaign as he worked his way through the crowd. I learned that he came from an old banking family, was himself on Wall Street, and that this was his first run for public office. I got the impression that the commentator, in his measured enunciation of the candidate's full name, felt the party's rejection was the best thing it had done in years.

I suppose I had heard the name before, but I really didn't pay attention to politics. I stopped painting to look at him. Up to that moment, I hadn't had a clear view of him through the sea of other faces and what I knew conditioned me to expect a patrician face. That was decidedly not the case.

It was a downright common, a homely, face. The most prominent feature, the nose, was large, even bulbous. An ill-restrained walrus mustache dangled beneath the nose, even more at odds with my expectations. It was a street-smart face. It was a face with a perpetual wink. If I had had to guess his occupation from his face, I think I would have guessed that he was a pool-hall hustler. It was a face I would have loved to paint.

As the camera closed in on it, I was struck by the fact that this was not the face of a man crushed by disaster. It almost could have been a victory. He was strutting like a cock: Stick with me, kid, we'll get there yet! I know a shortcut.

The woman he was holding by the hand looked much younger on closer view. The camera also had zeroed in on her as, hand in hand, the couple ascended the stage together. She was the one who seemed to realize that this was a defeat, an occasion to be suffered in dignity. She was taking the defeat hard. No one could doubt that, or the bravery with which she kept back the tears. While he waited for the crowd to become silent, she stood by him, composed, still holding onto his hand.

The rejected candidate finally was allowed to begin.

"I just want to tell all you wonderful guys that both Roxie and I ... "

His voice had a nice baritone roll. I could not hear how the sentence ended, for the sound was drowned by renewed applause. What I heard subsequently were disconnected phrases, soothing platitudes that seemed to flow over the audience like honey .

She did not speak. No doubt it would have been too much of an effort.

They left the stage. Her hand was no longer in his. For a moment the camera caught her alone. She turned and confronted it. She was not smiling. A smile would have been a veil that hid the truth. This was a face, uncomposed, vulnerable. She seemed to be looking directly at me. And it obliterated all other perceptions—of the ballroom, of her husband, of the painting I was doing, of Dr. Trueheart himself.

What I was feeling, I suppose, was the kind of effect that movie directors strive for all their lives, the kind of magical communion that lighting, camera angle, and so forth can create with an audience in a dark theater. Or make any man feel, despite the fact that he knows it to be the sheerest illusion, that he is, for the moment, the sole and exclusive object of a goddess' attention. It is Garbo in *Grand Hotel*, that klutz when moving, looking when still so ethereal. It is Elizabeth Taylor in *Butterfield Eight* before she opens her mouth. Roxie, whatever her last name was, was having just that effect on me.

It was that odd, adolescent experience of falling in love with an image. Even grown men can have it.

I am recording here my first awareness of the existence of L. Montcalme Carter and his wife, Roxanne, soon to enter my life. I once told my wife Lee about it, that I had seen her brother and his wife for the first time on TV. I think I said something to the effect that they had made a strong impression, in different ways, upon me—something very innocuous like that.

I lived to regret even that. Lee has remarkable powers of perception. And, as I have indicated, she is also an indefatigable spinner of myths. She thinks of me as the reincarnation of Jacob the patriarch, and she transmuted this episode into a veritable omen. In her version it was my first and blinding vision of Rachel at the well. Needless to say, my protests against all this mythologizing are in vain.

There is a postscript.

I awoke from my trance-like state to find that Dr. Trueheart was looking at me strangely. I had stopped painting. He had stopped dictating. He was regarding me for the very first time with interest. I was afraid he was reading my thoughts. I blushed.

"She's a patient," he said quietly. His voice was hushed, decibels below his usual mode of speech. "Old Southern family. Kentucky, I think. Wonderful carriage. Knows horses."

45

It was the first time I had heard Dr. Trueheart say anything not connected with his medical specialty. I picked up a brush and looked as if I were concentrating on a highlight on Dr. Trueheart's spectacles.

"They have a problem of fertility. Her husband brought her to see me. I did a thorough examination," he said, returning to his more familiar, didactic tone.

I was now painting furiously, wanting him to stop, in fear of his continuing, in fact prepared to throttle him if he did.

"I've never seen a more perfect pelvis," he intoned. "Or a more ample uterus." His voice trailed off. I thought I detected something almost reverential in the tone.

He allowed a moment of silence to follow this fond memory.

"I thought the problem was probably with the husband." That was the clinician speaking. Then he picked up his tape microphone and resumed his dictation.

O N A WINDY, WET NIGHT IN EARLY NOVEMBER 1966, I found myself on Eighth Street, between Fifth and Sixth, rather later than was my custom. I was coming from a party, and as I exited onto the street I was greeted by a shower of cold rain. I was unprepared for it. I was close to Sixth Avenue, but there was no cab in sight. I didn't want to go back to the party. Besides, I indulge in cabs only in emergencies. I was standing there getting soaked. An empty cab approached. I debated whether this really was an emergency. I decided it wasn't enough of one. I waved him on. I am pretty unworldly, I guess.

Anyway, out of the corner of my eye, I saw the lights of the cafeteria on the opposite corner and it was still open. I made a dash for it. I was inside before I realized that I was in the Waldorf Cafeteria. It had been my home away from home when the abominable Manny Shine was making out with some "debutante."

The decor was unchanged. It still had the garish, shadowless fluores-

46

cent lighting and the tubular stainless steel chairs of the 1940s, the tables
with the black formica tops, the imitation-leather booths along the wall.
At the serving area I poured myself a cup of coffee. A young Puerto
Rican girl was doing the night shift. That was different. In the old days,
it would have been an older woman from a Polish ghetto, with a heavy
accent. But some things just don't change: the coffee smelled and tasted
as vile as ever.

The place felt different in subtle ways. I decided it was the emptiness.
In the old days, even at two in morning, there would have been a knot
of Trotskyites—followers of one or another fractious group—
discussing the party line, sometimes several groups present together,
glaring at each other from opposite walls. But they were gone—maybe
dead, maybe living in Levittown. There were only two other customers.
They were at a booth in the back. The man's back was to me. He was
bordering on middle age, from the evidence of the graying red hair that
surrounded a large bald spot. What I noted about the woman were the
thick lenses of her glasses.

As I paid for my coffee, I heard shrill sounds coming from that table.
Minding your own business is a law of life for New Yorkers. So I chose
a table as far away as possible and chose a chair that put my back to
them. I hoped for the rain to end quickly and release me from this
dreary place.

But the voices carried, particularly the man's. It was a voice drenched
with drink. I could almost smell his breath from this distance. And
there was something familiar about it, the voice I mean.

"Don't give me that shit," he was yelling. "Don't give me *that* shit."

And suddenly I recognized the voice. It was Manny Shine. Shine
never could resist repeating a good line.

I turned around to look, as stealthily as possible. Shine's back was to
me, and my view of the pair was largely obstructed by the booth. But it
was Shine all right. The shape of the head under the corona of greasy
red hair confirmed it. If Shine is here, who is using the apartment, I
wondered, smiling to myself.

"What do you know about artistic feeling? The only genuine feeling
you know anything about is what happens when my cock is in you."

Manny was entertaining a young lady. It was like the old days, Shine offering some debutante the chance to ball one of the future greats. Now that he had truly arrived, no doubt the offer had become even more attractive. In the old days I had sometimes seen the beginning of Manny's affairs. I had always imagined them ending in a pleasant afterglow. Now I realized that this was not always the case.

The girl was sobbing steadily. I tried to ignore the discord. I wanted to get away before something violent happened. Then I heard the sound of a chair being knocked over. I was afraid to look. The noise that followed was that of scuffling feet.

"Where the fuck are you going? I'm just getting started on you."

This was followed by a thud, the kind that could only have come from flesh hitting flesh, his upon hers. I heard the sound of glass breaking. I turned around. Manny was standing, looking down in the direction of his feet. A blond girl in a camel's hair coat was lying there, face down, sobbing uncontrollably. Her hands were searching the floor for her broken glasses. Weaving unevenly, Shine seemed to be on the point of kicking her, but he was so drunk he staggered before he could steady himself to deliver the blow.

Straightaway, I was out of my chair. I didn't stop to consider whether to intervene or how. Later, I wondered whether I did what I did from hidden rage, pent-up year-long, at Manny Shine. And at his success! I have never thought of myself as a man of decision. On my way to the battle zone, my eye met that of the Puerto Rican girl. She was rigid, paralyzed with fear.

Shine did not see me coming until my face was right up in his. He had no chance to ask what I thought I was doing butting in on something not my business. "What the fuck do you—" He probably would have said it twice. It all happened so quickly. I put my hand up to Shine's unshaven face and my whole weight into his body, and I sent him reeling and spinning against the back wall. He didn't even have the chance to brace himself against my sudden charge. He lay there, stunned from the impact of the collision.

I felt the blood barreling through my veins. My temples throbbed with anger. I felt the vitality of that anger. As I leaned down to attend to the sobbing girl, I wondered whether Shine had any idea who his assailant was.

48

I got down on all fours beside her. I found her glasses. One of the lenses was shattered. I helped her to her feet. The cashier finally came from behind the cashier's stand to assist, muttering, "Pobrecita, pobrecita."

"Are you all right?" I asked.

Through her sobs, she nodded that she was. But I could see her nose was bleeding profusely. It had soiled her expensive coat. I took out some tissues from my pocket and put it up to her nose.

She started to get up. She put on her glasses and squinted with one eye at me. Manny was beginning to stir.

"Come with me," I said. I was overwhelmed by my own resolution. She let me lead her out. It had stopped raining. On Sixth Avenue I managed to hail a cab. Okay, this was an emergency. My idea was to take her to the emergency room at Bellevue.

"Where are you taking me?" she asked through the tissues.

"The emergency room at Bellevue."

"No, not there."

"But you need first aid. Something may be broken."

She felt her nose with her free hand. "No, I don't think so."

"You still need first aid."

My lodging and studio was on West Twenty-third Street. I gave the driver my address. And settled back to find that she was inspecting me through the unshattered lens and from above the bloodied tissues.

At my apartment, the nosebleed finally yielded to an ice pack, and I insisted upon applying a wide swatch of adhesive tape to her nose, even though she said it wasn't broken. Her face was swelling.

I gave her a stiff drink. She took a long swig of it.

I tried to imagine her face without the insults it had sustained. Manny's women had never been beauties. This was not a beautiful face, I thought. But there was something about this girl. She was not a debutante. She was older. Not simply experimenting. The clothes were tasteful and expensive. She wore no makeup. I didn't know her name yet, for she had not volunteered it. It was a clean, forthright face. When she put her glasses back on, her face changed. She closed one eye and squinted with the other through the unbroken lens. It made her look

49

much younger, like some precocious adolescent cursed with poor eyesight. I expected momentarily to find braces on her teeth.

"May I know the name of my—knight-at-arms?" she asked. Her voice was well modulated and in the mezzo-soprano range. It rose steadily until it reached "knight-at-arms." Then it hesitated a moment and plunged on, giving the phrase a musical ring. The effect was coquettish. Pleasantly so.

"Jack Birnbaum. And yours?"

"Lee Carter."

She looked around the studio. She took in the dais, the lights, the empire couch. Her eye fell on my easel.

"You are a painter," she said. I nodded assent. I finished the first aid. She suffered my final ministering acts in silence. "The man I was with is a painter."

I nodded. "I know. Manny Shine."

Her face lit up in surprise. "You know him?"

I nodded. "I once shared an apartment with him. On Banks Street."

"He still lives there." She fell silent.

"He was a louse," I said. Then I felt I had intruded where I shouldn't. "I'm sorry. I shouldn't have said that. But we didn't get along."

"You were right the first time. He was a louse. He is a louse. I should know." She laughed. It was a derisive little laugh, directed, I thought, as much at her own foolishness as at Shine.

"Funny, I should be at the Waldorf, tonight. I used to spend long nights at the Waldorf Cafeteria. When Manny was romancing some debutante."

She applied the ice pack to her nose again. "I am his most recent *debutante*."

"Oh! I'm sorry!"

"No need!"

"So, if you knew he was a louse, why? Or shouldn't I ask?"

"I don't know. I guess I'm not choosy."

"Do you want me to call someone? To tell them where you are? I mean family? I don't think it would be a good idea to call Manny. She laughed. Then she thought for a moment. "There's my brother." She made a face at the thought of calling her brother. "Now, he's not a louse. He's a real prick! Excuse the expression, but by comparison Manny's only a weenie."

I waited while she gave the matter further thought. She looked around again at the studio.

"Can I stay here tonight? I could sleep there." She pointed to the couch. "I'll call someone tomorrow."

I thought for a moment. Caution was beginning to replace resolve. After a moment, I responded. "I guess so. You'd probably be more comfortable in the bed. I'll sleep there."

Then I remembered I had someone coming in the next morning. She'd have to be out by nine. Or at least, stay out of sight.

LEE NEVER COUNTERED BY OFFERING THAT SHE SLEEP ON the couch and I keep the bed. She never even said she was sorry that she was putting me to any trouble. She never said she was grateful for my help.

And she made no move toward vacating the bedroom. Not the next day. While I was busy with my client she went out. When she returned, she had a new wardrobe. She smiled at me, slipped into the bedroom and came out to model it for my approval.

Nor did she show any signs of decamping the day after. She went out and this time returned with armloads of kitchen utensils. The bell rang repeatedly as she accepted deliveries of groceries, from faraway places, from Dino and Deluca, Sherry Wine and Spirits, and from a nearby Gristede's. She announced that she would make dinner. It was an absolutely magnificent dinner. And over dinner she told me she didn't see why I should continue sleeping on the couch. There was plenty of room in the bed for the two of us.

Next morning she was up before me. I heard her getting breakfast, trying to be quiet so as not to disturb me. Then she entered the bedroom, bearing a breakfast tray. She was wearing a new challis wrapper, and her long blond hair was tied in back with a red ribbon. I had not seen that tray before. I didn't own one. It was one of her recent purchases. On it was orange juice, hot croissants, orange marmalade, and coffee. I smelled the aroma—French roast.

She saw I was awake and smiled. She really had a disarming, innocent smile. A sunbeam caught one of the thick lenses of her new glasses. It made me suddenly aware that they were no longer a distraction. I was only conscious that she was, after all, a very comely creature.

She set the tray down on the bed and I reached up and put my arms around her waist and drew her mouth down to mine. She tasted of croissant and orange marmalade. She disengaged and got back into bed.

There was a moment of silence. Neither of us seemed to know exactly what to say. Lee found her tongue first.

"I am numb. You are a satyr," she said. Then she quickly added, so that I wouldn't get the wrong impression, "And I loved every minute of it!"

A week later Lee was still at my little apartment on Twenty-third Street. So far as I knew, she hadn't called anyone to say where she was. She took over the shopping, the cooking, even the cleaning. She stayed out of sight when a client came for a sitting.

She had examined much of my painting and said intelligent things about it. One evening, after another wonderful dinner, she asked me whether she could model for me. I set up and she took off her clothes, but we ended up on the floor under the hot, glaring lights, making sweaty, lubricious, unrestrained love.

By the end of the week, she had gathered the full history of my life. And I knew next to nothing about her. Except that she had a brother she didn't get along with.

It was, for a brief period, a floating island, a fairy story, an idyll, something out of the unexpurgated edition of *The Arabian Nights*. Spun by a blond, blue-eyed Scheherazade, with skin like alabaster. Circassian rather than Arabian, a preview of what Allah provides to the faithful in heaven.

One day, quite suddenly, she announced to me: "Our life needs organizing, Jack." She paused. "This place is too small for the two of us." She paused again.

"So, I've made an offer on the building."

I was astonished. It involved such big money, and it was so casual. It was a whim of the very rich. Very, very rich. It was the first inkling I had that she was rich. I mean *rich*.

"I've been talking to an architect," she continued. "We can remodel. It would be easy to expand our space, using this floor and the floor above."

The future, the permanence of our relationship, had never come up, not in our tenderest moments nor in our most serious ones. All of this happening at once took my breath away.

"I don't think I can let you do that, Lee."

She blinked her eyes at me. "Don't be silly," she said. "Think of it as my—dowry."

Her voice assumed that coquettish, mocking, lilting inflection she adopted when she really had something very definite in mind but sought to make it look like nothing special.

It was about this time that my family discovered that there was a woman living with me. It was Phyllis, my brother Morton's wife, who made the discovery. She had telephoned and Lee had answered. To Phyllis' inquiry who this was, Lee had answered simply, "a friend." To Phyllis that was sufficient incentive. That evening she and Morton just happened to drop in unexpectedly. They said they were in the neighborhood and just thought they'd pop in. I made the introductions, sat back, and watched Lee charm the pants off Morton.

I watched her adroitly maneuver around Phyllis. Phyllis thought she was being subtle in her probing, but Lee was enjoying playing the woman of mystery. It was rather like Phyllis' trying to read the labels on Lee's clothes while they were still on Lee's back.

Phyllis: How'd you two meet? Lee: We met through an old and mutual friend. Phyllis: Oh, who? Lee: Oh, probably somebody you wouldn't know, a minor painter.

Lee suffered the interrogation good humoredly. She left a trail of names: expensive schools, summer camps, spas, shopping. Phyllis was clearly impressed, even if Lee left the source of all this good fortune shrouded in mystery.

Two things became obvious to Phyllis. First, Lee was the real goods. Second, Lee was not Jewish real goods.

As they left, Phyllis gave Lee a little peck on the cheek, a kind of little welcome-to-the-family. Meanwhile, Morton was whispering to me that he thought Lee was great. Phyllis also gave me a peck. She used it to whisper, "Too bad she's not Jewish." I raised my eyebrows. "Your mother and father will have a fit."

By this time I was no longer living in a make-believe world. Somehow, it had begun to dawn on me that I might end up with a wife. But I resisted bringing up the subject of marriage. The thought of all the fuss, the hurly-burly that goes with getting married, the families meeting, the dinners, all of that kept me from broaching the subject. Meanwhile, Lee continued to remain reticent about her people. Whenever I asked, she said I'd meet them in good time.

It was actually Lee who first suggested that we get married. She did so by asking whether I wanted a rabbi to marry us. I said I didn't care. Wouldn't my family like it, she persisted. I replied that I didn't think I could find a rabbi to do it. After all, she wasn't Jewish.

"No problem," Lee said, "I'll convert. It's really no big deal. Like Elizabeth Taylor."

"What about your family?" I asked.

"What about them?" she asked sharply.

"Don't you want to tell them?"

"When the time comes," was all she said.

Then something happened that brought everything to a screeching halt.

I was arrested and charged with committing obscenity.

It was about one o'clock on a Friday afternoon, and the front door-bell rang. I wasn't expecting anyone. I called out to Lee, was she expecting anyone? The answer was negative. I went to the door. There was a man in a gray fedora and raincoat. He asked if I was Jack Birnbaum and I said yes. He said he was from the NYPD.

"You are under arrest," he said, and produced a warrant for my arrest. I was stunned.

"What have I done?" I asked, still numbed by the news.

"Purveying obscenity," he muttered.

"Lee," I yelled. She came running. "I am being arrested."

She looked at the officer for an answer.

"It's an obscenity charge," the man said matter-of-factly. "Something to do with some book."

The book in question was called *Gourmet Sex*, and it had just been published by Pleasure Principle Press. PPP was the brainchild of Mitchell Fairchild, whom I had known in high school as Mo Gutkind. *Gourmet Sex* was the first title that PPP published. Fairchild had written the text and I had done the illustrations.

It had taken over five years for *Gourmet Sex* to see the light of day, and I had almost completely forgotten I ever did those drawings. The only time I remembered I had done them was when I looked at the Caillou painting *La Blanchisseuse* (see *Catalogue Raisonné*, No. 8), which was based on Dorothea, the female model for *Gourmet Sex*. I was desperate for money when I took the job. And I never got paid anything at the time. And now in lieu of payment, I was being arrested.

I had met Mitchell Fairchild at a sidewalk art show, where he had stopped to admire a couple of my Marthe nudes—the ones I had done of Marthe while she was doing the odalisque. Remember?

I didn't recognize Gutkind, as I waited while he inspected the red chalk drawings. But he knew me. Then he bought them; we got into conversation; and I recognized him. It was then that he told me that he had gotten a degree in clinical psychology.

"My speciality is sexual behavior," he said. "Your drawings give me an idea. They are so full of—how shall I put it—endearing imperfections. Like that wonderful appendix scar! They remind me of Egon Schiele. I love it. Come see me!" He handed me his card, and I learned he was now Mitchell Fairchild, Ph.D.

I remembered Gutkind from high school as a humorless left-wing zealot. What I found in Fairchild was the same humorless energy, but now he was crusading for sexual pleasure. He had devoted his life, he said, to undoing the crippling effects of Victorian repression. What he had in mind was a collaboration on a sex manual. He would write the text. I would do the illustrations. "Drawing demonstrates greater seriousness than mere photography, don't you think?"

"You are aware of the standard work of Dr. Van der Veldt?" he continued. "No? Well, it's been the standard sex manual for many years. Too many years. Mothers all over America give it to their daughters before the wedding."

He put his fingers together in a prayer-like gesture. "The trouble is it's a wee bit sacramental. All that talk about the 'communion' of the partners! And the only kind of sex discussed is—well—orthodox."

He looked to see if I took his meaning. "There is still much need for the work of enlightenment, Jack," he said with a weary smile. "So I want to produce a new book—something that enlightened priests and rabbis could use."

"A how-to book?" I asked. He didn't smile.

"I can't pay you immediately. We'll work out a share of the profits."

I was desperate enough to take the job on "spec." Fairchild agreed to pay for materials and models. It never entered my mind that what I was doing was against the law.

Fairchild seemed to know exactly what he wanted. And I had great difficulty pleasing him. He provided me with models. Their names were Herman and Dorothea.

They were uninspiring to the point of being ill-favored. Herman was short, stocky, very hairy, and very heavily bearded. Passing him in the subway, you might have noted the Elvis Presley hairdo. But nothing else about him would have lingered behind in memory. He had a "Semper Fi" tattoo on his left breast and a livid seven-inch scar on his right side, a reminder of a near fatal automobile accident. Dorothea I found at first downright repulsive. She was thin and flat-chested. And she had a large, disfiguring birthmark on her left hip.

What I produced ignored these features. I produced pretty Hermans and Dorotheas. When Fairchild saw my first efforts, he flew into a rage.

"What's wrong?" I asked indignantly.

56

"I want Herman and Dorothea. Those two aren't Herman and Dorothea."

He threw my drawings back at me.

"They look like Herman and Dorothea, but where is his scar? Where is her birthmark? I want to see his scar and her birthmark. She's thin, she's flat-chested. I don't want Marilyn Monroe—make her thin and flat-chested."

"I don't understand."

"It's really very simple. This is a book for the Hermans and the Dorotheas of this world. It's a book for—and about—ordinary people, with plain faces, with birthmarks and disfiguring scars. They are not the kind of people you fantasize about. I don't want you idealizing them."

He calmed down. "And another thing. Just as important, Jack. Look at their faces. Do those people look as if they were creating bliss in each other? These are supposed to be people who are transported out of their fucking skins. Realism, Jack, realism, yes! But above all, rapture. Rapture!"

It was not a happy collaboration, and in the end I just gave up. I never got a cent in payment, and I never gave it another thought. That is, not until I was arrested.

I was taken to the police station, spent about an hour in a holding cell, and then was taken for arraignment by police car to the Manhattan County Courthouse. It was there that I saw Fairchild for the first time in five years. He looked scared, but he had had time to retain a lawyer. The latter turned out to be a cousin. The cousin suggested that he could also serve as my counsel. I was about to agree, when Lee burst into the courtroom in the company of a distinguished-looking gray-haired man. She threw her arms about me and told me not to worry. The cavalry had arrived.

"This is Sherman Linden. He's the best I could do in a pinch. Mostly he does mergers. I'm afraid this is his first First Amendment case. But it'll be good experience for him."

Linden shook my hand. When he withdrew his hand, he looked at it. I had the feeling he wanted to wash it.

We were all shown to a conference room. Fairchild explained that

Gourmet Sex had just appeared under his imprint, Pleasure Principle Press. No copies of it had yet been sold. Indeed, contrary to his expectations, no book dealers wanted to handle it. He still had almost a thousand copies sitting in his office. Linden asked how it had come to the notice of the police. He had given a couple of copies to patients, he explained. One, a woman who had broken off her therapy, had complained to the police that her sex therapist was a pornographer.

Had he charged her for the book or was it a gift, Linden asked.

Just a nominal sum, Fairchild replied, somewhat sheepishly.

Linden took the news gravely. He was silent for several minutes. Then he beckoned to Fairchild's cousin, and they went into conference. I watched them as they spoke. Fairchild's cousin's face was a study in deference. I concluded that Sherman Linden must be one heavy hitter. I was beginning to get the idea that Lee was not merely rich; she was Fortune Five Hundred.

When they returned, Linden, acting as spokesman for both, announced pompously, "We think with a little luck we can get the charge reduced. To Misdemeanor Purveying. You'll probably get off with a suspended sentence, a fine, and the confiscation of the materials."

Both Fairchild and I breathed a sigh of relief. I glanced at Lee. She was shaking her head.

"I wish I could have gotten through to Morrie Ernst," she murmured.

I thought the matter would end there. The judge also showed that he held my counsel in high esteem. The fine was small, thanks in part to the mere presence of Sherman Linden. Above all, I didn't want my family to know. Morton and Phyllis would never let me forget it.

But I was wrong. In the next six months *Gourmet Sex* seemed to have a life of its own. It began to circulate in a pirated edition. Fairchild disclaimed all responsibility. He said that all he knew was that the edition had been printed in Taiwan. I didn't know whether to believe him.

Then it began to draw attention. In a *Times* magazine piece on sexual mores in the age of the pill, a social psychologist named Dr. Beverly Chew recommended it. She called it "a no-nonsense book." She complimented Fairchild and me and deplored the fact that we had had to adopt such devious strategems to get it in the hands of readers. She thought the illustrations were "genuinely sensitive—a true representation of the pleasure two loving people could give to each other."

I read the piece while Lee and I were still in bed breakfasting. I groaned.

"What's the matter?" she asked.

I tossed the magazine section over to her. She read it and put it aside.

"Well," I said. "It's a bad dream. Why won't the whole business go away?"

"I knew someone named Beverly Chew at Sarah Lawrence. I wonder if it's the same person," Lee said.

She yawned and cuddled up.

About that time, I ran into HMB on a Fifth Avenue bus. I had gotten on at Washington Square, sat down, and started reading. I just happened to look up from my book to discover him studying me with interest. I returned to my book.

It was a long time now. He appeared not to have changed his almost clerical habit. The only change I could detect was a pair of enormous horn-rimmed glasses. The sight of him made my stomach churn.

He ignored the cold shoulder. "I've seen your recent work," he began. "It's not at all bad."

"Oh, come on, Harrummb," I said testily. "It's kitsch. I didn't know you had a taste for pornography."

"HMB does not disapprove, so long as it does not pretend to be more than calendar art. The genuinely *entartig*—I have in mind, among other things, a certain class of Japanese woodcuts, some of Toulouse-Lautrec's lithographs—also has a place in the temple of art."

I made a great show of concentrating on my book, but HMB would not let me alone.

"I would like to do a piece on your recent work."

I closed my book abruptly. The angry slam drew the attention of an elderly couple, who had been dozing in nearby seats.

"Oh, nothing critical. It doesn't merit my attention in that way. I was thinking of a First Amendment piece. Something on the rights of expression of the graphic artist."

He obviously would not be put off. I decided to change the subject.

"And what 'mischief' are you up to these days?" I wagged my fingers around "mischief" in imitation of his well-known gesture.

"I am in charge of Art Affairs at Time, Inc. I write. I advise the twenty-seventh floor on acquisitions. They are really quite knowledgeable up there."

"Ah yes, I think I remember a piece of yours. On furniture, I think."

"No. I think you must be mistaken. Oh, you mean that little thing in *Fortune?*"

My father would not speak to me. Morton and Phyllis, who did continue to speak, spoke of nothing else. Phyllis, especially. One Sunday, she surprised me by inviting us to lunch. I said that under the circumstances I thought we had better not come. She replied that despite what she thought, she would not let a single word on the subject pass her lips. "After all, Jack, we are family."

So we went. And it was a disaster. We couldn't even get through the shrimp cocktail.

Phyllis started by heaping praise on Lee. She loved her dress. She wanted to know who did her hair.

Then she got started. "You are such a brick, Lee. A real jewel. Twenty-four karat."

Lee blushed sweetly. "What have I done?"

"I mean to stand by Jack through all this. Not many women would. I wouldn't, I can tell you."

My brother tried to intervene. "Phil, we promised not to talk about this." But to no avail.

In a moment she was telling me how I had disgraced the family. How could I have produced such a disgusting book! How could I have shown a man and a woman doing such unspeakable things to each other!

Lee tried to come to my defense. I had done the drawings years ago, when I was very hard up. It was Fairchild who was really to blame. She didn't believe that stuff about pirated editions. It was Fairchild's—not my—promoting that had brought the book to everyone's attention. And ... but Phyllis wouldn't let her continue.

60

Phyllis' voice was shrill. I felt like I was listening to a fingernail scratching on slate. After a while, I tuned out. I looked over at my nephew and niece. The older, the boy, was just on the edge of puberty. His mouth was open. He was hearing about strange, mysterious, exotic practices. His father probably hadn't yet had the talk initiating him into the knowledge of the ordinary ones. I wished I could have slipped him, under the table, a copy of *Gourmet Sex.* I looked down at my unfinished shrimp cocktail. My virago of a sister-in-law was still doing her Madame Lafargue imitation. I looked over at Lee. I wanted her to intervene to change the subject. Anything! The name of her hairdresser, for God's sake!

But Lee wouldn't look at me. She, too, was concentrating on the as yet uneaten shrimp. From there she proceeded to an elaborate inspection of the not very interesting Waterford waterglass in front of her. I tried to nudge her hand, but she was deliberately ignoring me. She had an odd expression on her face. Unruffled, you might say. You know, studied.

No. 8 in the *Catalogue Raisonné* (see Color Plate 6) of the works of Jean-Jacques Caillou is a work called *La Blanchisseuse* (oil on cream primed canvas, 60 inches x 40 inches). The text reads:

A strikingly beautiful work of early proto-impressionism! The painting is usually assigned to the year 1868 on the basis of the fact that the young lady who is the subject has been tentatively identified as the model for a number of nude studies in red chalk on gray paper Caillou executed that year. Unfortunately little is known of these, since they were lost, presumed destroyed in the fire, except that the model is reported to have had a large birth-mark on her left hip. Here the model is shown fully clothed in a beautiful purple dress, wearing a bonnet of the same color, her hands folded in a white muff at her waist.

She is dressed for a Sunday outing. That the subject is of working-class origin is indicated by the title, "The Laundress." This is no great beauty. Her face is common, pert but by no means pretty. But the artist had endowed her with a charm that is undeniable. A smile spreads across her features, as if she were caught in the act of greeting the arrival of her young escort. Who knows, perhaps her lover!

One finds in certain Caillou works like this a quality remarkably like that to be found in certain eighteenth-century painters like Chardin. It is a celebration of the simple pleasures, the joys of leisure, here clearly a celebration of the leisure of working-class people.

The painting is in concept strikingly like a Renoir work executed five or six years later called "The Parisian." Compare the way Caillou lets the cream ground show through to form part of the symphony of colors of the background.

Iᴛ was not until Lee got pregnant that Monty and Roxie Carter descended upon me. You may find it hard to believe that I had no idea that she was one of *those* Carters. But it's true. Lee had purposely made a mystery of her family. All I knew was that she had a brother who was her mortal enemy and that his wife, whom she loved like a sister, had been forbidden to see her. Then the mystery had become part of the electricity of our affair, like my rescuing her from the clutches of Manny Shine.

After telling me she was pregnant, and then after our fervent declarations that we wanted to spend the rest of our lives together, and after acknowledging that for the sake of the baby we ought now to get married, Lee threw herself into the work of remodeling our apartment. The floor where I had lived and worked would now become simply my studio. The two floors above would become our home. She threw herself into the work with a fury. When she did something, I learned, it was never by half measures.

"What did you and your brother fight about?" I asked.

"What *didn't* we fight about? He's a racist, he's a bigot, he's a fascist. In short, he's a *schmuck.*"

Morton had found a rabbi who was giving Lee instruction. So far as I could tell, what Lee had so far acquired was a set of blessings and curses. She especially loved the use of the curses. She never bothered much with the difference between the sacred and profane.

62

"He's a Scrooge. You never heard anybody who can poor-mouth the way he can." She paused a moment.

"Poor Roxie, imagine having to live with that creep. And he says I need a keeper. He's tied up all my money. I've had to take him to court. What a creep!"

"When was that? When did you take him to court?"

"The case is still pending. How do you like that for meanness?"

"How are we—you—going to pay for this?" I waved my hand around the room at the unfinished masonry and plumbing, paint and plaster.

"Not to worry. I sold Connie some paintings. Consuela Connery."

"What paintings?"

"Some things of Manny's she's wanted."

There were constant comings and goings during the day—the architect, electricians, plumbers, carpenters. It interrupted my work, but I felt buoyed by all the activity. It was strange and exciting. My life was changing.

One day, I was working in a little corner from which I had managed to keep the workmen. There was a ring at the door. I thought Lee would get it. There was another ring, then another. Lee was upstairs and couldn't hear the bell. So finally I went. I was in the clothes I used for painting. I was bespattered from head to foot. I opened the door, expecting it would be one of the workmen. I was angry at the self-proclaimed urgency of this interruption.

I found myself face-to-face with a woman. She looked familiar. She was tall. Her hair was long, raven colored. Her eyes were dark brown, augmented by the subtlest of eye shadow. She took my breath away.

It took me a moment to realize where I had seen her before. Now she was wearing a Burberry, collar up, and carrying a collapsible umbrella. In her hand it looked like a riding crop. She was the woman I had seen on television. In the flesh, in living color! It was like catching sight of a celebrity, a world-famous beauty, whose name is on the tip of the tongue.

Then I put two and two together. Of course, this was poor Roxie, beloved of Lee, forbidden to see her by her monster, bigot, racist, poor-mouthing brother. And he was *that* Monty Carter, the banker, the recent candidate for lieutenant governor, rejected so unlamentingly by his party.

I was first of all aware of what an appalling impression I was making. I was aghast at my own stupidity. Waves of wonder alternated with waves of anxiety. Why hadn't I realized? I really wondered whether I was out of my depth. I stood there, mouth agape.

"Is Lee here? I am Roxanne Carter," the visitor announced. Roxie's voice was light and musical, in a higher range than Lee's. It pleased me. I remembered what Dr. Trueheart had said about her origins. I could detect no trace of the Old Folks at Home or the Camptown Races.

I was still silent, half hoping for more speech from this vision of delight.

"I am Lee's sister-in-law."

I finally found my voice and mumbled, "Come in. My name is Jack Birnbaum."

She smiled. *"I* jus' knew that's who you were." Just a touch in the emphasis of "I," no more than a whiff of the fresh smell of bluegrass. It was a genuine smile, the kind that expressed a pleasure really felt. She extended her hand. "Everybody calls me Roxie. I like it better than Roxanne. Which is part of my Southern Gothic past!"

I took her hand. "Jack," I said. All I could do was mumble. "Lee's upstairs. Excuse the confusion. I'll call her."

In the weeks that followed, I got used to having Roxie around. She and Lee were inseparable. The two of them would have endless discussions about matters of decorating and furnishing. Then I would be consulted. These were matters in which I had never really taken much interest before. We would go out for long lunches in little ethnic restaurants. "Everybody falls in love with Roxie when they meet her, " Lee said to me. "He's a real prince, isn't he?" I heard her say to Roxie.

When Lee was not there, Roxie and I seriously set about the business of getting to know each other.

I listened, with sympathy but also with great curiosity to her accounts of how she had had to negotiate the rough waters between brother and sister. And how she was faring now. At first she had to keep her visits to us clandestine. But then she decided to put her foot down. She told her husband that she had a right to see whomever she pleased. If he didn't like it, he'd just have to suffer it. And to her surprise, Monty had accepted it without a murmur. Well, almost without a murmur. The only condition he put on her coming was that he didn't have to see that "crazy bitch." He'd heard Lee was now consorting—"consorting" was the very word he used—with a pornographer. She said that she absolutely exploded when she heard him say that. After she calmed down, she explained that Lee's "beau"—"forgive the Dixie folkways, Jack"— was a wonderful man, a fine and serious artist, who made a decent living painting portraits of distinguished people. If he was nice to me, she told him, maybe I'd paint *his* portrait. Although God knows who would have thought he was distinguished, the way he ranted and raved about his relations. Of course, I'm an only child. But I'll bet you didn't fight like cats and dogs with your brother Morton!

I am afraid I'm giving you the wrong impression of Roxie with these paraphrases of our earliest conversations. At this remove, I can't give you a more precise image of her than this sort of line drawing. Perhaps all I can really convey is what I was feeling. Don't get the idea that she was a Scarlett O'Hara. She was no coquette. True, she could produce a fine pot of grits and honey when she wanted, usually telling, in a whimsical and exaggerated way, stories about her "fahn ol' Lexin'ton fam'ly." "We'uns done lost thah ol' manse durin' thah dupreshun. We dun los' ever'thin' but our stayndards of propah breedin.'"

She would quote her mother's admonishing her on what to wear, what to say, whom to see. "We keep our position here'bouts, Roxanne, by maintainin' our *standards.* Don't you *ever* forget that." Then she would add, "God, Jack, every time I hear the word 'standards,' I just feel like screaming."

I suffered with her through her stifling youth. I came to see what a burden it could be to be counted a great beauty when you are being groomed to play the part for life. She rarely spoke to me about Monty. I knew she had married him when she was still quite young. I could see the whole thing as the triumph engineered by a scheming mother. You can see the legend I was weaving around Roxie—the beautiful heroine

65

who early on makes a "brilliant marriage with a banking scion." Being happy didn't quite fit into the plot.

Roxie would, of course, never complain in so many words about the burden of great beauty, for she had somehow learned to ignore the heads that turned, to deflect the compliments offered. And she really hated it when someone made her looks a cause for attention.

She pried my stories out of me. And I told them to her with pleasure. Who can resist the laughter of a woman of marvelous beauty? She roared at Hack eating the rose. She made me repeat my description of Manny Shine, his combat boots and his "debutantes." And HMB. The very fact that I could make such a good story out of him was a kind of balm.

And then there was the fact that she and I became fellow conspirators. True, it was innocent conniving.

One day Lee was out and Roxie and I were alone. There was only the noise of a power drill whirring in another room.

"You don't know how *thrilled* I am about the baby. I am sure that Monty will be too."

She smiled at me warmly. Suddenly, she stopped. She seemed on the verge of tears. As she had been that night I had first seen her on television. We were seated on the couch in my studio. I suddenly realized I was aching to put my arms around her and comfort her. But I kept the urge in check.

"It doesn't look as if Monty and I will ever be parents. God knows, we've tried! And it will soon be too late! But you probably know all that already."

I said how sorry I was to hear that. Yes, I did know it already, I said, from Lee. I did not add that I had also heard about it from an independent source.

"The doctors can't find anything wrong with me. But I just can't seem to *conceive!*" She looked again on the brink of tears.

Again, I said how sorry I was.

"That's why this baby is going to be very special, Jack. To me and to Monty. Particularly to Monty."

I felt a moment of discomfort at her concern for him. I had by this time formed an image of Monty. He was someone, at the very least, to

66

be handled with kid gloves, yet better, to be avoided entirely. I felt a pang to hear Roxie speak Monty's name as if he and I already were fond relations. But why would my baby be so important to him?

"There'll be a new generation of *Carters*, Jack! That'll mean so much to him. I know it sounds stuffy, but you will be *kind* about it, won't you, Jack? You will be *tolerant* of us, won't you, Jack?!"

I wasn't exactly sure what it was she was asking. But I nodded. "For your sake, Roxie," I was about to say, but I was beginning to feel I had to keep a firm grip on myself where Roxie was concerned.

"And I think the baby will be a blessing in yet another way," she continued. She paused. "I think we could all get back to being family again."

She paused again, searching my features to make sure I understood. Frankly, I was still in the dark as to what had caused the rupture and I didn't think anyone ever would enlighten me.

"Neither of them is a *simple* person, Jack. Maybe that comes of being so rich, if you know what I mean. All I know is that I love them both very much. It hurts me to see them so angry and estranged. And it is so *difficult*. So difficult for *me*."

She stopped, but I did not think she was finished.

"Will you help me, Jack? I mean help me get them back together?"

I nodded and became part of Roxie's sweet little cabal.

I am taking all of this out of a photograph album that I long since put away in the attic.

I suppose it is only the doomed loves—the loves that are denied or renounced—that survive in the hereafter of memory, with that wonderful bittersweet corona of feeling. When we recall an early love that has flowered and then continues in some form to be part of our lives, a passion domesticated so to speak, we don't seem to recall the songs, the shows, the fashions of that magic era with the same pangs. When I think of Lee now as she was in those days, the memories don't resonate with the same throbs of pleasure and pain. The colors and forms in the snapshots of her—they seem to form a series. I will turn the page and find yet later ones. The photoalbum of Roxie, as I first knew her, comes to an abrupt end. I knew I had fallen in love with her. And it required an act of will to master my feelings. For, you see, I never could tell her that I was in love with her.

Wasn't I at the same time also in love with Lee? That's a good question. And honestly, I don't think at this remove I can answer it. I can't even recall asking it of myself. I took it as an established fact that I would marry Lee, for she was pregnant, and I was the father of the baby she was carrying. And I wanted to be married. But did I suffer from this dilemma of loving another woman? Most probably. But even then I knew that my love for Roxie would never bring me happiness.

There are other albums there as well, containing other, less fond photographs of Roxie and me. In some I see her using me in a cruel and careless way. In others, I must confess, I see myself sacrificing her to my own ends.

I COME NOW TO L. MONTCALME CARTER.

I had already formed an unfavorable picture of him. Monty did nothing to alter it by the way he chose to introduce himself to me.

One day I got a call from Mitch Fairchild. We hadn't seen each other since the trial. I thought he was responsible for the fact that *Gourmet Sex* was still bedeviling me. When he said who he was, I responded with the barest civility.

"I've just called up to warn you," he said. "The police have just been here. They want to know who is behind the reappearance of our book. I told them it wasn't me. I think they may be about to pay you a visit."

I assumed he had put the blame on me. I got nasty. I cursed him. "I'm not taking the rap," I shouted. I sounded to myself like Jimmy Cagney.

There was silence on the other end. Then, "Well, if it's not me and it's not you, who is it?"

The police never came. But I discovered that I was under investigation from another source. My father called. He sounded pleased with me for a change. It seems private investigators had just been to see him at his office. They wanted to check certain vital statistics, to get leads on persons who had known me in the past, that sort of thing. They told him that I was under consideration for a position that would require bonding. The idea thrilled my father. I had to tell him there must be some mistake. It must be some other Jack Birnbaum.

I didn't connect the two until I began to have the strange feeling that I was being followed when I left the house. Then, one morning, just as I was exiting, two men suddenly approached me. They flashed some identification before my eyes—too quickly for me to discover who they were. Then they each put a hand on an arm and led me to one of those threateningly large stretch limos, double-parked at the curb.

One sat in back with me, the other up front with the driver. The latter got on the car phone. I couldn't catch anything he said. When he hung up, the car pulled away from the curb. My companion ignored all my questions. I was in a sweat.

We headed downtown and ended up on Wall Street. I was escorted into a high-speed elevator and whisked to the top floor. It seemed to be some kind of athletic club. All around me were men of all ages in shorts and teeshirts, torturing themselves on rowing machines or at weight-lifting contraptions. None of them turned a hair in our direction. I wanted to yell "Help!," but my voice failed.

I was taken into a back room. It contained an array of large metal boxes, the kind in which one sits, with only one's head protruding. You know, the kind in which the body is steam-cleaned of both excess poundage and tension. There was only one figure in the room. Through the steam I recognized the well-known head of L. Montcalme Carter.

In the flesh Monty looked older than when I had seen him on TV. There were suspicious signs of cosmetic retouching about the face and the hairline. But nothing had been done to the nose. It was still a significant landmark. And the mustache that hung below was rather like a large military decoration.

Recognizing him, my fear immediately turned to rage.

He nodded to me and signaled to one of my guards to free him from the box. When this was done, he emerged. He was naked.

"I'll be with you in a moment," he said to me, and disappeared into the next room.

Five minutes later when he came back, he was fully and expensively clothed. He signaled majestically to my escort to leave us. He put his hand on my arm. I noted what a strong grip he had. I resisted his effort to direct me.

He took my resistance in stride. He smiled at me. "We can't talk here."

So I allowed myself to be led off to a small lounge, where he motioned me to a chair and offered me coffee. I angrily refused the coffee. But I needed the chair.

The little scene I have just related was, as I later discovered, a fairly typical Monty production. What better way to announce himself than to whisk me by force away to this Mount Olympus on Wall Street and then to appear to me in god-like nakedness? It was classical theater, pantomime, opera. First, a display of authority. Then what? In this case, a shower of grace. You see, Monty always enjoyed mollifying outrage.

"I'm Monty Carter," he announced after he had given his order to a barman. I remained silent.

"I'm Lee's older brother. Her only relative."

"I am fully aware of who you are," I sniffed.

He continued to smile benignly at me. "I'm sorry if I have inconvenienced you. You see, I very much wanted to meet you. And I wasn't sure that you would come. I preferred not to have my sister present."

I felt the spigot of Good Will being turned on. But I continued to burn.

"Do you usually operate like a mafia capo?" I asked.

He smiled, undeterred, determined not to take offense. For a moment, just a moment, I saw that twinkle I had first encountered on TV.

I continued. "I take it that Mutt and Jeff—those dear lads, your thugs—are the same who called on my father. And impersonated the police to Mitch Fairchild? That's against the law, Carter!"

"Monty, please, Jack!"

"You are considering me for a bonded position? What am I to be, your bag man? I've had no experience in that line."

70

I was surprising myself. The angry words tumbled out. Usually I keep my temper under control. But Monty laughed merrily at my fulminations. And I began to realize just how armor-plated he was. Nothing would stick, nothing would ruffle him. And somehow that perception forced me to bring my anger back under control.

"I think you can appreciate, Jack, that in *our* position—I speak in Lee's *best* interests too—we have to be careful. We aren't like other people."

"Oh, how so, Monty?" I asked, feigning innocence. "The very rich are different from you and me?"

He looked puzzled. The "you and me" perplexed him. He didn't recognize the quotation.

"It's something Scott Fitzgerald is supposed to have said to Ernest Hemingway. Hemingway thought it was dumb," I explained.

He took in my words solemnly. He didn't seem to like what he heard. Had I penetrated his armor? He looked at me for a very long moment in silence. Without smiling. He was, I surmised, not used to having wealth dismissed so frivolously.

"It's not so dumb," he said, quietly.

He looked as if he was wondering whether he should put me in my place and then decided against it. Better the man-to-man approach. I was still angry, but it was seeping away, giving way to detached, amused curiosity at his sheer gall. I was wondering how far he would go. I half expected he would put his hand gently upon my shoulder and look me squarely in the eye. A moment or two late, he reached over and fulfilled my intuition.

"Frankly, that's the problem, Jack. I mean between my sister and me. She thinks I am trying to run her life. You know I've blocked her trust fund? Hell, I'm a man of the world. I don't care who she is—consorting with—"

The funny thing was that Monty assumed he was flattering me in talking so seriously and confidentially to me. But he never stopped to consider that I might not like the tone of that "consorting." No offense, meant of course, old boy. If you happen to be the current clown in my sister's circus, well—

I felt the anger surging. He must have seen me stiffen. "Let me say that I'm very happy she's chosen a fine man like yourself. I know that you are not a bum. Well, I hope you won't take offense, but frankly you should have seen some of the others. But wealth—I mean the kind of *inheritance* Lee has been given—that's a *trust*. That's not to be squandered. That's not to be frittered away."

He took a sip of his coffee. And then he plunged on.

"Lee's been involved in some pretty bizarre business. Better I not tell you."

He paused to consider whether he should tell me. I knew he was going to tell me. And I wanted to stop him, but there wasn't time. "I mean I wasn't shocked when she took up with a man of color—I am not prejudiced against persons of color, Jack." I half expected him to add "or Jews." "But that character was out on bail for rape and murder. It was all politics, she said. Politics, my ass!"

He drank more coffee. "And then there was that creep Shine! Do you know him? She planned to build the Shine Museum. Even *I* had to buy a load of his crap. I hate it. And it's too big to store. I understand he's hot stuff these days. You want it? I'll give it to you as a wedding present!"

What he was telling me wasn't anything that Lee hadn't told me. Or would have, if I'd asked. I wondered why he was telling me. It was really none of his business. I was about to tell him so, but again I didn't get the chance to speak.

"And now there is this so-called Free Speech Foundation. The trouble with Lee is that she gets fired up. She gets carried away. I expect you to rein her in when you ... What's the matter, Jack? Didn't you know about that? Oh, I've let the cat out of the bag. I am sorry!"

I said something about having to leave. Did I have his permission to leave? He missed my sarcasm. He said he'd have his driver take me anywhere I wanted to go. I got up. He offered his hand, beaming. I hesitated and then took it. I hated taking it. I was "consorting" with the enemy. I felt disloyal.

"I want you to know I am delighted about the baby. And, of course, the upcoming marriage. I count on you. I am unfreezing Lee's trust."

I murmured my thanks. Lee's thanks, rather.

72

"Lee will be notified of the action in a day or two. In the meanwhile, I wouldn't mention that we've met, old man!"

I didn't tell Lee about it. I felt I should do so, but I vacillated for a couple of days out of fear that it would add more fuel to the fire. After that, particularly after she was notified that she could draw again upon her account, I was afraid it might have looked as if I had gone behind her back to plead with Monty. I was experiencing the guilt that is said to afflict some hostages. That's why I could never bring myself to ask Lee what role she had had in the reappearance of *Gourmet Sex.*

She took the news of the reinstatement with a shrug of her shoulder, as she passed the letter to me. It just so happened that Roxie arrived a moment later. She looked almosty girlishly breathless, pleased with herself. She had news to tell us, she said.

"Monty has agreed," she announced before taking her coat off. "We are all going to have dinner. At our place."

"Did you really have to do that, Roxie? I don't want to see—that *schmuck.*"

But Roxie was in no mood to have her train derailed. "Quit being a child, Lee. You are thirty-three years old. Marriages are *family* occasions. Help me, Jack. Please!"

I felt that I couldn't. I didn't know whether Roxie was aware that I'd seen her husband. I wanted to help, but I felt like a double-agent. So I kept silent.

Lee pouted. "I don't want to see—that *gonif.*"

I sensed progress. *Gonif* was less hostile than *schmuck.* I tried to signal to Roxie that she was making progress, but Roxie had her own head of steam up and was plowing ahead.

"There will be no talk of money. I get enough of that, without you, thank you," Roxie huffed. "And no politics. We accept that you have different views from *ours* and ask only for a little civility."

"Did you tell him I was converting?"

Roxie was silent. She obviously hadn't gotten around to that yet. It confirmed my suspicion she didn't know about my visit with her husband. Finally she said, "You *know* Monty won't object. He's not an anti-Semite."

"Oh, the hell he is not! For Christ's sake, Roxie, the man's a fuckin' Nazi."

Two steps forward, one back.

"Being a Goldwater Republican is not being a fascist, thank you. We have many Jewish friends, but you know that."

Lee snarled back savagely.

"Look, Roxie," I was trying to intercede before things got out of control. "Maybe this is not the time—"

Roxie ignored me. "Well, if you won't do it for *him*, Lee, you might think a little of *me*." On the brink of tears, she got up and rushed out of the room.

When she was out of the room, I turned on Lee. "That was bitchy of you," I said.

She looked at me. I really didn't have to say anything. She already had that little-girl look of contrition on her face, silently begging for forgiveness.

"She's been working hard on getting you and Monty back on speaking terms," I said. "And he has unblocked your funds. What more do you want?"

I heard Roxie leave the bathroom.

"Okay, Roxie, you win," she called out. "I'll see the *schmuck*," she said to me under her breath. As she reentered the room, Roxie was smiling beatifically.

W E DID BREAK BREAD TOGETHER, THE CARTERS AND the to-be-Birnbaums. I bought a new suit for the occasion. It was the first time I had a suit made to measure. I modeled it for Lee. I said I could be married in it, but first I'd wear it to the dinner. If Monty devoured me, she could bury me in it, I added. She said that wasn't funny.

74

It was gallows humor. I had good reasons for dreading that dinner. I was sure that it would slip out that Monty and I had already met. Lee would be furious—again with him, but also this time with me. Perhaps furious enough to call the whole thing off.

As we entered the Carter's Sutton Place duplex, we immediately began a complicated, duplicitous minuet. Lee put her cheek up so that her brother could kiss it. And Monty shaking my hand, as if he were seeing me for the first time, declaimed, "So this is *your* Jack. Welcome to my family, Jack!" Then he threw his arms around me in a brotherly bearhug. Looking over his shoulder, I spied Roxie, who was on the brink of tears. At the end, we all declared—to each other—that the evening had been a vast success.

I see Roxie today in my mind's eye, pretty, sweet, vulnerable Roxie, holding back the tears of happiness at once again "being family." She had bought the mythology about the rich and powerful. Maybe it was because of the lost Arcadia back in Kentucky; maybe it was because Monty had bewitched her with some cheap magic romanticism. But it was one of my fantasies that, like Saint George, I would slay the dragon, free her from that thralldom, take her by the hand, and lead her out into the light. I had, you see, my own fantasies. And I thought I had Monty's measure.

And in a sense I was right. Life for Monty was a constant indian-wrestle, a perpetual struggle for power. I said I *thought* I knew what made him tick. But he always seemed a step ahead of me. And I didn't count on Lee. For she could never resist the opportunity to test her will against his. So, I became, not entirely unwittingly, a satellite trapped in the force-field of two contesting wills. Rather like Roxie, I suppose.

Let me give you an example of what it was like to have Monty as a brother-in-law. It happened not too long after we were married. At the wedding Monty had taken special pains to charm the pants off everyone, my immediate family, my cousins, the dentist friends of my father, the mah-jong playing cronies of my mother, everybody. He made the protestations, usual at large weddings, of his high regard for his new brother-in-law. He made common cause with the rabbi against numerous, unnamed enemies of Israel. Phyllis, who could never resist a celebrity anyway, flirted with him shamelessly. But I digress.

A day or two later, I got a call from Monty. He wanted me to lunch with him. When I informed Lee, she said to make sure he picked up the bill. It's something Monty had once heard about the Windsors, she said. They always let somebody else pick up the check. I told her I was to meet him at the Merchant Bankers Club. She raised an eyebrow, but said nothing else.

At the appointed hour, I presented myself at the Merchant Bankers, which happened to be high atop one of the skyscrapers surrounding Wall Street. I was wearing my made-to-measure suit. It was a pin-stripe suit. Everyone else seemed to be wearing a suit of the same stripe. It made me feel somehow that I was not out of place.

But when I tried to enter, I was promptly challenged by a young man in a tuxedo. I gave him my name and said I was the guest of my brother-in-law, L. Montcalme Carter. Just as I had been told to do. He gave me a look I can only describe as searching. He went through his list of reservations.

"I do not see any reservation for Mr. Carter today, sir."

I assumed that being Monty's relation had its privileges. I said, okay, I'd just wait for Monty in the bar, which I could see from the entrance. I started to move in the direction of the bar. To my surprise, this impertinent flunky suddenly blocked my way. "That is for members only, sir." The officious fellow pointed to a seat in the anteroom.

I didn't have to wait long. Monty emerged a moment later. He was followed by a retinue of young pin-stripers. He conferred at length with one of them and then dismissed the lot. One slight figure remained. He seemed constantly to be fidgeting with his brief case. For some reason, a zipper on one of the pockets needed constant attention.

Monty spotted me and waved me over. He took my arm and approached the gatekeeper.

"Ah, Pierre, how is the wife and the baby? Beautiful baby. Are you ready for us?"

"I am sorry, Monsieur Carter, I do not find a reservation for you today.... And Monsieur Fred is on his way. He would like to speak with you."

In a trice, Monsieur Fred appeared. He was also a young man. He was wearing a double-breasted blazer. He had obviously been waiting in the wings for Monty to appear. He took Monty aside. The slight young man with the zipper problem repositioned himself in short, discrete motions, all the time continuing to worry about the zipper.

The colloquy started in stage whispers. With great rapidity it grew angry and audible. All those within earshot could hear every syllable of Monty's speech.

"This is outrageous! In this day and age! In this great country, that kind of bigotry has no place. Let me get this quite straight. You refuse to admit my friend, my relation, Mr. JACK BIRNBAUM? Simply because he is JEWISH? I don't believe it!"

"I am sorry, Mr. Carter. This is a private club and there are ..."

"Well, I for one will not tolerate it. You'll have my resignation this afternoon. By special messenger."

Monty turned on his heel and over his shoulder summoned me. He stormed to the elevator, shouting his apologies to me for the embarrassment I had suffered.

Hailing a cab, Monty gave the address of a French restaurant uptown and settled back in the cab. The young man with the zipper problem had disappeared. Then Monty gave me a broad wink.

"They are expecting us at Le Champignon," he said. Then he laughed. "Wait until they read about that in the *Post* tonight. With pictures."

I was suddenly aware of what had happened. I had never had such an experience before. I knew that there were clubs where I would not be welcome. It was a fact of life. And I was not accustomed to travel in circles where some such thing might happen. Suddenly, I understood Lee's raised eyebrow.

Then the shock gave way to fury.

"You staged all that!" I said, beside myself with rage. "How dare you!"

Monty ignored my rage.

"You used me. Jesus, what a fraud you are!"

Monty took my anger in stride. He smiled confidently—that street-smart smile. He put his hand firmly on mine. It was his gesture of placation. "It will look great, if I decide to run for mayor."

When I tried to withdraw my hand, Monty simply strengthened his grip.

"Listen, old buddy. There are some things that you have to understand. That's what I wanted to talk to you about. I am a public figure. I have to worry about my image. You'll have to learn to live with that. With being around public figures!"

"*You* live in the limelight. I don't want to be a celebrity."

"Like it or not, you will be. Just by being a member of my family. What any of us do—and it's Lee who worries me—is grist for the mill to my enemies."

We arrived at the restaurant. All I wanted to do was go home. But he had a firm grip on my arm and dragged me inside. There he was greeted as royalty. Before he had ordered, there arrived a plate of *hors-d'oeuvres variés*. And a waiter brought a bottle of wine for his inspection. He nodded absentmindedly. His wishes were well known here.

They went through the ceremony of pouring the wine before he accepted the bottle. Monty took a sip. "Taste that. It's in a class by itself. They stock it here just for me."

I took a sip. It was undoubtedly the best white wine I have ever tasted.

"What the Queen of England doesn't get, I take. And sometimes she gets a little less than she orders." He winked at me. I stared back, unappeased.

He carefully spread some caviar on a piece of melba toast and ordered me to open up. For some reason, I obeyed. Then he served himself. He rolled his eyes in pleasure. Dining with Monty was always a show. He reverted to being a little boy at a treat. But at that moment there was a point to all this display of discrimination and, at the same time, indulgence that cared not for cost. The privileges of being "family" were being pointed out to me.

"I am going to tell you something in confidence. I want you to keep it to yourself. You are not to tell my sister. There are people who want me to run for mayor. And I am seriously considering it."

I felt like telling him that I had already learned the news from Phyllis, who had no doubt spread it all over the upper West Side. But I was fascinated watching him eat. Monty's enjoyment of food was about the only thing one could count on as genuine in him.

"So that was why you manufactured that phony little Dreyfus affair," I said dryly.

He immediately turned on me, incensed.

"Now, wait a minute. I resent that. Do you think I'm some kind of hypocrite, that I share the anti-Semitism of those creeps? I couldn't be happier that my sister is married to a Jewish man. I can depend upon my Jewish friends. They are men of their word. . . . And they know how to keep their women in line."

I exploded into laughter, thereby drawing the attention of nearby diners to ourselves. Monty responded by nodding affably to one and all. The whole thing, especially Monty, was too absurd to get angry about.

And it was an absolutely superb meal.

When the bill came, Monty took out a pocket-calculator and went over the bill carefully.

"Your half comes to forty-seven fifty."

N OT LONG THEREAFTER LEE MISCARRIED.

It was a disappointment to both of us, but Lee took it very well. She said not to worry; we'd keep trying.

In a way Roxie and even Monty took it harder than Lee and I did. It was a period of tranquility in our relations. As a foursome, we often dined together. Lee showed a polite interest as Monty discussed—"in the bosom of his family," as he put it—the pros and the cons of running for mayor.

Before Lee miscarried, I remember several conversations about names for the baby. Monty was certain our child was going to be a boy. "I know that you Jews usually name children for deceased relatives and you chose biblical names," he said more than once, "but I would consider it a very great kindness if the baby could bear the middle name Carter."

"I know that you Jewish people don't usually designate godparents," he said another time. "But Roxie and I—well if we can't be parents, at least we could be godparents. Would that be possible?"

I responded by telling him: For God's sakes, stop with all this folklore. I don't subscribe to it. I am a humanist. Of course we'd be delighted to have him and Roxie as godparents.

I looked at Lee for confirmation.

"What the hell," she replied after a moment's hesitation.

"And I'd consider it an honor for the child to bear the Carter name," I continued magnanimously. Monty beamed and Roxie's eyes grew moist at the new warmth of our family relations. Monty started telling me how he'd already started using his influence to get Carter enrolled at his schools, Taft and Harvard.

Then Lee miscarried. For a while, we continued to flourish as a foursome. Monty was always making a great show of how much confidence he had in me. He used to put his arm around me and call me "old buddy."

He would call and suggest we have lunch. One day he said there was something he particularly wanted to talk to me about. I said fine. He suggested I meet him at "our old hangout" Le Champignon. My business had fallen off over the year, and I was determined to maintain my financial independence. I assumed he knew all that. So I suggested a less expensive spot. He said not to worry, so we agreed upon Le Champignon.

He waited until after we had finished our *Tournedos Rossini* (which he had ordered in advance), before broaching what was on his mind.

"There is a matter I must take up with you, old buddy. But I hesitate to do so."

"Go ahead, Monty."

"Well, it's your profession."

"My profession? I am an artist. What's wrong with that?"

"Well yes. I suppose so. But that's not really what your reputation is."

I felt my anger rising. "And what *is* my reputation, if I may ask?"

"No need to take offense, old buddy. I've never held it against you."
I waited.

"But it just doesn't look good—I mean it doesn't look good for the family. I mean—if one of its members is a—how shall I put it?"

"Is a what?"

"Is a pornographer. Now don't get offended. . . . "

I tried to insert a justification of the part I had played in what he was referring to. Perhaps that had been a youthful misjudgment. But was it going to haunt me for the rest of my life? Halfway through I suddenly began wondering why I was offering any defense. I trailed off into silence. Monty rushed in to the void.

"I want to offer you a job. It's a very responsible position, with a good salary. A job you'll find worth doing."

"Oh?" He had caught me totally by surprise.

"How'd you like to become director of the Carter Foundation?"

I had never heard of the Carter Foundation. Lee had never mentioned its existence.

"My grandfather started it. It's a small foundation. Really a family thing. Mostly charity, some educational support. Certainly not in the league with the Ford or the Rockefeller. But dollar-for-dollar, better value," he said.

"There ought to be a Carter over there, old buddy. I don't really have time for it anymore. Oh, I'll still be there in spirit—as chairman of the board."

Why me? I wondered. Why not Lee? But I was curious enough not to interrupt him.

"Besides, it will give you an income. It's not good for a man to be dependent upon his wife's money."

We were finishing our lunch. He was about to start with the ritual of the pocket calculator. I took my wallet out, I was expecting Monty to pick up the tab. But that was not Monty's way.

So I paid my half of the expensive lunch, musing at the same time that I would, no doubt, have an expense account if I were director of a foundation. As we got up from the table, I said I'd think it over. I wanted to talk to Lee about it, but I didn't tell Monty that.

He took my word as acceptance. I found him suddenly looking me over head to toe. It was definitely not an approving look.

"For God's sake, haven't you got another suit? You got married in that one! We'll go see my tailor."

I went home and talked the matter over with Lee. I was sure that she would hate the idea, so I presented it to her as a ploy of her brother's, nothing to which I had given more than a moment's amused thought. She was seated at her desk. I noticed the open book in front of her. It had Hebrew characters. I took a close look. She had begun to study Hebrew and was on lesson four.

"I am thinking of going back to school," she said. "I have always been interested in mysticism."

She went back to her Hebrew lesson. "I'm almost finished." I waited until she closed her book.

"How was lunch? Did Monty say anything about running? He is so gross! When is he going to learn that everybody knows what a charlatan he is!"

"As a matter of fact, no! He had an amusing little whim. He made me an offer. He wants me to think it over." I laughed at the caprice. Lee waited for me to stop. I could see I had piqued her interest.

"He wants me to become head of the Carter Foundation. Until today my knowledge of foundations was limited to the Rockefeller and the Ford."

"My grandfather established it when they passed the income tax. It's a tax dodge. You'd be a fish out of water!"

"I know. I didn't take him seriously."

Suddenly she was giving the matter serious thought.

"You know, Jack, maybe it's not such a bad idea. You'd have a decent income. You wouldn't be dependent upon me."

I was frankly surprised. That was the second time that day I'd gotten that counsel. I already had what I considered a decent income. Not in Lee's class, of course. But most of what the trust provided went to her charities and causes. She was not stingy like Monty, thank God. But she kept an eye cocked to what happened to the loose change. It's not a trait uncommon among the very rich. Suddenly I was aware of the attraction of a paycheck coming in regularly.

82

Lee was also intrigued. "We won't take less than six figures to start with. And a generous expense account!"

So I BECAME A BUREAUCRAT. I HAD NO TRAINING AND no talent for it. There would be continuing gifts to the foundation from various trusts Lee and Monty held, separately and jointly. There would always be the possibility of conflict. I was there to pour oil on troubled waters. Monty had intended that I would be a rubber stamp for him. I knew that. Lee thought I should promote her interests. I also recognized that. I should have known better than to allow myself to be used by both of them.

You see, I thought I was wise to Monty. I'd heard him say more than once he never did anything for just one reason. He would say it with a straight face to his fellow bankers, and they would nod sagely at this fiscal wisdom. He would say it with a wink to me, and I would smile back bravely and start figuring out what the other motives were. Somehow I always counted on staying one step ahead. And I almost never succeeded.

And I didn't reckon with Lee's seeing the foundation as a new toy.

It took some bickering but I got what I asked from Monty, which was, after all, only what Lee had suggested.

And I began to see the true motive when Monty began reading the art journals. Not that he had yet given up on any of his other interests, not publicly. Every so often, an item would appear in a political gossip column speculating that he was considering a run for mayor. But now after our Friday lunches at Le Champignon, which became a regular feature of my life, Monty wanted to tour museums and galleries. "I want your educated eye, old buddy!" he would say.

I got a yet clearer indication of his intent when he asked me to look

83

over the Purchase estate. The house in Purchase, New York, and its contents, the home of the grandparents, I discovered, were part of the joint estate. The contents were in storage in the city.

"The Carter collections will interest you, old buddy. Both my grandmother and grandfather collected on a positively munificent scale. Absolutely princely! You could afford to be princely before the income tax. My mother also collected. Poor Dad didn't have time. He literally killed himself keeping the bank from going under in '29. But he had wonderful taste. Just wonderful taste."

Monty took a bite of his salmon in dill sauce and purred with pleasure.

"My grandmother put together the foremost collection of Meerschaum glass in the world, you know!"

I showed myself impressed. Actually I had never heard of Meerschaum glass. Glass, as far as I was concerned, was somewhere in home furnishings.

"They are wonderful panels, the work of America's premier art nouveau designer. And full of a sublime religiosity not common in that movement."

I smiled appreciatively. Monty must have cribbed that. Before he had begun reading the journals he could not have made it all the way through "sublime religiosity" with a straight face.

"Anyway, why don't you take on the Purchase homestead and its contents? As your own mission. As a favor to me, old buddy."

Monty did not punctuate the sentence with a wink. It sounded innocent enough.

"I'd be delighted," I said.

Grandmother Carter's home in Purchase, long unoccupied, consisted of a hundred acres of park, in the middle of which stood a huge turn-of-the-century pink palazzo. It had been designed by Sanford White and was listed in various directories of historic landmarks. The driveway was lined with great stone urns done by an Italian sculptor of the period. The sculptor, I discovered, was best known for his funerary objects and mausoleums.

84

I went up to Purchase to visit the house. When I got back, I suggested to Monty that he and Lee think of donating the house and land to a religious order or school.

"That's an appalling suggestion," Monty said. "Would you suggest that Winterthur or Biltmore be turned into a playground for rich brats? It should be a public trust! A place of pilgrimage for school children, a place for senior citizens in their golden years. For chrissake, Jack, just think of that gorgeous Renaissance sculpture garden!"

I decided I had better drop the subject. I had had my first insight into what Monty wanted. He wanted a museum.

"Listen, old buddy, I'd like you to inventory the Carter collections. And then get somebody—somebody good—to appraise it."

I noted the plural on collections. Six months ago, Monty would not have referred to the "Carter collections." We were on the phone, so I couldn't monitor Monty's facial expressions. But I couldn't detect the speech analogue of a wink. He was dead serious.

So I dutifully complied. It took me several months.

Grandfather Carter had had a taste for Americana. He had bought heavily into western subjects, including a Frederic Remington of Custer's Last Stand. Other canvases were by artists distinguished enough in their time to be members of the National Academy of Design, but now they were largely forgotten. The latter included huge scenes of Père La Salle exploring the Mississippi and another of General Montgomery dying in the snow before Quebec. There was a large family portrait of a rich merchant and his family that derived from the late eighteenth century. It bore the attribution "Peale(?)," followed by "Rembrandt(?) or Raphaelle(?)." On one interpretation of the question marks, it could have been painted by any of them. On another by all of them. On yet another, by none of them.

There were drawings of American Indians and wildflowers by La Farge. And some sculpture by Saint-Gaudens. And a large collection of swords, armor, and escutcheons.

Grandma Carter's interests had been religious. Her acquisitions

85

included an Alma-Taddema of Christians praying. They were surrounded by ravening lions. She had also generously supported the work of the artist Johann Von Goethe Meerschaum. I now knew that the name was the name of the artist. I had imagined a kind of glass, somehow magically made of sand from the shores of Turkey. Meerschaum was a contemporary of Louis Comfort Tiffany and had originally trained as a painter. A little research revealed this to me.

The Carter collections contained the Meerschaum notebooks, the Meerschaum cartoons, and, of course, a very large number of glass panels. The subjects were usually scenes from the Old and New Testament. They had been executed by Meerschaum on Grandmother Carter's commission. They were all wired and illuminated from behind. They were executed on a grand scale.

When I had finished the cataloging, I went to a dealer who specialized in Americana. The dealer called me when he had finished his appraisal. I took him to lunch. We talked about other things until coffee. When the coffee came, my companion handed me a large envelope.

"I hate to do this after such a great lunch, Jack."

I had expected bad news.

"That bad?" I asked.

"Don't bother to read my report."

"Dreck?" I asked.

"*Le mot juste,*" he replied.

When I presented him with the appraisal of the Carter collections, L. Montcalme Carter exploded. He demanded a second opinion. I obliged. The second opinion was even more negative, if that was possible.

"Little do they know!" Monty snorted at our Friday lunch at Le Champignon. "It's a *heritage,* that's what it is. It should belong to the people. There should be a *Carter* Museum of Fine Arts."

Monty spread his hands out as if presenting to the world this porticoed Temple of Apollo. It was his first explicit mention of a Carter Museum.

When he heard that his old pal Joe Hirshhorn had gotten the federal government to build a museum to house his collection, Monty hit the ceiling. He described it as a "hustle."

"As an angry taxpayer, I protest," he said.

"That guy, he'll buy anything," he continued. "Just as long as he can get it wholesale. He even collects Manny Shine."

Then there was the sudden wink.

"But what a tax break!"

When the bill arrived, out came the pocket calculator. I wasn't really paying attention. I was considering this new direction to Monty's ambition. So far as I knew, he was still planning to run for mayor.

"Your tab is ninety-five. My God, that's highway robbery. The foundation can't afford to have you eating here regularly. You'll have to start paying for it out of your salary."

I had expected Monty's next suggestion. He wanted me to take it up with Lee.

It was now his idea to turn the Purchase house and its contents over to the foundation. "The tax write-off would be enormous," he said. "Absolutely enormous. We'll get the benefit of it for years."

I tried to take it up with Lee. I tried more than once. But Lee just couldn't be bothered. She was too busy then. She had started taking courses at Union Theological on medieval mysticism.

Monty had not expressed himself on the subject of Lee's new interest. But I am sure he regarded it as a blessing. What harm could Lee do reading Jewish and Arab mystics? He himself was growing almost obsessive on the subject of the Carter collections. It was about then that he announced that he had decided not to run for mayor. At the press conference he left his reasons something of a mystery. He was asked whether he might consider it in the future.

"All I have to say is not this time!" he replied with that characteristic wink.

But his sister's indifference to his now well-known ambition to establish a museum was frustrating. And nothing could really be done until the Purchase estate had been transferred to the foundation. Monty had long ago had the paperwork prepared, and he was champing at the bit. I took the deeds of bequest home with me, where they languished on Lee's desk for months. Whenever Monty brought the matter up, I'd bring it up with Lee. She always responded that she'd find time next week.

But then one day out of the blue, she simply signed the papers. "If he wants a museum, let him have his museum," she said with a sigh, delivering the papers into my hands. "Maybe, it'll keep him out of my hair." That was followed by a long statement in Hebrew she did not bother to translate. But I could supply a reasonable gloss—something to the effect of "vanity of vanities . . . "

When I looked at the budget of the Carter Foundation for the next year, I discovered that there was a whole new chapter in it devoted to "Collection Building." I was, as I have indicated, out of my depth in the job and far less diligent than I ought to have been, but I saw at once that if the Carter Foundation began to make purchases on that scale, it would soon be dipping into its endowment. And the source of revenues for collection building was unexplained.

I picked up the phone and called the chairman of the board.

"Does that mean *I* am to buy painting and sculpture? And if so, with what?" I asked Monty. "The papers are full of stories about the fleecing of the innocent. I had no idea this is what you had in mind when you asked me to take this job."

I was sure that my voice was betraying how nervous the whole idea made me.

"No, old buddy. Not to worry. There are *experts* to worry about that. What I want you to pay special attention to is *de-acquisitions.*"

"I don't follow."

"It's simple. We are going to get rid of the less worthy holdings of Grandpa and Grandma Carter's."

"You mean you want me to sell their stuff?"

"Maybe some, but later. Some of it, of course, we'll keep. But a lot of it we are simply going to give away. I've already spoken to some museums and schools. You'll be getting the paper work for—"

"For what?"

Monty thought for a while. "Well, for all that Meerschaum crap."

"Who would want *that*, Monty?" I asked.

"You'd be surprised, old buddy! Trust me. I know what I am doing."

It was about that time that Monty introduced me to Dr. Harald Jensen, assistant professor of art history at a state university somewhere in West Virginia or Ohio, I was never clear exactly where.

Monty brought Jensen to lunch and paid for his lunch, a sure sign to me that Jensen was worth knowing.

He was a young man in his early thirties. He was thin, almost to the point of emaciation. His features were sharp and angular. He was a dapper dresser. He sported a fawn-colored vest, with lapels, under his dark jacket. He called it a "weskit." His silk tie, pearl gray, went with it. To perfection. He was nearsighted, a handicap he corrected with the help of contact lenses, which gave his blue eyes an unnatural brilliance.

His speech had a measured quality that suggested the care taken to express the exact thought. There was something about it that made me think Jensen was always practicing elocutionary exercises. When Jensen said something he thought particularly worthy of note, his eyes seemed to take on a momentary sparkle, as if he were wired to some inner electric source that could be triggered by some imperceptible girding of his loins.

It was Lee who first began calling him Prince Hal.

"This is Dr. Harald Jensen, Jack. Jack Birnbaum, Dr. Jensen. Jack is from the Carter Foundation."

We shook hands.

"Dr. Jensen is one of the world's leading experts on art nouveau, Jack. If you don't know his book *Art and Craft, A New View of Art Nouveau*, you should. There is a section on Meerschaum in it. Dr. Jensen thinks Meerschaum has been grossly overlooked. He calls him the premier American Pre-Raphaelite. More important than Maxfield Parrish."

Fancy that! A couple of months ago Monty would not have had a clue what Pre-Raphaelite meant.

"How interesting. When did your book come out?"

"Very recently," Jensen said. "It's based upon my doctoral dissertation."

"I must read it."

"I think it says some *perspicuous* things," Dr. Jensen owned modestly, his blue eyes blinking momentarily like Christmas tree lights.

As we made our way through lunch, I kept wondering why Monty was concerning himself with the career of this distinctly odd bird. I tried to keep up my end of the conversation. I chatted with Jensen about apartment buildings in Paris, metro stations, Gallé, and Tiffany. I visited the suburbs, straying as far as *Jugendstil* and *Sezessionsstil*.

In my career as a foundation man, I had discovered that lunch is the time for displaying attainments in the social arts, for gossip, not erudition. And Jensen was obviously an expert in the art of lunching. He led me through the alleys and one-way streets of the art world, scattering little tidbits of color, as if he had all his life been conducting tourists through the galleries of the world. He knew of my connection with Hack Ferkin. He asked to see the catalog of *Sous Mer*, which he was sure would some day be, in itself, a collector's item. He professed himself curious about that "sadly neglected figure" Hack Ferkin. I am sure he knew about my connection with HMB, but he was too diplomatic to inquire about it.

The name Charles Labiche also somehow came up. I think I was the first to mention it. "He's the very best—donchaknow—absolutely the top on proto-impressionism," Jensen averred. I think it may have been my first encounter with the word proto-impressionism. That led me to recount the story of my own discovery of the work of a "minor painter of the period" named Jean-Jacques Caillou. And Jensen, of course, had already heard of Caillou. That made me a little suspicious, but he parried my suspicions by expressing a great interest in seeing the painting.

Most of this left Monty out. By the time the *salade verte* came (the vinaigrette dressing, according to his orders, had to be made with raspberry vinegar), Monty was growing very restive. He chewed his lettuce with noisier relish than usual. He waived dessert away and finally got everyone down to business over coffee.

"Now, Jack," he said, putting his hand on my arm, "you are my point man on the Carter Collections and I want you to be just as helpful as you possibly can to Dr. Jensen. He is to have all the access he wants to our collections. He has a particular interest in them."

I turned from Monty to Jensen. What precisely was the interest of this popinjay in the Carter Collections?

"I am planning to do a monograph on Johann Von Goethe Meerschaum. Or a series of articles," Prince Hal announced, modestly. "Thanks to the foundation."

"The *definitive* study," Monty interjected

"Oh, I see," I said. I did not really understand the game. "Of course. They are in the vault. But I'll take you whenever you wish. It will be my pleasure."

"Let him have his own key, Jack. He won't steal anything."

I had never known Monty to be so trusting.

It was sometime later that, searching through the foundation's files— something I was not accustomed to do—I ran across a file labeled "Jensen, Harald J." In it, I found from a few years before an application to the Carter Foundation for a grant. It was one of a not very large number received every year from college teachers seeking relief from the burdens of teaching. I could not remember the matter, but there was my signature on a letter informing Jensen of his good fortune. Oh well, my secretary, Miss Pomfret, had probably dispatched it in my name. She often did things like that.

Now, as I reviewed the project description, I saw that it did contain the name of Johann Von Goethe Meerschaum. The title of the project was "Glass Panelling, 1890–1920" and there was Meerschaum's name, but in the company of the more recognizable names of Tiffany and Wright.

But the foundation's investment paid off handsomely. First, there were the series of notes in the *Journal of Art Nouveau Studies*. Then there was the long article in the *Burlington Magazine*. His file of articles, all of which acknowledged the foundation's generous support, came to include other matters—for example, an article in *Christian Century* entitled "J. G. Meerschaum's Depiction of the Logos." And finally there was the long-awaited appearance of the monograph on Meerschaum (Art Books, 1971), in which the author gratefully acknowledged the subvention from the Carter Foundation that had made publication possible.

Sometime thereafter I received a call from the dealer who had made the first appraisal of the Carter Collection. He hemmed and hawed for a while and then got to the point of his call: "Jack, old friend, rumor has it on the street that the Carter Foundation wishes to sell a Meerschaum panel or two. I don't know why, since they are images of transcendent beauty. But maybe it's just because you have a surfeit of his work. But I'd consider handling the sale for you. I might even buy one for my own firm."

It was the first word I had heard about it. I said I'd get back to him. I called Monty. When Monty heard the news, he chuckled gently.

"Let's run up the flag and see if anyone salutes, old buddy. Pick one—hell, I don't care which one—and we'll see what Park-Bernet can get for it. Say, at a reserve of—I don't know. You set the reserve. Somewhere in the range of upper five figures."

The reserve price is a face-saving device, one of the courtesies of an auction house. It enables the owner of a work to "buy" his work back should it not reach a price at which he is willing to part with it. That Monty should be familiar with the concept of a reserve was not all that astonishing to me. He was, after all, a banker. So I set the reserve at sixty-five thousand, embarrassed to have to set so large a valuation on what I considered to be a piece of period junk.

When this small glass panel, depicting Saint Jerome with a lion, came up for auction, it met the reserve price and much more. I was flummoxed. But Monty was so delighted that he bought me lunch at Le Champignon.

PRINCE HAL BEGAN TO MAKE REGULAR APPEARANCES AT the Friday lunches and to come on the tours of the galleries. Between the second and third such lunch, I learned, just before it was announced in the *New York Times,* that Dr. Harald Jensen had been appointed

Curator, Carter Collections. I expected that I would have to find room for him in my offices. But when I brought the matter up with Monty, he played its importance down.

"It's nothing, Jack. He just gives me some advice from time to time. You know, sort of like B.B. I thought we should normalize his remuneration. It's actually a saving for the foundation. And the title will look good on his C.V."

Monty was full of initials today. "Like B.B. for the Gardner. You've heard of him? Bernard Berenson? If you weren't such a provincial modernist, you would have heard of him."

In "provincial modernist" I detected the influence of Prince Hal. At the last lunch, Jensen had delivered a lecture on the passing of the modern.

"I know damn well who B.B. was, Monty."

I suspected that there was more to the matter. I usually got more by not pressing. So, for the moment, I held my peace. Monty had recently raised my salary, saying how grateful he was for my shouldering a share of the family burdens.

But once Prince Hal was on board, there seemed a lot more paper work. Some of it had to do with gifts that Monty was presenting to the Carter Foundation, in his own name, or in the name of himself and his sister. Half the time I had no idea whether Lee had been consulted or not. When I would mention the matter to her, she would say not to bother her; she was too busy. Sometimes she would mutter to me that she vaguely remembered talking to Monty. About tax benefits, she thought. Maybe, that's what he meant. What's on your mind, she'd ask, looking up from some Arab or Jewish manuscript of the fourteenth century.

"Oh nothing," I would usually reply. "What do I know about tax benefits? I just don't want to get into any trouble."

Lee obviously wasn't greatly concerned. Why should I be?

Monty went public without discussing it with me. He planned to open the Carter Collections to the general public. He was interviewed by a TV reporter who had heard the rumors that Monty was planning to run for mayor. Monty jovially dismissed the report. He didn't have time to think about that right now. He was too busy. And he was having too much fun. With what, Monty, the reporter asked. All my time at the moment is taken up with a project that has been dear to my heart for many years, Monty said grandly. What's that, the reporter asked.

"I want—"

He turned shy, as he always did publicly when touching on something personal. He put his hand to his heart, a gesture familiar to Monty-watchers.

"I want the public to enjoy the magnificent art treasures that my family has collected—my grandfather, who established Carter and Co., my grandmother, and my mother. And all the others down to my own time. I feel very strongly that the time is past when treasures such as these should be the private preserve of the fortunate few. I have long wanted to bequeath them to the nation." His arms spread apart in an appropriate gesture of bounty.

Rumors began to appear in the papers about talks between the Carter Foundation and the Nixon administration (Nixon had enjoyed Monty's personal and generous support). A mall site was mentioned.

I knew that the cauldron had begun to bubble when I started issuing checks to a New York architect for renovation of a *Belle Époque* structure on East Seventy-second Street, not far from the park. The architect had labeled his drawings "Proposed Carter Museum."

The date and place for the meetings of those concerned with the Carter Collections—Monty, Prince Hal, and me, and sometimes the architect—were now a fixed part of my calendar. Always the last Friday of the month at noon. Always Le Champignon.

We were coming along very nicely. It was a Thursday, preceding one of our Friday lunches. Usually I was not in the office on Thursday. That was one of the days I was usually at home painting. Oh yes, I had not given up, although the Caillous for the years 1868 and 1869 tend to have a somewhat somber quality—still marvelous but, one might say, rather less celebratory. Anyway, I happened to be in the office that day, and I had an unexpected visitor.

I was not accustomed to being visited at all. But even more unusual was an unannounced visitor. When Miss Pomfret announced that there was a Mr. Jack Vendetta to see me, I didn't think to ask her who he was or about what he wanted to see me. Nor did Miss Pomfret volunteer. You see, I was by that time thoroughly bored with foundation work. I was thinking about sneaking off to an afternoon movie. But the name intrigued me. I wondered what line of business would go with a name like that. So I said to show him in.

Jack Vendetta was a smallish, roly-poly, jolly man. He took my proffered hand in one of his own and, with the other, presented his business card. Jack Vendetta was from the Internal Revenue Service. On sight of Mr. Vendetta, I had expected an amiable little encounter with chance. *Pas grand' chose!* Now I had to try to rise to the occasion. I suddenly felt my stomach rumble.

"I was in the neighborhood and just decided to drop in for a get-acquainted visit," Vendetta said with a smile. "I wrote the Carter Foundation a letter, but I never got an answer," Vendetta said.

"Probably went astray," I countered.

I called Miss Pomfret. She couldn't recall any letter from the IRS. But something about the way she said it sounded slightly unusual, evasive you might say.

"What can I do for you?" I asked.

"Oh, nothing special."

Vendetta had a reassuring smile. Evidently the anxiety had crept into my voice. "Just routine. Do you mind if I take a look at some of your records? It's really nothing that can't be explained, I am sure. But I am particularly interested in seeing some deeds of gift."

"Which ones?"

"From your foundation to the Museum of Pentecostal Art. That's in Oklahoma City. I expect you give so much away you don't even recall the matter."

I instructed Miss Pomfret to fetch the file and invited Vendetta to seat himself. I offered him coffee or sherry. He declined—in a quite gracious manner.

Miss Pomfret brought the file in promptly, and I told her to hand it to my guest. She hesitated momentarily as if she wanted to say something. Then she complied. I sat waiting while Vendetta read it. After he had finished, he looked up and smiled.

"Do you have a copy machine? Mind if I use it?"

I nodded and instructed Miss Pomfret to let him copy what he wanted.

Before he left, Vendetta came back in and once again shook my hand and thanked me.

"I am a big fan of Mr. Carter's. I've voted for him. Will you tell him that for me?"

I promised to pass the word along.

After he left, I went through the file myself. It was not large. It concerned the recent gift of several Meerschaum panels. I noted that I myself had presented the bequests on behalf of the Carter Foundation. There was nothing unnatural about that. There was my signature on the documents. I was not sure whether I had signed it myself or whether Miss Pomfret had used my signature stamp.

What surprised me was the valuations I had placed on the Meerschaums. They were all in six figures. I was sure I would never have done that.

I tracked down the original documents of acquisition by the Carter Foundation. They were all signed by both L. Montcalme Carter and Lee Carter Birnbaum. The valuations taken by the donors were significant enough, but still were well below the value of the gifts to the Museum of Pentecostal Art. Had Meerschaum panels appreciated *that* much in three years? Could the foundation's investment in Prince Hal have paid off *that* handsomely?

I called Monty at the bank. I got through to him with no trouble. I started right out: I'd just been visited by the IRS, and I didn't understand why. It had something to do with a bequest to the Pentecostal Museum. I thought the IRS was challenging the foundation's valuation of its gift. I gave him the figure. I said I found it astonishing.

Monty heard me out in silence.

"Why does the amount astonish you, old buddy?"

"Well for one thing it's more than twice the value when we accepted it three years before. It was high then. You may remember I thought we took too much—"

"I remember. But we got away with it then, didn't we?" he replied. "Not to worry, old buddy!"

"I think somebody tampered with the papers, Monty!"

"Oh, how?" he asked, in a cool and controlled voice.

And I suddenly had the feeling that Monty had been expecting my call. His response sounded rehearsed. It could only have been Miss Pomfret who had warned him. She'd probably been playing me false from the very start, that wicked witch of the west.

"I didn't put that value on the donation. Mine was identical with what we claimed when we accepted it as a gift. And I think the document was signed with my stamp. Somebody is trying to slip something by me."

There was a long silence at the other end. Then a laugh.

"I plead guilty, old buddy. But, trust me, it was okay. You'd already left the office, so Ruthie called me. She said she wanted to check the value. She thought something was wrong. It didn't seem to reflect inflation, reasonable market appreciation, that sort of thing. I suggested the new figure. She said she had to file it that day. So I said to use your stamp."

"How come nobody told me about it?"

"I guess it slipped our minds. Don't blame Ruthie. I'll take responsibility."

"And if the IRS comes after me, Monty?"

He laughed. "You are such a worry-wart, Jack. A first-rate collection is built by what it *de-acquisitions* as much as by what it acquires. Think bold! With a little finesse in the bookkeeping we were able to finance the Monet *l'Étratat*. And no one gets hurt."

I knew at that moment what I ought to do. Even before I hung up, I resolved to resign. But later I reflected on the benefits of my position. And I counseled myself not to do anything hasty.

Monty had a full head of steam up at lunch at Le Champignon the next day. The renovation of the building on Seventy-second Street was now well under way. And while I munched on my Beluga on melba toast, I let Monty and Prince Hal devote themselves to minutiae of paneling and drapes. No expense was being spared.

"God, I feel great," Monty interjected at one point. "I am building a monument. A monument!"

Over the entrée—mine was *Poulet Montmorency*—he and Jensen discussed the recent purchase of the Monet.

"Jack," Monty said, suddenly addressing me. "Send Wildenstein a check. They'll tell you how much."

I nodded, then turned my attention back to my chicken. In doing so, I was only peripherally aware of some business between the source of all this philanthropy and his Curator of Collections. It was a signal to begin an action, of which, in retrospect, I realize I was the target.

Monty began by clearing his throat. I continued devoting my full attention to my chicken. He then put his hand on my arm and squeezed it gently. I looked up, my mouth full of chicken and cherries. He smiled at me.

Monty, his hand still on my free arm, turned to Prince Hal.

"Do you know, Hal, how fond I am of this guy here? Have you any idea of how much joy he has brought into my life since he married my sister?"

His eyes began to cloud over. He gave my arm a gentle jab of buddy-ship.

I felt the warmth being radiated, but I returned his smile warily. I suppressed a shudder, remembering my visitor of the day before, the conversation with Monty, my resolve to resign. I thought I might be coming down with the flu. My eyes met those of Prince Hal, and I detected a momentary flicker of light. His eyes also seemed to catch, to amplify, to reradiate in my direction some of the waves of Monty's affection.

I blushed. "Cut it out, Monty. You are embarrassing me."

But Monty continued, "I've thought more than once that it ought to be called the Carter-Birnbaum Museum."

"Cut it out, Monty. You aren't serious. And if you were, I couldn't allow you to do that."

"I can't begin to describe what a difference this fellow has made in the life of my sister. He picked her up off the floor. Literally."

"For God's sake, Monty."

"No, I mean it, old buddy."

I tried to concentrate my full attention on the remains of my chicken.

"No, I think the museum ought to reflect in some way our friendship. Don't you think that would be fitting, Hal?"

"Absolutely!"

Monty went back to his steak, which he had hardly touched. Prince Hal followed. I now hoped that the subject was finished. But the continued silence of both men suggested they were giving it further thought.

"We could have a Birnbaum Room," Hal said quietly, tentatively, as if the idea had just occurred to him.

Monty gave it some thought.

"Go on," he responded. "I like that. What do you have in mind? A permanent exhibit of his painting?"

"That's not quite what I had in mind," Hal said.

"Why not? He's a good painter—if you like that modernist crap."

"That's just my point," Hal said, choosing his words with great care. "I am sure he is a very—" Hal searched for the right word and found it, "—*collectible* painter. But from what I've seen, I don't think his work fits in with the character of the Carter Collections. What I had in mind for the Birnbaum Room—"

Prince Hal's eyes sparkled with the inner light.

"—is a tribute to his *taste*. We could put the Monet *l'Étratat* in the Birnbaum Room for a start. We could house there all our impressionist paintings—all those we are planning to acquire."

"That's a *bully* idea, Hal. I like it. Very much."

Again the Jensen candle seemed to flicker with a sudden brightness.

"I just had another thought. Mind you, it's only an idea. It just came to me. I really don't know how Jack would feel about it." Hal stopped. He was now toying with the last morsel of steak on his plate.

"Out with it, man!" Monty commanded.

"We could put his Caillou painting there. Right next to the Monet. They were after all, colleagues, even friends. That is, if Jack would consent to donate it to the museum. Or maybe, the foundation could purchase it from him. Or he could give it to us on permanent loan until he felt—" Prince Hal's voice trailed off into silence.

The idea of allowing that cretin Jensen custody of my Caillou turned my stomach. Monty and Prince had their eyes on me, waiting for an answer.

"I think I am catching the flu," I said.

THE CARTER MUSEUM OF REPRESENTATIONAL ART opened its doors on East Seventy-second Street in 1972. It was the subject of a long review in *New York Magazine* by the noted art critic HMB. The title of his review was "Detritus," which sent most of his readers to their dictionaries. They learned there that the term derived from geology and it signified something worn out, worn away, or worn down.

HMB proceeded to heap scorn upon the "endless rooms" of large canvases depicting the opening of the West. He greeted the few Hudson River School paintings with the interjection, "Hudson River School, my aching foot!" He found the Meerschaum stained glass "painful." "I prefer the sly pedophilia of Maxfield Parrish to Meerschaum's degenerate saints."

HMB found the Monet *l'Étratat,* rumored to have been purchased for 1.2 million dollars, "one of Monet's rare lifeless canvases." He found another recent acquisition, a Vuillard, also purchased at a price "incommensurate with its quality," a mere "painting of wallpaper." The only painting he liked was a Caillou, said to be a portrait of Auguste Renoir.

"Finally, after nearly fainting from ennui, HMB found a painting he liked—by an impressionist master of whose existence HMB admits to having been previously unaware, one Jean-Jacques Caillou." But then, HMB continued, HMB ascended to the top floor, which contained—to his horror—several rooms of paintings by the late Sir Winston Churchill, said to have been "generously" lent for an indefinite period by the Churchill family. "HMB yields to no one in his admiration of Churchill the man, but does not feel called upon to review Churchill the painter!"

Accompanying HMB's review was an interview with the recently named director of the Carter Museum of Representational Art, Dr. Harald Jensen. It was an insert on the first page of "Detritus," and there was a small photograph of Dr. Jensen, full face, smiling, his eyes glittering like Christmas tree lights. It was obvious that Prince Hal was a tyro at the game of being interviewed, an unwitting victim of the wiles of HMB.

HMB: I have not yet had the privilege of visiting your museum. I wonder if you could tell me—

Jensen (smiling): You have a treat in store for you, HMB.

HMB: No doubt, but why is it called the Carter Museum of *Representational* Art?

Jensen: Well, speaking frankly, Mr. Carter—and, of course, his sister Mrs. Birnbaum— felt that that title would be more in keeping with the wishes of his grandfather, who started the collection, and his grandmother. And also with his own wishes. Quite frankly, Mr. Carter feels that the variety of abstract movements that began with Picasso and Braque are somewhat—shall we say—*over*represented? (Jensen giggles)

HMB: I am not sure I agree with you, but—

Jensen: *À chacun, son gout.* (Jensen smiles)

HMB: What do you regard as the "family jewels"?

Jensen (his brow furrowed in deep thought): That would be very hard to say. We think it is a small museum in which every item is a masterpiece. Rather like the Frick here or the Phillips in Washington.

HMB: Well, try.

Jensen: Well. We have a Monet *l'Étratat* that is—the only word that is adequate—is *ravissant*. We outbid the Met for it a few years back— those malefactors of great wealth. There are some other French post-impressionist paintings, among them a Vuillard that is positively delicious. And, of course, a large number of American painters who were the focus of Mr. Carter's grandfather's collecting. A first-rate collection of Hudson River painters, perhaps the best in any museum. And a very distinguished Peale.

HMB. Oh? Rembrandt or Raphaelle?

Jensen: Actually we are not sure which. But undoubtedly, one or the other. And several absolutely marvelous stained-glass panels by the great Johann Von Goethe Meerschaum. That's the area of my greatest expertise.

HMB: Meerschaum? Never heard of him.

Jensen (giggling): You are having me on, HMB. No. Really? He was a contemporary of Tiffany's, a member of the National Academy. Mr. Carter's grandmother was his chief patron. The Carters had acquired practically all of his work, the sketchbooks, the oil esquisses, as well as the glass panels.

HMB: You said had?

Jensen: Well, that's correct. Some of our holdings were sold off and some donated to other museums. A number are on exhibit in our museum.

HMB: You de-acquisitioned them—to use the barbarism current among you museum types?

Jensen: That's correct. It was an important part of our collection-building strategy, dontchaknow.

HMB: No, I don't think I do know.

Jensen: Well, it allowed us to buy on the present highly inflated market and to diversify. You have no idea how important it is to have a *concept* these days. For building a collection, I mean. I know it sounds crass and commercial, but it's become rather like an investment portfolio. You have to take account of all kinds of things. For example, donating the Meerschaums gave us tax advantages that allowed us to purchase other works.

HMB: Where are the various Meerschaums now?

Jensen (speaking swiftly, somewhat inaudibly): In various museums, such as the Museum of Pentecostal Art in Oklahoma City . . .

T HE YEARS I AM SPEAKING OF WERE NOT HAPPY ONES for our nation. Remember, they were the years of the Vietnam War. For me as well, they were years of wandering in the desert, so to speak.

It should not therefore come as a surprise that there is something dark and disquieting about a number of the Caillou works, which are attributed to the period leading up to and including the Franco-Prussian War. They are brooding, even foreboding works. They reflect a mood of persistent depression—that is how several critics have rightly characterized these works.

Take items 15 and 16 in the catalog. Both are pencil sketches on gray Siena paper. They are studies of soldiers. No.15 depicts a group of four soldiers unloading hay from a cart. No. 16 is a particularly bleak sketch of a dead Zouave lying by a road. The joint entry for both items notes that they are unsigned—"but of undoubted authenticity." It dates the sketches from 1870, possibly executed just months, or even days before the Prussian bullet found its target, ending the short life of Jean-Jacques Caillou. The note continues, "They are hasty but masterful products of the artist's hand, made during a period when paint and canvas were probably unavailable to it."

Then there is No. 13, which bears the title "Portrait of Unknown Woman." The entry for this item reads:

> This small portrait (12 inches x 16 inches) poses a problem for the community of Caillou scholars. No evidence has been unearthed that it was ever exhibited anywhere. Nor is there anything in the correspondence between the friends of Caillou that makes any reference to it. Nothing is known about the subject, although Dr. Harald Jensen—not an acknowledged expert on the impressionist master, it must be admitted—has conjectured that the subject was the artist's mother.
>
> There is some agreement that it is a late work, done no earlier than 1869, and possibly even in 1870, the year of Caillou's death.
>
> The style is reminiscent of the portraits of Paul Cézanne. It is the only one of Caillou's works that suggests a tantalizing connection between the two masters. It features the blacks and dark greens that Cézanne employed, the skin tones have that almost livid quality that Cézanne sometimes favored. Textural effects are accomplished with a palette knife, a technique favored by Cézanne. There is no record the two masters ever met, but it is far from impossible that Caillou met Cézanne, something of a loner in impressionist circles, through Pissarro and was an early admirer of this lonely and independent figure.

The military scenes were done at the time of the invasion of Cambodia. I had played hooky from the foundation and gone to see an exhibition of Winslow Homer's Civil War sketches at the Morgan Library. I got home. Lee was away, doing research for her dissertation. I turned on the news and watched a young soldier die right before my eyes.

The model for the "Portrait of An Unknown Woman" was a practical nurse, a lady in her early sixties we employed to help look after the infant who was born in 1973.

You may wonder why we waited so long. We certainly talked often enough about trying again after the miscarriage. But for Lee the time never seemed quite right. You see, she never did things by halves. First she started studying Hebrew, that in turn led her to the mystical writers of the Middle Ages. Not only the Jews, but the Arabs. And then, of course, she had to learn Arabic. She finished her course work at Union Theological and embarked upon dissertation research on a certain Neoplatonic tradition, I was never quite clear which writers or even which tradition. She was often away in Rome, Vienna, or Jerusalem.

I have always found it true that absence makes the heart grow fonder. After she was away for a while, I would begin to worry about the state of our marriage. Then she would come home and everything would be roses. She'd throw herself into my arms and call me her prince. It was a term of endearment I grew to like.

In 1972 Lee received a letter on paper redolent of myrrh and frankincense. It was written in Hebrew, in script of great beauty. Enclosed was a translation. The letter was signed by the Reb Joshua Ben-Ezra, the Congregation of the Lost Tribes. It bore an address on 125th Street.

The letter recounted the plight of a congregation of Israelites stranded in New York. It told of unavailing appeals to charity. It recounted stone-hearted rejection by the government of Israel. "For, we have yearned, dear Lady, to return to our home in Israel. We have wandered in this desert too long." Would she, "known throughout the length and breadth of Creation for her nurturing and succoring," not do something to alleviate their misery?

They had chosen well. Since her conversion, Lee had become a veritable pillar of Jewish charities in New York. She asked me to find out about the group first. That was easy. They were in the *Encyclopedia of American Religions*, a work indispensable to educational foundations. There I found an entry on the Congregation of the Lost Tribes.

It was in the section on Black Judaism. The congregation had been founded in 1965 by one Dr. Kermit Degraffenreid. Dr. DeGraffenreid had received his Ph.D. from Berkeley in 1957 in the sociology of religion. The topic of his dissertation had been "The Doctrine of the Lost Tribes in the *Book of Mormon*." Until 1964 he had taught at the California State College of Technology. That year he had been turned down for tenure and had filed suit against the State, accusing the chancellor of "racial bigotry and pseudoscientific prejudice."

A year later, he had been found, almost dead from dehydration, in the desert of western Arizona, raving that he had had a vision. He had, he said, been "commanded by JHWH to restore His People to their Homeland." (The congregation, the editors noted, were very strict in observance of the Torah and Mishnah; they especially took very seriously the commandment never to use the Lord's name.) Taking the name Joshua Ben-Ezra, he had moved to New York and started the Congregation of the Lost Tribes the following year. Little information, the editors noted, is available on the membership. Although it is reported to be predominantly black, there are no prohibitions on the admission of whites, indians, or asiatics.

According to the entry, the Lost Tribes Congregation is committed to a communal way of life. There are twelve tribes, one representing each of the families descended from the Patriarch Jacob. All of them observe the strictures closely. Among themselves, the members speak only Hebrew—of the biblical era—but with outsiders they are permitted to converse in unsanctified languages. According to the teaching, Jacob and his original progeny were all black, but some of the tribes became white over time, and others yellow and brown. It was a punishment for their intermarrying with gentiles and adhering to their idolatrous ways. Whites and asiatics are admitted only to the Tribe of Judah. According to unconfirmed reports, polygamy is practiced within the tribes.

Lee went to visit the Lost Tribes. She returned in a state that I could only describe as rapturous.

"Everything they do is covered by a *mitzvah*—that's a commandment. Literally."

I allowed I already knew what a *mitzvah* was.

"They wear *tefillin*. They dress in white—which is a symbol of purity. In a special kind of clothing. They have signposts—*mezuzah*—in every room. And they dress in clothes with fringes. The fringes are very significant."

She didn't immediately explain what significance. I waited in patience.

"And they never desecrate His name." She stopped for a moment, then she continued. "They keep the *kashrut*—that's the right term. Kosher is a corruption. There is sexual *discipline* between man and wife.

"What does that mean?"

"The period for conjugal relations is prescribed. A woman is in a state called *niddah* during her menstrual period and for seven days after. Before they can resume she has to immerse herself in a ritual bath. It's called a *mikvah*. She has to take off everything—even her nail polish. And they all sleep in separate beds—so that no man will come near a woman to uncover her nakedness while she is impure. Isn't that nice?"

I allowed that I thought that was nice. "Did you meet—what does he call himself—the *Reb?*"

"Of course."

"What's he like?"

"He's charismatic," she sighed.

"It's a communal life," she continued. "It's so *pure.*"

There was a pause. I felt a certain foreboding.

"Our lives need reorganizing, Jack. It is time our lives had greater purity."

And she immediately set about the reorganization. She started on me, I had to learn Hebrew. I resisted. She presented me with an electric razor, which I refused to use. I explained that I have always enjoyed the bracing effect of soap and water on my skin. I did not see anything simpler or purer about an electric razor. She explained. Electric razors are in accordance with the *halakha*. They are like scissors. Razors are not. I refused to let my beard grow. I did agree to letting the sideburns be lowered somewhat. But I stood firm against hair on my chin.

She threw out the dishes and replaced them with two sets. She hired a lady to cook kosher. She bought twin beds. She gave up her frequent profanity and admonished me when I used a four letter word. I was upset by the changes in routine. I didn't like having to bathe and dress up Friday nights, I didn't like the rigamarole with the candlestick, holding hands, and saying things I didn't understand.

But after only a few days, Lee had things well in hand at home. From then on, she spent more and more time with the people of the Lost Tribes commune.

One day she came home and proudly announced that her Reb was coming to dinner. Would he be bringing his wife, I asked. "Which one?" she responded. "Oh, no, but he's bringing the Translator. As a concession to you."

"I am honored," I said, remembering that the Reb spoke only in Hebrew. I touched my hand to my chest and then to my forehead.

"Don't be sarcastic, please."

I can't say that I was unimpressed with the powerful figure who graced my table, dressed all in white fringed garments. He was wearing a white *kippah* ("For G-D's sake, don't call it a *yarmulka*," Lee admonished me.). He was large, broad, intimidatingly virile looking. He was in his forties. His nose looked as if it had been broken in some gladiatorial combat. Lustrous, large, intelligent brown eyes shone forth from his dark black face. They were positively hypnotic.

When he opened his mouth for the grace, he chanted in a marvelous deep baritone. It was an evening full of *brakhas*, for bread, for meat, for vegetables and fruit from the ground, for fruit grown on trees, for any of five allowed kinds of grain. After each intonation of the blessing by the Reb, it was rendered into English—for my benefit—by a bespectacled, scholarly looking young man. He spoke a mellifluous, singsong English that revealed his West Indian background.

It was a meal of long silent communion between blessings, except when the Reb addressed a remark to one of us. At one point he looked toward Lee and said something in Hebrew. Smiling, she responded in Hebrew and the Reb laughed. I waited until he had resumed his eating and then looked expectantly in the direction of the Translator.

"He said, 'When three eat together and there is no word of Torah

107

exchanged it is as though they ate from pagan offerings.' And she responded, 'But if three have eaten at a table and spoken words of Torah, it is as though they ate at the table of the Lord.'"

I tried to look properly enlightened.

"Avot 2:4," the translator added.

At another point the Reb spoke directly to me. It was a long passage in Hebrew. Lee blushed becomingly, it was obviously a compliment. When he had finished, I looked expectantly at the Translator. He looked somehow harrassed. Finally he said, "It is a long passage difficult to translate. From the Song of Solomon. The gist is: your lady is unto us as is the Queen of Sheba unto King Solomon—beautiful and bounteous. Any man who is her consort is a fortunate man indeed."

I asked the Translator to relay my sense of good fortune to the Reb. And I nodded to him in an expression I hoped showed proper appreciation.

IN 1972 MONTY FINALLY THREW HIS HAT INTO THE RING. He announced that he could no longer resist the petitions of his many, many friends and well-wishers. He would run for mayor of the great City of New York—"my kind of town," he sang to the assembled press.

I heaved a sigh of relief. The Carter Museum would no longer be receiving the full brunt of his attention. He would, I was sure, no longer be available for lunch on Fridays at Le Champignon.

In January 1973 there was for me yet more momentous news. Lee informed me that I would be a father. She thought she was nearing the end of her first trimester.

"We are blessed, Jack. The special blessing of children," she said, taking my hand and placing it on her stomach.

It was a Saturday night. The Sabbath was over. My thoughts had been far away.

"What did you say?"

"I said we are blessed. I am pregnant."

It took a while for the news to seep in. I said nothing.

"I thought you'd be overjoyed."

"I am. Only we are a little old to be saddled with the responsibility of a baby."

"Pshaw. You love children. You will be a prince of a father."

As the news penetrated, I realized I should have seen the signs. She had missed the *mikvah,* a ritual which in the last year Lee had made a great to-do over. But then this latest reorganization of my life seemed to allow less and less time for conjugal relations. She seemed to be absent more and more, or too tired. Never less willing, she purred when I brought it up, but "well, *hors de combat.*"

"It will bring us closer together again," she now said. "Sometimes I feel we have been growing apart."

"Does this mean you are going to slack off on your activities?"

"Not on your life. I am determined to see the Lost Tribes reunited in Israel—before the baby comes."

The United Jewish Appeal had continued to be adamant in its refusal to help, and the Israeli Consulate in New York was stonewalling in the matter of visas—to use Lee's words. It was, she decided, time to "go public" with the plight of the Lost Tribes.

She had started the previous month by having the Translator go to the Fifth Avenue office of the Israeli Bank of Commerce and apply for a loan on behalf of the congregation. It was to tide them over until they could be repatriated. The bank turned them down, of course, in a polite letter saying that support of such activities was not within the scope of its charter. A copy of the letter was forwarded to a reporter for the *New York Post* and became the basis for a series of articles on the Lost Tribes.

The reporter had never heard of the Lost Tribes Congregation, but saw a good human interest story. He was granted an interview with the Reb. And the story he wrote reflected the Reb's point of view on some of the profane and sinful practices of modern Judaism—for which JHWH would continue to afflict the white House of Judah with plagues and locusts. First, the bank violated the several mitzvahs regarding charity—which in his view extended even to banks. Secondly, even if the Bank of Commerce regarded itself as bound by U.S. banking laws, they were clearly guilty of racial discrimination, a gentile practice that also violated the commandments.

Then Lee got me to lease the Carter mansion and its lands to the Lost Tribes Foundation. She had recently established the latter. The Purchase property was still under my control at the Carter Foundation.

"They need a *Beit Midrash*—a *Sefer* and a *Talmud*," Lee announced.

"What is that?"

"They are the schools. What kind of Jew are you? Besides, they need a place to pasture their flocks."

"Their flocks? They keep flocks on 125th Street?"

"No, but they need to learn how to keep flocks. Theirs is a pastoral way of life. Or will be."

"I can't do that Lee. A school's one thing. But Purchase has laws against pasturing flocks within the town limits."

"Okay, we'll use it as a school."

I accepted her concession, but I could foresee trouble. I was sure Monty would not like it. He would be sensitive about a group that could be regarded as controversial in some circles important to his election. And he would be sensitive about the use of a family home.

"But what about Monty? What if he notices that we've leased the house to the Lost Tribes? It'll make trouble."

"He'll blow a gasket, of course," she said winking at me. "When he finds out. At the moment he's too busy. With all that mayoral twaddle. We'll deal with Monty when the time comes."

She was right. Monty was too busy campaigning. The election was still far off, but he was too busy to notice what Lee was up to or pay attention to foundation matters. In March the Carter mansion was leased to the Lost Tribes Congregation. Every day I expected Monty to howl, but there was no word from him. It was now June, and Monty had not yet been heard from. It was a Sunday morning, early in the month.

That Sunday morning, Lee presented me with a new suit. It was all white. And of wool. The jacket was very long—a white version of the black caftans worn by the Hassidic Jews I used to see on Forty-seventh

Street. The hat, also in white, was a version of the headwear they favored.

"What is this?" I asked.

"We are showing solidarity with the Lost Tribes," she responded. "That's what we are wearing in the parade."

"What parade?"

"There is a big benefit today. For some cause or other. A parade. The Israel Symphony will play on the steps of City Hall this afternoon. We've got to be there."

I held up the vest. One put it on over the head. It had tassels at the four corners.

"What the hell is this? Why these tassels?"

"Please don't be profane, Jack. It's called a *tallit katan*. It's like the *tallit* worn in a synagogue, but the pious wear the *tallit katan* outside as a sign of their devotion. Usually under the shirt. But we are wearing them over the shirt today. And they are not tassels. They are *fringes*. I forget the right Hebrew word."

I sighed. You ask Lee something these days and she recites the whole encyclopedia. In biblical Hebrew.

At twelve we were dressed. Lee was dressed in a long skirt of similar material, as white and pure as mine. She wore a little bolero-like jacket over her loose long-sleeved shirt. On her head was something like a turban, with a long snood behind that completely covered her hair. Her face had grown round in her pregnancy. She was now in her seventh month. When she put on her thick glasses, she reminded me of a child wearing dress-ups from the attic.

"We are assembling at Fifty-seventh Street. They have put us at the end of the parade—the bastards. Pardon the expression. They tried to exclude us entirely, but I threw a tantrum and threatened them with a plague if they kept us out." She smiled knowingly. "A plague from the press. The power structure was frightened by the series in the *Post*."

We left our house, and I tried to hail a cab on the street. I hoped to G-D we didn't meet anyone we knew. Don't you know, you can never get a cab when you really need one! Finally one stopped. I wondered whether there was a suitable *barokh* for a taxi that stopped when you needed one.

We emerged on Fifth Avenue. It was an unseasonally hot day. As we made our way to the rendezvous, we drew the attention of various delegations dressed more sensibly for the weather. Then suddenly we were surrounded by a host of black faces. The Lost Tribes, man, woman, and child, were all assembled for the march—all in the same dress. I surveyed the crowd. Ours were the only white faces.

The Reb, dressed in ceremonial robes, gave us a patriarchal nod. The Translator positioned us at the very head of the crowd. "In a position of honor," he explained. "Only the Reb will be more exalted among the Lost Tribes." He pointed to the open sedan chair that would be borne by twelve stalwarts, one from each tribe.

The parade started. It was a long way to City Hall. I cursed those heavy wool garments. I looked over toward the Reb. Somehow he managed to look cool, serene, regal. By contrast, I was sweating like a pig. "You should pardon the expression," I told myself.

The Lost Tribes had hardly arrived at the entrance to the park adjoining City Hall when the Israel Symphony, Lenny conducting, launched into the "Star Spangled Banner," followed by the Israeli anthem. Then His Honor the Mayor, Monty's opponent in November, went to the microphone.

"Isn't this a glorious day?" he said to the cheers of the crowd. "We are here today to celebrate a fest—"

Quite suddenly, I was knocked off my feet by a great eruption. I reached for the nearest support, a park bench. I hadn't paid any attention when the host had stopped at the entrance to the park and maintained its position. I do remember wondering what had become of Lee. We were suddenly separated. I was, I suppose, too busy looking around for some inconspicuous Hebron at which to lie down by quiet waters.

But now I felt the tremor pass through my whole body. I looked back and was surprised to find no signs of chaos, no dust, no trees shaken or uprooted, no mangled bodies. I turned toward the source of the tumult.

It was an explosion of voices. It was the host of the Lost Tribes singing, singing in Hebrew. In a wondrous unison for such a large chorus, far larger than the combined Westminster, Mormon Tabernacle, and Robert Shaw groups. And so well rehearsed.

112

The Reb had dismounted and was raising his voice with his people. The first ranks had knelt to let the back ranks see the conductor. They were singing as one. They were singing the old spiritual "Let My People Go." Every syllable of the Hebrew was clear as a bell. All their eyes were glued on the figure conducting them. It was a glorious rendition. The unfamiliar language rang out with great majesty. And the whole thing was being conducted, even orchestrated, by my wife, raising her arms and moving her lips in stately and solemn direction. It was as if she had been trained to do it, as if she had been doing it all her life.

They had finished "Let My People Go" and were into "We Shall Overcome"—also in Hebrew—when the police arrived.

We were home by six, Lee shedding her clothing as she rushed toward the television. She flopped, in her sopping undergarments, into an overstuffed chair, fanning herself, as the local news came on. The Lost Tribes were the lead item. There were shots of the Reb, borne aloft on the shoulders of his people. There were explanations from the Translator. There was an interview with Lee. She and the reporter, Roland Something-or-other, were friends from way back, from Civil Rights demonstrations and anti-war marches. They called each other by their first names.

When it was over, Lee turned to me and announced proudly, "I have put the Lost Tribes on the map!" She waited for the national news. Maybe they'd made it there, too. They had. With a film clip of the singing. She was named in the piece, but there was no footage of her being interviewed. She was disappointed. "Wait till Monty sees this." Recovering, she doubled over her swollen belly in laughter.

Speak of the devil! It was not five minutes before the front door bell rang. Sundays we were usually without domestic help. I went to the door. There were Monty and Roxie—in evening kit. Monty, a whirlwind, swept past me without a word, trailing Roxie who was desperately trying to restrain him. In passing, she managed only the ghost of a smile at me. It stopped when she took in my white suit stained with sweat.

The brouhaha began even before I could regain the living room.

"What the fuck do you think you are doing?" It was Monty's voice.

"I am trying to cool off. You are fogging my glasses. And no profanity please. This is—" The middle was lost in the heat of Monty's rage. "—a house of piety."

Monty repeated his question. He was red faced with rage.

"I am trying to get my people repatriated. They are displaced persons —the world's oldest," she said, coldly. "What's wrong with that?"

"'My people,' my ass," Monty said. He spat the words out. "You are doing it for revenge. You are out to wreck my campaign. What have I ever done to deserve this?"

"Calm down, Monty," Roxie tried to put her arm on his shoulder. He rejected it angrily. "Jack, get him a drink of water. He'll be hyperventilating in a minute. And he is scheduled for an important speech in Brooklyn. The B'nai Brith."

I went into the kitchen. Over the running tap, I could hear the shouting. Now Lee was mad.

"It's my money as much as it is yours," she was shouting, as I handed my brother-in-law the glass. Monty flung it away. The glass landed harmlessly on the carpet, the water and ice spilling across the floor. Roxie was in a panic. She picked up the glass and went in search of a paper towel.

Monty turned to me. "And you, you Judas!" Then he began hiccupping. "You are in on this," he managed to get out between hiccups.

Roxie forced him into a chair and ordered silence. Lee made no move. She sat there, majestic in her late pregnancy, in her panties and bra. Monty was holding his breath. After a moment, the hiccups ceased.

"This is a fine show of family loyalty, I must say. Do you know what kind of damage you've done to my campaign?"

Ice had replaced fire, rhetoric-wise.

"There are some things more important than being mayor of this Gomorrah. Like getting my people home."

"Oh, for God's sake, stop calling them 'my people.' He's a charlatan, don't you know that? And you're his patsy!"

"How dare you call him a charlatan—you—you Nazi! You are the patsy. One of the world's richest men trying to buy his way into office."

"Now stop this both of you!" Roxie yelled and broke into tears. Then she ran out of the room.

"And you." Monty turned and looked at me. "Explain to me just what those black bastards are doing in *my home*. They are running a sheep farm up there. And goats! How dare you let them use *my* home as a kibbutz."

"I don't know anything about that, Monty. I let them have a lease for a school. Do you, Lee?"

Lee made no answer.

"Do you, Lee?" I repeated.

She mumbled something.

"I didn't hear you," I said.

"It's not a kibbutz. It's a summer camp. Why shouldn't a school run a summer camp? Lots of schools do. How did you know about it?" She looked at her brother.

"It'll be on the news tomorrow," Monty replied, his anger still white hot. "The town has kicked up a helluva ruckus. It's had an avalanche of protests. 'Your people' are being kicked out on their self-righteous asses."

"By whom?"

"By me—that's by whom!" he yelled at her. He began hyper-ventilating again, loudly enough to draw Roxie from her sanctuary in the other room. She pulled Monty up and immediately insisted that they leave. He went kicking and yelling—between hiccups.

THE NEXT DAY VERY EARLY I RECEIVED, BY SPECIAL MES-senger, a letter informing me that the board of directors had relieved me as director of the Carter Foundation. There was no explanation.

But Monty was on the morning news. The footage of him immediately followed film clips of a shepherd, clad in spotless white, holding a large crook, curved at the top, herding a flock of bleating goats into a pen. The letter still in hand, I sat watching the stately shepherd and his bleating goats. They reminded me of a particular Meerschaum panel I assumed was still in the Museum of Pentecostal Art. As the reporter spoke into the camera, signing off from Purchase, one could still hear the bleating of the goats and the ringing of their bells in the background.

In the clip that followed, Monty denied any knowledge of the Lost Tribes's existence. It had been arranged behind his back by someone at the Carter Foundation, he claimed.

"That's Jack Birnbaum," the reporter said. "He is your brother-in-law, isn't he?"

"Unfortunately. He is now *former* director of the Carter Foundation, Leslie. The Carter Foundation is conducting an in-house investigation. Dr. Harald Jensen is in charge. Speak to him."

"Into the Purchase kibbutz?"

"That and other matters."

"What other matters, Monty?"

"Well, it's too early to go into the details. But Dr. Jensen is charged with finding out whether revenues from the sale of valuable art works—and from tax credits—were diverted to the support of those *mishuguners*."

In early July of 1973 I was called before a federal grand jury and questioned about certain reports I had filed with the IRS, concerning donations by the Carter Foundation of certain works of religious art to the Pentecostal Museum in Oklahoma City. I acknowledged, under questioning, that the works were grossly overvalued. Yes, that was my signature. I had signed the reports to the IRS—or let my signature stamp be used. But I also said that I honestly could not remember placing those valuations on the Meerschaum works. The judge admonished I was under oath; I had better answer truthfully or indictments of Conspiracy to Commit Fraud or Perjury, or both, might be returned. I stuck by my story. Had the figures been altered without my knowledge, my lawyer asked me. It is possible, I replied.

Soon after, on a Saturday night in early August, Lee awoke me from a sound sleep and said she thought her time had come. We rushed her to the Carter Pavilion at Maimonides Hospital. She had donated it to them at the time of her miscarriage. Throughout the night the doctors and nurses kept assuring me that everything was proceeding normally. But I spent a sleepless night in the waiting room. At six I was joined by Roxie, who, despite the rupture in relations, had continued to function as an unofficial emissary.

Lee was delivered of the baby at 6:45. "A beautiful baby girl, eight pounds, two ounces," the doctor announced and departed.

I was admitted to my wife's room at 7:30, while Roxie went to the nursery to see the baby.

Lee was still groggy when I entered. She smiled at me beatifically as I came through the door, stretching her arms out to me. I knew that without her glasses she could hardly recognize me. She threw her arms around me, and I squeezed back gently. We both exclaimed simultaneously how delighted we were to have a baby.

"What are we going to call her?" I asked.

"We haven't talked much about names, have we?" she asked. "How about Sheba?"

"If that is what you want. Now sleep."

I walked to the nursery, where Roxie was inspecting the new arrival. As I approached, I sensed something amiss. It was something about the expression on Roxie's face, the kind of confusion that would spread over her face when she was called upon to deal with a social crisis and didn't quite know how to cope. She spied me approaching and followed my approach with her eyes, as if warning me to expect a shock.

I looked down at the crib containing the squalling infant.

Sheba was black.

ITEM NO. 17 OF THE *CATALOGUE RAISONNÉ OF THE WORKS of Jean-Jacques Caillou* is called "Harlequin and Columbine." The entry reads:

Oil on pale primed canvas, 30 inches x 42 inches.

The subjects are, of course, the familiar figures from the *Commedia del Arte. Arlequino,* the buffoon, is shown here in the standard dress, tights and a close-fitting shirt, of a pattern of black diamonds on a white background. On his feet are ballet slippers and in his hand is the magic wand, which is part of the costume of this traditional figure. It is pointed in the direction of his companion. He is without the mask which usually covers the upper part of the face. He is standing, three-quarter face, looking in the direction of his companion and pointing with the right foot. *Colombina,* his lady, portrayed full face, is dressed in a pink tutu. She is captured in the act of curtsying, as if acknowledging the applause of an unseen audience.

All this suggests that these are figures from a ballet, rather than a play or pantomime, but what is unusual is that the background does not suggest a stage but a room in a house or apartment. In the center, between the two figures, can be seen a marble mantle. To the right, the upper back of *Arlequino* is reflected in a mirror. To the left on the wall above the table is a small painting. The subject is a blackamoor, in a seventeenth-century courtier's costume. It may be intended to copy a well-known work of Velázquez, a painter much admired by the proto-impressionists.

Some scholars, most notably the French art historian Charles La-biche, have seen echoes of Edgar Degas' larger and better known portrait of the Bellelli family in this work of Caillou. Like Degas, the painter here also employs the full repertoire of his techniques not to *prettify* but to *dramatize* his subjects. Instead of showing *Arlequino* dead-pan and *Colombina* as flirtatious—the usual convention in *Commedia del Arte*—there are strong tensions between the two in this painting. *Arlequino* is here seen looking veritable daggers at his companion. His gesture with his wand seems to want to make her disappear. *Colombina,* on the other hand, seems to be making a strenuous, not entirely successful, effort to ignore his anger. On her face is a little frozen smile. At the same time, her features are contracted in a kind of squint—as if she were accustomed to wearing glasses and needed them now to see her audience.

Very little is known about the circumstances of composition or the date of this very beautiful painting. It must also be noted that it is unsigned, but it has been accepted without reservation by the community of Caillou scholars as an authentic work of Caillou.

On the surface, we maintained the appearance of a family united in the joy of a new baby. Sheba was indeed a blessed event from the outset, a real love. I welcomed all those exhausting things, the routine of the two o'clock feeding, the frequent diaper changing, walking up and down the room with the baby when she wouldn't go to sleep. It put off having to deal with my own hurt.

Almost the first thing Lee said when she came home from the hospital was, "Jack, our life needs reorganizing." Out went the two sets of dishes. Out went the kosher cuisine and the cook. She had the upper floor repainted, and after the painters were finished, I noticed that the mezuzahs on the front door and in every room had also disappeared. None of this was lost upon Roxie, who was a constant visitor and a frequent assistant in the care of Sheba. But she kept her own counsel.

When Lee and I were alone, we maintained an unruffled tenor of behavior. If anything, we were more considerate than usual of each other, but it was all façade.

I am sure that Roxie was aware of the reserve with which we treated each other. But she kept her own counsel on that as well. Monty, of course, was never present. We had not seen him since that day in June. He made no effort to come by, so I did not have to face the prospect of forbidding him my door.

In the course of the redecoration Lee asked me—apropos of nothing in particular—whether I wanted a new bed. No, I said noncommittally, I was very happy with the one I now slept in. I did not go out of my way to say *"single* bed I now slept in." Lee accepted my answer—evenly and without comment.

That Lee had ceased her activity on behalf of the Lost Tribes did not go unnoticed. There were intimations in the press—usually in connection with Monty's campaign for mayor, which most observers felt was at the moment too close to call.

Then there began to appear stories in those tabloids that prey on the appetite for malicious tales—the kind available at the supermarkets where most of the voters did their shopping. They said that Lee Birnbaum had recently given birth to a black baby, whose father was reputed to be the leader of a sect (in Harlem) that claimed descent from the Lost Tribes of Israel.

Political wisdom dictates that it is usually better to ignore than to deny. But the story was doing too much political damage. So a spokesman for the Carter campaign issued a blistering denunciation of the sleazy campaign of innuendo being waged against the candidate. Because they could find no blemish on the candidate's record, his opponents had turned to slandering his family—and in the lowest forms of journalism that existed.

To friends of the Carter family, Roxie confided that Lee was too busy with a new baby at the moment to continue her campaign on behalf of the Lost Tribes. In conversation with more casual acquaintances, she managed to insert the news that Lee and I had adopted a darling black baby girl, to the delight, she added, of Monty and herself. Roxie was especially nervous these days, it seemed to many. Not just that slightly flustered, schoolgirl, unable-to-cope manner that was part of her charm, but nervous! They put it down to the ravages of campaigning.

In any case, no member of the Carter family was present when the Lost Tribes Congregation embarked on the two specially chartered El-Al 707s in late October for their return to the Promised Land. Negotiations had been started with Panam by the Carter Foundation—in the strictest secrecy—around the middle of September, but Panam, while it could handle the *kashrut* commandments, could not accommodate the other *mitzvah* pertaining to air travel. Needless to say, I had no part in those negotiations.

According to a later report in the *Times,* quoting an unnamed El-Al employee, before the Lost Tribes embarked, the Reb pronounced in his rich deep baritone the *barokh* appropriate to the journey, long by airline standards, short by biblical ones. The Carter campaign, which had several friends close to the Israeli government—which had hastily granted the visas—breathed a sigh of relief. But it was too late for Monty Carter to regain the ground he had lost in Queens and Brooklyn. The incumbent was returned by a healthy majority.

It was not until early November, weeks after the departure and just after the election, that the whole painful business finally came up. It was Lee who forced the discussion. I think I would have continued to act like someone out of Noël Coward play if she hadn't brought the matter up.

Roxie, who had assisted her in bathing Sheba, had just departed. We were sitting together in the living room after supper.

"Poor Roxie, she wants a baby *so* much."

I nodded. At the moment, that was a subject I was not much interested in pursuing. There was a long silence, in which neither of us could think of anything witty to say.

Then Lee said, "Jack, I'd like to explain."

I didn't say anything immediately. It was another painful silence. Then I managed to say, "You don't have to. When have I asked you for explanations? Loving is not having to say you are sorry—as somebody says in a movie. Or a popular song. Or something."

"You've had no reason to ask before."

"Who says I am asking now?"

"Now you have the right."

There was another long silence, which she broke, choosing her words carefully.

"You are a prince, Jack. As a husband and now as a father. You know I know that. But he was—*is*, as far as I am concerned—a prophet."

Another long silence.

"So?"

"So, you can't say no to a prophet."

I considered that statement a long time. It seemed, at the moment, irrefutable. Try as I might, I couldn't find any balm to the wound. So after a while, I got up and excused myself.

Nothing appeared to change. The new baby continued to be adorable and adored. It was the center of everyone's attention. But a few weeks later, Roxie asked Lee what she was now "reorganizing." Lee said it was nothing. She had decided to occupy the room next to mine because my snoring kept her awake at night.

I T TOOK LEE ABOUT SIX MONTHS TO FIND A NEW DIREC-tion for her life. I was having breakfast—it was rather a late breakfast —when my wife suddenly appeared in the doorway with a suitcase.

"Where are you going?"

"To Switzerland. Here is the address where you can reach me if you need me. I've already said goodbye to Sheba. I'll be home in six weeks."

"Am I permitted to know the purpose of this trip?"

"Of course. My life is an open book. I am going to attend a seminar at the Jung Institute. I plan to become a therapist. It is time I did something useful with my life. I want to leave the world a better place than I found it."

"You can't say that you haven't tried in the past."

I was afraid she would think I was being nasty. "No sarcasm intended."

"I know. But not just with money. There are people out there who need help, personal help, individual help. There are people out there who need to reorganize their lives. Anyway, I don't have any more time." She came over and kissed me on the cheek. And I reciprocated.

"I am a fortunate woman. I leave Sheba in the best of hands," she called out.

"I know. I am a prince," I said under my breath. I heard the door slam.

That was on a Tuesday. I spent the rest of that day and also Wednesday in the studio. I had resumed my career as a portrait painter, and I was flourishing. The biggest artists' management agency in New York had

122

asked me to do all of its artists. The portraits were to be displayed in the anterooms of their offices. I had already done Lenny. I was working at the moment on Itzhak. Pinky and Glenn were waiting in the wings. I worked now mostly from photographs, requiring only a few sittings from the subject late in the project. I thought of myself now as the descendant of a distinguished line of society portraitists. There was still, I told myself, a *beau monde,* and I would be its John Singer Sargent.

I was finishing the portrait of Itzhak, putting in highlights, a touch on the violin, another on the glasses. The glasses made me think of Lee's thick lenses—rather fondly. Absence makes the heart grow fonder. Or as Hack was fond of saying, absinthe . . . and so forth. The phone rang in the studio.

"Jack?"

It was Roxie.

"Hi, what's up?"

"I've been trying to get you for two days."

"I've been home. Lee's gone to Switzerland. She'll be back in six weeks."

"I know. She told me."

Roxie sounded flustered.

"When I wanted to call, Monty was always here."

I got the message. I thought momentarily of Monty. The grand jury had not returned any indictments for conspiracy to defraud or tax evasion. I suspected that Monty had pulled some strings to see that I wasn't indicted. Nothing that could involve him, of course. Somehow, the size of Monty's defeat had washed my soul clean of most of my bitterness toward him. Now the thought of him rankled only slightly. He was no more than a nuisance. Maybe, I would never see him again. And that would be a blessing.

"Anyway, I thought I'd come over."

"When?"

"Now?"

"Nobody is here but Sheba and me. The help is off on Wednesday afternoons."

"That's okay. How about if I bring lunch?"

It passed through my mind that maybe it was Lee who had put her

123

up to it. "Look in on Jack, Roxie. Don't let him become a hermit," I could almost hear her saying. I felt a twinge of guilt. I had been cold toward Lee for too long.

"Fine. Sheba goes down for her nap by one."

"I'll be there by twelve. That way I can see Sheba."

"See you then."

I gave the matter no further thought and went back to Itzhak. I resumed my work on the highlights. Stepping back to view Itzhak's glasses, I thought I had captured very well the twinkle in the eyes, merely suggested in the photograph. The most recent dab of paint spoke volumes.

Roxie arrived a little before twelve. I took Sheba out of her playpen —where she had been contentedly spending the morning sucking on a rattle or ringing a bell—she was really no bother, the little lamb—and carried her upstairs with me to greet Aunt Roxie at the door.

Roxie looked especially ravishing. Her raven hair—was she retouching it these days?—was still silky and beautiful. It fell around her neck and curled under in a kind of extended page boy. She was wearing a knee-length frock of blue shantung silk. An off-white shawl of some soft woven fabric covered her shoulders. She looked more beautiful than ever. Her hands were full of packages.

Sheba smiled at her Aunt Roxie. She was almost as familiar as her mother. And giving the packages to me, Roxie took Sheba into her arms, carrying her into the kitchen and putting her into her highchair.

I had now begun to prepare Sheba's lunch, Gerber's carrots and milk. Roxie announced that she would feed Sheba, why didn't I lay out the lunch?

"Are you sure it's no trouble?" I asked.

She replied, "Of course, not. Haven't I done it before?"

"Okay, I'll get you an apron. That's a particularly fetching frock."

She started feeding Sheba. Unwrapping the packages, I proclaimed my delight. What an elegant lunch she had brought—cold salmon, Caesar salad, and a bottle of white Margaux '66.

"Is this a special occasion?" I asked.

There was no answer from the direction of the highchair. Then after

124

a moment. "Let's eat downstairs in your studio. Is there a place to eat down there?"

"Yes, but not worthy of this repast."

"That'll be just fine."

I arranged the meal on the good china and set it on the small table downstairs where I sometimes took my lunch when I didn't want to be interrupted. I set the bottle of Margaux in a silver cooler, I fussed with the table arrangement. Then I waited. Finally I heard her descend.

"I've put Sheba down."

She stopped momentarily to admire the portrait of Itzhak.

"You've caught the twinkle. That's Itzhak. To a tee."

I held her chair for her and she bestowed a smile upon me as she sat. There was something different about Roxie today, something out of character, vaguely disturbing.

She took a mouthful of salmon. I raised my glass in a toast to her.

"Perfection," I exclaimed after sipping it.

"I'm glad all that business with the grand jury is at an end," she said. After a moment, she added, "It wasn't your fault, you know. The values were altered. They thought you had put them too low."

I knew who *they* were, but I let it pass without comment.

"In the end, no harm was done," I said, feeling charitable. "Let's forget it. This is too good." I was aware of how hungry I was.

But she wasn't prepared to let things pass.

"He uses everybody. He uses you; he uses me. The only one he can't use is Lee. She's too smart for him. And it makes him furious."

This lunch is beginning to take a curious turn, I thought. It's becoming a tête-à-tête. I wasn't sure I wanted one. What a bonafide heel Monty was—that I was always ready to discuss. But I didn't want to discuss my feelings about Lee and the whole business with the Reb. That was too painful.

I should add that at that moment I knew exactly how I felt about Roxie. I recognized that it had been a crush, nothing more. She was now familiar, a sister-in-law, someone my wife loved, whom I loved—but without magic. I concentrated on the insidious bouquet and fruity charm of the wine.

"And he's such a miser," she continued. "You can't conceive how much he spent on that dumb mayoral race! Have you ever seen him pick up a dinner check at the Champignon? My God, he's impossible, Jack. Why have I stayed married to him all these years?"

I could think of an answer, *You love being filthy rich, Roxie.* But candor was not required. That's what I would have said, and then added, *I suppose I do too. But in your case you get the added satisfaction of having fulfilled your mama's ambitions.*

But I was relaxing, seizing the moment, so I kept my thoughts to myself.

"And you?" she continued. "It hasn't been easy, God knows. I love Lee. In some ways I even wish I could be more like her. She has such energy. But she tries one's patience. They both manipulate everyone. It is wrong that anyone should have that much money. Wrong! Wrong! Wrong!"

I wouldn't have put it that way, but I thought it a sentiment that did her credit. Perhaps it was the wine. I raised my glass. She responded by raising hers, and we clinked.

Suddenly she changed direction.

"Why haven't you ever painted me, Jack? You've painted Lee. But not me. Haven't you ever wanted to?"

"Of course," I said. At one time nothing could have pleased me more. Was that the reason for the lunch, I wondered? Was it the wine or the portrait of Itzhak that had put the idea into her head?

"Somehow I didn't think you would like being a model. I think you'd fidget too much."

"Maybe. But I am willing to give it a try."

"Sure. If that is what you really want, Roxie."

She clapped her hands in glee, like a little urchin from the mountains of Kentucky.

"Can we start right after lunch? Will Sheba sleep?"

"Sheba usually is down for a long time in the afternoon."

"Great." She got up from the table. "How about over there. On that great old Empire couch."

It was a prop I still kept around the studio. I smiled at the thought of Roxie, shy, proper, easily flustered, sitting on it, her hands folded in the lap of her silk shantung frock, holding the pose.

126

"Okay," I said. "But it's not very comfortable." I went over and dusted it off. I seated her on it, fixed her hands in her lap, turned her head, brought over a studio light, then another on the other side. I stepped back.

"Should I smile?"

"No, you wouldn't be able to hold it! I'll provide the smile. I think I'll only make some sketches today. I can work from them. That way you won't have to pose. Not until the final stages."

"Okay, but before you begin, may I have some coffee?"

I went upstairs and made some coffee. I looked in on Sheba, who was breathing deeply, sucking contentedly on her thumb. I started downstairs, rattling the two coffee cups. When I got to the bottom, I turned to smile at Roxie. She was no longer sitting upright. She was reclining on the couch, facing out frontally, clutching her shawl around her shoulders. She was looking up at me. She was naked—in the *maya nuda* pose.

I took a breath. She was now in her forties but absolutely ravishing. Small breasted. The curve of her hip was—"I never saw a more perfect pelvis"—the words seemed to leap into my mind. I was puzzled. Then the image of Dr. Trueheart followed and I suddenly felt like a peeping Tom. I think I blushed at the intruding memory. I was suddenly quite confused.

I put her coffee on the floor near her. I gently moved her foot, then her hand. And I tried to be matter of fact, but I was afraid that my hand was trembling. The thought had crossed my mind during lunch that she was sending me signals of a sexual nature. But I think I had dismissed that. We had been too long in the familial roles. Now when I saw her naked, I decided maybe all she wanted was for me to paint her that way. At least that's how I would respond. So, wordlessly, I retreated and took up a pad and pencil. Frankly, I was surprised by her whim. The whole thing seemed so out of character, so narcissistic. But, okay, if that's what she really wants—

I sat down at the desk and began sketching, quickly putting in the upper outlines. Then I lightly sketched the breasts, the navel, the pubis, with its discrete scattering of dark hair. I concentrated on the paper in

127

front of me. I worked quickly. Then she moved. I adjusted. Then she moved again.

"Roxie, you are fidgeting. I can't work with you fidgeting," I called out to her.

I looked up at her. There were tears in her eyes. Then suddenly she burst out crying. She sat up, grabbed her clothes, and dashed into the bathroom. Through the door, I heard her sobbing. I waited for the sobs to subside and for her to emerge. When she didn't, I knocked. She didn't answer. After a moment, I opened the door gingerly. She was standing in her bra and panties, her back to me. Silently, I took a tissue and offered it to her over her shoulder. She blew her nose.

"I am sorry," she said. She started putting on her pantyhose, "I'd better go. I've embarrassed you."

"No," I said, taking her hand and patting it. "I was surprised."

"You were so cold. I was just another client. I felt ashamed. And I shouldn't. Jack, I'm forty-two years old and I'm still acting like I just got off the train from Lexington. I couldn't bring it off."

She began sobbing again. I gently took her in my arms and patted her hair. She allowed me to do so. When she stopped crying, I left my arm around her waist.

"Understand Roxie, I have done many nude studies. You maintain a certain distance. You just don't think of the model in that way."

I thought that would comfort her. But she looked again as if she would break into a flood of tears.

"That's not what I meant," she sobbed. "I couldn't even *se-se-seduce* you." She got the words out between sobs.

"Seduce me?" I asked. "Why would you want to seduce *me?*"

She was crying again, still in my arms, her face buried on my breast. I reached behind and got another kleenex and held it up for her to blow her nose.

"Because I want a baby. Jack, you are my last chance. I want a baby *so* much!"

"Come on, Roxie. Let's sit down and drink our coffee and talk about it. You want a brandy?"

She shook her head affirmatively, her head buried on my shoulder.

I went upstairs and got two ponies of cognac and brought them downstairs. When I got there, she was seated on the couch, fully dressed, drinking her coffee. She had recomposed herself. She smiled wanly at me as I handed her the pony. I sat down on the couch beside her.

"It was a dumb idea," she said. She paused for a moment. "I guess it's because I've been to a new doctor. We both went. The problem, it seems, is not me. It's Monty. His sperm count is too low."

I gave that serious thought. That's what Dr. Trueheart had suspected years before. "Haven't you considered artificial insemination?"

"Monty would never tolerate that. My idea was to have you get me pregnant and let Monty think it was his. Like it was a medical miracle."

"But why *me*, Roxie?"

"Because I thought you'd be willing. And I could trust you. And the time is right. Lee's away and you and Monty aren't speaking. God knows, as much as I love Lee, she has given you cause." She stopped, then she added as an afterthought. "And because I thought you might have been in love with me at one time. Were you?"

I nodded. "I suppose I was—in a way—but it was with an idea. It's a ghost I am not sure that I want to disturb now."

"So it wasn't very wrong to want you to make love to me, was it?"

"It's not a matter of right or wrong, Roxie. We are playing with feelings that ought to be left undisturbed."

"Jack, do this for me. You don't know how I envy Lee. It's my last chance. Truly." She put her arm up and started teasing the back of my neck. She took the pony from my hand and suddenly she was in my arms, pressing her lips to mine. At the same time, she reached down and unbuckled my belt.

"Shall we—?" She didn't finish the sentence. I think she wanted to say "fuck." It was a word she never used. And she couldn't use it now. What would her mother have thought?

The frontispiece of the *Catalogue Raisonné of the Works of Jean-Jacques Caillou* is the famous "Odalisque," which appears in the painting "The Portrait of M. Auguste Renoir." According to the catalog, entry number 12, this canvas, an oblong, 30 inches wide by 48 inches high, is "perhaps the most beautiful of all the many splendid works of Caillou's refined sensibility." But, the author of the catalog admits, it is the most difficult to discuss in terms of influence and relations, both with respect to Caillou's other work and to the work of other painters. He continues:

It is surprising that the nude was not a subject for oil much favored by the original impressionists—after the scandalous *Déjeuner sur l'herbe* and *Olympe* of Manet. Only Renoir undertook many nude studies and, of course, Degas—but at a later period, and then mostly in pastel. But then Degas considered himself an impressionist only intermittently.

In any case, all the impressionist nudes strive for *intimacy* rather than *sensuality*. This one is an anomaly, since it harkens back to the cool nudes of Ingres and the title given to this work is therefore not inapt. All of which makes this painting something of a throwback to the orientalism and exoticism of French romanticism. Such art, beautiful though it may be, requires studio conditions. The impressionists rejected these conditions when they moved out of the studio. It is probable that this, more than any other factor, explains why nude studies fell out of favor with the impressionists.

Moreover, Caillou's "Odalisque," when studied under X ray, reveals an underpainting—rather, the preparatory outlines for another painting (see Plate 12a). The configuration of the finished canvas has been rotated ninety degrees. The X ray reveals that the canvas had been a study of a woman in her bath—of the type of Degas' *études de toilette*. The female figure is seated upright in the water and only her upper torso is sharply outlined. One arm reaches out for a towel to a clothed female figure on the left, not shown in full.

The towel bears an insignia which can barely be discerned. It appears to resemble a Star of David. Its presence is part of the whole mystery surrounding the underpainting.

I went into it without illusions. I knew that Roxie didn't love me. I told myself that over and over again, hoping that would be sufficient innoculation against being twice smitten. I was still telling it to myself when I realized that all I was living for were those Wednesday afternoons.

It was an idyll, very sweet, very short. It went on for the six weeks Lee was in Switzerland. And suddenly it was over.

It was Tuesday and Lee was due back the following Monday. Sheba had just gone to the park with the nurse. The maid was out shopping. I was working on the portrait of Glenn, but really daydreaming. The doorbell rang. I was not expecting anyone. It rang again impatiently. In haste, I put down my palette and dashed up the stairs. I was breathless when I got to the front door.

It was Roxie.

She was wearing a one piece wool outfit. She looked absolutely radiant. She threw her arms around me, ignoring the fact that I was wearing a paint stained smock.

I kissed her on the lips. My whole being was communicated in that kiss.

"I've missed my period. I've missed my period," she murmured ecstatically, pressing her body against mine, brushing her lips on my cheek. "Isn't that wonderful?"

"Are you sure?"

"Practically. I'm as regular as clockwork."

I was faced suddenly with the end of our afternoons together. Disengaging, I asked, "It's over then?"

"Ah, baby," she took me in her arms. "It was beautiful, my dearest one."

"Was?"

"We shall always have the memories." She put her hand gently on my cheek and then let it play teasingly along the thin line of the mustache that I had begun to grow shortly after we became lovers.

"Roxie, I can't—"

"Don't!"

She wouldn't let me say it. She put her finger up to my lips again.

"But—"

"Lee will be back Monday."

"We could start anew—you, me, and *our* baby!"

"Jack, be sensible!"

She looked deeply into my eyes. And she saw the pain that was there.

"With what? Do you think Monty would let me go? And there's Lee. I won't hurt her! I simply won't!"

"But—"

"You love *her*—deep down." There was a pause. "You may be angry with her right now. But you will get over that."

"It's *you* I love, Roxie."

"But *I* don't love *you,* Jack. Not in that way."

I felt the words sting, then I felt the surge of tears. I fought to hold them back. I looked away and then glanced at her furtively. She was resolute, even ruthless. There was not the least suggestion of a tear in her beautiful eyes.

L{EE CAME BACK FROM SWITZERLAND WITH A FULL HEAD} of steam. I took Sheba out with me to Kennedy to meet her. I saw her from afar as she barged through customs. Our lives before her departure had acquired a certain façade of good humor that was never entirely convincing. But now I had something to hide, and I was afraid that I would give myself away.

She was talking, at the top of her voice, to a distinguished gray-haired man just behind her. Then she caught sight of us, waved, abandoned the man in mid-sentence, and ran to embrace us. The customs guard stopped her and made her go back to complete the routine. She was in the company of the man when she exited from the customs hall. She dropped her bags and put her arms out to take Sheba, at the same time calling out to her companion.

"Goodbye, Dr. Menninger. Give me a ring sometime. We'll continue our discussion."

The man looked harassed. He waved momentarily and then quickly resumed his passage. Its speed suggested it was flight.

"Poor man. He's so orthodox. All that Freudian nonsense. He thinks *it* is the path to true enlightenment. He's so wrong."

"*The* Dr. Menninger?"

She kissed me on the cheek. She took note of my new mustache, but she made no comment on it.

"One of them, I forget which. He was on my flight. We argued all the way home. Shall we go?"

It was obvious that Sheba, after a short interval of wondering who this stranger was, recognized someone from her past and began the process of making the delinquent a slave once more. But sitting on her mother's lap, she soon fell asleep. Lee immediately began the process of true enlightenment on me.

Through dinner she carried on nonstop. Now that we had arrived at the age of maturity and were free of economic and social pressures, we could concentrate on "integration."

"Integration?"

"Of the persona and the ego. It's something like the Buddhist concept of *mandala*." She paused to take a breath and then started up again.

"Jungian analysis is very good for people experiencing midlife crises, my dear," she continued. She reached across to me and squeezed my hand. "I have been much worried about you these last years."

I summoned a smile, a somewhat weak one.

"The first thing is to locate your mythic *Dasein!*"

"Mythic *Dasein?*"

"*Dasein* is the German word for 'being,' but 'presence' is better. *Sein* means 'to be.' *Da* means 'there.' The idea is that all of us carry an unconscious feeling toward the Feminine—*Die Weibliche*. It's part of the collective unconscious—*Die gemeine Bewusstlosigkeit*." It is differentiated into archetypes which we Jungians give names derived from mythology. Mine is Erda, the Earth Mother."

She took a sip of wine.

"We must discover yours."

Lee never did get around to asking what I'd been up to. And for that I was grateful. That night she gave no sign that she wanted to resume conjugal relations. She was cheerful, good-humored, and busy. Next day, she resumed running the household and the lives of everyone associated with it. She shopped around for a therapist with whom to start her training. She joined a therapy group of fellow Jungians.

Roxie turned up the day after her return. She said she had dropped in a couple of times during Lee's absence and apologized, in her flustered way, for not being able to come more often. Lee promised to help her discover her mythic Dasein. Roxie threw me a look of patient suffering—but it was nothing personal. Just joint martyrdom. It was, I told myself, time to restore the photo album to the attic.

Several weeks later, I was out all afternoon on an errand. I had thrown myself into my career as the heir to Sargent, and it was paying off. I came home to find Lee waiting for me in the living room. She was decked out in a gold lamé gown, the kind of feathers she had scorned for years. It was too tight for her, but she had struggled into it. She had had her hair done. She was waiting for me impatiently.

I went over and with all deliberation poured myself a drink.

"Are you going out?"

"Not me, Jack. Us. We're due at the Champignon. You don't have a lot of time. I've laid your dinner jacket out."

I hadn't been to Le Champignon for well over a year now, not since the break. Actually, I missed the fare. I tried to look as if I were giving the matter serious consideration. "What's the occasion?"

"We are dining with Monty and Roxie."

I stopped my glass at my lips. I drew myself up to my full height. I tried to assume a posture of outrage at the very thought. Lee sat there impassively. Her expression, as well as her dress, told me she was prepared to outmaneuver my every thrust and parry.

"I know what a prick he is, you should pardon the expression. I know how he used you." She paused. "But Roxie is pregnant. And *she* wants the reconciliation. *We* can't deny her that! So get ready to tough it out!"

I said nothing. I concentrated on her choice of the conjugal *we*.

"So get a move on. Do it for her!"

Hadn't I already done enough for Roxie?

I indicated my assent silently. I started for my bedroom, feeling like I was the main character in one of those second-rate stage vehicles for has-been actors, full of double entendres, ad-libs to the audience accompanied by broad winks, the kind to which my father had not felt it fit to take my mother.

"And for God's sake, don't let him outfumble you for the check."

134

She obviously wouldn't take no for an answer. Considering how long it usually takes to get a table at Le Champignon, I wondered how long this had been in the works.

I dressed myself in a brocaded tuxedo Monty had had his tailor run up for me when I'd started at the foundation. In my misery, I recalled how much the wretched thing had cost me. And I couldn't remember ever having had a good time in it. I felt like I was going to a wake with gourmet refreshments. I rehearsed in my mind a toast to Roxie that would not betray me. Or her.

Monty and Roxie were waiting for us when we arrived. Roxie was in silk harem pants and a long caftan-like jacket of deepest blue. There was just the barest suggestion of pregnancy. I couldn't help but note that she didn't bulge in the same places that Lee had. But all that did was remind me that she was no longer mine. At this point I couldn't even look at Monty. Lee made a great show of delight at the news. Le Champignon is a small place and Lee's voice carried. Before the maître d' had a chance to welcome us, he and all his guests were privy to Roxie's pregnancy. I expected all present to rise and applaud.

Roxie disengaged and came up to me and went through the ceremony of offering her cheek for the buss of her brother-in-law. "I am so, so happy," she said to the public, blushing prettily, sweetly flustered by the attention she was receiving. "You'll act normal, won't you?" she whispered in my ear. Over my shoulder, I watched Monty enfold his sister in his arms. Now it was time for me and Monty to play to the audience. Thankfully, Monty took the initiative.

He threw his arms around me and said, "Hello, old buddy. *Great* seeing you. Isn't it marvelous?"

Monty is a master of public acts. What could I do with all those people watching—stiff-arm my brother-in-law?

"I am *so* happy for you and Roxie!" I said, trying to project my voice. I looked around the room. We all seemed to be acting as if we were on the balcony at Buckingham Palace.

Only the maître d' stayed in character. He simply greeted us as old friends and said slyly he'd been so pleased he'd been able to find room for us on such short notice—and for such a happy occasion.

It was, being a public occasion, Monty's party. Almost immediately he started buttering me up. It was as if the waters had never been turbid with anger, nor had there ever been lapses in family loyalty, nor any embarrassments with the Internal Revenue Service—all costly at the polls. All was forgiven. It was so much water under the bridge, not worth mentioning.

"Jack, I've been talking to Dick about you. I've had a couple of meetings with him."

Dick? Of course, that Dick, the one in the White House! I couldn't resist the temptation. "Which *Dick* is that, Monty?"

Monty ignored the jibe. He was soaring. He wouldn't have allowed it to go unanswered in the old days.

"He wants his portrait painted. I said I knew just the man. I didn't mention that he was my brother-in-law—naturally. What do you say to that? Of course, you would have to go down to Washington, but it'd be a big commission."

The nation was not yet reeling under the Watergate revelations.

"That's very nice of you, Monty. But are you sure the President of the United States would want his portrait painted by a pornographer? Besides, I can't at the moment. I am doing a large family portrait, which also involves travel. To Hyannisport."

It was a lie, which made it all the more gratifying. As a matter of fact, I had more commissions than I could handle and at prices I considered extortionate. Monty shrugged it off. He was too jubilant to suffer the slings and arrows of outraged brothers-in-law.

But both Lee and Roxie blanched. Lee shot me a penetrating look. Usually I could be counted on to rise to the occasion and behave. Okay, I'd behave. But I hated the whole idea.

To create a diversion, Lee reached down into her purse and produced a small package, beautifully wrapped, and presented it to Roxie.

"A small gift," she announced. "Open it."

"What's this?" Roxie asked, fingering a dried stem that was part of the wrapping.

"Don't you know? Guess!"

"It's mandrake root!" Roxie said, laughing. "You are a little late." She unwrapped the package. It contained a used wooden baby rattle.

136

"It's Sheba's," she said. "You gave it to me. Now I am giving it to you."
Roxie leaned over and kissed Lee. Joy was unalloyed.

"Mandrake root, doesn't that have something to do with fertility?" Monty asked.

Roxie nodded.

"That quack of a doctor kept saying my sperm count was too low," he began. "Little he knows. Superstitious bastard. I'd have been better off drinking mandrake milkshakes and eating mandrake salads."

The reference to mandrake root had gotten Monty started. He didn't seem to know that it was folk medicine for the *female*. Until dessert we were treated to an analysis of the shortfall in his sperm count. He discussed it as if he had found an accounting error in a report of quarterly earnings.

When the check arrived, Monty picked it up without fumbling. I felt like applauding. There was silence all around the table. Roxie was waving to someone at a nearby table. Lee discreetly looked away. Following the leader, I dropped my napkin and had difficulty retrieving it from the floor. I stayed down there until I saw the waiter disappear with the check.

There was one point of the dinner during which I displayed a degree of generosity that caught Monty, and everyone, by surprise. It seemed to seal our reconciliation.

After the presentation of the rattle, I reverted to the subject of portrait painting. I looked at Monty, my face alight with an idea that apparently had just occurred to me.

"I can't really fit in your friend in Washington, Monty. But I have an offer for you. I'll waive my usual fees, which you would find exorbitant anyway, I dare say!"

The old street-smarts were showing when he returned my look.

"What's up, old buddy?"

"Why don't I do a portrait of Roxie? You know, I have never painted her. I could even do a mother and child, if you'd prefer."

Out of the corner of my eye, I saw Roxie blanch. I saw the face of Monty, who was in the center of my field of vision, light up with pleasure. A free portrait of his wife and child. I expected a counterproposal: Why not all three of us, old buddy?

Roxie's protests that she couldn't sit still, especially now that she was pregnant, were overridden by the enthusiasm for the idea shown by the rest of her family.

I thought we had carried it off. Roxie had played her part. She had reverted to her persona as wife to an important public figure, retiring by nature, flustered by any public attention, putting up with it for her husband's sake. And I, in turn, was merely her amiable clown of a brother-in-law.

But as we entered our own home, I was experiencing some anxiety. It was occasioned by Lee's silence in the cab ride home. Somehow, inexplicably Lee might have taken the measure of the situation. I'd never made the mistake of underestimating her. Sometimes she even seemed to have mystical powers.

When we got home, she made straight for bed, while I went in to see how Sheba was.

She was curled up with a large teddy bear, sleeping soundly, breathing regularly. I put my hand to her forehead. She had had a slight fever when we'd left. I had given her a couple of baby aspirin. Now she did not feel feverish. I pulled the blanket up over her shoulders. Her eyes opened slightly, mere slits. She gave me a quick smile and immediately resumed her untroubled slumber. I stood there for a moment as she kicked the blanket off.

I went around turning lights off and went into my own room. I had started to undress before I realized that I was not alone. Lee was in my bed. She hadn't been there since before the birth of Sheba.

It only increased my anxieties. I went about my preparations for bed, deliberately, in silence. I came out of the bathroom with the feigned air that nothing unusual was about to take place.

It was not something I wanted, but I knew I would go through with it as if I had been waiting all along for her to take the initiative.

And after it was over, we lay there in the dark, she on her side of the bed, I on mine. Neither of us seemed to know how to break the silence after this familiar, perfectly satisfactory conjugal act. It was, I suspected, Lee's way of letting me know that she forgave me my transgression. It was my way of reassuring her that I had no intention of deserting her and Sheba, at least not in the immediate future. But I was afraid that she would want to talk about it. And my feelings were too raw and confused for me to want that.

Then I heard her crying softly.

I sighed. We are going to talk about it after all.

But no, she was not crying, she was laughing. Not robustly exactly, as was Lee's usual way with laughter. But neither was it bitter.

"What's so funny?" I asked defensively.

"Oh, nothing!" she said. "I was just wondering how I was going to explain this to my therapy group." One night a week she met with her group. I pretended not to see the point of the jest.

"I was just wondering how to characterize you. Archetypically speaking," she said.

I had by now picked up enough to know that, according to Jung, each of our lives is to be understood in mythic terms. "We Jungians do not subscribe to the Freudian superstitition of determinism," my wife was fond of saying. Lee had suddenly become interested in mythology. Her room was full of books about the Greeks, the Norse, the Mayans, Buddhism.

I switched on the light. I did not feel that it was the kind of discussion I wanted to have in the dark.

"I finally know who you are." Now she was laughing uproariously.

"Just don't tell me I'm a prince, for God's sake."

She kept laughing, but it was not at what I had just said.

"You are not going to tell me? Who am I? Apollo? Rama? Loki? Surely I am not Buddha! I am certainly not Buddha."

"Wrong religion. Don't you know? We even have the right names."

"I still don't follow you."

"You are being so dense, *Jack*. Don't you know anything about your own religion? You don't know about *Jacob* and *Leah* and *Rachel?*"

She could not restrain herself. I was afraid her laughter would wake Sheba.

"What's so funny is Monty as Laban. But it fits. He's such a gonif. And Roxie?" She went off into more gales of laughter. "You saw her before you met me. At the well, you might say!"

She started to laugh again. I wanted to interrupt to tell her that she was wrong. I'd actually seen her first. I'd helped her find her glasses and stop her nosebleed. I didn't want to remind her of that. Besides, she would not enjoy having a good myth ruined.

"No, it was on the telly!"

When she stopped laughing, she said, "I even have the weak eyesight Leah has in the story. But I don't belong. I'm not the Leah-type. I can't play the scorned wife."

"Oh? And who are you? Archetypically speaking!"

She gave me a mock quizzical look. She rolled her eyes and gave me an affectionate pat.

"I am from another culture. I am Earth Mother. I figured that out long ago."

"I don't think a misalliance with Manny Shine and an indiscretion with the Reb qualify you for that," I answered.

She yawned. "Why don't you shave off that silly mustache? It doesn't suit you."

I wanted to say that Roxie liked it, but I thought I'd better not.

"Turn out the light and let's go to sleep," she said. I dismissed the whole discussion from my thought. I put it down to Lee's current enthusiasm for mythology. Actually, there was something more important I wanted to think about. You see, at dinner I had had this sudden idea about how to make Roxie a very rich woman in her own right.

THE BIRTH OF L. MONTCALME CARTER V A FEW MONTHS later created only a minor flurry on the New York political scene. Monty had announced a little while earlier his availabiity for the U.S. Senate seat to be contested two years hence. When the baby was born, the event was hailed as a sign that a seasoned campaigner was still vital enough to fight the good fight. *People* ran a picture of Monty, with the by now familiar Carter grin, holding the baby up for everyone to see. The slug carried a quotation from the new father, something to the effect that the country needed younger and more vigorous men.

I had to wait, it seemed forever, for the execution of the commission to paint Roxie. It was now to be mother and child. It was evident Monty was enthusiastic and Roxie resistant. But Monty's will finally prevailed. "Nothing fancy, mind you, Jack. You are not Van Dyck. I'll settle for Sargent," Monty baited me on the phone.

Fatherhood had seemed to mellow Monty Carter. He was even tolerant of his sister's attempts to search out an appropriate archetype for him. When Lee had started teasing her brother about his mythic persona, I experienced a pang of anxiety. But she had avoided mentioning Laban—not that Monty—or Roxie for that matter—would have paid much attention.

"I think it's very decent of you to waive your fee, old buddy. But then, we're family."

"*We* sure are, old buddy," I responded with a throb in my voice.

I wanted to lure Roxie back to my studio. In the months since she had succeeded in conceiving and producing the Carter heir, I had myself been giving birth to something that even then I recognized as a turning point in my life. I was, of course, now a very busy painter of portraits, but I do not flatter myself that my success was anything more than good product for the dollar. In those moments when I looked inward and reconsidered my goals in life, I now began to see my way dimly toward that great exhibition to which I have previously alluded. I could now see a major celebration of the work of Jean-Jacques Caillou. It would be the signal event in the restoration of his reputation. And what more fitting place than the Carter! It was the home of Caillou's portrait of Auguste Renoir, on permanent loan from Mr. and Mrs. Jack Birnbaum. And if I succeeded in my new project, the Carter Museum would become the home of several more Caillous, thanks to the generosity of L. Montecalme Carter and the Carter Foundation. And there would be an added benefit—one of those sizeable numbered accounts in a Swiss bank in my own name. The whole idea was so delicious.

It was at the dinner when we celebrated Roxie's pregnancy that the idea first occurred to me. The scenario had been a little different then. Roxie would be lured to my studio, accidently discovering my secret work. She would be overwhelmed by its beauty. (Make no mistake, she is not a phony, like her husband. Roxie has real understanding of art.) A little later I would suggest to her that we could sell them, and on the proceeds we and our baby could live very comfortably in Europe.

Now Roxie was playing a slightly different role in my fantasy. I had come to accept that she and little Monty would not be running off to Europe with me. Perhaps my ardor had even cooled a shade. No matter! She was going to become the angel of Caillou collecting, prodding her husband and the museum into acquiring each new Caillou as it came on the market. I never intended to make her the target of my mischief. I thought of her, like myself, as a victim, a sacrifice to the Carter household gods. Besides, if I were to succeed, I would need her as confederate. And with Roxie I counted on material reward as a greater incentive than love (an idle lure) or revenge (she probably did not feel as ill used as I did). So she would also be offered a numbered Swiss bank account.

I had come to appreciate the wisdom of her own maxim: if you must cheat, safer to keep it in the family.

Roxie appeared in my studio at the hour we had arranged. She was dressed in a skirt of deep blue velveteen with a matching cape. She had let her raven hair grow long. She said she was trying to look younger. She attracted less attention when she took the baby out in his carriage, she said. I expected her to bring the baby, but she had come alone. So much the better.

She looked ravishing, and I told her so. She gave me back a simple thank you. It was tinged with caution. It was the first time we'd been alone together in the studio. And it was proving difficult.

"I don't see why you want to do this, Jack. I hate the idea, " she said as I directed her to a Regency chair and put one of Sheba's dolls in her lap. I ignored her complaint. I explained that all I would do today was make some outline sketches in charcoal of the pose I wanted to capture.

She nodded her head petulantly. I started to work. Then my charcoal piece broke. I cursed. She looked at me startled. I explained that I was out of charcoal. I would have to run out and buy some from a nearby art supply store. She drew her breath in an expression of vexation. I said I'd be back in a trice.

You see I had carelessly left open the cabinets in which were stored the Caillou canvases, always kept under lock and key. I had removed every other distraction from my studio. Roxie, who was a fidgeter anyway, would have no choice but a little innocuous snooping. Put yourself in her situation. I figured it was a reasonable invitation to accidental discovery.

But when I returned, she was still sitting in the chair. She was nearing the boiling point. She had not accepted my invitation to prowl.

It took another visit. She brought the baby. He was wide awake. Little Monty was a colicky baby. I could hear him crying from upstairs. That would please Roxie. I would cancel the sitting, perhaps the whole project.

This time I had one of my Caillous out on the easel—the snow scene, "Louveciennes, Road to Versailles" (1868). The entry in the catalog, number 3, reads:

> Caillou, "Louveciennes, Road to Versailles" (1868). There are several studies of the same subject from this year—by both Monet and Pissarro. Pissarro was living there in 1868. Impressionist painting of this period is full of studies of the same scene by different members of the group. That is because they liked to paint together, each working on the same subject, making suggestions to one another, even occasionally retouching one another's works. The above study is seen in Caillou's "Portrait of M. Auguste Renoir" in the Carter Museum in New York City. It was once assumed that the picture on the wall in the latter was one of Monet's snow scenes, now lost. The discovery of this painting, also in the Carter Museum, makes it clear that Caillou was among the company in 1868.

I had recently been working on it. I was dissatisfied with a detail here and a detail there. I was a fusser, like Caillou's fellow at Gleyre's studio, Claude Monet. I had read a recent article about Monet, which had tried to explode the myth that he always did his canvases in one sitting *en plein air*. I had often worried about the difference it might make to my

143

work that I never worked out of doors. But forgery is studio work. It is a more deliberative process—unfortunately.

I knew that Roxie would immediately recognize the canvas as the one on the wall in the Caillou in the Carter. I would be at my easel working on it when she came down the stairs. I would call attention to something mysterious I was working on by quickly, stealthily putting another larger canvas over it.

She entered with the screaming baby at her shoulder. I feigned not to notice. When she had descended the stairs, I suddenly saw her and, in obvious confusion, put down my palette and went over to a pile of canvases and picked one, a long finished portrait of Pinky, to position over the one I had been working on. The baby was still shrieking at the top of his form. But I could see she had taken note of my stealth.

I seated her in the chair. She was jiggling the baby at her shoulder, trying to make him quiet down. I excused myself for a moment. I had to clean some brushes. I would do it in the bathroom.

When I got back, I made a detour around my easel to the chair I would use to draw her. I could see she had moved the portrait of Pinky. The baby was sucking his thumb and showing signs of going to sleep. I pretended to begin to work.

She subjected me to a long searching stare, as if she wanted to ask me something, but at the same time was afraid to hear the answer.

"What's that, Jack?"

"What's what?" I asked, feigning a yawn.

Roxie got up from her chair and walked over to the easel. She took the portrait of Pinky off the easel and deposited it on the floor. The baby stirred. Roxie ignored it. "That!" she said, pointing to the "Louveciennes."

"Oh, that," I said. "It's a copy of a Monet. One in the Metropolitan."

I yawned again. There was no such painting in the Metropolitan. I knew Roxie knew there was no such painting there.

"No, it's not," she said. She paused. "There's no such painting in the Met."

I was silent.

"And it doesn't have Monet's signature. It is signed J-J-C."

"So?"

144

"So, it's one of the paintings on the wall in the Caillou painting. The painting at the Carter. *Your* painting."

"So?"

"How did you come by it?"

"I bought it."

"No, you didn't. It's still wet." She put her fingers on the canvas.

"Don't touch that! You'll damage it," I yelled at her.

"Sorry. Just tell me the truth." She paused. "You painted it."

I didn't speak.

"You are a bad liar, Jack. You forged it."

"I suppose you *could* call it that. I'd prefer not to. Let's just say I painted it."

"It's marvelous. Are there others?"

I didn't answer. Little Monty had begun to cry again. Roxie rocked him at her shoulder, and when that didn't quiet him down, she simply ignored him.

"May I see them? Won't you bring them out?"

"They are not very interesting. Please stop it."

"I'd like to see them." It was a command.

"Please, I'd like to see them," she repeated, softening the command to a request.

"No," I said. "I don't think I want to show them to you."

"Why not? Are you ashamed of them?"

I reddened. "No. It's just that they are not ready to be seen. They're a—a hobby. Yes, a hobby. They're personal."

"A secret?" she teased.

"Okay, they're a secret. Even Lee doesn't know about them. You are the only one besides myself who knows they exist."

"Since when do we have secrets from each other? I am your friend, your lover. I am the mother of your child," she said, having to raise her voice to be heard above the bawling Monty.

I sighed. "Roxie, I don't pry into your secret fantasies. . . ."

She laughed, "Where do you think you've been in the last year, my darling?"

In the end, I, of course, gave in. As I began trotting them out, I remembered other private showings of my work—to my friend Henry

Berger and later to Hack. I felt just as vulnerable now as I had then. I brought them out, one by one, beginning with the "Woman Contemplating a Vase of Flowers." Next I brought out the "Odalisque," the one on the easel. That finished the sequence of paintings referred to in the portrait of Renoir. I followed them by "The Boat House at La Grenouillère," then "The Bathers" and all of the others. I put them on the easel, one by one. During the hour or so it took, Monty howled constantly. But his mother was otherwise occupied.

"They are stunning. Beyond words. You really did all these?"

I nodded.

About half way through, I knew how deeply she was affected. As I took one off the easel and replaced it with another, she could not hide the excitement at the prospect of yet another one.

"They must have taken you years."

I was pleased. I thought that Roxie was actually looking at them as if she were viewing them in a museum.

"You are a genius."

I shrugged that off.

"No, they belong in a museum."

"Well, maybe a loan exhibition," I conceded with modesty.

"The nude, the one on the easel in the painting in the Carter, is that me?" she asked.

I blushed. "I was inspired," I said.

The strategy I had decided on was to initiate Roxie in stages. First show her the goods, then broach the idea of making the Carter Museum their permanent showplace and center of Caillou scholarship.

It was only a few days later that Roxie called and said she was coming to see me. She didn't mention the portrait I was doing. And I noted when she arrived that she had left little Monty at home. I pretended to make preparations to work on her picture.

"Stop that! You can turn the portrait out in your sleep. That's not why I am here."

"Oh? *Why* are you here?"

"I want to make you a proposal."

146

I waited. She was looking at me rather slyly. I had never seen Roxie look that way.

"Have you tried selling any of them?"

I was surprised. Perhaps it showed on my face.

"No," I said, solemnly. "How could I?"

"Why not? Don't you intend to?"

It was now clear to me that I would not have to recruit Roxie. So on the spur of the moment, I decided to let her recruit me!

"Oh, I've had an occasional fantasy. Nothing more, mind you. But it's tricky. Not to say, criminal."

"So, why did you paint them?"

"I am not sure I can explain that to you."

"But you'd like to see them exhibited?"

"I suppose so."

"And you'd have to offer them for sale then, wouldn't you?"

"I haven't thought that far ahead. Why are you *so* interested?"

She smiled. Again that sly smile! It was so out of keeping with the face she presented to the world, the face I had once adored. And perhaps still did.

"I have an idea," she continued. The words were tumbling over each other. "Well, the germ of an idea. Is there anyone who might have a special interest in Caillou paintings?"

I smiled inwardly. She even had the same inspiration I had had. Outwardly I appeared to gave it the most serious thought.

"I don't know," I said. "The Carter, I suppose. If any."

"Precisely!"

"So what?"

"Don't be dense!" she said, impatient with me. "It would be perfect!"

I could not believe my ears. Roxie was suggesting to me that we fleece the Carter? And her husband?

I continued to play dumb. "What would be perfect, Roxie? I don't understand."

She sighed at my obtuseness. "The idea is that we sell your Caillous —at least some of them. There are probably too many to unload them all—to the Carter Museum."

I tried my best to look shocked.

"Why not?" she asked.

I played devil's advocate. "First, it would be a crime. I am not the criminal type. Neither are you. Even if we were, we don't have the marketing skills. We couldn't bring it off."

"Jesus, Jack, don't be such a jerk. We are already halfway there. We have the paintings that everybody will take as Caillou's work. We can get the marketing skill."

She had an answer for everything.

"Besides, selling them to the Carter guarantees we don't go to jail. Monty wouldn't press charges—even if he ever learned they were forgeries."

"Why not?"

"He'd be too embarrassed. If it ever came out that his own wife had fleeced him—"

I couldn't help laughing. Roxie was enjoying the idea so much and my laughter encouraged her to go on.

"Besides, it would vastly improve the museum's image to be the home of the Caillous. Imagine—the Caillou Room or even the Caillou Wing.

"Don't get carried away."

"You are intrigued, don't deny it. I don't think it would be hard to get Prince Hal interested. All we have to do is get word to Prince Hal that a Caillou has come to light—we'll have to work out the details there—and Monty will be greedy to snap it up. Count on it. You don't know how eager he is to make the Carter Museum of Representational Art respectable. Positively greedy!"

"But Roxie, that is *our* museum. It's the *family* museum." My voice was laden with sarcasm. "Lee's and yours and mine as well as Monty's. It's robbing Peter to pay Peter."

"Oh, for God's sake! Don't go getting sanctimonious on me." She had entirely missed my sarcasm. "I've been married to one of the nation's richest men for twenty years. And if he left me, I wouldn't have the proverbial pot to—you know what! I am not getting any younger. I don't know what'd happen if some little bimbo came along. And don't think there haven't been a few already! I want some *insurance*. For me *and* for my son. Who is, incidentally, also your son."

148

She was vehement. She was unflustered. She was suddenly—I searched for the word—determined. No, that was too weak. She was *formidable*. Said with the French inflection. I had never before thought of Roxie as *formidable*.

"What do you think Monty'd do if he found out about you and me?" she asked harshly.

"Does he suspect?"

"No. But Jack, you have to do this. You just have to. For the sake of your son."

I looked at her in astonishment. Would she stop at nothing? This was a new woman. Suddenly she realized that perhaps she was fishing in troubled waters. She flashed a winning smile at me. She was trying not to look so *formidable*. Then she winked at me and I laughed. Winking was Monty's thing. I hated being winked at. When Monty did it, I always knew I was about to be used. Okay, this wink was the wink of a co-conspirator, but it sent a shiver up and down my spine.

"For God's sake, quit winking at me," I said. "Okay," I conceded, "I'll rob Peter to pay Peter's wife."

"We'll split fifty-fifty," she answered.

THAT NIGHT I HAD A DREAM. IN IT, ROXIE WAS MY WIFE. Monty was also in it. Monty was very wroth with me, and I was defending myself. He claimed that I had been cheating him. At first I thought he had come to know about the baby, but then I realized it was not about that at all. What it was all about was never clear in the dream. But Monty kept poking his finger into my chest and accusing me of being a thief. "You are a thief, Jacob," he said over and over again. "I am falsely accused," I kept replying. "Who is this Jacob, Monty, you think I am?"

Then I awoke. And remembered Lee's crazy talk about my archetype's being Jacob.

In the morning I searched the house for a Bible. There was one in a bookcase in the living room and another one among Lee's books in her bedroom. Both were in Hebrew, so I ended up going to a bookstore and buying one. When I got home with it, I found out it was the American translation done by Goodspeed. I remembered Lee, with her new passion for mythology, scoffing at "demotic" translations. "They always *de*-mythologize," she said. It would have to do.

I found the story of Jacob in Genesis and read it through avidly. According to Lee, it was part of the collective unconscious of my people. She had referred to the story of Jacob and Laban, Rachel and Leah, as if I were already familiar with it. But I wasn't. Now I found the story absolutely engrossing. I noted the part about the stolen blessing and the flight. Every good little Jewish boy is supposed to know that story. Maybe I did know it once, but the collective unconscious must reckon with individual memory lapses. It gave me pause. After all, my father's blessing took the form of dentistry. And I had rejected that. Nor had I stolen the blessing of my brother Morton, which was medicine.

I read how Jacob had first caught sight of Rachel at the well, where she was watering Laban's flock, and had fallen in love with her. Okay, I had first caught glimpse of Roxie on TV, a good enough surrogate. I read how Laban had given Jacob Leah for his wife when he thought he was getting Rachel. "Yah, yah," I thought, again skeptical of Lee's powers. Then I got to the story of the speckled and spotted kind, and I read it over and over again.

> "Let me go," Jacob says to Laban, "that I may depart. . . . Give me my wives and children, for whom I have worked for you. . . . "
> But Laban said to Jacob, "The Lord has blessed me because of you. Name me your wage and I will pay it. . . . "
> "I will go on pasturing and tending your flock," Jacob replied, "if you will do this for me: go through all the flock today, and remove from it every speckled and spotted sheep . . . and any of the goats that is spotted and speckled. . . . At some future time, whenever you may come, my honesty toward you will answer for me in the matter of my hire; if there is any one among the goats that is not speckled and spotted, . . . it came into my possession by theft."
> "Good," said Laban, "let it be as you say."

150

After years of laboring for Laban—seven years for Leah when he wanted Rachel, and then seven more years for Rachel, and then some—Jacob could no longer have been a young man. He certainly should have acquired enough sense to realize that he was dealing with a real crook. All this I understood. And it seemed to make the case for the biblical Jacob being my mythic Dasein—if I had one. But then I was again puzzled by Jacob's breeding methods. Maybe a less demythologized translation would have been better.

It was the business about Jacob's taking fresh boughs of poplar, almond, and plane and peeling them so that white stripes showed. He placed them in the water troughs where the sheep came to drink before reproducing, thus procuring unto himself further lambs that were striped, speckled, and spotted. Maybe that was biblical superstition. After all, those were the days before scientific sheep breeding. But then I read the passage in a different light. It was, I concluded, a very doubtful piece of sheep dipping. Jacob was trying to make the genuine article look striped, speckled, and spotted. Jacob was giving Laban back a little of his own medicine. After all, Laban had hoodwinked him often enough. Now the wink was—so to speak—changing hoods. And the Lord was looking the other way—so to speak.

True, there were certain places where the biblical archetype just didn't fit. Leah's children were all of Jacob's seed. A mere detail. My own seed had made Laban's child. There was nothing parallel in the story to a nephew's being the son of his own uncle. For a moment that gave me pause. Now I was thinking about contributing to Laban's goods, not taking from them. Another mere detail. After all, I was reading the American version. Maybe something had been lost in translation.

Roxie came back to the studio a couple of days later. I got all the Caillous out of the cupboard. I got a tape measure. I called out to her the measurements of each canvas and its title. She recorded them in a notebook. In the course of doing all this, I suggested that since our last meeting I had concocted a plan.

I started outlining it. "We won't start with any of the paintings in theportrait. They'll come later—after we have planted the idea that there are lost Caillous to be found."

"Why?"

"First, because they will command a bigger price if it's already known there are Caillous about. We start small. A private sale. Maybe something fishy about the provenance—a rumored theft or contested ownership, something like that. The Carter has to acquire it by private sale. Maybe a little bit suspiciously. Do you follow?"

She nodded.

"We, of course, arrange for Prince Hal to get a sniff of the contraband. Later, he can boast how he got it on the cheap."

"How does Prince Hal discover—?" she started to ask.

I interrupted her. "I was coming to that. Do you remember the name of that dealer in Zurich who tried to sell Prince Hal the stolen Gainsborough? You remember, the one that Monty wanted him to buy?" I asked.

"Ellenbogen. He's a crook," she replied. "Why go to him?"

"For just that reason. Because he is a *known* crook. Has he ever been caught selling a forgery?"

"How should I know?"

"Find out if you can," I told her. "Our first Caillou was stolen."

"Oh?"

"During the war. By the Nazis. From a family in Lyons. It's on the Interpol list of paintings that have never been recovered."

She laughed. "How can that be? You bought the portrait at a junk sale, and you painted all the others."

"So I did, my dear, but hear me out. I have been doing some research. There is a painting on the Interpol list that fits. 'The Bathers,' 60½ x 54 cms., said to have been painted by A. Renoir, 1869, purchased by Georges Pourbus from Durand-Ruel Gallery, Paris, 1891. Missing from the Pourbus house in Lyons since the liberation of Lyons in 1944. There's a recorded bill of sale, but no known photograph. No record of its having been exhibited anywhere. The Caillou bathers is smaller, but that's dandy. The canvas could have been reduced, couldn't it?"

"But that's a Renoir; it's not a Caillou!" she said.

152

"All the better."

"I don't follow you."

I was feeling very confident. "Don't be dense." Maybe bordering on the insufferable. "We offer it to Ellenbogen as a Renoir. I can paint over the signature. Overpaint it with Renoir's signature. There's that figure in it that looks like the one in Renoir's 'Boating Party.' When the painting is examined by the experts, under the X ray or whatever, they'll see the Caillou signature underneath."

She was beginning to understand. "That's brilliant. A previously unknown Caillou."

"Which nobody will suspect is a fake."

"Because it is being offered as a fake Renoir. Beautiful."

She was looking at me as if she had never seen me before, as if I had just unlocked the mysteries of existence to her. I basked in that admiring look. Then the suspicion dawned on her lovely face.

"You've been planning this all along. You wanted me to discover them. And you just pretended to let me persuade you. Jack Birnbaum, you conned me!"

Then she laughed. I smiled.

"You look so superior," she said. "You're silly."

I got back to business.

"We get less for it. It's like the supermarket. They offer you coffee at half price to get you to come in. What's that called?"

"The loss leader!" she said.

It was Roxie who came up with the idea of how to approach Ellenbogen. What she worked out was based upon my premise of a Renoir stolen in the waning days of the Second World War from Lyons. Most probably, by someone in the retreating German Army. She spent weeks watching old Marlene Dietrich movies, playing old Dietrich records, and then trying to change her voice—to speak in a throaty singsong, to speak an English that betrayed a hidden German origin.

Months went into the planning. Then Roxie telephoned Ellenbogen, announcing herself as Elsa Schmidt from Toronto. She said she had a Renoir for sale. She planned to be in Zurich in the near future. Ellenbogen agreed to see her.

So, the both of us went to Switzerland. She supposedly was visiting a sick aunt in California. I let it be known that I'd had an inquiry from the Holy See. Lee was too busy with her analysis to be troubled with the comings and goings of her husband. Monty nodded at the news. She had done it before.

Our first stop was Geneva, where Roxie opened a bank account in the name of Elsa Schmidt. The next day was the day planned for her visit to Ellenbogen's in Zurich.

It was a little gallery at a very good address. It was the kind of place where in the window would be a seventeenth-century Dutch still life ("Unknown Master" from Utrecht), a deer or rabbit pelt hung up to dry, some such thing, or a painting of the Rialto Bridge in Venice, one that might have been taken for a Guardi.

Ellenbogen would have smiled affably if someone had inquired, "How much is that Guardi in the window?," complimented the questioner on his connoisseurship, and suggested politely it was probably beyond his price range. Later, if the questioner raised doubts about its authenticity, he would have corrected himself, "Sorry, did I say Guardi? I mean 'after Guardi.'"

The "old master" in the window changed every so often. Inside, there was usually not much to be seen on the walls. One might wonder how the gallery could afford the rent with so much obvious kitsch. The answer was that the good stuff could not be shown.

It was in the vaults of a local bank. Most of Ellenbogen's clients didn't just walk in off the streets, and he didn't advertise in *Burlington*. If one was in the market for his kind of wares, one already knew that he had what one wanted. If one was selling and he was interested, he didn't ask too many questions.

On the day of her visit, we breakfasted at the hotel in Geneva, and then I took Roxie to the train. She had a small traveling case with her, as well as a flat paper parcel. She would be back that night. At the station I watched as Roxie disappeared into the ladies room. A few moments later, a woman emerged in a mink stole, a stark black dress. She was wearing a pillbox hat with a veil. She was carrying the traveling case and a flat paper parcel. She looked like something out of a 1940 Hollywood movie, black and white. I followed her at a discreet distance as she checked the traveling case. I conjectured she was in deep mourning. As she passed me on her way to the train, I thought I saw this woman of mystery wink at me from behind her veil.

I returned to the hotel on the shores of Lake Geneva. I was therefore not present at her interview with Herr Ellenbogen. What follows is a reconstruction from what she told me when she returned that night.

Roxie arrived, toting the wrapped "Renoir." She announced herself as Elsa Schmidt and said that she had an appointment with Herr Ellenbogen. The elegant male clerk announced himself as the party in question and said in perfect English how delighted he was to make her acquaintance. You are not Swiss, Herr Ellenbogen. No, dear lady, I am not. You speak wonderful English, Herr Ellenbogen. These days one must, dear lady, he sighed. "Just to survive," he sighed again. He rubbed his hands, signaling eager anticipation.

The preliminaries over, she hoisted the canvas onto a nearby table and began fidgeting with the knots.

"Not here, dear lady," Ellenbogen said, a bit anxiously. "We will be more *comfortable* in my office." It was a nice bit of business on her part. She was now, in Ellenbogen's eyes, a newcomer to the ways of the art market. He led her to his small office at the back of his shop, furnished in eighteenth-century antiques, produced by a shop on the Via Bardi in Florence. It had a comfortable musty smell that mixed with Herr Ellenbogen's subtle but pervasive cologne water. On the walls were a couple of well-known Dürer etchings. They were real, but if one inquired about the price, he would reply that they were not for sale. He would not say that they actually belonged to a furniture maker in Florence and were on loan from him. The furniture maker was a first cousin. And a partner.

Ellenbogen offered coffee, liqueurs, which Roxie declined. He put the wrapped parcel on the table and with practiced fingers undid the knots. He removed the painting and placed it upon an empty easel. It was a gilded antique easel. For several moments he studied the painting and said nothing. Then he went to his desk and procured a magnifying glass. And he went over the painting with great care. When he got to the signature, he lingered upon it. Finally he put the glass down and fixing Roxie with an amiable, somewhat ambiguous smile, said, "Yes!"

That was clearly intended as an exclamation, not a question. Roxie did not quite know what it meant.

"You agree it's a Renoir?"

"I agree it *could* be a Renoir, dear lady. We will need to make some little researches, run a few tests. Can you leave it with me for a while?"

Roxie showed disappointment on her beautiful face. She was in a hurry. In the art world it is disastrous to show that you are in a hurry. It reveals your amateur status.

"How long?"

"Who knows!" Herr Ellenbogen was again not asking a question.

"Are you interested in buying it?"

He put his hands up in a sweet little gesture, like a puppy inviting one to rub its stomach. He smiled.

"Unfortunately, at the moment, I am overcommitted. But I would consider acting as your agent, if it is genuine. As a matter of fact, I do know a gentlemen who has expressly asked me to look for a Renoir. At the right price. What would you be thinking about asking, Mrs. Schmidt?"

Roxie looked uncomfortable. "I don't know about these things, Herr Ellenbogen. I was thinking about a hundred fifty thousand."

It was an absurdly low price.

"Dollars?"

"Dollars, of course. You see we need to raise cash. But I must stress it is imperative that our name be kept out of it. If there's a danger that it might become known that we are trying to sell, I'd have to withdraw."

Ellenbogen shook his head in sympathetic understanding. He probably was already entertaining doubts about Elsa Schmidt from Toronto.

"I promise complete confidentiality. You will suffer no embarrassment, dear lady. But I am bound to inform you that I may not be able to sell this painting—even if I am satisfied it is a genuine Renoir—at that price."

The year before, Sotheby's had sold at auction a smaller Renoir for one million two. It had been knocked down at such a low price because the canvas was not in the best state and, although its credentials were impeccable, it was an inferior painting. Ellenbogen knew this was a much better one. He also knew why this was a private sale. Forget the tale of financial woe. He could tell a hot picture when he saw one. He was counting on a solid six figures. After all, could the lady sue?

"What will your fee be, Herr Ellenbogen?"

"Fifteen percent of the sale price is usually the standard brokerage fee in a private sale, dear lady."

Roxie nodded. "Well, I guess I have no choice. You see we need to raise capital as quickly as we can."

"I am sorry to hear that, dear lady. Now I am afraid, I must ask you some questions. I shall not pry. But I have to make some researches into this beautiful painting's provenance."

"Provenance, what does that mean?"

Ellenbogen smiled. "Its origin and history. The documentation if there is any. When it was sold, resold, where it has been exhibited."

"I don't know anything about that."

"How did it come into your possession?"

"I inherited it from my father. He died two years ago."

"And his name was?"

"Oh, dear." Roxie pretended not to want to reveal his name.

"Kerwin. Gustav Kerwin," she whispered.

"Do you know how it came into his possession?"

"He *bought* it. Did you think otherwise?"

"Of course not, dear lady. When and from whom?"

"I am afraid I don't know. I think it was during the war. He was stationed in Lyons, France.

"In the Canadian Army?"

"No."

"Ah!" Ellenbogen did not pursue this line of questioning further. A little glint of satisfaction showed in his eyes. At the mention of the French city, he knew exactly which missing Renoir he was dealing with. The Interpol "Stolen and Missing List" was mother's milk to him.

"Do you have a bill of sale?"

"I am afraid not."

"Never mind, I will search for one. It is part of my labors on your behalf. May I ask, dear lady, who sends you to me?"

Roxie had expected this question much earlier. But Ellenbogen was really something of a klutz. Everybody in the business knew he fenced stolen art.

"I got your name from a friend of a friend." She mentioned the name of a curator who had recently bought a hot cylix that had gone missing from Turkey a few years before. There had been rumors then of Herr Ellenbogen's good offices. He smiled and wrung his hands in satisfaction.

Roxie knew he had fallen for the bait. Before she left, she had a receipt from him for the painting and a copy of the provisional contract empowering him to act for her in its sale. He was to make contact via the bank in Geneva.

Roxie returned to Geneva that night. It was late when she got back to the hotel. I was already in bed in my own room when my phone rang. I was summoned to her room. The door was unlocked and she bade me enter. She had loosened her dark hair, which fell around her shoulders. A bottle of champagne was on the table. She was holding the champagne glass up to the light, watching the bubbles rise to the surface, smiling mysteriously to herself.

She flashed me a smile. It was full of triumph. "Get a glass from the bathroom and join me. We are celebrating."

I obliged. I looked at her peignoir hanging on the hook and her mules neatly arranged beneath them. I wondered why she had not wanted two champagne glasses when she ordered the bottle. Then I remembered the shy, correct Roxie of old, who was careful about even the breath of scandal.

I rejoined her and asked if she were not very tired.

"Yes. But I am too excited to sleep."

She started telling me of her visit to Ellenbogen. It was short. It was exciting. It was gleeful. She made it sound like a horse race. She had won by four lengths.

"God, I loved every moment of it," she said.

She got up and moved toward the bathroom. "I am going to take a shower," she announced. I got up to go. "Don't go," she said over her shoulder. It sounded like a command. I sat down again.

158

In the shower I heard her singing to herself. It was an old Marlene Dietrich song, from *The Blue Angel*—"*Ich bin von Kopf bis Fuss auf Liebe eingestellt.*" She was still singing it when she stepped out of the shower. I heard the sound of her powdering herself. And then she stepped out of the bathroom.

She was wearing only her mules. The dark hair falling around her shoulders gleamed with little beads of vapor from the hot bathroom. She had a bemused, odd little smile on her face, as if she had just discovered the principle of buoyancy.

"You know, I was just thinking about my mother." She laughed and walked over to the bed. Kicking the mules halfway across the room, she got into the bed.

"I was thinking. For the first time in my life, I don't give a damn what my mother would say."

She was like some figure in a trance. I was not clear what it was she wanted of me. I searched her features for an explanation.

"Well don't just sit there, lover-boy. All this conspiracy has made me horny—very, very horny!"

N EXT DAY ON THE FLIGHT HOME, I THOUGHT ABOUT the end of our adventure in Switzerland. Was it in fact a new beginning for us? Was it time to take the photograph album out of the attic and put a few new leaves in it? Roxie had been carried away by the excitement of the day. And I—how did I feel? I was drinking a glass of champagne. I watched the bubbles percolate to the top. I felt like a naughty boy having a treat. Nothing more.

For months nothing happened. I lived my workaday life, outwardly collected, inwardly scorched by the fire of impatience. Roxie, surprisingly, had discovered the well of patience. On the rare occasions when we spoke, she kept counseling me to keep cool. But finally even she could not stand it any more.

She called Ellenbogen, pretending to be in Toronto, and, sounding desperate, she inquired if he had made any progress.

He chuckled. He said, "These things take time. Patience, dear lady."

She was not at all reassured by his little words of comfort. Breathing hard, she hoped to communicate, at great distance, her anxiety for results. She wondered to herself—but aloud—whether someone else might not have better luck in finding a buyer. He listened patiently and then said, as if he was announcing news of the Second Coming, "But we have established that it is indeed from the hand of Auguste Renoir. Beyond a shadow of a doubt. If you wish, I can confirm the experts' finding by letter. To your bank in Geneva. Very good, dear lady. Trust me, dear lady, we shall have no trouble selling it."

She had no sooner hung up on Ellenbogen, then she called me at the studio. I was busy finishing a group portrait of the Beaux Arts trio. I had had to have a large Steinway moved to my studio, and it cluttered up the place. I excused myself and went to the phone upstairs. Lee was out—as usual. I listened to Roxie's account of her conversation with Ellenbogen.

"It's obvious what went wrong," I said after she was finished. "The jerk didn't even know enough to look at the underpainting of the signature." Raking light would have immediately revealed that the Renoir signature had been added after the painting was finished.

What do we do now, Roxie asked. Maybe he really has a buyer, she mused.

"What can we do?" she asked again.

It was my turn now to take a page from Ellenbogen's book of common prayer. "Patience, dear lady."

But Roxie had other ideas. She started a rumor campaign. She told people in the art world that she had heard from an unnamed friend about a Renoir in Zurich that was about to be offered in a private sale. To other people she reported that she had heard that the gorgeous Renoir people were talking about in Zurich was really a fake. She made sure the rumor reached a *Rome American* reporter who was reputed to be working, in cooperation with Interpol, on a story about art theft.

160

She did this without consulting me. When she told me, I got angry. I was against that kind of aggressive salesmanship. She also got hot under the collar. The art of forgery, she said, lies in creative marketing. At any one moment there are hundreds of forgeries in the market. In the end I cooled down. I decided that Roxie really knew what she was doing.

She kept her ear to the ground. The first word of success came from Prince Hal. He reported to Monty that he had recently heard of a "gorgeous Renoir" in Zurich. Was Monty interested in his looking into the matter for the Carter?

Then it happened. I saw the news first. It came in the form of an art note in the back pages of the *Paris Herald:*

Zurich, May 2 (1975)—A suit has been filed in the Court of Common Pleas, Cantonment of Zurich, by the French government to recover a painting alleged to be from the hand of the impressionist master Auguste Renoir (1841–1919). The painting is currently in the custody of Zurich art dealer Otto Ellenbogen. The suit alleges that the painting left France without the export documentation required by French law. According to M. Charles Labiche, curator of Impressionist Painting at the Louvre Museum in Paris, the painting, "The Bathers," was taken from the Lyons home of one A. Pourbus, by the Gestapo in July or August of 1944. The French government, in the name of the Pourbus' heirs and the Louvre, asks for its restitution to France.

In August, there was another piece, this time in the *New York Times,* entitled "A Purloined Renoir":

Zurich, August 20—The Court of Common Pleas in Zurich is expected this week to render its verdict on the ownership of a Renoir painting that has become the focus of a campaign by the French government and the international police agency Interpol to stop the traffic in stolen art works.

Every year, important works of art are reported missing or stolen from museums, private collectors, or smuggled from countries in which they are dug up. The traffic in such items has a long history going back to antiquity. Some, like the Greek cylix recently taken from a town in Turkey, later turn up in prestigious museums. That work was reputedly sold to a museum for four million dollars. Others are never seen again but find their way into the possession of private collectors.

The French government, in an effort to enlist the support of European governments in stopping the trafficking in art contraband, is making a test case out of the Renoir canvas. It is believed to be the painting looted from a private home in Lyons in 1944 by the Gestapo. The painting, shown above, is a study of bathers. It bears the signature A. Renoir and the date 1869. Art historians consider it an important find, since it contains a figure, believed to be the art critic Aristide Duran, who also appears in Renoir's well known 1881 canvas, "The Boating Party."

This Renoir canvas only surfaced again this year after being on the Interpol list of missing art for many years. It reappeared when an unknown party brought it for sale to the Zurich art dealer Otto Ellenbogen. Although the painting is now in the custody of Swiss authorities, Ellenbogen has refused to identify the owner.

The case currently being heard in Zurich is being followed closely by governments throughout the world. It is rumored that in case of a judgment favorable to the French government, the government of Greece may institute a claim for the restoration of the Elgin Marbles.

The Court of Common Pleas is expected to render its judgment next week, after the completion of tests and the hearing of closing arguments.

A week later the *New York Times* carred an item on its front page headlined "STOLEN 'RENOIR' NOT A RENOIR."

Zurich, August 28—The Court of Common Pleas of the Cantonment of Zurich today dismissed the suit of the French government for restitution of a canvas alleged to be by Auguste Renoir and stolen from a private home in Lyons in 1944.

It accepted the findings of a team of experts that the painting was not by Renoir but by an obscure painter named Caillou. When the canvas was x-rayed, Caillou's initials were discovered. They had been painted over and Renoir's signature added. In the judgment of the experts, this had probably been done in this century, exactly when they could not say.

But the evidence of the forged signature was sufficient for the finding that the plaintiff had not successfully established that the painting was the one removed from the private home in Lyons in 1944. It therefore ordered the canvas to be restored to the art dealer Otto Ellenbogen.

Two weeks later I was taking Sheba to the doctor. She had a low-grade infection, nothing serious but persistent. I was still working on the group portrait of the Beaux Arts trio. I had promised to have it done three days before. Usually I worked very quickly in the early stages but suffered agonies in finishing a work. It was Lee who had made the appointment with the doctor.

"Do you think you can take Sheba to the doctor this morning?" she asked me at breakfast.

She was up very early that morning. "I am due on the Phil Donahue show. My group is discussing archetypes and their influence on our behavior."

Outwardly I kept my peace. I was reading the *New York Times*. I knew that it would be I who took Sheba to the doctor.

When she asked me to pass the toast and I ignored her, she perceived that I was displeased. "You are not the only one with a career to worry about, you know," she said, flouncing out. That confirmed that I was taking Sheba to the doctor.

At ten o'clock Sheba and I were sitting in Dr. Rathbone's waiting room, amid a covey of mothers and children. We were coloring a picture of a doctor holding a stethoscope to a little girl's chest. It was a book provided by the doctor. On a wall nearby there was an exhibit of like pictures, some signed in childish scrawl. Sheba wanted to give the doctor in her picture a dark skin. That's fine, I said. I didn't think Dr. Rathbone would appreciate that. Dr. Rathbone's views on the matter were not known to me. But they probably would be very soon.

"Is there a *Mr.* Birnbaum here?" a woman called out from the reception desk.

I was the only man in the waiting room. Who else could it be? I raised my hand, feeling a little as if I were in the first grade, asking permission to go poddy.

"There's a phone call for you," she said, peremptorily.

I went to the phone. It was Roxie.

"I tracked you down. The Bank called. There is a message from O.E." She was speaking in code. She was excited. She was bubbling over with the sheer love of intrigue.

"He's had two offers for the merchandise. One from a firm in New York."

That could only be Prince Hal.

"The second is from the outfit in Paris."

"A French buyer?"

"Be careful, for God's sake. It begins with an *L* and has—let's see—six letters. And it ends with an *e*."

I was astonished and forgot myself. "The Louvre wants it?"

"For God's sake, Jack!"

I looked around. My outburst had drawn no attention to me from the mothers and children.

"They are having a bidding war." She laughed. It was a giggle, a little like Sheba's. "I just thought you'd like to know. That's why I tracked you down."

"Caveat emptor," I said before I put the phone back on its hook.

In September there was yet another article, this time in the Arts and Leisure section of the Sunday *New York Times*. It was entitled "Resurrection of an Impressionist Master." It contained a full-page color photograph of "The Bathers" and another somewhat smaller photograph, but also in full color, of the "Portrait of M. A. Renoir." It bore the byline HMB which, so the *Times* explained in a little note at the bottom, were the initials of the doyen of American art critics.

The article began: "Last week, the Louvre Museum, not known for its swashbuckling in matters of acquisition, did an absolutely amazing thing. It paid three-quarters of a million dollars for an art work it had previously labeled a stolen Renoir."

After identifying the real painter and recounting "the comedy of errors" in Zurich, HMB proceeded to give the known details of Caillou's life, describing the only other known Caillou, the one in the Carter Museum of Representational Art—"it is about the only reason to visit that bastion of the banal."

I surmised that the chief source of information was an old article in the *Burlington* by Labiche. Without credit, I noted.

HMB's description of "The Bathers" was glowing: "Painted back before 1870, and unknown until rediscovered this year, what glorious, ebullient feasts of light and color this painting is! More than one viewer has commented on the figure of the bather playing the wood flute. What a bittersweet little drama of frolicsome seduction! Caillou's painting is a celebration of the ordinary life of the late nineteenth century, which could hardly be improved upon."

HMB finished his paean (it could hardly be described as anything less) by calling attention to the now two known paintings of Caillou:

For my part, I think it is time for a major reappraisal of the works of the whole Renoir-Monet circle in the 1860s. It is a well known fact that these painters traded canvases freely. Is it possible some other Caillou master-piece has been misattributed? HMB is reminded of the history of Ver-meer's work. That seventeenth-century master, perhaps the greatest of all the Dutch painters, had to be rediscovered in the last century (by the Frenchman Burger-Thoré) after his canvases were sold and resold as the works of de Hooch, even Rembrandt, and other Dutch masters of the same period.

THE INSTALLATION OF THE RECENTLY REDISCOVERED Caillou in the Louvre was something we had not counted on. As I have said, the plan was to keep it in the family. That it had gone astray we chalked up to our own inexperience. We did not let it deter us. We would do better next time.

We started planning for the debut of the third. Roxie did not feel we could meet in my studio any longer, nor did she think we could talk freely on the telephone. She devised a schedule for meetings on a park bench in Central Park, just off the entrance at Fifty-ninth Street and Columbus Circle. She devised a code for confirming meetings and cancelling them: three rings and hang up, if the *treffe* was on, five if it was a no-show. She was becoming addicted to this life of intrigue.

This time we knew we could reckon on certain advantages. The art world was now positively pullulating with expectations. The paintings were, I suppose, forgeries. That's how they would be reviled if their true origins were discovered. But they were also poetry—the products of profound experience recollected in tranquillity—something like that!

The gross hand of your commercial *faussaire* could not be detected in them.

We could not rush things, of course. A wait of at least a year—two would be better—was called for before another Caillou could make its appearance. It was good that it took time to launch a campaign and let it come to fruition. Roxie always insisted that in order to satisfy a need you had to create it in the first place.

"It is time for the Monet," she announced, one spring day a year later. I was munching popcorn, and she had just finished a Good Humor. We had been watching a troop of girl scouts roller-skate into the park, followed by the den mother, also on roller-skates but less confidently.

"I take it you are alluding to 'The Snow Scene at Louveciennes.'"

She nodded. "We shall write to your friend at the Louvre. What's his name?"

"Labiche. He's not my friend. I haven't been in contact with him since he established the first Caillou."

"No matter. Send him a photograph of the snow scene. It's a favor for a friend. A naive friend who is confident she has bought a Monet. On the cheap. You have doubts. It is from a dealer here that you suspect. You don't have to give his name. You want Labiche's opinion. Has he seen this painting before? You think it might have been exhibited as a Monet in a show back in the 1930s, challenged, and then withdrawn. There was such a show in Paris and with a Louveciennes snow scene. The cartouche said Monet or Pissarro."

I didn't like the scenario. She stopped and noted the disapproval on my face.

"Just wait a moment until I finish. Now, there's also a so-called Monet, also a snow scene of about the same size, that found its way to New York after the war. Lots of people saw it. You can tell that to Labiche. It was sold and resold as 'very possibly a Monet.' Do you follow?"

I saw the strategy immediately. The m.o. was a variation on the one we had already used—only this time, a Caillou would not masquerade as a stolen painting, but as a suspicious painting, a painting already seen but unfortunately misjudged. It had a history of being "very possibly

166

Monet." With the picture in hand, Labiche would, of course, instantly recognize the image from the portrait of Renoir. Was he not the authority on the work of Caillou? He would be called upon to examine the canvas itself. He would search for and find the obscured initials J.J.C.

A "very possibly Monet" equals an "authentic Caillou." Labiche would chuckle to himself, recalling a well-known anecdote about Monet. Monet had late in life reputedly been confronted with a work attributed to him. "Of course, it is forgery," he is reported to have said, cheekily. "Just look at that signature. It is better than I could have done."

I was developing this scenario in my head when she asked a second time, "Do you follow?"

"I think so. I want Labiche to put the quietus on this misrepresentation. And I send him the photograph of the Caillou."

"Good. But you can't give him the lady's name. She is too well known. She would become a laughingstock if it were known she had purchased a forgery. So what do you think?"

I was considering the idea. It made me uneasy.

"I don't like it. There is no 'cut-out,' as there was last time. And the art world is not going to ignore the documentation on this sale. They are going to look carefully to see if it will lead them to other Caillous."

Roxie sighed, impatiently. "But Labiche will recognize that it is a Caillou, right?"

I nodded my assent.

"So, he'll ignore the paper trail that indicates it was sold as a Monet," she continued. "That's the beauty of the idea. Maybe, he'll even buy into the part about its being the questionable Monet in the 1930 show. Even better. It was never identified as an outright forgery; it was merely a misrepresentation."

"I don't like writing to Labiche in my name. Certainly I would recognize the painting if he can. No, it will have to be a third party who gets in touch with Labiche."

"But we are going to have to take risks, Jack. There's no other way. I don't think we can use the stolen-by-the-Gestapo thing again."

"Agreed, *chérie*. Maybe we ought to cut the risk by producing all three of the paintings in the portrait. *Tout d'un coup*."

"No! The price will go up every time a Caillou appears." She answered emphatically. "We aren't giving them away. Stop with the French. It's an affectation."

I had hardly noticed I was doing it.

"I don't want another partner. I'm greedy," she said with an attempt at humor. But I knew she was really serious.

"Not a partner, a dupe, a patsy," I allowed. "And there is another problem. How are we going to sell this time?"

"I thought we'd agreed. Sotheby Parke Bernet auctions it off after it's been authenticated."

"Then there has to be an owner. No Marlene Dietrich lurking in the shadows. Not this time."

She was silent. Then her face suddenly lit up.

"Look, maybe you won't like this, but I think the art world is nutty enough to swallow it. *I* am the one who thinks she got stuck with the phony Monet. God knows, I'd be a laughingstock if anyone found out. What would I tell *Princess Grace?* We change the scenario slightly. *I* am the one who gets suspicious. I read about it in a book on art forgery. Otto Kurz's or somebody. So I go to Prince Hal with the painting. I have the documents that say that this one was in the 1930 Monet show. I produce the book in which it says that at least one of the Monets in that show was a known phony and ask Prince Hal to verify. I suggest he contact Labiche."

"Suppose Hal recognizes it?"

"Don't be silly. He doesn't know anything about paintings. All he knows about is antiques. And so what?"

"It's right under his nose, my Caillou."

"Not to worry. It's all a big blur to him. If he does, all the better. We sell it straight to the Carter."

"So now, Labiche recognizes that he is looking at a Caillou and that the provenance is suspicious." I said, "So, where does this painting come from?"

Roxie started laughing madly. "You just don't see the point, dear one. *No one* knows. They take it as a Caillou just because its provenance is a complete mystery! It's like an old Hollywood movie. A gambler buys a stake horse on a whim. Call the horse Old Glory. Old Glory is a lovable old nag but a loser, but she ends up winning the Kentucky Derby."

"I still don't like it. There will be a lot of publicity. We'll be vulnerable."

"We've got to take the risk, Jack. Sooner or later, we've got to take risks. Sotheby's won't agree to auction it if they don't think the seller is kosher."

"What do we do if Ellenbogen recognizes you as Elsa Schmidt?"

"I don't think he will. I'm not exactly unknown, you know. He's already had plenty of time for that."

"That's not good enough!"

"He won't squeal. He can't afford to. He's a crook."

"But he can still blackmail."

"He can threaten to, but I won't let him. He can't prove it."

"I still don't like it!"

"One thing at a time. I don't think we can afford to let more than one go this time. But maybe in the next sale, we can market several."

"There's one other thing."

"What's that?"

"How are you going to handle Monty? He'll claim it as his own."

"The hell he will. I don't buy that family loyalty crap. If he wants it, he'll have to buy it from me. I'll fight him."

She gave me a wink. I was beginning to feel uncomfortable with Roxie. She seemed suddenly to want the spotlight. I never did like self-advertising. I thought it one of the most vulgar manifestations of free enterprise.

But eventually I came around. I insisted upon certain precautions. We were going to have to have some documentation.

The documentation was to be provided by one Signor Giorgio Barzoletto. For a few weeks that fall, Signor Barzoletto would appear in New York and stay at a hotel on the east side that catered to travelers from Rome.

His business card would carry a Rome address, telephone (if anyone called, an answering machine would report that Signor Barzoletto was abroad and would return the call as soon as he returned), and a telex address.

Signor Barzoletto made the rounds of the art world in New York, Boston, and Philadelphia. With museum curators, he called ahead for an appointment. The same with the more reputable dealers. With the less reputable dealers, he simply sent his card in. In conversation he made vague reference to partners in Sicily. He spoke absolutely abominable English. He reminded one museum curator in Boston of an old Fred Astaire movie—he couldn't remember which one, because so many of them had *opera buffa* Italians in them.

Everywhere he went he carried a large portfolio, with etchings, drawings, and photographs of paintings. His sample case was full of phony Picasso and Matisse drawings, plus photographs of paintings that were "in the company vaults" in Rome. Some were photos of items on the Interpol missing list, others were known items of dubious provenance, including a snow scene identified, *tout court,* as by Monet, Claude.

Signor Barzoletto's second visit was to the gallery whose owner had done the initial appraisal of the Carter holdings. It now advertised itself as holding "American and European Masters." After inspecting Barzoletto's offerings, the owner threatened to call the police.

Barzoletto had better luck at the Carter. He sent his card in to Prince Hal and was invited in.

Prince Hal came from behind his *directoire* desk, his eyes sparkling. Barzoletto took Prince Hal's hand a bit tremulously. Prince Hal held it.

"I say, you remind me of somebody, Signor—"

"Barzoletto at your service, Signor," he said, clicking his heels.

"Give me a moment and I'll remember ... "

"Soma peopula taka mea fora Chico Marxa," Barzoletto said, with a warm smile.

"That's it. Have a seat, Signor Barzoletto."

He showed Prince Hal his wares. The director of the Carter showed no interest whatsoever in the "Monet." When he came to the Picasso drawing, he stopped.

"Oh, I say, isn't that something?"

170

It was one of the Minotaur series. It showed two women making very explicit love to a bull.

"*E vero. Bellissima!*" he said, blowing a kiss with his finger.

"How much are you asking for that?"

"*Alla mia casa a Roma* ita woulda be—" he counted on his fingers, "*Venti mille.* That'sa ina dollari!"

Prince Hal shook his head, "No, I don't think so, Signor Barzoletto. The Carter is in the market for a Picasso. But that's not quite what Mr. Carter had in mind. Something more Rose or Classic period would be to his taste."

Signor Barzoletto threw his hands up in the classic *che fare* gesture and asked if it would do any good to show his wares to the Mister Carter. Prince Hal doubted it but said he could try. He wrote down the address and telephone number for his visitor.

When Barzoletto called at the Carter residence, Mr. Carter had unfortunately been called away suddenly, but Mrs. Carter received him graciously. It was to her he sold the snow scene by Monet, Claude.

She had a rather large canceled check to prove it.

I was, needless to say, Signor Giorgio Barzoletto.

On the day of the auction, the television cameras and lights made the auditorium at Sotheby Parke Bernet look like a movie set. The Caillou snow scene had been on exhibit there for several days. Sotheby's had publicized the auction under the title "Impressionist and Post-Impressionist Masters." The Caillou was clearly the star of an otherwise undistinguished lot. Its only rival was a Maurice Prendergast.

The suggested value in the catalog was four million dollars. Nobody took that figure seriously. To those in the business, that meant that the owner had put a reserve of 3.5 million on it. The auctioneer would knock it down to a ringer in the audience or to a fictitious party if the bidding stalled at less. "Sold to Mr. Slade," or "Mr. Tate's is the winning bid," he would announce with an open smile. Everybody would recognize the harmless deception. It's bad for everybody's business for him to have to say, "No sale."

It had been ballyhooed as the event of the season. The *New York*

171

Times in its feature on the upcoming sale had reported that several museums—the Cleveland, the Norton Simon, the Dallas, as well as the Metropolitan and the Louvre—were anxious to acquire the new Caillou. Nobody from these museums would be there to be identified, of course. They had representatives known to the house. It was rather like Carnival in Venice. So many people were in disguise.

The day before Roxie had been on the six o'clock news on television. The interview with her was cheek-by-jowl with a feature on the recent winner of the New York State Lottery, a pizza cook from Sunnyside. Did I detect a little bias in the editing? Katherine O'Connell, called by her colleagues and fans "Kathy O," was asking Roxie how she felt about "serendipity." Roxie made a little moue and pretended not to know what that meant.

"It's when *you* go shopping at Alexander's," Kathy O explained.

Then Kathy O wanted to know what Roxie was going to do with the money. "Donate it to my favorite charity," Roxie said. Kathy O beamed, not knowing that Roxie was at that moment her own favorite charity.

For an event like this, one needs a ticket. The house, knowing who practically everyone in the audience is, positions the buyers so the auctioneer can see the likely bidders. This is necessary for the bids are made by a prearranged code. No feverish waving of hands here. No numbered placards, as in smaller road shows. One dealer may put his gloved finger discretely to his nose. The finger must be gloved. Ungloved it does not signal a bid. He's not really scratching; he is deceiving the opposition. Another lady favors the auctioneer with a sudden come-hither smile. She isn't trying to seduce him, for she's a well-known womanizer. She's entering her bid.

In the middle of all this, where they could be seen by everybody, sat Roxie and Monty. She was "Queen for a Day." Monty didn't like it one bit. She had refused all his appeals to family loyalty and then subjected him to this show, in which he didn't get top billing.

I made no effort to get a ticket. I was one of the children of paradise, standing amid the crush in the back of the room. Two well-dressed gentlemen stood next to me—minor dealers I surmised. They were busy identifying the players in the seated audience. Sotheby's should issue a playbill, I thought.

"I see Gimpel. I wonder who Wildenstein is representing. You think they might want it for the house?"

"No, too speculative. I hear Cleveland has asked them to act. Who do you think Genevieve is fronting for?" He nodded in the direction of the womanizer.

"The Louvre. I hear Labiche has the hots for this number."

"For Genevieve?"

"Don't be cute. For the Caillou."

One of the men nodded to me, giving me a twinge. Perhaps he recognizes me, I thought. I probably should not have come, but how could I stay away?

An impeccably dressed, handsome, gray-haired man named George P. S. Biddle mounted the lectern. Rumor had it that once, for a lark, he volunteered to stand in for Cary Grant in a movie in which Grant was playing a playboy named Biddle. Biddle acknowledged Roxie's presence with a sly smile. With cheeky charm, he explained to the audience the auction rules. Bids are final. They are to be secured by check, no less than twenty-five percent of the purchase price. It all sounded like a Monopoly game was about to begin. "We will begin with item One-A, eighteenth-century Shiraz carpet. Shall we start the bidding at ten thousand dollars?"

He soon had a bid. He was now asking eleven thousand. The carpet went for eighteen thousand.

"To Madame Gerstein, *antiquaire de Greenwich, Conn,*" he announced in purposely fractured French, giving Gerty Gerstein an unlooked-for plug. Gert is a fixture in the suburbs of the art world. It was a rare success story. She had started professional life as a hooker. Dwelling on the lady's present profession was intended to add a little humor for the initiated. Come to think of it, Gert did look rather like *une ancienne poule.* Or should that be *une poule ancienne?* Appearances are not always deceptive.

The next item was a piece of Persian glass, early nineteenth century. It was time to tune out for a while. It would be hours before they came to the main event. The bidding for the vase had started at two fifty. It had jumped to five hundred with no trouble at all. Biddle was anxious to dispose of this bauble, which, comparatively speaking, was small change. His eye scanned the audience and rose to us children of paradise. He took a bid from a lady in my environs. All eyes turned toward her. She was a comely little thing.

"I have six hundred. Do I hear seven? No? Going once. Ah, I have seven hundred!"

My eyes were still on the comely lass. She gave an audible sigh. It was obviously one of relief, and caught the attention of Biddle.

He smiled at her. "That was fun, wasn't it?" he said with his endearingly mischievous little twinkle. She reddened. The urn went for twelve hundred, again to the unsmiling, businesslike Madame Gerstein.

About an hour later, the Prendergast, a painting of Central Park, came up for sale. It fetched a price in lower six figures. To a dealer known to my neighbors.

"Who is David buying for? Can't be himself. He's not in that league!"

"Some obscure museum in the midwest. In North Carolina, I think."

"That's not in the midwest," the other replied.

It was now time for the Caillou. There was a noticeable murmur in the crowd when it was announced.

"Shall we have the seventh-inning stretch?" Biddle asked, again all cheeky charm.

People got up to stretch. Almost immediately Biddle cleared his throat, the audience hurried to resume their seats. "Shall we start the bidding at one million five? And go up in increments of one hundred thousand?"

He acknowledged a bid immediately. I looked to see who the bidder was. I hadn't the faintest idea.

"The Met's in. The talk on the street is that they are using two agents, in case one gets lost in traffic. What's their limit, have you heard?"

"Five mil. That means they expect to get it below five."

I was so fascinated by the running commentary, I had missed the action. The bidding had already jumped to "three mil."

"Do I hear three point two? A bid of three point two from the Honorab—Oh dear, my apologies Freddy, but there's a bid of three point three over here."

"Who the hell is the Honorable Friggin' Freddy representing?"

His friend whispered something in his ear. "You don't say! You mean

174

we are going to have to go all the way to Saudi Arabia if we want to see that painting?"

By now it's over four mil, and the Honorable Freddie has folded, followed by Cleveland, Dallas, and the Norton Simon. The Met is still in, seeing and raising a young Japanese.

"Who is he?"

"He's simply called the Rising Sun! Nobody knows his name yet."

My eye fell upon Roxie and Monty. Roxie sat there, regally. Why not? We were four mil richer and still going up. Four mil four.

Monty was making some kind of hand signal, laterally, not to the Cary Grant at the lectern. Ah, I saw the target. It was Prince Hal. He was no novice at the game. He was sitting on the aisle. I recognized Hal's signal to the auctioneer. It was a grave, gentlemanly nod, the kind one preppy gives to another to show that he doesn't favor just *anybody* with a nod. I wondered whether he and Biddle had been at school together. Prince Hal got the bid at four point eight. We were now way beyond the reserve price. Whoopee.

The ranks of bidders now began to thin out. Just the Met, the Rising Sun, and Prince Hal were in when it reached five point five. The womanizing Genevieve, invited to submit a bid over five, did not deign to smile. The Met wouldn't go beyond five point seven, the bid of the Japanese gentleman. At six million, Prince Hal's bid, the Rising Sun lowered his flag and surrendered.

"I have six million. Once, twice. Sold to Dr. Jensen."

As the crowd made for the exits, I saw Kathy O interviewing Roxie. Monty was off camera, glowering. He's not used to being off camera, I thought, particularly after he has just coughed up six mil.

I caught the interview on the six o'clock news.

"Well, how do you feel about the sale, Mrs. Carter?" Kathy O asked.

Roxie batted her eyes. "Just like Shirley Temple. I think that was Shirley Temple"

Kathy O looked perplexed. For her, history started with "I Love Lucy."

Roxie explained. "You know, the child star? In the movie the kid is given the claim horse nobody else wants. And it wins the Derby for her." Kathy O smiled, still not comprehending.

That sounded pretty saucy. She is enjoying the celebrity status. She is beginning to treat my Caillous as if they are a line of cosmetics she is marketing in *Vogue*. I was beginning to worry about Roxie. Pride goeth before a fall.

MONTY HAD INSTALLED MY PORTRAIT OF ROXIE AND the baby over the mantle. He had the room redecorated in colors that flattered it. Lee and I had been invited to dinner when the redecorating was finished. He admired the portrait greatly. He gave me a bear hug. He lavished attention on me. I was saluted in every other sentence as "old buddy." Lee inspected the canvas, but reserved comment.

Over the years, the comments of other Carter intimates were reported to me. Close friends often professed to admire it publicly, but privately complained that I hadn't really captured Roxie. The baby couldn't have been rendered better. He was so like Monty! Look at that famous nose! But Roxie? I had missed her sweetness. She was too—"I really can't find the right word!"

"*Formidable?*" "The very word!"

"Woman Contemplating a Vase of Flowers" made its debut a year after we started our planning. It went to the Carter. I blush at the thought of how much they paid.

Roxie had discovered that in 1920 there had been a large exhibit of Renoir canvases, some judged to be questionable, at a gallery in New York. Renoir had died in 1919.

Among them was a "Woman with Vase of Flowers" bearing the signature A. R. There was no reproduction in the catalog. But the dimensions of the canvas were wrong. That so-called Renoir was far too large. I had to take mine off its stretcher and alter the edges. The edges

176

had been covered with only a ground layer. Now I had to make it look as if my canvas had been cut down. That was not impossible, but it was risky. It invited the attention of technical experts. And I was anxious to avoid that.

The artist's son, the great actor Pierre Renoir, had seen the show in New York and written to the gallery owner, expressing doubts about the whole show. The canvases were purported to be a gift from Renoir to a friend and admirer. According to Pierre, his father, Auguste Renoir, would never have been guilty of such prodigality. After the painter's death, they had been sold in France to an American antique dealer, who had asked the gallery in New York to undertake the sale.

The expert who had prepared the catalog defended his certification against Pierre's doubts: Pierre was not an art expert. Moreover, he hadn't been there in the studio when the paintings were done. Therefore, he couldn't impeach them on the utterly irrelevant grounds that his world-famous father was not capable of charity on that scale. *Zut alors,* wasn't it possible that at least *some* of the canvases were genuine?

From Roxie's point of view, the pearl in this oyster was the idea that my Caillou Woman-With-Flowers had been, so to speak, hidden in plain view. It had remained in Renoir's possession all those years. Maybe Renoir had given it away at the end of his life, thinking it was his own work. The experts who examined the alleged Renoir would of course uncover the J.-J.C., which would establish its true authorship.

"Won't that be suspicious—first an alleged Renoir, then an alleged Monet, now another alleged Renoir?" I asked as we sat on our bench just inside Central Park.

"No. I don't think so. There is a precedent. You don't know about Vermeer?"

I allowed as I did. "The art world has come somewhat to expect it," she said.

"Oh?"

"Experts on impressionist art, dealers in European masters, pray every night for God to send them a 'so-called' or a 'very possibly'—even something they've seen before—which will turn out to be the next Caillou. The hunt is on. In our kind of marketing, nothing succeeds like success."

I allowed that it sounded plausible. She was too wound up in our next move to make a reply.

"I have an idea where the next one will be found. Some place the dealers wouldn't think to look. How about Gertie Gerstein's barn?"

"Dirty Gertie from Bizerte?"

She smiled. "The same."

"I didn't know you knew her."

"In the old days Monty was a client. Now she is *my* friend. She owes me a favor."

I didn't press for further details. I already knew about Gert's barn in Connecticut. It was where set designers went for period furniture. "That's where people in too much of a hurry to furnish their houses go. I don't get it," I said.

"Didn't you find the first Caillou in the flea market?"

"But that was Paris. Years ago."

"It doesn't matter. It's still every dealer's fantasy of how to make a killing. And where do you think Gert picks up her junk? On Staten Island? No! She makes the rounds—Portobello Road, Place de Clignancourt, the Arezzo antique fair. Monthly. And Gert has another advantage."

"What's that?"

"She never has the slightest idea what she paid for anything or where she got it. Her bookkeeping is legendary."

"She is a partner on this one? I don't like taking partners. You said you didn't either."

"No, she is not a partner. She is a witting agent. Not, of course, to the fact that the painting is a forgery. But she'll do it for me. And for the commission. Trust me."

"We are riding for a fall."

"Don't be so negative."

"She's an airhead."

"She'll work out okay. And it'll be a private sale. We can't risk the Shirley Temple routine again. It won't play in Peoria. This time we play to Monty's tragic flaw."

"Which one?"

"To be remembered as the grand old man of Caillou collecting. This

178

is the scenario: Gert's in the museum one day and happens to look at the Caillou portrait. She sees the woman with flowers and a bell rings. She bought something like that, who knows when, and thinks she still has it around. She spends days rummaging through her junk and comes across it.

"She may even be able to produce a bill of sale that leads—or seems to lead—back to the antique dealer of the phony Renoir show in 1920. She calls Prince Hal and asks to show it to him. Since all the Caillous but one are in the Carter, the prince is now claiming to be the leading authority on Caillou. He issues the certificate of authenticity. The Carter buys it. How does four million sound?"

"Too round."

"Four million two hundred fifty?"

"Better."

"We'll worry about the details later."

It was a variant of the no-provenance scam, in a way. But once seen, the initials J.-J.C. on "Woman Contemplating a Vase of Flowers" (as it would come to be called) would lead naturally to the conjecture that it is a wise son who really knows his own father. Auguste must have given *something* away—like a Caillou.

Roxie called Gert. "The leading antiquarian in Greenwich, Connecticut," as Gert now calls herself, was in fact in Roxie's debt. It was a matter of a bounced check—years ago. Monty was going to put the sheriff on Gert. Roxie intervened. There were other little scrapes Roxie helped Gert out of. And Gert had become a one-woman Roxie fan club.

So Roxie invited Gertie to lunch at '21,' saying she had news to impart.

Gertie waltzed in, in a huge black felt hat, a mink, and a flood of good will. Some dissatisfied customer once dismissed Gert as a walking oxymoron. Roxie was sitting in the lounge in a tan Republican cloth coat and a tearful expression. They spied each other. Roxie rose and the two women embraced.

"God, I wish I had your looks, Roxie. I could have made a fortune without ever getting out of bed." Gertie loved to talk about the good old days. Nowadays, she made it sound full of Dutch and Lucky.

They were shown to a table.

"How's Monty? I read in the news he's going to run for something, I forget what. Doesn't he ever stop?"

"Don't believe it, Gertie. He's got other things on his mind at the moment."

"Is that a martini you are drinking? Bring me one, too, sweetie. So what's on Monty's mind?"

"Me," Roxie said, looking Gertie straight in the eye.

"You? I'll bet you're always on Monty's mind, the *alter cocker!*"

"Not that way. Monty and I are talking about separating."

"WHAT?"

"Shsh."

"I don't believe it. You've been married twenty years. You and Monty are a fixture. My God, what's next? Grace and Ranier? Elizabeth and Philip?"

Roxie smiled wearily, trying to look like Saint Catherine on the wheel. "Come on, Gertie. You're my friend. You know Monty. From the old days! He's never been faithful. You know what he is like. At the moment, he's balling some TV bimbo."

Gertie was surprised at Roxie's language and her bitter tone. They were both out of character, a clear sign of the trial Roxie was undergoing. She put her gloved hand across the table on Roxie's and squeezed. "He's a *schmuck*, you should pardon the expression. I knew it when he was one of my gentlemen callers. . . . Before your time, my dear. Still it's hard. Does anybody know?"

"No, not yet."

"You need anything? God knows, I owe you. Honest, if you need anything, honey. Listen, take a little advice. Have you seen your lawyer? He's a mean man. If you leave before the settlement, you'll get peanuts."

"Don't worry about it, Gertie. I made a killing about a year ago. That's when all the trouble really started. He's never forgiven me for making him pay. I won't starve. Let's order."

Gertie was well known for the quantity of food she could put away in a sitting, and Roxie's news didn't seem to suppress her appetite. After the oysters Rockefeller, she had rack of lamb, a Caesar salad, and a Napoleon. So, it wasn't until coffee that Roxie got around to the point.

"Gert, I do have a favor to ask of you."

"Anything, anything at all, baby."

"I have a painting. I want you to sell it and keep me out."

"Me?" Gertie laughed. "I got *schlach*, sweetie. Not even kitsch. *Schlach*. Old masters I am not known for—today." She smiled. "Only in the old days."

"I know. How'd you like to find a masterpiece among the *schlach*? I'll pay you the regular commission—fifteen percent. I think your share would be in six figures."

"What is this masterpiece?" Gertie's voice had dropped to a whisper. She knew when discretion was called for.

"It's a Caillou. A woman with a vase of flowers. And it's got his monogram—J.-J.C."

"Where did you find it?"

"I bought it at the same time as I bought the snow scene. From the vanished Signor Barzoletto. He showed it to me first. I recognized it immediately. He had no idea what he had. When I also saw the other, I couldn't believe my eyes. Two birds with one stone."

"Wow, why is it the rich have all the luck? So why didn't you let Sotheby's sell it for you at the same time?"

"I was going to hold it for a while and let the price go up. Now I think I'd better unload it in a private sale."

"Why don't you just go to one of those Madison Avenue creeps?"

"Two reasons. First, I want it to go to the Carter. Second, Monty doesn't know about this one. If he found out I was the seller, he would be sure to make trouble. He'd claim it was community property or something. Then I'd probably have trouble selling it to anyone. No, it's got to look as if I have nothing to do with it. You could say you just found it in a pile of junk. You don't even know exactly when you bought it. It could have been ten years ago. Will you do it, Gert?"

"Sure, kid. What have I got to lose?"

"Thanks, Gert. You are a real friend."

I

N LATE 1980 THERE WAS TALK IN WASHINGTON THAT L. Montcalme Carter was in line for an important government post. Monty, of course, made frequent denials that there was anything to the rumors. The only thing he could confirm, he told the press, smiling graciously, was that he and the president-elect were friends. "From way back!" he added, bringing the interview to a close.

Over breakfast, reading yet another rumor about her brother, Lee said to me, "Monty is fishing."

"What makes you think that?" I asked, not terribly interested.

"Who do you think started those rumors in the first place, my prince?" she replied.

The rumors persisted into the spring. By then, it was clear that he was not in line for a position at Treasury. Now they centered on the Court of Saint James. Or the Élysée.

Monty told the press he had no idea where the rumors came from. Yes, he had talked to "Ron" at Christmas time. But he and Ron always phoned each other on Christmas eve. "We go way back, you know," he said.

Then the constant rumble out of Washington, which was keeping the defeated candidate's name before the public, suddenly came to an abrupt end. Not that his name wasn't still before the public.

One Katherine O'Connell, long known to watchers of the six o'clock news as Kathy O, had just published a book: *Kathy O, Her Story.* (It was one of those "as told to . . ." jobs.) It retailed her struggle with the local station that had been her employer until June of the last year and then had abruptly dismissed her. She was at the time three months pregnant.

The station, of course, immediately issued a statement, saying that they did not have a policy of discriminating against pregnant anchorpersons. Kathy O had been let go because of declining ratings.

182

In the book Kathy O discussed her life with the frankness and courage that are marks of the times. She drew a picture of herself as a dedicated professional, but not a woman to be denied the fulfillment of motherhood. She drew witty, barbed portraits of the many personages in art, politics, and journalism whom she had known intimately. There were tales of the famous, the rich, and the powerful. Defenders of the book said it was not—emphatically not—a mere kiss-and-tell book. She included snapshots in the middle of the book, taken with her Polaroid.

Prominent in the text and photographs was the name and face of L. Montcalme Carter. Kathy O first met him while covering an art auction. It had been love at first sight—on both their parts. In her portrait Monty was "decidedly not a simple man." "The rich and powerful rarely are," Kathy O noted trenchantly. Among the foibles she recounted was a certain tightfistedness with money. In the last chapter, dictated from the bed of motherhood, she announced her plan to call the baby Monty Carter O'Connell.

In Washington, they thought Kathy O's timing was abysmal.

Monty could not be reached for comment, but a statement was immediately issued by his press representative. It denied all knowledge of the mother. The next day he declared his previous comment "no longer operative." Mr. Carter recalled Kathy O, but only professionally.

On the six o'clock news, there was a clip of Monty's press representative, saying that his employer was out of the country and would have no comment until he returned. Under further questioning, he admitted: yes, the record would have to be amended. Mr. Carter did know Katherine O'Connell.

"In the biblical sense?" a reporter asked poking a microphone in his face.

Monty's press spokesman pushed the microphone away with a look of repugnance. He said, "Mr. Carter has the highest regard for Miss O'Connell's professional and personal integrity. He is sure that ultimately she will admit that she has made a terrible mistake."

The next issue of *People* magazine (Monty had never considered the crowd at Time Inc. particularly friendly) featured Kathy O on its cover, smiling and presenting her baby for everyone to see.

183

The accompanying story rehearsed her fight with the station. It quoted the station manager—rather sourly—calling Kathy O "a power groupie." And it also quoted Kathy O (again holding the baby up to the camera): "Just look at that schnozz! Can you have any doubts who his father is?"

Reading the *People* story over breakfast, Lee Birnbaum had commented, "It's the old story."

"What old story?" I asked.

"Europa and the Bull. That's her mythic Dasein. She has fantasies of being ravished by a bull."

I absentmindedly nodded my agreement and went back to reading the newspaper. Lee went to the phone and called her brother.

"Damned, if he doesn't look like you. He has the Carter nose," she said. Monty evidently did not understand that she was trying to make light of the matter. There was an angry stream of half-finished sentences, and a number of vulgar expressions. Then he started hiccuping.

Roxie Carter had never really believed that her husband could be unfaithful to her. Not in her heart of hearts. She had been hearing the stories for years, and she could even bring herself to repeat them to close friends like Gert when they served her purposes. But she hated the idea of playing the injured wife, of people being especially kind and considerate to her because of the hurt they knew she must feel. Thank God, her mother was dead. If she weren't, Roxie knew she'd be breathing down her neck. With tales of how brave women in Lexington, Kentucky, women with standards, had coped with just this situation.

So she went on with her life, but avoided people who might try to penetrate the screen she had erected around herself. She gave instructions to the maid to say she was away. She did, however, talk to Lee. They lunched. And Lee told me about it.

"You think she will leave him?" I asked.

"No."

"Why not? She doesn't love him. Who could?"

She shot me a sharp look. It was obvious that not only Monty, but I, had been a subject of discussion. I was filled with anxiety. I told myself to be careful.

"No, she doesn't. But she can't conceive of an alternative life."

"Why not? She's a wealthy woman in her own right!"

I had a sudden attack of panic. I had given the game away. The thought also occurred to me that perhaps Roxie had in a rash moment taken Lee into her full confidence—about the Caillous.

"Roxie has a long-suffering Dasein. She's not like me."

"I mean she cleared a lot of money from the auction of that Caillou—I forget its name. Several million, I seem to remember."

Lee nodded. "But her life is here. For good or ill. With that monster!"

She fell silent. I had a premonition that it was not the end of our discussion, just the intermission.

"We also talked about you."

"Oh?" I asked. With nonchalance, I hoped.

"I made it clear that I considered it a *loan*."

I smiled.

"And that I forgave the loan. But that I was not prepared to extend a line of credit."

Roxie also talked to me, a few days later at our regular rendezvous in the park. She was wearing a scarf over her hair, sunglasses, all the trappings of incognito celebrity. I asked her how things were going.

"We go through the daily rituals. But I refuse to speak to him. Little Monty is very confused about what is going on."

"What are you planning to do?" I asked. I meant it to be a general question. I meant it as a prelude to saying that Lee and I would do anything we could to help. But Roxie took the question to be about business.

She flashed me that sharp and hard little smile.

"It is time to start planning for the reappearance of the "Odalisque"— surely the most beautiful of all of them," she said matter-of-factly.

I was stunned by her detachment.

"It ought to make us very wealthy. Very wealthy, indeed!"

I nodded.

"I have special plans. Monty will buy it personally, not out of foundation funds. He will pay plenty for it. It will be a gift to me. It won't go to the museum right away. It will hang above the mantle—where your other portrait of me is now. You know that's the only one of your works I really detest?"

I mumbled my apologies.

"It will be retribution," she said with a crooked smile.

I thought our meeting was at an end, but she did not get up to go. She wanted to tell me something else.

"By the by, Jack, do you know about the Carter's plans for a Caillou spectacular?"

I was surprised. I counted the known number of Caillous. They were not enough for a "spectacular." "No. It's a bit premature, isn't it? Let them wait a couple of more years."

"It's Prince Hal's idea. The museum's holdings, plus the one in the Louvre—all the known Caillous—are to be exhibited along with works from the same years by Monet, Renoir, Bazille, and Pissarro. He plans to include several Gleyre canvases, including one the museum recently bought on the cheap. The focus is going to be the students of Gleyre. All in all, he is hoping for fifty works."

My heart leaped up.

"He was surprised when the Louvre agreed to lend 'The Bathers.' They wanted a trade for some Meerschaum panels."

I evidently looked surprised. "The Louvre is planning an art nouveau spectacular. You will be getting a call from Prince Hal."

I cocked an eyebrow. "About what?"

"He sounded me out as to whether you would welcome his suggestion. He is wondering whether you and Lee might not like to donate the portrait of Renoir. It's only on loan. He thought you might think it a nice gesture of loyalty to Monty and me."

She uttered a bitter little laugh. "His very words. He is such a pissant."

The Kathy O story persisted into the spring. It just would not go away. When *Kathy O, Her Story* left the bestseller lists, the author instituted a paternity suit.

A few days later, at dinner, Lee introduced that as the topic of con-

186

versation. I knew something serious was on her mind, for she had been silent through most of the meal. And she had waited until after Sheba had left the table, before she began.

"Jack, you've got to do something," Lee announced, gravely.

"About what?"

"About Monty, of course! He's planning to fight the suit. You've got to convince him to settle out of court."

"Oh? Where'd you hear that?"

"From Roxie. He thinks he can win. He's going to use the low-sperm-count defense. It will be another Roman Carnival."

"So?"

"So? Surely, you of all people see the implications."

"Oh, I see what you mean."

"Good. You must talk to Monty. Try to convince him to drop the suit."

I was nonetheless astonished at the suggestion. "You want *me* to talk to him? You are out of your mind, Lee."

"Of course you can't tell him the truth, if that's what you thought! Do you think I am an idiot? Just remind him of what he owes to the family. Tell him he owes it to Roxie and to little Monty to spare them further grief. Tell him to think of the family! It is something only you can do. Take him to lunch tomorrow. At Le Champignon. Give him all that 'old buddy' crap he always gives you. Tell him to quit shooting himself in the foot."

"Won't he suspect I have what you might call an ulterior motive?"

"No, I don't think so. If he were having any suspicions, he wouldn't be thinking of all that low-sperm-count jazz. What's important is not allowing anybody else to suggest he might have reasons for doubt. . . . Oh, and one thing more—"

"Yes?"

"This time you pick up the check."

I rose to the occasion. I took him to lunch. I cudgeled Monty's arm. Then I admonished Monty sternly that he should cease shooting himself in the foot. He must bring to an end "this time on the cross for all who love you. But especially you must do it for Roxie and little Monty." And, bleary-eyed after a second bottle of La Tache '58, Monty threw his arms around me and promised that he would settle out of court. As I paid the check, I chuckled to myself that at least I could afford the whopping bill.

In return for consideration, the amount of which she was not to divulge, Kathy O also promised she would henceforth make no further reference "to any relations she might in the past have had with Lawrence Montcalme Carter."

But the Kathy O story would not die.

We were sitting watching the TV one night that summer. Lee was poring over a large map. When I asked her what she was doing, she said she was studying the map of West Virginia. Why, I asked. Oh, no reason in particular, she said. Then she suddenly looked up at the screen.

"I know her. It's Betsy Somebody-or-Other. I went to college with her."

I looked. "Her name is Betsy Browne. She hosts a program. It's called the 'Betsy Browne Reports,'" I said.

I had watched her rise to eminence from the hurly-burly of TV news. She was known for nonconfrontational interviews with the rich and famous. But she was a mousetrapper from way back. She plays along with the mouse, asking questions that gets him or her talking about his or her own agenda. Then snap, she snares them with a question they don't expect. The victim squirms, squiggles, blanches. He or she is too flummoxed to give a coherent answer. Then cool as you please, she thanks the victim for being there with her and so gracious. Then she signs off.

Lee had gone back to the map of West Virginia, and I was about to switch the set off when I was struck by the familiarity of the room behind Betsy Browne. It was the living room of the Montcalme Carters! I called out to Lee. She looked up just in time to see the camera pan to Monty and Roxie. They were sitting on a couch opposite Betsy. They were holding hands.

Lee and I exchanged looks. "Monty, you oaf," Lee said. "You simply can't resist a loaded gun."

188

BB: What a beautiful place! But you'd expect that of patrons of the arts like the Carters. It's the perfect setting for you, Roxie. I have a confession to make. I've always been green with envy. In all the years we've known each other, you always managed to make heads turn. How do you manage to stay looking so young and beautiful?

Roxie blushes, fidgets.

Roxie: Betsy, you are embarrassing me.
BB: I didn't mean to—sincerely. (BB allows a significant pause. Now, for the supposed agenda.) You guys have been through a rough time this last year. If it hadn't been for the book and then certain well-publicized legal problems, Monty, you might have been our ambassador to London or Paris right now. Has it ended your political ambitions?

The camera shifts to Monty. He smiles. The smile of a sadder but wiser man. The camera lingers on his face.

Monty: To quote Sherman, Betsy: "If drafted, I will not run. If elected, I will not serve."

The camera goes back to Betsy.

BB: But surely, you must have been aware of the risks. You've lived in the public eye too long.

Camera on the obviously contrite Monty.

Monty: I know. I let everybody down. I let all my supporters down. I want to take this opportunity to tell them how sincerely sorry I am. And my family. What I have subjected them to was—unforgivable. That's the only word for it. But—

The camera pans to the still joined hands of Monty and Roxie. Then back to Monty.

BB: You wanted to add something?
Monty: Yes, but not in my defense. I think we all ought to pause and reflect on the way the press invades our private lives these days. I am not

talking about you, Betsy, of course. But you have to admit that there are a lot of irresponsible people in your profession. My God, the things they say in those rags you can pick up in the supermarket. And they go scot-free. Nobody in public life these days is safe from that kind of filth. I'll bet you—even you, Betsy—have suffered from that kind of smut.

The camera goes to Betsy, who smiles a little stiffly. But it doesn't linger. Back to Monty.

The fourth estate needs to police itself. Why, back in the old days when Jack Kennedy was cocking around Washington—pardon the expression—everybody knew it. But then the press had the good taste to keep it out of print.

The camera goes back to Betsy. She looks surprised. She does not know quite what to say.

Monty (continuing with his planned agenda): But that's not to excuse my mistakes—

The camera is back on Monty's face, which shows real anguish.

No, that's too weak. I've fallen from grace. I had everything a man could wish. A fulfilling life, a wonderful wife, a great family. And I risked all that—

Monty holds up their still joined hands for the camera to catch.

But one thing I want you to know. We've come out of this time on the cross—Roxie and I—with a marriage that is stronger and deeper than ever.

The camera takes in Roxie's beautiful face. Roxie is struggling to hold back the tears. Then back to Betsy. Betsy, by contrast, is suddenly looking very much in control.
Uh-oh, I thought. She is about to catch the mouse.

BB (enunciating with special care): Monty, there is something that puzzles me. I wonder if you'd like to clear it up?

Camera on Monty, to capture the moment the trap is sprung.

I have it—on good authority—that you and Roxie have had problems in the past with infertility. Something to do with a low sperm count? I was sorry to hear it.

The camera is still on Monty. His eyes shift from side to side. He has not expected this line of questioning.

You could almost certainly have won your case. Why did you settle out of court?
Monty: I wanted to spare Roxie any more anguish.
BB: Was that the only reason?

Monty looks dumbfounded. He looks as if he simply doesn't understand the question.
Watching Monty squirm, squiggle, and go white, Lee gasped. My heart was also in my mouth. My hand went instinctively to cover my mouth.
Suddenly the camera is on Roxie. Roxie is fit to be tied.

Roxie: I'll handle this, Monty. . . . Yes, Betsy, we have had problems conceiving a child. And yes, you are right about the reason. But, as my dear mother back in Lexington used to say, if at first you don't succeed, you try, try again. It's an old home remedy, you know. We tried and we tried and finally we were blessed with a son. Maybe it was a medical miracle. But miracles do happen, thank you.

The camera goes back to Betsy. She did not expect an answer from Roxie, but this is the real stuff. It is footage that is just too good to break off.

BB: Roxie, would you care to assure our viewers—
Roxie: Now you listen good, sweetpea—

As the camera moved back to Roxie, I became aware of the drawled speech. It was Scarlett O'Hara. It was Blanche Dubois. This is the new Roxie. There is fire in her. Oh boy, is there! She's a bona fide, fire-

191

breathing dragon. If Betsy Browne were not made of ice, all that would be left of her by now would be a little pile of ashes.

Ah hail fum Lexintun—that's in Kayntuck, y'all—an' mah mutha, that's Mizz Ditmars—y'all ask anyone in Lexintun about Mizz Ditmars —she wus sum lady, I can tell you. An' she didn't raise no daughta to be a tramp.

The camera goes back to Betsy, who is speechless, but knows she has to recover.

BB (mumbling somewhat): Thank you, Mr. and Mrs. L. Montcalme Carter. You are, as always, the soul of graciousness. It's been a real pleasure.

Lee doubled over with laughter. I found myself rising to my feet and applauding.

I COME NOW TO MY EVENING OF TRIUMPH. THE CARTER opened its gala, "Proto-impressionism," with a black-tie affair. Naturally we received an invitation. We were "Honored Friends of the Museum," were we not?

I had been in a state of elation for almost a month. Even Lee, who was usually too busy to notice, and these days was rather more mysterious than usual, had taken note of my mood. "You are in a particularly good mood these days, my prince," she said to me, looking up from her papers. I was so absorbed with my dreams I didn't bother to inquire what was so engrossing to her. Even Sheba noted my buoyancy. "Daddy, you are singing again. How can I practice if you are always singing?" Sheba had started to study the flute. According to her teacher, she had real talent.

In order to fit into my brocaded dinner jacket, I had had to lose fifteen pounds. Even those draconian deprivations had not dampened my mood. When the evening arrived, I cast an approving look at myself in the mirror. I looked like I should be endorsing Scotch in the *New Yorker* or saying, "Do you know me?" on television for American Express.

When I saw Lee dressed to accompany me, I experienced a shock. Over the years she had put on weight, but by that insidious process that keeps those in daily contact from realizing, except at rare moments, the change in appearance. Now I was suddenly aware of it. I was also aware that her blond hair, now hanging down to her shoulders, had strands of gray. Maybe the process had started long ago and she had some time in the not too distant past stopped trying to conceal it. But it was her oufit that administered the real shock. The dress was a gauzy, bleached material of no discernible cut. And worst of all, around her forehead she had placed a tiara of fresh laurel and berries. She reminded me of a figure in a painting that I couldn't immediately identify. I sighed. It was too late to try to persuade her that her costume was not fitting for the occasion. We left for the museum.

We arrived fashionably late. The large room that usually housed the Meerschaum panels had been cleared—several were already at the Louvre show.

Prince Hal was greeting guests at the door. I tried to steer past him, but he grabbed me by the arm.

"This evening we put the Carter on the *Carta Mundi*," he whispered to me, then giggled, the sparkle of his contacts punctuating his little sally.

"I beg your pardon?" I said.

"We're on the *map*. With this show we tell the Metropolitan to move over."

I got it. I acknowledged with the ghost of a smile. He was really full of himself.

I cast my eye around the room. It was stunning. The walls had been covered with brocaded paper—very *Deuxième Empire*—and the tables and chairs were of the period. I was enchanted. Prince Hal had done beautifully. I was entering a *salon* of the 1860s. I knew I was in my milieu.

I spotted Monty. He was wearing tails. He was one of the few men in full evening regalia. The tails somehow made him look older. His nose dipped more pendulously, his mustache drooped more rakishly. He had a certain weary, dissipated grandeur. He looked very much *Monsieur le Duc*. I felt an unexpected flush of sympathy for him. Roxie was not far away, chatting up a storm. She was ravishing in a red sheath. Her hair was swept up and crowned with a diamond tiara. I was also momentarily caught up in the general admiration for *Madame la Duchesse*. But then I preferred her in her more familiar role. She was now altogether too much in control.

"Oh, God."

It was the voice of the show's producer. I turned toward Prince Hal. He had finally spotted Lee, who had emerged from behind me. It was an unrehearsed response. And she answered by sticking her tongue out at him.

"This isn't the Art Students' League Ball!" he said petulantly.

I quickly steered Lee past him. My face felt flushed. Then my eyes swept the walls. And the whole busy scene vanished from my mind. Suddenly it was as if I were alone in the room.

There are often moments of sheer magic when I enter a gallery of great paintings, sometimes even very familiar ones. They take my breath away, those moments where I encounter a whole room of Velásquezes, or Titians, or Cézannes, all seen at once. In a small distinguished museum I visit often, the Frick for instance, I even expect to be overwhelmed with a feeling of awe that every one of the paintings in the room is a masterpiece. Then I go to a particular painting and take up the proper viewing angle and distance for its study. I am rewarded, but in a different way. For me these first panoramic visions are the closest I will ever come to the bliss of being received into heaven.

I experienced this reverence at that moment. I caught sight of my Caillous among the Monets, Renoirs, Bazilles, and Pissarros with which they were hung. The blood pulsed wildly through my temples, I felt flushed by heat and then chilled by cold. My skin prickled. I thought I might faint.

The Caillou portrait of Renoir was paired with the Renoir portrait of Bazille—also a very great painting. The Caillou snow scene was hung

194

next to two views of the snowy road. Not one, but two—count 'em—of the Louveciennes pictures—Monet and Pissarro! The study of the woman with flowers was hung next to a Renoir painting of a woman holding a bunch of flowers. For "The Bathers," a quite small oil, Prince Hal had found another counterpart, the glorious "Boating Party" of Renoir, which belongs to the Phillips in Washington. My heart skipped a beat at its sight. The resemblance of one of the male figures in the Caillou to a figure in the Renoir was perhaps a little too obvious. But at the same time I marveled how well my little painting held its own against Renoir's much grander work.

I did not feel at that moment that I had brought off a hoax. I wasn't conscious of my own cleverness. I did not feel wickedly superior. *Au contraire*, I felt positively humble. But so *exalted!*

I warned myself that I was not Jean-Jacques Caillou; I was Jack Birnbaum, in a brocaded dinner jacket, and I must play the part expected of me. I must play the worldly clown. I took Lee by the arm and steered her through the crowd. I tried to ignore the throng of partygoers in evening finery who seemed to retreat to make a path for us. I overheard a woman's voice behind me say, "It's the fairy godmother! But where is Cinderella?" I did not look around. I took a firmer grip of Lee's arm and hoped she hadn't heard.

We arrived at Roxie's side. The three of us exchanged cheek pecks. We chatted in the pointless party fashion. We appraised the size and quality of the crowd. Roxie turned to respond to another greeting. Lee and I circulated. I was dying to get away to the paintings. We approached Monty, who was in conversation with a tall man I recognized to be the director of the Met—not the opera, you know, that other one. He was, of course, one of Monty's intimate friends. In addition, there was another man, shorter, whom I did not recognize. All of them were in gala finery. Monty blanched at the sight of his sister, but sought to cover himself by ignoring her and going through the "old-buddy" arm-punching routine with me. I suffered the ritual in silence. Then I complimented him on the great distinction of his soirée.

Monty made the introductions. Lee and the director, it turned out, went way back together; they had peed in each other's sandpiles in kindergarten, or some such thing. They had not seen each other for a long time and were soon on a voyage of discovery: whatever happened to what's-his-name . . .

I did not get the little man's name. I burned to put myself in front of the paintings. I just managed to catch that he was someone from the Louvre. I smiled and shook his hand absent-mindedly. He took mine rather more enthusiastically. Then I discovered he was addressing me in French-perfumed English.

"—belongs the—how to say—credit. *Sans nous, rien ne serait possible, vous savez.*" He tapped his chest. He was smiling at me.

I smiled, not comprehending the secret he believed we shared. I wished I had paid attention to his name. He seemed to know me, and I hated not being able to place him.

"It was your—how you say—*'oeil'* and my—how you say—*'recherches.'*"

Evidently, I was still looking blank. He pointed to the Caillou portrait of Renoir. And all of a sudden I understood. He was Charles Labiche. I took his hand again and pumped it enthusiastically.

"Of course. I am so sorry I didn't recognize you. It's been so many years."

Pas de quoi he nodded with Gallic good humor. I insinuated my recognition of his important status. I thanked him for his efforts to support the loan of "The Bathers" to the show. We discussed the exciting story of that painting's discovery and his role in establishing that it was indeed a Caillou. Then he inquired discretely as to my *place.*

My position? I explained that I was by profession a portrait painter and that I was also the husband of Montcalme Carter's sister.

"Zat lady is your vife?" he said, with the Gallic rise of the eyebrow.

"Yes," I said. "She is a psychoanalyst. A Jungian, which is rare in New York. Most psychoanalysts here are Freudians."

Perhaps I had overexplained, but he took that information in with Gallic seriousness.

"She's very wrapped up in her work," I continued.

He nodded again. "She reminds me of a picture. In your National Gallery. A figure in a painting of Bellini. *Très amusante.*"

He obviously meant the "Feast of the Gods." I said I thought the resemblance was intentional. I smiled in appreciation. I did not want to nullify the impression.

"I appreciate your saying so. You have—how to say—*'l'oeil'*!"

He gave me a millisecond's worth of smile. I wanted to change the subject. "And how is Marthe?" I asked.

Now he looked confused. "Marthe?"

"Marthe de Saint Veran. I am afraid I have lost touch with her."

"Ah, her! She and my cousin, they divorce each other now many years since. I also 'ave lost touch."

There was a pause in our conversation. Then I said I had a special interest in his views of the newly discovered Caillous. Could we go over and look at the paintings?

He welcomed my invitation.

I watched him as he viewed each of my works. He stood in front of first one, then another of the Caillous impassively. He looked first at the Louveciennes snow scenes—first the Caillou, then the Monet, then the Pissarro scene. Then he went back to Caillou and looked closely at the brushstroke. Then he straightened himself up to his full height—he was quite a short man—and put his hand up. Again it was a Gallic gesture. All brevity, if you know what I mean! "*Ah, ça!*" he sighed with deep satisfaction.

When we stood before the woman and the vase of flowers, I suddenly experienced a deep feeling of its inadequacy—not that it was bad, but that it wasn't quite finished. It needed stronger highlighting, a touch more white in the broach at her throat, some other small changes in the vase of flowers. I said something to this effect to Labiche, something about its lacking a certain luster. He listened to me, then shook his finger excitedly back and forth in front of my face, uttering that strange clucking sound that in French means "Don't touch" or "For shame." Here it meant simply "You are quite wrong!" It was the balm to my ache to retouch.

He paused longest before "The Bathers." I was wondering why he lingered over that painting when he had had every opportunity to study it at home. He looked at the small work with fierce concentration, then moved over to "The Boating Party," then back again, and once more to the Renoir canvas.

"*Regardez ça,*" he said, pointing to one of the figures in the Caillou. "*Et maintenant ça!*"

He was pointing to the mustached figure in a striped undershirt, with a boater on his head. "*Épatant!*" he said. I put my hand over my mouth. I was sure I was about to be exposed.

But I managed to keep my sangfroid. "I see what you mean," I said. "There is a strong resemblance, now that you mention it. It's mostly the man's stance. I hadn't seen that before. Renoir has simply rotated the figure."

"*Exactement.* Renoir mus' 'ave zeen zat *forme* and recall' it ven 'e came to paint 'is own *chef-d'oeuvre.*"

Labiche left me, and I continued my devotions. I hardly noticed when a silence fell on the crowd and Prince Hal started to make his remarks inaugurating the show. I held my position at the wall where all the Caillous were installed. Only phrases of his preening sycophancy penetrated the shield around my communion with these masters of the century past. Phrases about Monty's "peerless generosity" failed to arouse a snicker from me. I was simply in another, nobler, world. Even the pangs of Monty's villainies seemed now the merest of trifles. I was literally immune to the tomfooleries of Prince Hal. More than once, he asserted to the assembled "Friends of the Carter, and Special Friends of the Carter, and let us not forget the Honored Friends of the Carter"—that this night was "a triumph long to be remembered in the history of art statesmanship."

I felt an arm gently take my elbow. I turned to look into the beautiful dark eyes of Roxie Carter. She was smiling at me. For a moment I had the impression she had just stepped out of one of the paintings. In the rush of warm feelings I had toward all things bright and beautiful, I wanted to take her in my arms. Then I noticed that Hal's remarks had come to an end; guests were leaving; the caterers were champing at the bit to return to Le Champignon. I suddenly awoke to the fact that I had not visited the buffet in the next room. And I was famished.

"I haven't had a chance to talk to you all evening," she said. "But I've been watching you. You haven't moved. What a triumph!" She gave my hand a secretive little squeeze.

198

I beamed at her. She was my old, dear, lovely Roxie. The only one in this vast crowd who really understood me.

"Now listen, I've been doing some research . . . "

The change was instantaneous. We were back to business. ". . . Caillou's mother had a house in the Vosges. That's were he stored his paintings when he went off to war. What if—"

"Not now!" I said impatiently. "We can talk later. The usual time and place!"

She nodded.

She broke off eye contact and looked around the room. Her eye suddenly fell on a little knot of loiterers. They seemed to be attending upon a bald man. His back was to me. He was, like every one else, in evening dress. He was talking in a loud voice, animatedly, about the need to distinguish postmodernist kitsch from the *authentic* postmodernism. As he turned slightly, I thought he looked vaguely familiar. With shock, I recognized the spectacles with the large black frames. The shock must have been apparent, for I found Roxie was saying something to me.

"Is there something the matter, Jack?" She turned and looked at where I had been staring. "Do you know him?"

I nodded.

"He asked me," she said, "whether I'd read HMB's piece on the 'Woman with the Vase of Flowers.' I said no, I hadn't. I thought he was talking about someone else. It didn't dawn on me that *he* was HMB."

"Himself, you might say."

"Does he always talk in that bizarre way?"

"Always."

"Well, whoever he is, he is one of your greatest fans."

"I beg your pardon?"

"He said that after tonight, they are going to have to rewrite the history of impressionism."

Iτ WAS A LITTLE OVER A MONTH LATER THAT LEE AN-
nounced she had something important to tell me. She said she had
already talked to Sheba. That sounded ominous. "It'll keep until breakfast, I suppose," she said. Over the years many of our most important
parleys had taken place over breakfast.

So at breakfast next morning, right before Sheba left for school, she
put her hand on mine and announced that she had recently bought ten
thousand acres in the West Virginia mountains. "It will be my permanent residence," she said solemnly. It was a place called Baldhead. She
didn't particularly fancy the name, but the county commissioners were
agreeable to a name change.

"I am thinking of 'Bliss.' My address will be: PO Box 1, Bliss, West
Virginia. Don't you think that's nice?"

I allowed that I did.

"For the time being, I think Sheba had better spend the school year
with you. The schools are terrible. I plan to do something about that,
but it will take time!" She turned to Sheba, "You do want to spend the
summer with me. Don't you, honey?"

Sheba nodded her head enthusiastically. She smiled, exposing the
braces on her teeth. "I've got to go. I'll be late. I have a flute lesson this
afternoon, Daddy."

She arose, came around the table, gave me a hug, then planted a kiss
on Lee's brow. A moment later I heard the front door slam. She seemed
to be taking the news in stride.

Lee's hand was still on mine. I withdrew mine.

"Do you want a divorce?" I asked. My voice sounded shaky to me. I
wasn't at all sure how I felt about this idea of Lee's.

"What ever gave you *that* idea?" she responded.

"That's usually what is happening when a spouse decides to set up a
separate residence."

200

"Jack, why would I want to divorce *you?* You're ... well, you're still my *champion.* Ever since that rainy night—"

"So, why are you moving to West Virginia?"

She took a sip of her coffee, while deliberating. "I have wanted for a long time to establish ... I suppose you could call it a retreat. A place where troubled souls can find the ground of their being. Get in touch with who they really are. You can't do that in New York. It's a place of disguises. . . . You have your own life, of course. I'm proud of you. I am not worried about you. You are always welcome in my tent, my dear!"

She took another sip of coffee.

"Roxie is going to look in on Sheba—and you!"

She giggled. I studied her, wondering what was so amusing.

"I was just thinking how *functional* polygamy really is. I'm so glad it's part of your mythic Dasein." Her hand resumed its place on mine. " ... Jacob."

It was the first time in some time she had mentioned my archetype. And I found it disturbing. She and Roxie had talked about this move. And about me. It always disturbed me to know that Lee and Roxie had talked about me. They were still very close. Could Roxie have said something about our partnership? It suddenly struck me: that also had its place in my mythic Dasein. I remembered the part about Rachel's stealing of Laban's household gods.

Lee was still smiling at me benevolently.

"I'm sure there won't be any complications," she said. "Thank God that sexual business is no longer ... a possible source of conflict ... between the three of us."

I happened to agree with her. But it was not something I wanted to discuss. She was not finished, however, with the subject.

"You know, the Freudians make too much of sex. All that folderol about the pleasure principle. Oh, maybe it has some truth as far as men are concerned. But in women, the basic need is to give nurture."

A few weeks after Lee left, I had a commission in London. Sheba went to stay with Roxie. I crossed on a Concorde. I had just finished an excellent repast of kippers and eggs. I was drinking a second cup of coffee, thinking of nothing in particular, idling through the complimentary

201

Times of London when a headline caught my eye. I read the story—in one gulp, so to speak.

ANOTHER CAILLOU IS DISCOVERED

Zurich, September 16—Reports are circulating in the art capitals of Europe of the existence of a newly discovered painting by Jean-Jacques Caillou (1841–1870).

Caillou is the forgotten French impressionist, a friend of Renoir, Monet, and Bazille, several of whose works have been rediscovered during the past ten years. Previously attributed to Renoir and Monet, the Caillou canvases have commanded enormous prices for an artist all but unknown to the art public ten years ago. The price in a private sale to the Louvre Museum in Paris in 1975 was rumored to have been three quarters of a million dollars. A Caillou more recently auctioned at Sotheby's went to the Carter Museum in New York for six million. The Carter has also recently acquired, in private sale, yet another Caillou, for which no price has been disclosed.

According to the reports circulating here, the most recent Caillou to be rediscovered is the largest of the Caillou canvases, measuring approximately 90 x 60 centimeters. The subject is a nude female in a dramatic pose. Reputedly it is a student work dating from the early 1860s, exhibited with great success at the Salon of 1865. It is depicted in Caillou's "Portrait of A. Renoir" in the Carter Museum, which was purchased by artist Jack Birnbaum in Paris in 1949 and acquired by the Carter in the late 1960s.

The "Odalisque," as it has come to be called, is currently undergoing restoration. It is expected to be offered for sale later this year by a dealer in Zurich. The dealer is said to have purchased it from a Canadian, who is also thought to have been the seller in the 1975 sale of "The Bathers."

My first thought was that Roxie had acted on her own. I feared our success had gone to her head. She loved all the cloak-and-dagger, the cover stories, the disguises. I tried to remember the last time I had seen my painting. It had been only a few days ago, in my studio. That was comforting. It wasn't Roxie.

When I got to London, I took a taxi from Heathrow and checked into Brown's. Since I had begun painting the leading figures of British public life, I was invited to openings and parties. I had privileges at a good club and a studio was available to me near Burlington House. There had even been feelers from the Royal Household.

It was a little after one in the afternoon, about eight in the morning in New York. I put in a call to Roxie. The maid said that she and Monty had just left. I tried to concentrate on something else—a party I was to attend at the Albany that evening. I couldn't banish the news from my mind. I called down to the desk and had them check into flights to Zurich. A moment or two later, they called back. There was a flight at two-thirty and a flight back at eight o'clock, each lasting a little over an hour. Okay, maybe I could still make the party. I had the desk book me a place.

I hesitated for a few moments before I put in my next call. Had the real painting been discovered? Somehow, I doubted that. Was somebody else producing Caillous? If I had a rival, was he as good as I was? I hated the idea that I had competition.

In this unsettled frame of mind I called Zurich. When I reached the number, I asked to speak to Herr Ellenbogen. I almost hung up when they went to fetch him. I knew I was acting on impulse. That was bad. But I had to see that painting. When a voice said, "Ellenbogen speaking," I toyed with the idea of reverting to Signor Barzoletto. But that would have required rehearsal. I had missed the chance.

"Hallo! Ellenbogen here."

"Mr. Ellenbogen, my name is Jack Birnbaum," I said in English.

"Ah, Mr. Birnbaum, what an honor!"

"You know who I am?"

"Of course. You are the brother-in-law of the distinguished American connoisseur, Mr. Montcalme Carter. And the very distinguished painter of portraits."

"You are too kind. I am in Europe on business. Mr. Carter has asked me to undertake a commission. He wants me to look at the new Caillou. I was wondering if I could make an appointment to see it."

"Ah, you have seen the item in the press? But permit me to ask how, Mr. Birnbaum, you knew that *I* have the painting for sale?"

"Ah, so my guess was right, Herr Ellenbogen. It is you."

"Yes, I have the honor."

"It wasn't hard to guess, Mr. Ellenbogen. You were involved in a prior Caillou sale. Was it in 1970?"

"No, 1975."

"May I come to see it, sir?"

"But, of course. When would you like to come?"

"I have business in Zurich this afternoon. Is that too soon?"

"No, I am expecting some people who've expressed an interest in seeing it. I see no reason why you should not be among them."

"I was hoping for a private showing. Mr. Carter wants me to act confidentially."

"They should be gone by five-thirty. I can stay open for a while if you can get here by then."

"Perfect. Thank you, Herr Ellenbogen."

"Thank *you*, Mr. Birnbaum."

I just made the plane to Zurich. All during the flight I kept thinking I was acting rashly. My temples pounded wildly. Assuming my own work was still in the cupboard at home, I told myself that I must now suppose Ellenbogen knew that the Caillous were forgeries. Putting it out that the painting came from the same source as his other sale! I marveled at the cheek of the man, appropriating our story for *his* forgery!

But could I exclude the possibility that finally a genuine Caillou had surfaced? On consideration, the answer was affirmative. If Ellenbogen thought it was genuine, it would have been unveiled to the public with great éclat, not insinuated into the *Times of London*. I went back and forth between scenarios as to how I should react when I saw the painting.

At best, all these surmises explained only why we had never been contacted by Ellenbogen after the Sotheby auction. We had expected to be. We had even prepared for the contingency. We had considered buying Ellenbogen off or making him a partner in some future sale. You have to expect such things in our business!

Roxie, I knew, would be furious with me. She had little enough respect for my business talents. And here I was encroaching on her territory.

"Why are you doing this?" I heard myself ask aloud. It roused the man in the next seat from the reading of his newspaper. He looked at me and smiled.

The very form of the question warned me that I was overwrought. I felt near panic. "Get a grip on yourself, Jack," I counseled—silently this time. "Why are you talking in this second-person way? You are not suffering from jet-lag. There is no jet-lag on the Concorde." I heard the sentences echo through my consciousness. I looked at the man next to me to see if I had again been thinking aloud.

He smiled again. And said something I didn't catch.

"I beg your pardon?"

"Je le regrette, mais je ne parle pas anglais," he said. I smiled and nodded absentmindedly. He thought I had been trying to start a conversation with him.

But then my tension seemed to pass as suddenly as it had come on. I was vaguely aware of falling into one of those trance-like states, halfway between waking and sleeping. It was like coming out of anesthetic. I knew I was still in the plane, but the man sitting next to me was not the foreigner who didn't speak English. It was Monty! Roxie was across the aisle, and next to her was little Monty. Lee and Sheba I could not see, but I believed they were in the seats in front. Out of the window below I could see a river. The captain announced that we were crossing the Rhine. That's not the Rhine, I told myself. It is the River Jordan. We are awaiting permission to cross over. I was aware of vague noises like the bleating of sheep. In SwissAir? I was hallucinating. Somewhere in the deep recesses of my mind, I knew it.

I was waiting for Monty to say we could go. Suddenly, it was not Monty. It was a stranger—saying something in English but with a German accent. He looked a little like HMB, but he sounded like Ellenbogen—something about, "Come and wrestle with me." I agreed and we wrestled. It was all very indecisive. I was sure that the stewardess would appear and tell us to stop fighting.

Then suddenly I woke up. I was thinking of Lee and remembering that conversation long ago. The man in the next seat was gently nudging my shoulder and pointing to the seat-belt sign. I thanked him and fastened my seat belt. We were about to land in Zurich.

I reached Ellenbogen's a little before 5:30. I stood outside in the twilight, to make sure there was no one else about in the shop. I studied a nineteenth-century landscape in the window, labeled "Fjord Scenen, von Knut Nielsen (1874)." I felt calm and collected.

I entered. The shop was empty. The front room had an old-fashioned atmosphere. It did not look like a gallery, but more like one of those gift shops to be found in places like Zermatt or Davos that sell nothing more threatening than foreign newspapers. The tinkle of the old-fashioned bell had summoned someone from a back room. A bald man, with a fleshy nose, dressed in a formal, rather old-fashioned way, was approaching. It had to be Ellenbogen.

The man approached and offered a friendly hand.

"Mr. Birnbaum? I am quite overwhelmed that you favor me."

I mumbled something about his kindness in seeing me on such short notice. He did not try to talk to me in anything but English. That was reassuring. In my tentative grip on self-control, I wasn't sure I could manage anything but my native tongue.

"May I offer you some tea, some coffee, or a liqueur?"

"No, thank you."

"Then let us go see my picture. I know, of course, that you were the first to discover Caillou way back. Thirty years ago, wasn't it? It is a legend in our profession."

I nodded.

"But I, too, am proud of my place in this marvelous story, although the last time," Ellenbogen laughed in modest self-deprecation, "I thought the painting I had was a Renoir."

"An understandable mistake." I smiled back at him, forgivingly.

We had arrived at Ellenbogen's office. Ellenbogen proceeded to an easel, and with a flourish took the velvet drape off the painting. He turned on the light attached to the top of the easel. He stepped back and let me inspect it.

It was a canvas of the same size as my own. I needed to step back to find the right viewing distance and angle. There were the familiar features of the odalisque, the towel, the hand raised to hold it. But the effect was muted, one might even say deadened. Decidedly unlike the warm effect of my own version. It was as if this one had been copied from some glossy reproduction of the portrait. Oh, it had a certain unbridled sensuality, true. But the immediate effect was of the kind

206

produced by one of those nineteenth-century photographs of the naked female—you know, a bit naughty, salacious. The lights and the darks were wrong. As if they had been air-brushed into a semi-chiaroscuro.

And yet there was something familiar about it. On the fringes of my consciousness was the feeling I had seen it before.

Ellenbogen was looking at me, waiting for my reaction.

"Hhhhm," I said.

"Glorious, is it not, Mr. Birnbaum?"

I ignored the question. I went up close to the canvas to observe the brushwork. It was too smooth, too finished. Again it looked like an *imitation*, not an innovative treatment of a familiar subject, reflecting the new experimentation in oil with the light values of the indoor photography then coming into vogue.

I nodded to Ellenbogen that I was done with my inspection. Ellenbogen turned the light off and replaced the velvet drape over the picture.

"May I inquire, dear sir, what is your opinion?"

I was feeling anxious again. You must guard against speaking your mind, I told myself. And yet I seemed unable to heed my own counsel.

"It's a forgery. I have no doubt of that."

I now expected Ellenbogen to protest, but the man just wrung his hands and smiled.

"Of course, it is a forgery, Mr. Birnbaum. You know that. I know that. The painter knows that. Mrs. Carter knows that. Fortunately for all of us, that is the extent of those—as one says in English—in the know."

"It's a bad forgery, Ellenbogen! It is—*unworthy!*" I said, suddenly, surprised at my own passion.

Ellenbogen inspected me with curiosity.

"Unworthy, indeed! I admire your choice of adjectives, Mr. Birnbaum. Of whom? Do you really know of *worthy* forgeries? I only know of forgeries that escape detection or are found out."

I made no reply. I went over and, removing the drape and turning on the light, I inspected the painting once more. It was an abominable painting, I now saw, truly without merit. It would not escape detection. I was sure of it. And yet it was so familiar. And then it struck me. Like a thunderbolt. Suddenly I could see Marthe's naked body glistening with sweat from the battery of lights. Of course, I smiled, now knowing the hand, not to say the body, of the forger.

"And this one has been certified. Make no mistake," Ellenbogen broke into my thought. "I have a certificate of authenticity. But I suppose in a way you are right. May I say, sir, that I think you are a real genius? I had not heard that Mrs. Carter paints."

"Do you mind, since you are being so honest with me, telling me who painted that?" I asked.

He smiled and tapped his nose in a gesture that said "that is my little secret."

"Please give Marthe—I understand she is no longer la Comtesse de Saint Veran—my fondest regards. I am afraid I have lost touch with her."

Ellenbogen stopped smiling.

"Well, I shall take my leave. Thank you."

I made for the door.

"Oh, Birnbaum," Ellenbogen called after me, "I take it I can count on your—cooperation? However worthier your works are, I do not think that Mr. Carter would be pleased to hear that his brother-in-law has swindled him of several millions of dollars. And his wife, too. For shame!"

I left his premises without replying.

I cancelled my London engagements and flew back to New York. My stomach churned, my bowel rumbled. I tried to think, but the Concorde is not the place for reflection. It is a place to enjoy the conquest of jet-lag, in the secure knowledge that the statement you will receive next month will not affect your standard of living. Neither the conquest of jet-lag nor the insignificance of next month's statement provided any solace on that trip.

I had only recently become a member of that academy of *savants et artistes* whose names but not whose faces were recognized by the public. I was mentioned in *People,* my advice was sought by advertising agencies as a discriminating consumer. I snapped my fingers at these vanities. All that would in the course of time be forgotten. On that flight home, what I perceived was a threat to my place in history. In the revised history of proto-impressionism, Jean-Jacques Caillou had become a figure to be reckoned with. He had a place alongside, even equal to that of his friends Auguste Renoir, Claude Monet, and Frédéric Bazille. I, Jack Birnbaum, could not let Jean-Jacques Caillou fall from that state of grace.

I T WAS MORNING WHEN I ARRIVED BACK IN NEW YORK. I was suddenly dead tired. I almost fell asleep in the taxi that took me in from Kennedy. Once home, I dropped my bag and poured myself a very large scotch, hoping it would induce a deep sleep. I wouldn't think about anything until I could do so with a clearer mind. I flopped on the bed without undressing. But once there, I could not get to sleep. I got up and went to the studio cupboard and found my "Odalisque." I put it on the easel and studied it. I looked at my own work and was consoled by it. It was a work of cool sensibility. The lighting was right. The skin tones, with their highlights, nothing short of exquisite. It was the work of an artist of great promise. Gleyre, the master with whom they had all studied, all those friends, had thought so. He had a higher opinion of Caillou than of Monet, of Renoir, of Bazille.

I put the canvas aside, feeling refreshed. Now I could sleep. I fetched a blanket and stretched out on the Empire couch. As I nodded off to sleep, I told myself that the best medicine would be work. I would set to work planning a new Caillou canvas.

I was awakened by the ringing of the phone. I felt disoriented. It took a few moments for me to determine I was back in New York. I looked at my watch. I had been asleep less than an hour. I roused myself and dashed upstairs to answer the phone.

When I said hello, my voice was husky with sleep.

"Jack?" It was Roxie.

"Roxie? How'd you know I was back?"

"I called you at Brown's."

I was suddenly frightened that something had happened to Sheba. "Is something wrong? Is Sheba okay?"

"Sure. Have you seen the papers?"

"Yes. There's an odalisque and it isn't mine. Where did you see it?"

"In today's *New York Times*. How did you find out?"

"Yesterday's *Times of London*. Ellenbogen has it. I've seen it. It's a forgery."

"You've *seen it?*"

The tone was harsh.

"When I read the item, I flew to Zurich and saw Ellenbogen."

"Are you mad?" The volume had been turned up to *angry*.

I tried to keep calm. "It's a bad forgery. It is unworthy. Now we know why he hasn't tried to horn in. He knows about us but is going into business for himself. Look, can we talk about this later? I'm exhausted."

"Okay. Where?"

"Here. Can you bring Sheba back after school? Tell her I got sick in London. That's the reason I came home so early. But I'm okay now."

I went back and slept a couple of hours. I had set the clock so I would be wide awake to face Roxie.

Roxie arrived with Sheba about four. I made tea. Sheba insisted on seeing whether I had a temperature. I explained to her that I was now fine. It must have been something I ate. And that I had come home because if I was going to be sick, I wanted to be sick at home where she could take care of me. But now I was fine—really. When she was satisfied, she deposited her bags in her room and a little while later I heard her practicing scales.

Roxie began immediately. She thrust the *Times* piece at me. It was short and didn't add anything to what I already knew. But she didn't wait until I had finished.

"How dare you! I am *furious* with you."

She didn't have to tell me that.

I proceeded to recount my conversation with Ellenbogen and gave her my opinion of the new painting. I told her I even knew who had painted it. As I talked, she pouted. Her face was dark with anger. It took on a somewhat bloated, sulky look. I had never seen her so angry.

"I don't know that what I did changes the situation very much," I said to placate her.

She began to calm down.

"I suppose not. Except that now we know we've got competition. What do you think we should do?"

I didn't know what to say. In the last few transactions Roxie had clearly been in charge and I hadn't tried to change that. Anyway, it was a rhetorical question. I didn't really want to talk about it. I wanted Roxie to go away.

"I suppose we don't have to do anything at this point." she said. "Just wait and see what develops."

I nodded. I hoped the matter would end there. I wanted to get to work sketching.

"If it is as inferior as you say, then someone will denounce it as a forgery, Labiche or somebody. But suppose nobody does?" she asked.

Suddenly I was interested in what she was saying. I simply had assumed everybody would see that it was unworthy. I had never thought of the possibility that it might be accepted as the work of Jean-Jacques Caillou. Now that I thought about it, it was a real possiblity. Badly restored, but a Caillou just the same, some so-called expert on Caillou would say. It was the kind of apology Prince Hal would make.

I suddenly had the feeling I knew what she would say next. And I was suddenly assailed by the dread I had experienced on the plane home. I thought of Lee's expression "the ground of being." That's what this fraud threatened. I had spent years suffering the whims of Carters— Lee's caprices, Monty's villainies. And suddenly Roxie appeared as one of the despots to whom I had also too willingly submitted.

"Well, I guess we'll just have to let Ellenbogen have his fun."

She flashed me a smile, the kind she favored me with when she wanted reassurance. She wanted to be sure that I was in agreement.

"I can't do that," I said.

It came out, straightway, without a conscious resolve, but barely above a whisper. I was surprised at myself, since I have never considered myself a man of decision. Indeed I didn't feel so much that I was making a critical choice. I was feeling that I could not have done otherwise. And I was refreshingly clear about *that*.

"What did you say?" she demanded, reddening.

"I said I can't simply do nothing."

"What does that mean?"

"If nobody else denounces it as a forgery, I will."

"What? What the hell is the matter with you?"

"Nothing. I won't let that miserable pastiche be sold as a Caillou. It is *unworthy!*"

"You keep saying that. That's what you said to Ellenbogen. So what?"

"It doesn't deserve to be there with the others. It's unworthy."

"Will you quit saying that!"

"It is not the work of a master."

"Oh, for God sake! They are all *forgeries.*"

"Are they?"

"Of course, they are. *You* painted them, didn't you?"

Her voice had risen several decibels very suddenly. She was practically shrieking at me. I was afraid Sheba would hear, but the flute is a pretty shrill instrument.

"Roxie, lower your voice. Sheba might hear you."

She ignored me. "And we sold them as *Caillous,* didn't we?"

Again, I didn't answer.

"Then they are forgeries. And you and I are guilty of fraud. Do you want me to go to jail?"

I was silent.

"Do you want to go to jail?"

Again I was silent. Then I found my voice. "If no one else challenges that miserable imitation, Roxie, I will." I said quietly. "It is something I would have to do."

She gave me a last angry look. Then she decided to change her tack. She was going to make me see reason.

"Look, my darling Jack. This is sheer madness. All we have to do is stand pat. Let somebody else raise a question about the picture. Just keep quiet and it will all blow over."

I said nothing. Roxie took my silence as a sign that she was making inroads into my resolve.

"No one is going to challenge the others. I bought the paintings from Signor Barzoletto. Everybody believes there is such a person—thanks to you. And if it comes to that, I can produce bills of sale for them. We are in no danger, believe me."

She searched my face for reassurance. Then, she continued. "And about Ellenbogen, well, we have no worry. He is trying to sell the 'Odalisque' as coming from the same source as 'The Bathers.' He won't rock the boat, believe me. All we have to do is stand pat. We hold onto ours. We let him try to sell his."

She had been sitting on a couch. I was now standing at the window. Suddenly she got up and came over to me at the window and put her arm on my shoulder. Then she pressed her whole body against my back.

"Trust me," she whispered. Then she seemed to have been struck by a further argument. "Maybe it would be better if we destroyed our 'Odalisque.'"

I was aghast at the idea. I was offended by the notion that it was "ours."

"No!" I said violently, springing free from her grasp.

My vehemence caught her unprepared. She was momentarily frightened. And that made me realize that I myself was very angry. I let the anger drain away. After a few seconds she also relaxed.

"Okay. It was just a thought. Can I have another cup of tea?"

The tea was cold, so I went and made another pot. When I came back, she was standing by the window, looking out at the traffic. As I handed her the cup, she bestowed on me a dazzling smile. It was a smile reminiscent of earlier "snapshots." It was a lover's smile. It was no longer business. She turned and took her tea to the chaise longue. She put the cup down and patted the seat for me to sit by her.

I obliged. She ran her hand over my back.

I knew I had ceased to be in love with her. It was as if those old photos had faded with age.

"Maybe we should be grateful to Ellenbogen," she purred.

"Whatever for?"

"For making us face things. Lee is off playing goddess. If you want, I could leave Monty. Sheba is almost my own. And little Monty, well. . . . We could be a family, a real family."

I felt a surge of anger at the word, the phrase. It sounded like Monty speaking, exhorting, blackmailing.

Evidently the emotion showed on my face.

"Why not?" she asked. She was angry with me again. And once again, I was angry with her.

"Because you won't leave Monty, Roxie. You don't want to. And why should you?"

"Because I love *you*. And you love *me*."

"Don't," I started to say, hesitantly. "I did. Maybe you did. But that was ... sometime ago."

I tried to say it gently. I took her hand and pressed it in a gesture of propitiation, knowing that the pressure was a fraud, a mere defense against further anger. But there were tears in her eyes.

"Let's be realistic," I continued, moved by the force of the truth. "Monty's not young. Neither am I, for that matter. You've got a big investment in him. And too little in me."

She put the cup down and rose to her feet. She was angry. This time it would simply not go away.

"You'd better remember your own words, Jack. You are losing your grip on reality."

IN RETROSPECT, I THINK DR. TODT WAS PROBABLY RIGHT. I lack the criminal social pathology necessary for art fraud. My handling of Ellenbogen certainly indicates that. My response to his *Odalisque* had been on the plane of its artistic merit. I should never have let go unchallenged his allegations that the other Caillous were forgeries. I should have bluffed, threatening Ellenbogen (and Marthe) with exposure if they persisted in seeking a buyer for that blasphemy of a painting. I did in fact entertain that idea in the subsequent months, when Roxie and I were no longer speaking to each other. But it was only *esprit d'escalier*. Frankly, I simply couldn't believe that no one else would come forth and say that it was a forgery.

And I was engaging in some broader and more serious soul-searching. Perhaps at fifty-five, it was time to take stock, I told myself.

My life suddenly seemed to me to be a mere thread of chance. I was the pawn of fortune, both good and bad. Sometimes, I didn't know which. Take Lee. What if I had headed for Fifth Avenue? What if I had not had the whim to play knight errant? I couldn't decide whether she belonged in the debit column or not. Take Monty. He certainly, if anyone, was a debit. Clearly, Monty was a curse. But no, wait a moment. He was, after all, the purchaser of most of the Caillous. He had been made—true, unwittingly—to make some restitution for a lifetime of mischief. The thought gave me some pleasure. I decided I could no longer reckon Monty a debit in my account at the Bank of Fortune. Take Roxie. At the moment, I'd rather not think about Roxie.

Take my career. I had prospered as a portrait painter, a blessing I owed in the first instance to my father. He hadn't wanted me to be a painter in the first place. That all seemed like winning a lottery, nothing really to my credit. Portraiture is, to be sure, an honorable trade, but the work could just as easily be done by a photographer. It is a craft. A living, not a lifework.

The trouble, I told myself, is that you have this childish belief that you had a destiny to fulfill. Where did you come by that bizarre notion? Was it HMB—the abominable Harrummb—to whom you owe this curse? He was the one who told you that you had a calling and that it wasn't dentistry; later he said he was sorry, he had made a mistake and maybe your destiny was dentistry after all.

You have slipped into the second-person again, I noted, and that is a bad sign. I was convinced Harrummb had shackled me to the idea of having a lifework. (He was clearly a debit in my account at the Fortune Bank.)

But I could not rid myself of the idea that I had a lifework. The only things I could identify as worthy were what the art world might dismiss as mere forgeries. If the art world ever were to come to know. How could I explain all that to Roxie—or to anyone? It would sound so immodest. It would sound like the ravings of a madman, worse, an adolescent.

I tried to bury this moral accounting. I was preparing a huge canvas. I had in fact already composed the entry in the catalog.

It would be No. 19: "The Afternoon Garden," 60⅞ x 90 inches (date of composition unknown).

So far as can be determined, Caillou never exhibited this work. It probably dates from the year before his death. The composition owes something to a similar work by Frédéric Bazille, a painting of the latter's family on a terrace at the family home, now in the *Jeu de Paume* in Paris. The Bazille painting was exhibited in the *Salon* show of 1868. This type of subject matter, figures in a garden setting, had been previously explored by Caillou's friend Claude Monet ("Women in the Garden," 1866). Caillou acknowledges this debt, albeit somewhat slyly, by including his friends among the people enjoying the spring afternoon. Bazille is recognizable as the tall man on the far left of the painting. Monet is the seated, lower-right figure catching the rays of the afternoon sun on his upturned face. Jensen ("Caillou and the Students of Gleyre," *Burlington*, 1980), speculates that Caillou was reciprocating Bazille's compliment in including him in his somewhat earlier work.

The composition is explained by two of the vectors determining the direction of progressive French painting in the 1860s: the depiction of the pleasures of everyday life and the adventure of painting *en plein air*. The favored painters of the Second Empire, such as Winterhalter, would have posed these figures more formally and in an indoor setting. They would have chosen their subjects from the upper classes, while the younger impressionists chose their subjects from the bourgeoisie. The Barbizon painters, on the other hand, preferred scenes from country life, for example peasants at work.

The locus has been identified as the public garden in Illiers. A photograph of the garden made in 1899 (see Plate 22A) shows that it had not changed much from when Caillou painted it in the late 1860s. The town was later celebrated by Proust in *Swann's Way*. The author gave the town the name of Combray.

This is the largest known canvas of Caillou and is a beautiful example of the "adventures" of proto-impressionism out of doors. Never again would the styles of Monet, Renoir, Bazille, and Caillou be so similar. It was no wonder that Caillou's work could so easily have been miscataloged under the name of one or another of his friends. The dark shadows and strong light bouncing off the white vestments contrast with the modulated chiaroscuro of academic painting during this period. In the latter, the shadows would have been rendered by smooth layering of thin coats of translucent black. Here they are thickly impasted greens.

We can only conjecture what the path of this brilliant young painter would have been if a Prussian marksman had not tragically ended his life.

During those months we had little contact, Roxie and I. Sometimes she came to fetch Sheba for an outing in the company of little Monty. But I avoided her, and when she was in the house kept to my studio. And she never tried to seek me out.

I was making slow progress with "The Afternoon Garden." For weeks at a time it remained in the bathtub in the studio, for that was the only place large enough to store it. It wouldn't fit into the cupboard with the other Caillous. The muse of painting, I felt, had deserted me.

One day I felt my muse return. I arose very hungry. Hélène, our Haitian maid of all work, scrambled me some eggs, which I ate while scanning the *New York Times*. It was full of dreary news: in Washington there was indecision, the crime rate was rising in New York, domestic oil reserves were being depleted faster than expected, the city was bankrupt, inflation was in double digits. But nothing on the front page was threatening enough to cast a shadow on the bright day of work ahead. My money was safe in Swiss banks; and I already knew to avoid Central Park.

Then I caught the item at the bottom of the page and it made my blood run cold. It was slugged with the headline "CAILLOU CANVAS PURCHASED FOR RECORD SUM." The text reported that the Carter Museum had just purchased a recently rediscovered painting by the French impressionist Jean-Jacques Caillou. No description of the painting was given in the first paragraph, but it could only be the detestable "Odalisque."

I read further. Yes, it was the abominable forgery. The article quoted Prince Hal as saying it was "the jewel in the crown." Yes, it was the very painting quoted in the portrait in the Carter. No, he didn't think he could say how much had been paid for it, just that it had been a private sale, financed by a generous gift from Mr. and Mrs. L. Montcalme Carter. The last sentence quoted "informed sources"—undoubtedly that blabbermouth Jensen—as putting the price at ten million dollars. Record sum, indeed! It was blackmail.

I threw the paper halfway across the room. I tried to banish it from my thoughts. But it kept galloping back. I pondered the significance of the purchasers being the Carters and that they had bought it for the museum. Why had Roxie changed her intention to hang it over the mantle? The answer seemed all too obvious. The painting had lost its personal significance. The body modeled in it was not her body. Relations between us being what they were, it would no longer be a delicious private joke.

I went to my studio and made preparations to paint, but I could not work. My mind would not focus. My hand shook with rage. My muse had deserted me again. I decided to take a long walk.

The walk in the cool air seemed to have been the right therapy. Once back, but feeling I still needed reassurance, I swallowed two tranquilizers. One would probably have sufficed, but the date on the bottle showed that the pills were old. I sat down and placed a long-distance call. To Paris. To the Louvre. To Charles Labiche, the dean of experts on proto-impressionism.

When I got Labiche on the phone, I announced myself and Labiche graciously remembered me. He said kind things about the little show the Carter had mounted, how long ago was it?

I got down to the reason for this call. I wondered if, by any chance, he had seen the new Caillou. Only a colored photograph, he answered. The dealer had been very guarded about letting it be shown, even to the Louvre. Didn't you find that suspicious, I asked. Ah dealers, Labiche replied with a conversational shrug. "I've seen it," I announced. "*Vraiment?*" asked Labiche, with that questioning tone that the French seemed to acquire at their mother's breast. "As a member of the family, but also as the discoverer of the original Caillou," I improvised quickly. No need to tell Labiche where I had seen the painting.

Then I said, with great deliberation, "I think it is not authentic, Monsieur Labiche." I was immediately gratified to hear Labiche reply that he too had doubts. But then in the sequel he let me down. Labiche allowed that he had "doubts yes, but, there are always doubts. I will reserve judgment until I see the original. It is, after all, the work of a student, and *ça expliquerait beaucoup, vous savez.*"

We had talked mostly in English. French is, of course, the language of skepticism, but Labiche balanced that with the Gallic devotion to Sufficient Reason.

I said I was sorry that I had interrupted his academic slumbers. He asked if I felt well. Fine, I replied.

218

I began that very evening drafting a "Note on a Recently Discovered Painting of J.-J. Caillou." Halfway through, Sheba burst into my studio. Her flute was in her hand.

"Daddy, how can I concentrate with you shouting?" She looked around the room. Her little face screwed up in perplexity. "Is there someone in here with you?"

"No, my dearest. I am alone."

"Oh, I thought there was someone here. You kept calling out to somebody. Daddy, are you all right? You never used to talk to yourself."

She put her hand on my forehead to see if I was running a fever, the little Florence Nightingale.

"What are you doing?"

"I am writing an article," I said.

"Oh," she said, as if that explained everything. Then she left, and a moment or two later I heard her again running up and down the scales.

I finished my brief note that night, about four in the morning.

I delivered it next morning to the editor of the *Bulletin of the Metropolitan Museum*. There was no love lost between the staff of curators there and Prince Hal. One of them, I remembered, had once referred to Prince Hal in print as "that dandified dealer in junk." I left buoyed by a feeling of righteousness. But the editor called me at home later that night, saying he was returning my contribution. They had a backlog, he said. Then something about its being "marginal to the interests of the museum and its staff." I got the real message. The Met didn't want to run the risk of exposing itself to a lawsuit. Calling a fellow curator a junk dealer is one thing, specifically questioning his merchandise quite another.

So I contacted the editor of the Sunday *Times*. I had done his portrait some years before, and it was now hanging in the *Times'* conference room. I wanted, I said, to write a piece for the Sunday magazine on Caillou. He probably knew that I was, after all, something of an expert on the man's work, having rescued from obscurity the first recognized work of the master. What I had in mind was a general retrospective on all the known paintings, complete with glossy photographs, including the recently discovered "Odalisque."

The editor sounded favorable to the whole project, particularly in view of the upcoming installation of the new acquisition. He couldn't give a definite answer, of course. He would have to talk to Dr. Jensen first, to get the Carter's cooperation.

On the whole, what I wrote was cautious, and scholarly. The only part of the article that might raise an eyebrow or two was the evaluation of the new painting. I noted the "lifelessness" of the fleshtones, the "mere adequacy" of the draftsmanship ("how different in this respect from the other Caillous"), the "pedantic" chiaroscuro. I liked that! I wondered how this painting could have been the one which burst "with such *éclat*" on the *Salon* of 1865. Reproductions had not been available before the sale ("And why not?"). I declared my certainty that "other connoisseurs" would share doubts about the picture's true "worth" ("possibly even about its authenticity").

I concluded with the conjecture ("and it is only a conjecture, mind you") that it might be a copy "from the same epoch." But even then it was at best "a study," possibly made by a student of no great promise. After all, copying paintings was a standard part of the training in those days. Someone could simply have added the J.-J.C. recently, since the sudden reappearance of the other works. The article was girdled with the qualifications of honest scholarship. They gave it, I thought, a certain ring of authority.

It appeared on the very day of the painting's installation at the Carter, a Sunday night affair, by invitation only, black tie. I did not plan to attend.

I was awakened from a sound sleep. The phone was ringing. I looked at my watch. It was two o'clock in the mornng. Nobody calls at that hour unless they are announcing the end of the world. I picked the phone up and said hello.

The voice on the other end announced icily, "This is Roxie, Jack."

"Hello, Roxie. It is two in the morning, what's wrong?"

There was a pause.

"You had to do it," she said.

"Had to do what?"

"Don't play games with me. You had to trash our painting. I've read your article. I'm so mad I can't sleep."

"Oh, so now it is 'our' painting? Who does that 'ours' refer to? I rather think I am not included."

She ignored my remark.

"Monty's so furious he can hardly speak."

"He is wondering what happened to family loyalty?" I asked innocently.

"Don't be flip. He called his lawyers. On Sunday, yet!"

"Are you worried about me, Roxie? Is that why you are calling—at two in the morning?" My voice was dripping with sarcasm.

On the other end, I could hear her quiet sobbing. For a moment, I regretted my savage tone.

"How could you do this to me?" she sobbed, as she hung up.

I did not return to sleep immediately. I pondered the import of this call. Had she wrung her hands and made a tearful confession to her husband that his Caillous were of the spotted and speckled kind? But in my wildest imaginings, I could not conceive of such an outcome. If there was one thing Monty hated, it was looking like a victim.

WHEN I WAS SERVED WITH THE LEGAL PAPERS, MY BELIEF was confirmed. The plaintiff in the suit was the Carter Museum, the defendants, myself and the *New York Times*. Monty would never have subjected himself to possible public ridicule if he had any inkling he had been taken. I wondered what story Roxie had invented to explain my motives. Perhaps my lack of family loyalty had seemed sufficient. Oh, well, it wasn't my problem! I really didn't ever expect to see either of them again.

I saw my lawyer, I talked to the *Times*. Not to worry, they all told me.

They don't have a case. They cited precedents in which some party of the first part had been sued by a party of the second part for calling an attribution of a valuable painting into question. The plaintiffs had never collected a cent. It will be a three-ring circus for a while, my lawyer said, pausing significantly. I could fill in the blank: "But that's really nothing new, is it?"

I went about my business. I tried working on "The Afternoon Garden," but my muse had fled again. Then I got a call from Los Angeles, a commission from a studio mogul. He expected I was busy and he might have to wait. I said no, I had time during the next few days to make a beginning. I needed a change of air, I told myself.

I was gone three days. I returned mid-afternoon, feeling invigorated by the way I had been courted in L.A. I hadn't eaten on the plane and Hélène fixed me a bit of lunch. It was gumbo. I ate it with relish. I prepared for an afternoon of painting. The fugitive muse had been on the flight with me, traveling alongside me—in business class.

As I descended the stairs, I felt the rush of excitement, the welcome home of the familiar contours of my studio. I took "The Afternoon Garden" from the bathtub and positioned it on the easel. I was dissatisfied with the figure of Bazille. The face was not right. But in imagination I now saw this painting as a work of tremendous scope, the very epitome of proto-impressionist values, a scale model of the world of impressionism that was to follow.

I donned my lab coat and was already mixing colors on the palette, when I was attacked by a twinge of anxiety. Something was wrong. I had sensed it, but it was lost in the rush of feeling at being home again in the studio. My eye studied the entire studio. It looked all right, the normal mixture of order and confusion. And then I saw what I had perceived only subliminally. It was the cupboard in which the Caillou canvases were stored. The doors were standing partially ajar. And I could see the lock—the one Roxie had insisted that I put on it when we had started in business together. It was broken. I dropped the palette in panic and rushed to it. I poked my head in.

The cupboard was bare.

I felt hot and cold. I gasped for air. My first reaction was to rush to the desk, where the catalog was stored in the middle drawer. It was still

222

there. It gave me a momentary surge of reassurance. But then no one had known about it, not even Roxie. It was a part of my fantasy life. I had wanted to keep its existence even from her.

I put it back and rushed upstairs. I found Hélène in the kitchen. She watched me enter from the studio with terror. It crossed my mind for a moment that I must have looked to her like Charlie Manson.

"Somebody's been in my studio, Hélène. Someone's taken some paintings. Do you know anything about it?"

I was shouting and that only served to throw her into a greater state of terror.

"Only Madame Roxanne, Monsieur Jacques," she stammered after she recovered her voice.

"When?"

"The day before yesterday."

"And you let her? Why, for God's sake?"

She retreated to the opposite corner. She was afraid I was going to strike her.

"She say you call her from L. A. You tell 'er to deliver to a gallery. She say you forget before you go. She takes them paintings away in a truck."

She began to cry. I tried to calm down enough to ease her fears of me. "It's okay, Hélène. You haven't done anything wrong. I am not angry with you." I patted her on the shoulder and told her it was not her fault.

I went into the bedroom, picked up the phone, and dialed. I was so angry I had to dial three times before I could get the number correct. The Carter maid answered. I asked for Mrs. Carter. She recognized my voice and went to fetch her. Then she came back and told me that she was sorry but Mrs. Carter had just stepped out. Did she know when she would be back, I asked. No idea, the maid said, was there a message?

"Just tell her she is a murderer! A female Hitler! A Prussian viper!" I screamed into the phone. I had meant to say "sniper." Then I burst into tears. And I cried like a baby.

I must have fallen asleep. I awoke and looked at my watch. It was still afternoon. It had been the narcotic, self-induced sleep of the deeply troubled, from which the sleeper awakes to the renewed nightmare of his existence. They all flooded back, those ghosts. I went into the bathroom and looked at the wild figure in the mirror in the splattered lab coat. I slapped my face very hard. Yes, you exist, I told myself. But who exactly is this you? Someone who has been "rubbed out." You are a man lobotomized, deprived of your history. A man with a catalog but no lifework. Who knows where it all now rests? At the bottom of the East River? In some polluted Jersey wetlands? The image flashed through my mind of my canvases, tossed out of a speeding car, moving through Jersey, or encased in cement offloaded some distance from Sheepshead Bay.

It was unbearable. I rushed out of the house onto the street, past Hélène, who was looking very anxiously in my direction.

It was a chilly day and I immediately felt the cold through my lab coat, but I could not go back. I wandered, not really knowing where. Momentarily it registered that I was at Gramercy Park. I was surprised that I had come east.

The well-dressed inhabitants of the neighborhood scurried past me. A man was coming out of the Player's Club. I recognized him. A man in his sixties, a fixture on the Broadway stage, I had done his portrait for the Schuberts. He was famous for his King Lear. The man's name escaped me. "Aging Thespian" was all I could think of. He looked my way, recognized me, and then in horror quickly looked away. As if I were the raving King Lear! As if I was about to capture him and make him the unwilling audience to my one-man cabaret of woes.

I suddenly thought of a modish woman my own age I used to see. I didn't know her, I had never talked with her—well, not exactly—but I knew all about her troubles. I used to encounter her in the checkout line at Zabar's, ranting and raving at the top of her voice about somebody named Josie. Josie stole her paper every morning and then put it back on her doorstep before she was supposed to discover its absence. She'd deliberate at the top of her voice about this injury, while everybody else in line pretended to be scanning the front page of their Sunday *Times*. Then she'd pay for her bagels and lox, just as sane as you please.

There was a figure, a man, reclining against the iron grillwork of the private park, looking at me with interest. He looked as if he hadn't been out of his clothes for a week. His face had that odd hue that looks like theatrical makeup. Underneath all that grime it was a nice face, a sensitive face. I felt the man's eyes studying me as I passed. At some

224

other time, when I did not have this heavy sack of defeat and failure, I would not have been too busy to offer this derelict something to ease his pain.

Sometime later, I surfaced again to the realization of where I was. I was sitting in Bryant Park, near the library. I was shivering. I felt a gentle prod on my shoulder. I was sharing the bench with someone. I recognized the derelict I had encountered near Gramercy Park. Was this a chance meeting, had our paths just managed to cross again? Somehow, I wasn't surprised to find us together on the same bench. In between the two of us on the bench was a hot dog and a cup of steaming coffee.

"You were talking to yourself," I heard the man say in a low voice.

"Are you talking to me?" I asked.

"You were saying something about someone named Odal. Odal Something. Some French woman. You called her unworthy. You were talking to yourself. You don't want to do that. They'll call the cops. They'll take you to Bellevue. You wouldn't like that. I know. I've been there. And to Islip. You wouldn't like Islip either."

"I beg your pardon?"

"You a priest or a rabbi or something? You don't look like a man of the cloth. Maybe a butcher?"

"No."

"I didn't think so. Maybe a man of the cloth. You kept saying something about a calling. I didn't understand. I just want you to know you're not alone, friend, in this vale of tears. Believe me."

I felt the hand on my shoulder. It was not unwelcome. The man was gentle and well spoken.

"In my case, it wasn't women. It was cards. I had a good practice in Boston, but I gambled it away."

"Were you a doctor?"

"No, a dentist."

I made the effort to rise to the occasion. "Thank you for your concern.... Can I offer you a little help?" I reached into my hip pocket and pulled out my wallet. I offered him a fifty-dollar bill.

"Hey, get rid of that wallet. Someone is sure to snatch it. Put your dough in your shoes." I continued to hold the bill.

"No thanks, that's too much. I'd do something foolish with it. You got a twenty? I could get a room to myself. With a bath. And a hot meal."

I fished out a twenty and got up to go.

"Hey, if you don't want your hot dog, can I have it?"

I waved my assent.

"You take care of yourself, you hear?"

I continued to wander aimlessly, a stranger on familiar streets. Then I recognized that I was on Seventy-second Street, one block from the Carter Museum. Suddenly I was seized by something so compelling I couldn't do anything but submit to it. I had to revisit once more the Carter's collection of Caillous. That was my destination when I had left the house; that's why I was here. I found myself running as if my life depended upon it. It was as if I would die if I didn't reach the lifegiving medicine in time. I need their reaffirmation.

But the Museum had already closed.

The thought of going home and coming back tomorrow never crossed my mind. I was afraid to leave. If I left, they too might vanish. I would stand guard until the museum reopened in the morning.

So I hung there all night. In the lab coat that now made me feel like a butcher, in his locker, slapping his arms together to keep the chill at bay. A police car cruised by occasionally. Every time it came by, I was afraid that the policemen would challenge my presence, threaten my slim hold on my existence. When I spotted the car, I would take evasive action by walking around the block.

I managed to evade the patrol. In the morning, I watched as the museum personnel entered. I saw Prince Hal far off as he got off the Madison Avenue bus. He made his way jauntily down the street, in that shallow, self-satisfied way of a man who has never had the concept of a lifework. But once more, I felt I had to conceal myself.

A few moments later, in my spattered lab coat, sleepless, unshaven, unbreakfasted, I was once more at the door, just in time for the museum to open. I scurried past the attendant at the door before he had a chance to take note of my unkempt condition.

I found the room where almost all that remained of Jean-Jacques Caillou resided. At first I avoided looking at the grotesque imposter. I

226

knew immediately that something of the great proto-impressionist still survived in the other few works. He would survive as long as they continued to exist, perhaps as long as civilization itself. I felt warmed— as I had not felt warm in almost twenty-four hours—by the shower of form and color that flowed over my being from the paintings on the wall.

My MEMORIES OF THAT DAY ARE FRAGMENTARY. I had no idea how long I remained in that room in the Carter. Later, I could recall, in very disconnected form, a conversation I had then with a stranger, a young man in a brown corduroy jacket. The youth was carrying a magnifying glass.

This interloper had started it. He didn't seem to be put off by my dishevelment.

"You are wrong," he had said.

"I beg your pardon. Are you speaking to me?" I asked.

"You said these are the only Caillous that have survived the Holocaust. I don't know what that means, but it's wrong. There's another Caillou. It's in the Louvre. I've applied for a grant to see it."

I didn't like this interloper. "I wasn't aware I was talking to you," I said testily. I wasn't aware that I had been talking at all.

The young man was undeterred.

"I am writing my dissertation on Caillou. I think it will revise the standard history of proto-impressionism. Are you some kind of conservator here?"

I did not answer.

"But you are right about one thing."

"What's that?"

"The 'Odalisque' is a fake."

I found that I was beginning to warm to this interloper.

I also vaguely remembered seeing Prince Hal, barely poking his head

227

into the room and fixing me with a stare. The director's eyes had momentarily taken on their customary iridescence, but the little laugh that usually accompanied that *son et lumière* was absent.

I also remembered—but through a glass darkly—the moment when the room suddenly filled with men in blue uniforms, that is along with two others, in white. The latter were brawny men. Monty was there, and I wasn't sure that I was not dreaming. At first Monty seemed to lurk in the background, as if he were a bystander passing an idle moment at a construction site.

But a moment later he approached boldly. He put his hand on my shoulder. I expected him to make the jab of buddyship at my biceps. But all he said was: "Hello, Jack." His voice was full of compassion. I looked around expecting to see the TV cameras.

I brushed his arm away. The effort cost me. My legs were beginning to feel like jello. Monty continued to look solemn. As if he were visiting a terminally ill friend. He looked old.

"What do you want?"

"We want to talk to you, Jack. Hélène called us. You didn't go home last night. Roxie and I think you need medical attention."

"Go away."

"We have a court order, Jack. It's just for a medical evaluation."

"Go away. And take your friends with you."

I turned and headed back toward the wall of Caillous. I was having trouble keeping my balance. The white coats were upon me immediately. My first thought was they were helping steady me. And the least I could do was to be courteous. Then suddenly I found myself lying horizontal on something that looked like a trolley. One of the white-coats was strapping me down. Another was doing something I could not see. Suddenly I felt a sting in my buttock. Just before I blacked out, I thought I caught a glimpse of Roxie. But I couldn't be sure. It could have been simply a flustered bystander trying not to look embarrassed at what was happening.

When I awoke, I was in bed. But it was not my bed. It was one of those hospital things, hinged so that they can be elevated and lowered. I looked around the room. There was a wardrobe and a chest of drawers.

An open door led into a bathroom. I knew I was in a hospital.

Outside of the door, I could hear a furious argument in progress. A female voice was shrieking at someone. Her antagonist was a man. It was very one-sided. The male voice could hardly get a word in, broadside or edgewise.

The female voice was familiar.

"Will you get that microphone out my face?" the male voice shrieked. "This is a hospital. Clear out all of you, or I'll call the police."

"Go ahead, you tight-assed quack. If anyone goes to jail, it will be you. I'm his wife and that gives me certain conjugal rights. Like, if anybody commits him, it will be me. Now get out of my way before I coldcock you. Come on, Sheba."

It was Lee. And Sheba. I felt vaguely comforted.

"You can't go in there. I haven't finished my evaluation. He's here by court order."

"You know what you can do with that. Better, stuff it up *his* ass, that *schmuck!* If you have any doubt, I am referring to my brother, Mr. Lawrence Montcalme Carter. The middle name is M-O-N-T-C-A-L-M-E. Make sure you spell it right, will you, dear?"

I was sure the addressee was part of the the fourth estate.

A moment later she burst into the room, followed by Sheba, followed by a thin, white-coated man with glasses. I vaguely remembered having seen the man before. Lee was dressed in a long white gown. She had bowed to the cold weather. Over her gown she had thrown an old fur coat, now somewhat ratty. She was wearing Adidas. She was bareheaded, her flowing gray-blond hair held in place by a laurel wreath. She was Juno descending from the heavens. Then came her court, a solid mass of blue jean pants and jackets, cameras, microphones, and recorders. She turned, her finger outstretched in an imperious gesture, pointing to the door. Don't anger Juno. Silently, obediently, the press trooped out.

She came over to the bed and took my hand.

"How are you feeling, honey?"

"Like I was on the Jersey side of the river Styx," I muttered, still confused.

She smiled. "I'm taking you home. Sorry about the fourth estate.

I thought I might need reinforcements. Where are your clothes?"

I waved toward the cupboard and then smiled at my child. She smiled back, showing her white brace-laden teeth.

"How long have I been here?" I asked.

"Not long. Hélène called Roxie when you didn't come home. They had you committed yesterday. And Sheba—the darling—called me. Smart, isn't she? Can you get out of bed? Here, Sheba, help your father."

Lee was helping me on with my pants, while Sheba assisted me into my shirt.

"I warn you, Mrs. Birnbaum—"

"Get off my back, you pest, or I'll turn you into a kudzu vine. Or something still more noxious."

Dr. Whatever threw up his hands and retreated.

"Now, you just let me handle the press, Jack."

I stayed in bed for a day or two until the drugs wore off. The phone kept ringing. It was mostly the press. Lee handled all the phone calls. Yes, our lawyers have asked the Justice Department to look into filing kidnapping charges against that Nazi. Of course, I mean my brother. Yes, you can quote me. They have assured us that, at the least, he will be charged with violating my husband's civil rights. No, I have nothing further to say about libel or slander or whatever. That's all I have to say for the moment, thank you. If the caller persisted, she wouldn't simply hang up on him. She'd bestow a variety of curses and maledictions on those who called back. She'd threaten to visit on them Hydras, Medusas, Furies, the whole mythological zoo.

On the second day I felt well enought to respond to Lee's questions.

"I don't understand, Jack. Why should they want you committed? Just because you said that you thought they had bought a phony? Okay, I wouldn't put that past Monty! But, Roxie? How could she do this to me?"

"Sit down, Lee. It's a long story."

She sat down. And I began telling her. I didn't spare any details. I told her how it had begun as a pastime, how it gave me far greater pleasure than anything in my professional life. The idea of selling them to the Carter had occurred to me the night we'd all four dined together at Le Champignon. It was probably inspired by low motives of revenge against Monty, I said. But I admitted that my intent in drawing Roxie in was the hope of inducing her to leave Monty for me. I related how, surprisingly, she had taken to crime. I gave Lee an accounting of the amounts that Roxie and I had stashed away in Swiss bank accounts. By this time, Lee was open-mouthed in amazement.

Then I turned to the story of the "Odalisque." I broke down when I began telling Lee about Roxie's theft of the remaining Caillous. I wasn't sure that she could understand that part of my story, I was sobbing so. I admitted I had probably exhibited enough symptoms of irrationality to convince a judge that I needed to be committed.

I looked at Lee. She was staring at me. She was literally struck dumb. We were both sitting there in silence. Finally, she broke the silence.

"You are making all this up."

"No, Lee, every word of it is true."

"But, Jack, you're such a—"

"Don't you dare say it. Go down to the studio. In the desk, center drawer, there is a notebook. It says, *Jean-Jacques Caillou, Catalogue Raisonné*. Bring it back up here."

She was a long time returning. When she came back into my bedroom, she was reading it, shaking her head in disbelief. When she finished, she put it down. She sat down. Then she started laughing. She couldn't stop.

When she got control of herself, she said, "You are such a straight-shooter. And Roxie? Who would have thought she'd have the nerve! I remember once she was with me when I got caught shoplifting. She was so embarrassed. And then the only way she could be unfaithful to that prick was to seduce her brother-in-law. All in the name of the sacred cause of motherhood. No, I can't believe it."

"We did it. I painted them. She took over the marketing. She became something of a marketing genius."

"Did you really do all these paintings?" she asked, leafing through the catalog.

"Yes. Oh, number nineteen in the catalog, I've barely started."

"Why, for heaven's sake? It wasn't money, was it?"

"No it wasn't money. I am not sure I can explain. It would sound silly."

"Try me."

"Well, look at my life. What have I been? A painter of portraits! I just didn't want to be remembered as a hack."

"So why didn't you go back to serious painting?"

"Who'd have taken me seriously, Lee? I mean, my kind of art? I paint small, Lee. I don't do walls." I stopped for a moment. "Besides, I love impressionism. I love Caillou."

She laughed once more. "It's the craziest thing I ever heard of. A forger does *imitations*. Who would look at them if there weren't *originals?*"

"I know. But I wasn't doing *just* imitations," I said.

"What kind of immortality can a forger have? If he's successful, no one will ever know his name."

I didn't have an answer for that.

She started laughing again. Again she was finding it hard to control herself. When she got some control, I began to tell her about our adventures in selling the paintings. Roxie's visit to Ellenbogen set her off again. It was minutes before I could get to my masquerade as Signor Barzoletto.

"Funny! Funny! Funny! But why did Roxie do it? She never loved you. She told me that herself."

I thought about how to respond. "To begin with, she wanted security. She was worried what would happen to her if Monty left her. But then I think she just plain discovered the joy of being naughty."

Lee thought about that.

"That makes sense. And he's *such* a fucking monster."

Suddenly she got up. I heard her searching for something in her bedroom. After a few moments, she emerged. She was holding a book in her hand.

"Listen to this. 'When Laban was away shearing his sheep, Rachel stole the household gods that belonged to her father, and Jacob—'"

"Lee, stop with the biblical gloss."

"No, it's proof."

I sighed. I was tired of my mythic Dasein.

"It's a double score for Rachel. First Laban, and then Jacob. You can read the passage as just household *goods* from Laban, but, if you put Jacob in the picture—and that's you, Jack—they were Laban's household *gods*. Laban's goods, Jacob's gods!"

I threw my hands up. It was no good arguing with her. She slammed the book closed. "I believe," she said firmly.

A FEW DAYS LATER, WE WERE BREAKFASTING TOGETHER. Sheba had already left for school. I was reading the paper when Lee broke in.

"There's one thing I still don't understand, Jack. Why did you kick up such a fuss about the odal—what do you call it?"

"Odalisque."

"That's it. So, it's a phony. Nobody knows but you and that French broad who painted it, and a couple of other people. What's the harm?"

I folded the paper. I looked at her and in my most solemn tone said, "Because it diminishes Caillou's reputation as a painter, Lee."

She looked as if she was about to laugh, but was held back by the seriousness of my expression.

"Monty will drop his case, if we don't sue him," she said, trying to change the immediate subject. "That's what the lawyers think. He might want a public retraction. A simple statement that now you think you were wrong in the article."

I shook my head slowly, "I could never do that, Lee."

She considered my answer soberly. "I was afraid you were going to say that." She paused. "I talked to the lawyers yesterday," she said. "They say the opposition has a snootful of depositions—that guy in France—Labiche—a couple of full professors from NYU and Columbia, and even that character HMB. They think we ought to settle out of court."

"No chance," I said with continued firmness.

She sighed. "I knew you were going to say that." She fell silent. "You aren't going to do something foolish, are you Jack?"

I made no answer.

"Roxie's destroyed all the evidence," she continued.

"I can do another. I've already started on it."

"You'll go to jail. Roxie will go to jail. Not that I mind, after what she did to you."

"I don't care."

"You are crazy, Jack, you know that, don't you?"

I looked down at my plate. I didn't want to answer. I would do what I had to, crazy or not. Suddenly I heard her laughing. I looked up.

"So what are we waiting for? Let's plan our campaign."

"Timing in such matters is everything," Lee said a few days later. "How soon can you deliver a finished product?"

We were in my studio. I thought about it. "It will take me six months to finish."

"Too long. You can only have three. Fred's booked beyond three months."

"Who is Fred?"

"Who is Fred? He's only the most distinguished maker of documentaries in the whole world. You haven't heard of him?"

She dropped the name. I allowed that I might have heard of him.

"He's coming next week. That only gives us five days to prepare the script."

"What script?"

"You are going on television, Jack. It's part of a series of hour-long programs to be shown on PBS. They are calling it "Creativity." Bill Moyers will be host. It'll feature various artists in the throes of creation, suffering the pangs, worrying aloud about their problems, that sort of thing—the Rolling Stones, George Balanchine, Helen Frankenthaler, and then you."

"What? How'd you get me into that crowd?"

"Jack, you've got to quit thinking of yourself as a hack. Besides, they needed an angel and I agreed to pick up the tab. They agreed I could be Mrs. Anonymous."

She smiled, then she continued.

"They don't know that you'll be creating a forgery. Fred knows, of course. He loves the idea, that's how I could get him on such short notice. But PBS thinks they are getting you painting Margaret Thatcher. How does "Jack Birnbaum Creates a Forgery" grab you as a title?"

"Fine," I said, with a noticeable lack of enthusiasm.

"There is one problem. I don't want you looking like a nerd. I don't think we have time to get you a coach. Try to be confident. You know, lots of *chutzpah.*"

I wasn't required to answer. Lee was merely thinking through the project aloud. "There are two other things. First, we need a continuance—"

"What's that?"

"We need to put the court date off until we are ready to blow them out of the water. We'll say you need time to recover from your ordeal and then—"

She paused.

"Do we still have title to the portrait—the one you bought in Paris? You didn't forge that one too, did you, honey?"

"The answer to your first question is yes. It's still on loan to the Carter. The answer to your second is no. It is the work of J.-J. Caillou."

"Good, we can get it back."

"Why?"

"We'll need it as a point of reference in the film. You can use it to explain the technical things. Like brushstroke."

Lee got a continuance of four months on *Carter Museum v. Birnbaum and New York Times.*

But the matter did not entirely disappear from public attention. When *Birnbaum v. Carter and Psychiatrists' Hospital* was entered on the court docket, a TV reporter got to Monty. It appeared on the six o'clock news. He was in Washington testifying at a Senate hearing on third-world debt. Afterwards, he held an impromptu press conference. A reporter pushed a mike right up into Monty's face and asked, cheekily, "Did you have your brother-in-law committed to silence him, Monty?"

Monty took the question in stride.

"Nothing of the kind." he said. "Roxie and I were genuinely concerned about Jack's mental health. It seemed to us—on more than one occasion—he was showing delusional symptoms. We are deeply anguished by his troubles. Deeply."

People magazine featured Lee Carter Birnbaum on its cover, in a photograph taken at the time of my release from the hospital—in her long goddess gown and Adidas, her ratty fur, her stringy gray hair held in place by a wreath of laurel and myrtle. The article on page three was titled "Does Madness Run in the Family?" It regaled its readers with an account of the suit and countersuit. It intimated that this was but the latest in the public brawls between different branches of the old banking family. Jack Birnbaum, "Portraitist to Celebrity," had a long history of psychological problems, the article said. And then it recalled Lee's well-known sponsorship of the Congregation of the Lost Tribes.

At about the same time, items began to appear in the art news columns of various journals, at home and abroad, reporting the discovery of yet another canvas by Jean-Jacques Caillou. It was rumored to be the largest of the known works. One report said it would cover a whole wall. Another said it was a picnic scene, possibly containing images of Caillou's family and friends. The French expert on Caillou, Charles Labiche, was reported to have said that it was the most glorious Caillou so far to be discovered. Another report quoted M. Labiche as saying he knew of no such painting. According to yet another report, the canvas, now called "The Afternoon Garden," had been consigned to Sotheby's in London, where it would be put on auction in the near future. A further report carried Sotheby's denial that any such painting was in its charge.

T

HERE WERE PROBLEMS AT THE PUBLIC TV STATION. THE well-known maker of documentaries—some said he was the world's greatest—was known to be finicky about his editing and was always late in delivering the finished product, never allowing enough time for an adequate review before screening. It was always necessary to give the legal staff full time, for his subjects were always controversial. After previewing this one, it was found to pose difficulties. For *Carter Museum v. Birnbaum and Times* was already into its third day, and the film touched on issues under adjudication. More important, as the station's legal counsel pointed out repeatedly, broadcasting the program would be, from the legal point of view, rather like airing a course of instruction in the use of burglar tools.

Nevertheless, art triumphed. Those in charge of programming felt they had a strong Emmy contender. And there was, after all, the issue of freedom of the press. Besides, the "anonymous" sponsor of the series, Mrs. Lee Birnbaum, was on the phone every fifteen minutes. After much negotation, it was agreed that the series host would issue the appropriate caveats. And they would change the lead-in and title. From "The Art of Forgery" to "Jack Birnbaum, Portraitist to Celebrity." Next morning, they'd act surprised.

With a rerun of a favorite episode of "Fawlty Towers" in place of the regularly scheduled installment of "Creativity," the hour documentary was shown a week later than originally scheduled. "Timing is everything," Lee Birnbaum had said, and she couldn't have been more right. The plaintiffs had that very afternoon finished their case by calling Mr. Henry Berger, better known as HMB.

> Plaintiff's Counsel: What, Mr. Berger, was your reaction to the painting in question?
> Berger: When I first studied it, I felt it did not sufficiently confront my sensibility. But then I had recently quarreled with—a lady.

237

Plaintiff's Counsel: But you found reason to change your assessment?

Berger: Oh, yes. When I went back a few days later, refreshed and reconciled, I was struck by the fact that, although a student work, it was by a student of the very greatest promise. And the student was father to the master, you might say.

Plaintiff's Counsel: Does this happen to you very often, Mr. Berger?

Berger: People who read my work know that it is part of HMB's credo that incorrigibility is a form of immodesty. In the case of this painting, I changed my mind.

Plaintiff's Counsel: So you are now prepared to accept the Carter's "Odalisque" as a genuine work of Jean-Jacques Caillou?

Berger: Without a scintilla of doubt.

Plaintiff's Counsel: Thank you, Mr. Berger.

"Jack Birnbaum, Portraitist to Celebrity" starts with the artist attaching a large canvas to the wall. The sound track picks up various studio noises, including the voice of the painter (that's me, of course), his back to the camera, muttering something about the canvas already being primed. He is saying something to the effect that usually a thin layer of lead white will do splendidly. He then begins sketching in charcoal the outlines of figures, trees, a path, a bench, a couple of wrought iron chairs. "The kind one must rent in a public park in France from the most disagreeable old crones in existence," he says, smiling agreeably in the direction of the camera.

All the while, the credits are still rolling. Another voice, more distinct, female, off-camera, is saying, "For God's sake, quit mumbling, Jack!"

A voice-over narration—it is a strong female voice, cultivated enough but not one that is familiar—is meanwhile describing his very successful career as a portraitist. Now he has just finished the outlining. He turns full-faced to the camera, a man bordering on sixty, with thinning gray hair, wearing a very soiled lab coat. The female voice-over is saying that he is not the kind of man you'd pay much attention to on the street.

When that is finished, the artist says, with a shy, winning smile, "If you are thinking of a career in art forgery, I recommend French impressionism." At the beginning, his words come haltingly; at the end of the sentence they have a real zing to them.

The camera follows him around as he squeezes paint onto his palette, moves over to the canvas, and begins painting in the tree trunks. "Don't try the Italians or the Dutch, don't really try anybody before 1860. Why not? It's the technology. With X rays, spectography, and all that stuff, it's just too hard. Starting about 1860, an artist could buy standard materials. Like these. See?"

He holds up some tubes of oils to the camera. The camera comes in close enough to read the label: burnt sienna.

"They are readily available at your local art supply store. Just make sure the base is poppy-seed oil. That way your painting won't crack the way old masters do. That's because of the linseed oil. It's fast drying. Face it, forgery is not a business for the impatient."

He fills his brush and starts painting. Then he turns away from the canvas toward the camera. "Also avoid the new synthetic bases. They dry very fast and they don't crack but—"

A voice, the same off-camera female voice—which is, of course, now recognizable as the narrator—prompts the artist. "Enough already with the technology. Anybody interested can write to 'Birnbaum on Forgery.' We'll give them a PO Box number at the end of the program."

"I think we'll call this painting 'The Afternoon Garden,'" he says. "Yes that will do fine." He steps back from the canvas. Then, pointing to the tree trunks with his brush, he says, "That, of course, is black. I'll give it time to dry and then add dabs of raw umber. To add texture."

The off-camera voice is heard to say, "That's better, dear."

While he paints in foliage, he amplifies on his reasons for preferring the impressionists. He interjects these comments between instructions on how to do the foliage using opaque viridian green mixed with white, brushed on over dry transparent green paint. He discourses on his choice of brushes. He makes insightful comments on the use of "descriptive brushstroke" and the subtle difference between, for example, Monet and Cézanne.

He remarks upon the fact that several of the impressionists lived very long lives and, as a result, did huge numbers of paintings. He cited the cases of Renoir and Monet. He tells funny little anecdotes about their inability, late in life, to say whether or not they had done a certain contested painting. He finishes with the well-known lesson about Corot (which he prefaces by remarking that he was, to be sure, not an impressionist): During his life, Corot painted over a thousand pictures, two thousand of which hang in American museums.

The off-camera female voice is heard to laugh uproariously.

Some time has now passed. The artist has turned to paint the clothing of the three distinct groups of figures on the canvas. Pointing in turn to each of the groups, he notes that the impressionists began avoiding a central focus in their compositions. He then discourses on matters of lighting. He gives some instruction on the use of warm versus cool colors for lights and shadows.

This leads him to make some trenchant remarks vis-à-vis the decline in *chiaroscuro* painting in the last half of the nineteenth century. Again, he seems to take refuge in technical matters.

"Yeah, yeah, Jack," the off-stage female voice is heard to say. "Leave the erudition to Kenneth Clark."

He turns to painting an ample female figure, seated, in the upper left, diagonal to the afternoon sunlight. She is in a full white dress. He has already painted in the bright white of her garment, and now begins with the shadows. When he is finished, he steps back and exclaims, "I think we'll give her a blue bonnet. With a veil. Yes, a veil will be just the thing. But we'll do that after we do her face."

He turns to the camera. "I don't know how seriously to take the *plein air* part of the impressionist revolution. At least, the business about setting up the easel and in one fell swoop capturing the light on canvas. Probably it is not a myth, but it ought to be taken with a grain of salt. Even the most committed *pleinairistes* must have done a lot of the finishing back in the studio."

"Get on with it, Jack"

"Be that as it may, forgery is a studio art."

He illustrates how to do highlights. He waxes eloquent on the wet-on-wet technique by which the shimmer of points of lights is achieved. He speculates on who invented the technique. All the while, palette in hand, he is stepping back to inspect his work.

"There, doesn't that just make you shiver?" He is pleased with this latest addition to the image.

"Now faces," he announces.

"Come on over and look at this." The camera follows him until he

240

stops in front of the portrait of Auguste Renoir. "It's a portrait of the great impressionist Auguste Renoir done by his friend, Jean-Jacques Caillou. Caillou might have been an even greater painter than Renoir if he hadn't stopped a Prussian bullet when he was only thirty years old. What a tragedy! Oh, don't worry, the painting is kosher. But what I want you to notice is that the face is not the most important thing in the picture. It's not the personality; it's the activity that is important. His friends would no doubt say, 'Oh that's old Auguste!' But note, he is in profile, his face is in shadow. The hand holding the brush is a more salient detail than the contours of the face. What Caillou has captured is the intense concentration of Renoir on what he is doing."

"Now I've done hundreds of portraits," the artist continued. There I concentrate on the face. I have to satisfy the family and friends. Otherwise, I'm out of business. The point is: painting faces is no big deal when you are forging an impressionist painting. The face is no more than a cartoon. I could paint recognizable faces when I started taking art lessons by correspondence. To make a long story short—"

"Not short enough, honey."

"They were a gregarious bunch, our impressionists. They loved to party. And they'd put fellow artists, friends, mistresses, their children, even critics into their crowd scenes. There's a famous Manet of an open-air concert that puts the poet Baudelaire in a prominent place. Maybe it was a private joke. Baudelaire wanted artists to paint ordinary life.

"Sooooo, I'm going to put some of my contemporaries into 'The Afternoon Garden.' And first of all, my lovely wife, Lee."

Lee appears on camera. She is wearing a full-length, summery white shift. On her head is a blue bonnet. It has a ribbon that falls on her bodice. It also has a veil. On her feet are the Adidas.

"Never mind the Adidas," the painter says, smiling into the camera. "They won't show."

Lee stumbles as she comes on screen. Recovering, she says, "I'm as blind as a bat without my glasses."

The viewer can now put a face to the off-stage female voice. The painter leads her to the ice-cream parlor chair, sits her down, and arranges her for a three-quarter face pose.

241

"Put the veil up, Lee, if you would." She obliges. She smiles in the direction of the camera. Which she cannot really see.

"Just look natural, dear. And not at the birdie," he says. And giggles.

It takes him three minutes to put features on the seated female figure in the upper left of the canvas. She is in partial shadow. The veil will be painted later.

"Thank you, dear."

Lee waves in the direction of the camera. It is obvious she can't see a thing without her glasses.

"Now there are these two children playing ring-around-the-rosy. I want you to meet my daughter, Sheba. She'll be the model for one of them."

Sheba enters. In a white dress with a black lace apron. She is grinning broadly, absolutely delighted at the prospect of being in the film. She looks directly at the camera, smiling, showing a full mouth of pearly teeth, somewhat obscured by braces. The artist arranges her in the pose he wants. He has already painted most of the figure on his canvas. He tells her not to move.

"This is a little like the old Edward R. Murrow show, isn't it? Remember, the one in which he comes right into your living room?" The artist says this over his shoulder. He is now relaxed, seizing the moment, you might say.

Again he is done with the face in a trice. It is a virtuoso performance.

"That was very good, dear," Lee says, again off-stage.

"Trick of the trade. Your shopping mall Rembrandt could have done it," he says modestly.

"That leaves the little boy in the ring-around-the-rosy. And the man and woman in the lower right. For them, I'll work from photographs. First, the woman. I was commissioned to do a portrait of her and her small son a few years back. She's the wife of a well-known public figure. I think he's some kind of politician. Here, take a look at this photograph of the portrait I did. I'll have to turn her face so that it is in profile, jutting out here from under the shadows of her parasol."

Again, he works with quick, assured, small strokes. "Now the little tyke." Enlarged somewhat, to allow for growth since the time of the

242

portrait, the baby on her lap in the portrait becomes the other child playing ring-around-the-rosy.

The artist moves back to inspect his canvas. "Now the man in the panama hat. He is talking to the woman with the parasol.

"Come over here, I have some pictures of the lady's husband."

The camera follows him over to a wall and dwells on a large display of memorabilia. There is a large colored poster of Monty, with his hand on his heart. Above it says "Carter for Lt. Gov.," below "Monty's Your Man." Then there is an oversized campaign button whose legend in a circle around the photograph reads "Send a Message With Monty." That was from his brief campaign for the Senate. There is a blow-up of a news photo of Monty from his mayoral campaign which captures the famous Monty wink. And, finally, there is Kathy O's Polaroid snapshot of herself and Monty in the Bahamas.

"I am rather partial to this one," the artist says, pointing to the last.

There is one more sequence to "Portraitist to Celebrity." The painter is shown first at a distance inspecting his work. Then he takes up a thin brush and positions himself at the lower right of his canvas.

"The last step before varnishing—you might incidentally throw a party in your studio for the varnishing; it's an old custom among painters—is the signature. You see this dark patch down here. It blends with the surrounding. Well, it's an overpaint. There's something I haven't shown. We had to wait for the paint to dry. Fred, can you give me the clip we made of this area before the overpaint? Thank you."

The image of the area is shown. Clearly visible are the initials J.B. on the canvas. The camera returns to the artist; the clip is finished. Then the camera follows his hand back to the dark patch that now completely covers his initials.

"We are now going to sign this glorious impressionist work. It is from the hand of the genius whose life was so tragically ended by a Prussian bullet."

He paints J.-J.C over the overpainted patch. It is quick. It is authoritative. Then he turns to the camera and smiles.

"Actually the signature is nothing more than a marketing device. I flatter myself that 'The Afternoon Garden' would have been recognized and sold as a Caillou even if I had left the signature out."

He smiles again.

"But if you are going to sign your work, you need to practice the signature. It has to be right. Recognizable yes, but not too careful."

He smiles again. Fade-out music is heard. It is an old Hank Williams record—"Your cheatin' heart." Above it, you hear the artist saying, "I could do Caillou's initials in my sleep."

The last words you hear are from Lee, off-stage: "You tell them, honey."

THE NIGHT BEFORE I WAS TO REPORT TO THE FEDERAL Penitentiary at Lewisburg, I had a dream. The setting was biblical. I was standing by the waters of a stream. It was one of my recurring biblical dreams in which I was returning to the land of my fathers. I knew vaguely that my families were with me, although I did not see either Lee or Roxie. I was awaiting the arrival of someone whose permission was necessary for our passage across the waters. In my dream I think I expected any moment now to see Monty.

A figure came striding toward me, a tall, imposing figure with a crook. I took the man for Monty, then I saw, even at a distance, it wasn't him. I felt a sense of disappointment, but I couldn't immediately make out who it was. Then, when the figure got close, I saw that it was my father. Even in my dream, I found that curious because I knew my father had died a couple of years back. But I recognized that it was my father. First because the crook had turned into a putter and because he was wearing the abbreviated lab coat he wore when he was working on a patient's teeth. Indeed, the biblical landscape, rocky, with sparse vegetation, had become something very green. I realized that suddenly I was on a golf course.

Even in golfing knickers and supporting himself on a putter, my father wore the expression of anger I had known as a boy when he was trying to keep control of himself. That often occurred right after I had done something to offend him.

I wasn't sure what I had done, but, as in the familiar scenario, I began to prepare to fend off my father's angry, sarcastic recital of my transgression.

"I am sorry, Dad."

I looked at him. He no longer looked angry. Just perplexed.

"For what, my son?"

"I have stolen your blessing. And I have squandered it."

"You always were a spendthrift!"

"I have not been true to my calling. Give me a vocation. Let me tend your goats."

"You are an artist, Jack. In the land of your fathers, artists do not tend goats."

"I have failed you, Father. I have forged. I have worn my brother's skin. In a manner of speaking."

"So what do you want of me now?"

"Another blessing!"

The old man's face darkened with anger. He raised his putter. I was suddenly afraid he was going to smite me. But he gently rested it on his shoulder. Then he smiled at me.

"Stop with this blessing business," he said gently. "This is the twentieth century. We don't give blessings."

I awoke. I was immediately aware of what I had to face that day. But I felt refreshed, quite at peace with myself.

This book was set by SkidType of Savannah, Georgia, in Minion, a typeface designed by Robert Slimbach for Adobe Systems. The design is derived from no single source, but is a synthesis of historical and contemporary elements inspired in the main by the old style typefaces of the late Renaissance. Mr. Slimbach chose the name "Minion" partly because it was an early designation of type size, but also because the word connotes the unobtrusive and useful qualities possessed by a highly valued servant.